CHRISTMAS EVER AFTER

Also by Karen Schaler

FICTION

Finding Christmas

Christmas Camp

Christmas Camp Wedding (novella)

NONFICTION

Travel Therapy: *Where Do You Need to Go?*

CHRISTMAS
EVER AFTER

KAREN SCHALER

HAWKTALE
PUBLISHING

HAWKTALE
PUBLISHING

Printed in the United States of America

FIRST EDITION

As a work of fiction all names, characters, places, and events are products of the author's imagination or are used fictitiously and are not to be interpreted as real. Any resemblance to real events, locales, organizations, or persons, living or dead, is completely coincidental.

Cover design by The Killion Group, Inc
Chapter title and chapter opener © Elena Zlatomrezova/Shutterstock.com
Edited by Double Vision Editorial
Interior design by Radiant Content & Design

Library of Congress Cataloging-in-Publication Data has been applied for.

ISBNs 978-1-7347661-3-4 (trade), 978-1-7347661-1-0 (hardcover), 978-1-7347661-2-7 (ebook)

PUBLISHER'S NOTE

The recipes in this book are meant to be followed exactly as written. The publisher and author are not responsible for any of your adverse reactions to the recipes found in this book, or for your individual allergies or health issues that may require medical assistance.

Praise for Karen Schaler

Praise for Karen's *Christmas Camp*

Praise for Karen's *Finding Christmas*

Dedication

For all the great loves in my life,
thank you for giving me the gift of true love.
And to everyone still searching for their
Christmas Ever After,
keep your heart open and always believe...

Chapter One

R iley Reynolds heard them moments before she saw them. People were singing Christmas songs, different Christmas songs, all at the same time, in exuberant, joyful voices. There was "Joy to the World," "We Wish You a Merry Christmas," and "Hark! The Herald Angels Sing."

"What in the world..." Riley said as she stepped out of the hotel elevator into the lavish lobby of the Royal Grand Central Park, one of New York City's finest hotels, and found more than a hundred high-spirited Christmas carolers. They were all wearing elaborate, vintage Victorian costumes and passionately singing as if their entry onto Santa's Nice List depended on it.

Riley barely had time to take it all in before she was surround by one group of carolers singing "Joy to the World."

"Joy to the world, now we sing
Let the angel voices ring...
Joy to the world, now we sing
Repeat the sounding joy..."

Riley quickly moved to the right and the left trying to get by them. She had a car waiting for her out front to take her to a live TV interview on the top-rated Sunrise in the City national morning show to promote her next romance novel. She didn't have time for these carolers to repeat anything.

"Help!" she called out, joking, but instantly regretted her request when one of the handsome male carolers took her hand and spun her around for a dance as he kept singing.

"Joy to the world, now we sing..."

"No, no, no," she said, laughing as she was twirled around. "I gotta go."

When she let go of her dashing dance partner's hand, a new group of carolers singing "We Wish You A Merry Christmas" circled her. Every time they sang *"We wish you,"* they'd point at her on the word *YOU.*

She felt like she was trapped inside the musical production of Charles Dickens's *A Christmas Carol*...on steroids.

Then the two caroling groups faced off and got louder.

"We wish you a merry Christmas," the first group sang.

"Joy to the world," the second group of carolers countered.

"We wish you a merry Christmas," the first group sang louder.

"This is insane," Riley said, still laughing. When she finally saw a small opening to get by the carolers, she made a run for it. She was almost to the hotel's front door when a third group of merry carolers, singing "Hark! the Herald Angels Sing," started coming toward her.

She narrowly escaped them by dancing her way around them just as the doorman opened the door for her.

"Thank you!" Riley said to the doorman, breathing a huge sigh of relief. She looked back at the carolers, shaking her head. "This is..."

"Amazing!" the doorman said.

Riley gave him a skeptical look. *Amazing* wasn't the word she was about to use. She had been thinking more along the lines of *insane, crazy, nuts,* but not *amazing.*

"What is all this?" she asked, not able to help herself.

The doorman was now happily humming along with the carolers singing "Joy to the World."

"Dueling Christmas carolers," he answered and then continued humming.

Riley laughed loudly. "Wait. What?"

"You know, like dueling pianos," the doorman said. "But instead this is with Christmas carolers. There's a big competition this weekend at one of the Broadway theatres."

Riley shook her head in amazement as she headed out the door. "That's really a thing?" She looked at the carolers, then at the doorman again. "You're not making this up?"

"Oh, it's as real as Santa's reindeer," the doorman answered with a grin.

Riley's steps faltered.

"What?" she asked, even more confused. "So it's *not* real?"

But her question was forgotten when a gust of wind caught her black scarf and sent it sailing down the street.

"Oh no!" she called out as she raced after it. She had just splurged and bought the scarf yesterday. It was from a top designer and pure cashmere. The scarf danced in the wind before falling to the curb right next to a black town car. It was the only car waiting.

"My car," she said, breathing a sigh of relief as she snatched up her scarf and quickly grabbed the back passenger's-side door handle. But when she opened the door to hop in, she found three carolers, singing "White Christmas."

The car's driver, an older woman, was singing right along with them.

Startled, Riley jumped back. "I'm so sorry. I thought this was my car."

When the carolers just kept singing, Riley quickly shut the door. She'd had enough Christmas carolers for one day.

When she stepped back on the sidewalk and looked around, she didn't see another car waiting. "Where's my car?" she said to herself, growing more confused by the moment.

When her phone rang, and she saw it was her new publicist, Mike Conneley, she took a deep breath. She knew without even answering that he probably already had his tinsel in a tangle.

Before she even had a chance to say hello, Mike jumped right in.

"Riley, where are you?" he demanded. "The car service just called and said they've been waiting for you for ten minutes, but you haven't shown up."

"I'm right out front," Riley answered as she paced back and forth in front of the hotel. "There aren't any cars here waiting for me. I mean, there was one, but it wasn't mine."

It was starting to snow.

Riley looked up at the sky in disbelief as chubby snow-flakes started to fall.

They were moving so slow you could catch them, but right now the only thing Riley was catching was grief from Mike.

"You need to find your car *now*," Mike barked. "Or get a cab, I don't care. Just get here."

As Riley watched the snow start to fall faster, beginning to cover the sidewalk, she gave her stilettos a nervous look.

"It's snowing," she said with disbelief. "It wasn't supposed to snow today. It was supposed to be sunny and clear. I am not dressed to go wandering around trying to find a car that isn't here."

"Then grab a cab. Just get here! You're on live in forty-five minutes," Mike shot back at her. "I called in a lot of favors to get you this interview."

"Then you should have made sure a car was here for me," Riley grumbled under her breath.

But Mike didn't hear her. He'd already hung up.

The snow and the wind were picking up fast. Riley quickly put up the hood of her black wool coat to try to salvage her TV-ready hair and makeup.

"This is unbelievable," she muttered to herself as she stepped out into the street, slipping and sliding in her stilettos as she tried to hail a cab.

But all the cabs raced by her.

She was about to give up and head back to the hotel when all of a sudden, she heard loud Christmas music. This time the Christmas music wasn't carolers, but a car radio on the street blaring "We Wish You a Merry Christmas."

"Need a ride?"

Riley whirled around to see a cab had pulled up.

"Yes!" she said, relieved, but as she made a run for the cab she forgot about her high heels and practically fell onto the front of the car before jumping in the back seat.

"Thank you so much!" she said, out of breath. "I need to go to twenty Franklin Street as fast as you can."

As the cab pulled back into heavy traffic, Riley texted Mike.

I'm on my way!

When they passed Rockefeller Center, Riley peered out the window at the spectacular Christmas tree, watching silvery snowflakes swirling in a winter dance, pirouetting perfectly before gently resting on the tree's branches. The tree's twinkling red Christmas lights magically illuminated the plaza, but right now, the only red lights Riley cared about were all the brake lights in front of them.

Her cab was barely moving.

She fidgeted in her seat. At this rate, she'd never make

her interview. The snowflakes were getting bigger and falling faster.

"This traffic is crazy," Riley said, turning her attention to the taxi driver. "Is there any way out of this? Another way we could go that would be quicker? I'm really running late."

The driver was happily humming along to the Christmas classic playing on the radio, "Let it Snow!"

The irony was not lost on Riley.

When the grinning driver turned around and smiled at Riley, she did a double take.

He had white hair, a white beard, and twinkling blue eyes, and looked suspiciously like…Santa Claus.

She'd jumped into the cab so fast she hadn't noticed what he looked like, but now she couldn't miss how he was wearing a bright-red jacket with white fur trim.

"Ho! Ho! Ho!" the Santa driver said with a big belly laugh. "You just need to *believe* I'll get you to where you need to be on time."

But right now, all she could *believe* was that her Santa driver had spiked his hot cocoa this morning or was on a sugar high from eating too many Christmas cookies.

She cringed as her phone dinged with another text from Mike. The text was in all caps. She hated when he did that.

WHERE ARE YOU?!!!
YOU'RE LIVE IN 20 MINUTES!!!

If she missed this interview Mike would serve her up like a turkey at a Christmas dinner. Her publisher and agent were counting on her, and right now she couldn't afford to do anything to upset them.

As her cab crawled forward, she looked around and looked behind them.

There was no escaping the glaring red brake lights.

She couldn't believe this was happening. She was never late. She prided herself in always being organized and showing up early to everything, and she would have been early if the car Mike had set up for her had actually arrived.

She knew she was lucky she'd been able to get a cab at all. When she'd lived in Manhattan, she'd always battled to get a ride whenever there was any kind of bad weather. All this gridlock was one thing she didn't miss about living in the city.

She also couldn't figure out where all this snow was coming from. She had checked her weather app right before leaving her hotel room. There had been no snow in the forecast. None. If there had been, she never would have worn the shoes she was wearing. Now her brand-new black suede stilettos, with their spiky sky-high heels, which had seemed like such a perfect choice, were mocking her.

Wearing the right shoes always gave her a boost of confidence, and that was something she needed today. If she'd known it was going to snow, she would have worn power boots, not power heels. She frowned as she looked down at her soggy shoes and wiggled her cold, wet toes.

She looked back at her taxi driver, who was now munching away on a candy cane. She needed this jolly good fellow to be the real deal for a second.

"Santa?" she said, leaning in, realizing how ridiculous she sounded but willing to play along in this Christmas fantasy if it meant saving her interview.

Stopped at a light, her Santa driver immediately turned around and smiled at her. "Yes," he answered with a twinkle in his eyes.

"Does this ride come with a Christmas wish?" Riley asked. "Because my wish would be to get to the TV station in the next five minutes. If you can make that happen, I'll double your tip."

Santa chuckled as the light turned green, and he did some serious maneuvering around traffic to get them onto another street. As they started moving faster than Santa's sleigh, Riley held on tight and thought she might just get her Christmas wish after all.

Not that Riley believed in things like Christmas wishes.

She'd outgrown that whole idea a long time ago. When she was little, growing up as an only child in a small town outside of Seattle, every Christmas her dad used to read her a holiday story he'd made up himself, every night before she went to bed around the holidays. It was their special time together. Riley smiled wistfully, remembering how much she'd loved his stories when he'd add beloved elements from familiar fairy tales. Some of her favorites has been his *ChristmasElla*—about how Cinderella spent her Christmas—*Snow White and the Seven Christmas Eves*, and *The Little Mermaid's Christmas Wish*, and the list went on.

Riley believed her dad's Christmas storytelling was one of the reasons she'd wanted to be an author. She loved how the stories always took her to another time and place, to magical worlds where Christmas wishes and dreams came true, and there was always a happily-ever-after.

But when her father had gotten sick and passed away when she was just eight, the stories had stopped, and she had stopped believing in things like Santa Claus and Christmas wishes.

Riley still remembered how heartbroken she and her mom had been that first Christmas after her dad had died. Nothing had been the same. Christmas wasn't even Christmas anymore. So the next Christmas, her mom had taken her to Hawaii where, instead of celebrating the holiday, they'd had a wonderful beach vacation. This had started a new tradition, and every Christmas after that they always went to Hawaii and escape all the holiday hoopla.

Basically, they just skipped Christmas and all the traditional Christmas activities like baking cookies and decorating a Christmas tree, and spent their time going sailing, snorkeling trips, and taking surf lessons.

Growing up, Riley had always looked forward to their annual Hawaii trips. When her friends had told her she was missing out, she had thought they were the ones who were missing something. She loved her time at the beach with her mom, and as she got older, she never missed celebrating the kind of traditional Christmas she could barely remember.

When Riley was a freshman in college, her mom had remarried and continued their Hawaii tradition with her new husband, Terry. Riley was, of course, always invited, but she'd been too busy with school, taking extra classes over the Christmas break, to make it to Hawaii.

She honestly hadn't minded missing her annual Hawaii trips because she was so focused on graduating early so she could save money on tuition and rent. Going to school in Southern California was spendy, but she'd felt it was worth it to go to one of the best broadcast journalism schools in the country.

After hearing stories from her high school English teacher about how hard it was to make a living writing books and movies, she'd decided it was safer to be a TV news reporter than an author. That way, she would still be telling stories, and hopefully they'd be stories that would make a difference and help change the world for the better. She'd always promised herself that someday she'd go back to trying to be an author, when she was more established and had some money in the bank so she wouldn't have to worry about paying rent.

It hadn't at all worked out the way she'd planned. She'd actually written her first novel when she was flat broke, but one thing had stayed the same. She always worked Christmas, no matter what job she had. It was the perfect opportunity to get ahead at work while everyone else was taking time off.

The irony was that after her last summer romance novel had the lowest sales numbers in her career, her publisher had decided writing her first Christmas novel was the best way to win back her readers. And the plan was for her to start promoting it now during the Christmas season to get a bunch of buzz going early, even though her book wouldn't be coming out until next Christmas. So now she was going to have to write about—and promote—a holiday she had expertly avoided all these years.

When she'd tried to get out of it by telling her agent, Margo, the Christmas novel lane was already overcrowded with best-selling authors, Margo had shot her down. Margo had insisted that Riley needed to do whatever the publisher wanted. Margo was confident Riley would have no trouble writing a holiday happily-ever-after.

But Riley wasn't so sure. Still, realizing she didn't have much choice, she was trying to give herself a holiday attitude adjustment and decided everything would be fine. She would just google Christmas and figure it out.

But first she needed to get through this live interview Mike had set up for her. And even though she had no clue what she was going to write about, Mike had pitched the story to *Sunrise in the City,* promising that they could have the exclusive on her big announcement, which included a unique twist.

Riley laughed a little just thinking about it.

Of course, Mike had been the one to also come up with this *twist.* He was from Los Angeles, and he was all about trading favors and leveraging contacts. Mike was only a few years older than she was, but he had this superior attitude that always made her feel like he was her boss, instead of the other way around. While she didn't always appreciate his holier-than-thou attitude, the bottom line was Margo insisted she needed him, and Margo hadn't steered her wrong yet.

Riley also knew they had to act fast to get the attention away from her last novel, *Heart of Summer,* which had been such a big disappointment for everyone.

Margo hadn't minced words when she'd said this was do-or-die time, and that they needed to make some big changes to get Riley back on the best-seller list where she belonged.

Since Riley had started writing lighthearted, uplifting summer romance novels six years earlier, every book, even her first, had been a bestseller. In reviews, her loyal readers used adjectives like smart, funny, relatable, authentic, and *heartfelt* to describe her writing. But when *Heart of Summer* was released, those same loyal readers had been disappointed, saying *Heart of Summer* was missing the…heart.

There had been no one more disappointed than Riley to hear these reviews. She always put everything she had into her stories, and while she had struggled writing this latest novel, she didn't think it was something her readers would pick up on.

She'd been wrong.

It was almost as if her readers knew her better than she knew herself. She had written *Heart of Summer* after breaking up with boyfriend, Tyler. The crazy part was one of the reason's she'd ended their relationship was so she could concentrate on her writing career, a move that had apparently backfired, according to her book reviewers.

Margo had been even more blunt, saying that her last *two* novels had fallen flat and were missing what made her fans love her so much—a voice that spoke to them, that they could relate to.

So Margo had found Mike, the powerhouse publicist with an ego to match. He was all about doing whatever it took to make headlines and get media attention. His latest idea was to have Riley host an author event at a Christmas Camp over a weekend at a charming winter lodge in the Rocky Mountains. At the event, Riley would not only be talking about her first Christmas book coming up, she would actually be asking her fans at the camp to help her create that story by telling her what kind of things they wanted to see in a Christmas novel. In addition to getting feedback from the guests she met, there would also be an ongoing social media campaign following her at Christmas Camp, where her fans anywhere in the world could also share their story ideas with her online.

Mike believed this kind of unique interactive experience would help Riley's fans feel more connected and personally invested in her next novel, and hopefully, that would translate into more sales and put Riley back on the best-seller list. He also believed all the publicity could help boost sales of *Heart of Summer.*

Margo and the publisher had loved the idea. Margo also thought this Christmas Camp would help Riley get her Christmas creative juices flowing. This was critical because Riley needed to get a story outline to her publisher by the end of the year.

Riley was assured that one of Mike's friends, Luke, whose family owned the lodge, would be planning everything for the Christmas Camp and all she had to do was show up and host an opening-night reception and interact with the guests. The guests would be some of Riley's top fans who had been handpicked by her publicity team during a special social media campaign.

Riley had to give Mike credit for one thing. He'd been right about how popular this whole interactive storytelling idea would be. Within an hour of her publicity team announcing that she would be doing the Christmas Camp on social media, more than twenty thousand people had applied to attend.

While Riley had been stunned by the response, especially before they'd even posted a schedule of exactly what the Christmas Camp was going to be like, Mike had said it was proof that Riley's Christmas Camp would be a win-win for everyone.

The lodge would get the publicity it wanted, and Riley would get a huge publicity boost herself, along with some great ideas for her Christmas novel.

Riley was counting on those ideas because right now, she was Christmas *clueless* when it came to what to write.

She was smart enough to know that the people who loved Christmas *really* loved Christmas. They were the kind of people who signed up for a Christmas Camp having no idea what it was. If she didn't write something authentic, her fans had already proved they'd see right through her.

She hoped Google didn't let her down and planned to start researching all things Christmas as soon as her interview was over.

If she ever got to the interview.

She laughed a little to herself.

This whole thing is crazy.

If someone had told her she would be here, in a cab driven by Santa during a freak snowstorm, racing to make a live interview announcing her upcoming Christmas story and Christmas Camp, she would have said they were nuttier than a nutcracker.

Another text from Mike lit up her phone.

THE PRODUCER IS GOING TO CANCEL YOUR INTERVIEW! WHERE ARE YOU?!

She winced. She could practically hear him yelling through her phone. She was just starting to text him back when the cab came to a screeching halt.

"We're here!" her Santa driver announced in a jolliest of voices.

Riley looked up, and sure enough they were right in front of the TV station. Her laugher came from pure relief as she handed him a generous tip.

"I don't know how you did it," she said, shaking her head in amazement. "You're the best! Thank you so much!" She hastily put the hood of her coat up, opened her door, and immediately got blasted with an icy mix of whirling wind and snow.

"Whoa!" she exclaimed, blinking several times to get the snowflakes out of her eyes. "This weather is ridiculous!"

"Ho! Ho! Ho! It's Christmas weather," the Santa driver answered back with another big belly laugh. "Merry Christmas. Good luck with your Christmas book!"

"Thank you!" Riley shouted back as she got out and shut the door behind her.

As she made a mad dash for the door, she realized she had never told her Santa driver about her book. Confused, she glanced back at the cab.

But it was gone.

When she turned around and continued rushing toward the door her power heels hit a patch of ice, and everything moved in slow motion as she felt herself fall.

Chapter Two

A man, also heading for the door, reached out and grabbed her arm, saving her just in time. "Are you okay?" he asked, sounding genuinely concerned.

Riley, her heart racing, looked into the bluest eyes she'd ever seen. For a moment she forgot she was standing in the middle of a snowstorm. Her writer's mind was too busy trying to figure out if she'd describe this man's eyes as sapphire or cobalt blue.

When she realized she was still clutching his coat in the death grip, she quickly snapped back to the reality and remembered her manners. "I am so sorry!" Riley said breathlessly. "I didn't see you." Her last words were lost in a gust of wind.

"Let's get inside," the man said, opening the door for her while still holding on to her arm, making sure she didn't slip again.

Riley gave him a grateful look "Thank you so much."

The man smiled back at her. "Glad I could help. Wait, you're…"

But whatever else the man was about to say was cut off by Mike hollering at her. "Riley, over here!" he called out.

He was standing by the TV station's spectacular twelve-foot Christmas tree. While the tree glittered in all its festive glory, Mike simmered in all his impatience. "Riley, come on.

I already checked you in. We need to go. Now!"

As Riley rushed toward Mike, he kept waving her forward.

"Come on. Come on. Come on," Mike called as he strode toward the elevator, impatiently pushing the "up" button. It was already lit up, but that didn't stop Mike from jabbing at it several more times.

Riley got to the elevator just as the doors opened. As she slipped inside, she mentally braced herself for what she knew was coming. And Mike didn't disappoint. Before the doors had even closed, he was already letting her have it.

"Riley, do you know all the strings I had to pull to get you this interview?!" Mike demanded.

Riley fought to keep her cool. "Yes, I know, Mike. You've told me over and over again. I'm sorry I'm late, but it wasn't my fault. The car never came, and I was lucky to even get a c—"

Mike cut her off by holding his phone up to her face. "You're live in eight minutes. Eight minutes! The producers are freaking out. I had to say you were already here in the bathroom. They were going to give away your spot."

Riley let Mike fire away at her. Even if she couldn't control the weather, or her weather app, or the town car not showing up—which Mike had scheduled, not her—she didn't want to waste time arguing with him. She knew there was no point. Right now, she needed to concentrate on was making her live interview and making Mike, her publisher, and her agent happy.

"I'm sorry, Mike," was all she said. She knew he didn't want to hear anything else.

As Riley undid her coat and shook off the snow, Mike gave her a sharp look and frowned. "I told you to dress *festive*. You're wearing all black. You look like you're going to a funeral."

Riley looked down at her black leather pants and a fitted

black cashmere sweater. She met Mike's disapproving stare with a forced smile. "This is all new and in fashion. We're in New York. Everyone wears black."

Mike shook his head. "But not for an interview about *Christmas*. You need to be wearing red. Red pops. Red is Christmas. And you need to fix all this," Mike said as he circled his hand in front of her face. "You're a mess."

"Wow, you're great for a girl's confidence," Riley snapped back at him as she dug a compact out of her bag.

When she checked her reflection in the mirror, she winced. Mike was right. It wasn't pretty. She was a hot mess. She looked like Rudolph with a red nose and a flushed face. Her shoulder-length hair was all tangled up from wearing her hood, and the static electricity in the air had the ends of her hair flying everywhere.

Mike had told her to come early for hair and makeup, but thankfully, she had worked as a television news reporter for ten years and knew to always come camera ready, just in case. This was a great example of why because at least some of the makeup she'd put on had survived the storm.

She was trying to tame her wild hair and touch up her cherry-red lip gloss when the elevator door opened, and Mike ushered her toward the studio.

"Tom's not doing the interview," Mike said. "He had a family emergency so a reporter is filling in hosting this morning."

Riley's steps faltered. "What? Mike, you know I'm not a fan of these live interviews, but I agreed to this because you said it would be Tom. He knows me. He knows my books. I've done lots of interviews with him..."

"Well, you won't be doing an interview with *Tom* today," Mike said impatiently. "You're lucky you're doing an interview at all. This new guy's name is Joe. Let's just get you in there before you miss your spot. You're a pro. It doesn't matter who's interviewing you. You've been doing this for years. Just do what you always do."

Riley didn't like his dismissive tone. "Mike, I know you've just come on board working with me, but remember I'm the one paying you, you work for me, and I'm a pro doing interviews because I prepare. I've already talked to Tom about the questions he was going to ask me. I explained to him that we're still in the planning stages for this Christmas Boot Camp thing…"

"Christmas Camp," Mike interrupted her. "Everything's branded as *Christmas Camp.* You have to get the name right."

"Got it. Christmas Camp." Riley said. "Christmas Camp, Christmas Camp, Christmas Camp."

Mike wasn't amused.

Neither was Riley.

"What I am trying to say is that Tom agreed to steer clear of any specific questions about what we'd be doing at this camp since I have no idea what activities the owner has planned. So I don't want this new guy asking questions I can't answer. Has he been given the questions Tom was going to ask me?"

"Yeah, yeah, we're all good," Mike said as he waved a producer over to them.

Anything else she wanted to say was cut off when a producer and audio tech surrounded her and started getting her mic'd up for her interview.

"We're sticking to the topics Tom and I went over, right?" Riley asked the producer now. "My writing process, how my life as a TV reporter has inspired my writing, and then the basics of this Christmas Boot C— I mean Camp, Christmas Camp, that I'm doing?"

But instead of answering, the stressed-out looking producer took Riley's arm and practically ran her over to where she'd be doing the interview. "We need to get you set up. Now," he said. "Sit here." The producer sat her down on in a director-style chair next to the host's empty one.

The set looked like a living room that was decorated for Christmas. There was a beautiful Christmas tree with gold and white lights surrounded by lots of colorfully wrapped presents.

"Don't worry," a man said as he walked over to Riley and sat down in the host's chair next to her. "You just need to answer the questions."

The fact that he was shuffling through his note cards and never once made eye contact made Riley worry even more. She also didn't like his tone. It was dismissive, not welcoming.

She sat up straight and spoke a little louder. "And you are?" Her own tone had bite to it.

It didn't faze him. He glanced up at her like it was a bother. "I'm Joe Bramson. I'm taking Tom's place today, and we're on in two minutes."

Riley instantly held out her hand. "Riley Reynolds. Nice to meet you."

But Joe was already back to going over his notes and didn't see her outstretched hand.

Riley quickly withdrew it. "Okay, then," she said under her breath as she studied him. Nothing about Joe surprised her. He was your typical on-air guy with polished good looks. When she self-consciously tried to smooth down her own hair, she was relieved to see a hair-and-makeup person hurry over to her.

While they only had time to brush her hair, spray down the flyaways, and do a final powder, it made her feel a little more confident that she wasn't going to look like a *total* hot mess on national TV.

"You're going to do great," the makeup artist whispered in

Riley's ear as she dusted her nose one more time with translucent powder. "I love your books. You're one of my favorite authors."

Riley smiled and touched her heart. "Thank you. That means a lot to me."

"I haven't had the chance to read your latest summer novel, but I will," the makeup artist said.

Riley fought to keep smiling. All she could think about was that she hoped she didn't let down another fan with her latest novel.

"There," the makeup artist said with a satisfied smile. "Much better. Good luck! I'll be watching." She gave Riley a thumbs-up as she hurried off the set.

Riley smiled back at her, thankful for her kind words. She loved her readers. Her loyal following had made her the author she was today, and she never took that for granted. Since her first novel, she had gotten hundreds of thoughtful e-mails from readers saying how her books and love stories had positively impacted their lives. Whenever she started a new novel, she always felt like she was writing for them, and she never wanted to disappoint them.

That's why she felt she needed to do whatever it took to get back on track, even if that meant going *way* out of her comfort zone by hosting this Christmas Camp Mike had come up with and then writing a Christmas love story.

She rubbed her hands together to calm her nerves. They felt cold and clammy. She usually didn't get nervous before an interview, but then she also didn't usually do a live TV interview talking about Christmas, a topic she'd spent her whole adult life successfully avoiding.

Plus, she'd spent more than a decade in front of the camera as a TV reporter herself. Her college education and determination had paid off when, after climbing her way up the ladder, working in one small market after another, she'd landed a national correspondent position in Washington DC. The difference was, as a reporter, she was always the one in control, asking the questions. Getting interviewed and having someone ask her questions was a whole different ball game.

As she glanced over at Joe, who was now smoothing down his hair and adjusting his tie, she made the snap judgement that he wasn't going to be a very good host. When she'd worked as a journalist, she'd hosted countless live shows, and she knew the number-one rule was to make sure your guest was comfortable before the show started. That was how you always got your best interviews. Watching Joe ignore her, and how he only seemed concerned about how he was going to look on camera, made her thankful she didn't have to work with guys like him anymore.

When she looked over to Mike for his support, she found him talking to a cute production assistant who seemed charmed by him.

Clearly, she was one-hundred-percent on her own here.

As she sat up straighter and ran her hand over her hair, trying to tame the stubborn flyaways, she gave herself a little pep talk.

The interview was only a few minutes. The time would go fast. Her goal was to focus on promoting her first Christmas novel, and getting her fans excited to follow along online and send in their suggestions and ideas. She already had the perfect line rehearsed for when she was asked what her Christmas story would be about. She was going to try to build suspense by telling everyone it was going to be like nothing she had ever written before but she couldn't give anything away yet, and then she would encourage people to follow along on social media for the very latest.

When the producer started the countdown to air, giving them the ten-second warning, she took a deep breath. She could do this.

Easy peasy.

When they were live, she relaxed a little as she listened to

Joe introduce her as a beloved best-selling author who wrote the kind of love stories every woman wanted to be in.

When Joe seamlessly moved on to announcing that she'd be doing a Christmas novel for the first time and getting inspiration for that book from a special Christmas Camp she was hosting this year, Riley was relieved everything was going as planned.

As he continued to talk about when and where she'd be hosting the Christmas Camp, they rolled video to show the Christmas Lake Lodge in Colorado's Rocky Mountains, and Riley was impressed by what she saw on the monitor.

Mike had shown her some quick pictures of the lodge, but they hadn't done it justice. From what she could glimpse now from the video, the place looked enchanting, like something out of a storybook. It was outlined with hundreds of white Christmas lights and overlooked a beautiful lake.

She was still taking it all in when Joe turned his attention to her.

"Riley, thank you for joining us this morning," Joe said with a perfect TV smile.

She smiled back at him. "I'm happy to be here, Joe. Thanks for having me."

Joe glanced down at his notes and back up to her. "Riley, you've had quite the career, working as a TV reporter, then as a travel writer, and now as a best-selling romance author. You've made a very successful living writing about love and relationships, about meeting 'the one' and happily-ever-afters."

Riley smiled and nodded. "Thank you."

When Joe continued, he looked her in the eye for the first time. "But isn't it true that you, yourself, have never been married, and that before writing *Heart of Summer*, you ended your last relationship and now your book sales are down?" he asked pointedly. "How can you continue to write about happily-ever-afters when you've never had one of your own?"

Chapter Three

B lindsided and stunned, Riley felt the room start to spin as all the Christmas decorations blurred into one big holiday nightmare.

When she looked over at Mike for support, her panic grew when she saw he looked just as alarmed as she felt. Heart racing, she fought to keep a smile on her face as a wave of embarrassment washed over her. Every second of silence was suffocating her, but she knew she needed to say something—and fast. She was on live television.

She'd been right about Joe all along, and she wasn't about to let a self-serving, wannabe TV host define who she was and wasn't.

She met his bold stare with one of her own. She didn't blink.

"That's a great question, Joe," she said with a sweet smile, the kind of smile that anyone who knew her would recognize as a warning. "I've actually been very blessed because I have known great love in my life, what it is to feel love and to be loved. But you know not everyone's happily-ever-after looks the same. You don't have to be married to know what love is. I write about love because I think it's the most powerful human emotion we have that connects us all. Wouldn't you agree, Joe?"

When Riley locked eyes with Joe, she saw he wasn't going to back down easily. So she did the only thing she could do. She prepared for a battle.

"So let me get this straight," Joe said. "You're saying you *have* been in love? That you have found 'the one' like you write about in your novels?"

Riley answered quickly, too quickly. "Yes."

"Yet, you're not with that person now," Joe said, continuing to prod her. "Have you ever wondered 'what if'?"

Riley laughed to mask her growing resentment at having someone pry into her personal life on live television. "Of course. Hasn't everyone?" She smiled into the camera.

"So then what happened?" Joe countered quickly. "Where is this love of your life?"

Riley instantly realized her mistake. What she'd meant to say was that all the love stories in her novels were inspired by *different* loves of her life, not just one person. She was trying to figure out the best way to clear it all up when she saw the floor director give Joe a wrap signal.

Perfectly on cue, Joe looked into the camera. "Everyone, we need to take a quick commercial break, but stay with us, because when we come back, we'll have more with best-selling author Riley Reynolds and this mysterious love of her life who has inspired her romance novels right after this break."

As soon as they were off the air, Riley gave Joe an incredulous look. There was a rational voice inside her head telling her to stay calm and professional and that getting upset wasn't going to help anything.

But she didn't listen to that voice.

Instead, she listened to the voice that told her to get the heck out of there as fast as she could. She rapidly removed her mic and stood up.

Joe looked surprised. "Where are you going? We're not done yet."

Riley laughed as she stared down Joe. "Oh, we're done. *So done.* I came here to talk about my new Christmas novel and Christmas Camp project, and you're trying to turn this into some tabloid tell-all. That's not what I signed up for."

As she started to walk away, Joe shouted after her. "If you walk out on this interview, you'll never get booked on this show again," he threatened.

Riley laughed and kept walking. "That's the best Christmas gift you could ever give me!" When she passed Mike, he was surrounded by two frantic producers and the handsome guy from the lobby who had saved her from falling. She didn't even have a chance to wonder what the lobby guy was doing there because her power heels were hitting their stride and she wasn't about to slow down for anyone.

"Riley, wait!" Mike exclaimed as she headed for the door. "You can't leave!"

Riley picked up her pace. "Watch me!"

When she got to the elevator, she impatiently pushed the button several times. "Come on. Come on. Let's go. Get me out of here," she said under her breath.

But when the elevator door opened, she was swallowed up in a group of singing Christmas carolers coming out the elevator. They looked just like the carolers in her hotel lobby. They were happily singing "Deck the Halls."

"Deck the halls with boughs of holly...
Fa la la la la, la la la la (fa la la la la, la la la la)...
'Tis the season to be jolly...
Fa la la la la, la la la la (fa la la la la, la la la la)..."

"Seriously?!" Riley exclaimed, feeling anything but jolly as she dodged one caroler after another to get inside the elevator and then pushed the "down" button as if her life and sanity depended on it.

Chapter Four

Luke stood next to Mike and watched Riley storm off the set. Cleary, Luke thought, she wasn't having a good day. First, he'd barely saved her from falling when she was running into the building earlier, and now she was running out the studio. He shook his head in amazement.

"I don't think she's coming back," Luke said.

"Riley!" Mike shouted again.

But she was already gone.

"She better come back," a producer said, glaring at Luke. "We're live in ninety seconds."

Luke looked at the livid producer and held up his hands in front him. "Hey, you're talking to the wrong guy. I don't have a horse in this race."

The producer whipped his attention over to Mike. "You get her back here or you're going on. We still have three minutes to fill."

Mike, as cool as ever, smiled at the producer. "Not a problem. Luke can go on. He's the resort manager where Riley's hosting the Christmas Camp. He can tell you all about it."

Luke's jaw dropped. "What?!"

An audio tech was already trying to get Luke mic'd up.

Luke took a step back. "Wait. Stop. No," he told the tech. "I'm not going on."

Everyone looked at Mike.

Mike locked eyes with Luke. "You have to. Riley's gone."

"Yeah, I'm aware," Luke said. "I saw her storm out of here. But I'm not doing any interview. I'm a behind-the-scenes kind of guy. I was only supposed to come to meet your author. An author *you* told me was this wonderful, charming, friendly woman who my guests would love.

"We're on in forty-five seconds," the director shouted.

Mike kept smiling his confident smile. "Look, Luke. I'm helping *you* out here, remember? I'm getting you publicity. That was our deal. So just go talk about your lodge, the Christmas Camp, what Riley's going to do, whatever you want. It isn't brain surgery. Just fill the time, get your free publicity, make everyone happy."

Luke looked at Mike as if he'd sprouted two heads. "You want me to go on national TV, in front of millions of people, and just...wing it?"

Mike smiled and patted him on the back. "Exactly. No big deal."

Luke couldn't believe this was happening. He hated doing interviews and public speaking, and besides, the only thing he knew about Riley was from the press packet Mike had sent him, and that only talked about her novels. He was starting to think this whole Christmas Camp idea was a bad idea. A really bad idea. Of course, it had all been Mike's brainchild.

Mike had been one of his college roommates. The two of them, along with their other roommate Jeff Jacoby, had done everything together. When they had graduated, they'd promised to always have one another's backs, no matter what. While Mike had gone on to be a top publicist and Jeff had earned his own accolades as an architect, Luke had been interested in the field of hospitality and finding creative and cost-effective ways to help make hotels and resorts more sustainable and eco-friendly.

Over the years, Mike had helped them both, usually offering unsolicited advice about how to get press for whatever projects they were working on. So when Jeff's dad, Ben, who owned the charming Holly Peak Inn up in the mountains of western Massachusetts decided to franchise his annual Christmas Camp for grown-ups, a Christmas-themed week filled with holiday activities to help people "disconnect to reconnect with what truly matters most at Christmas," Mike had stepped in to help with publicity.

When Mike recently learned Luke's mom, Margaret, was selling the family's Christmas Lake Lodge so she could retire in Florida, he'd persuaded Luke to hold one of Jeff's dad's Christmas Camps at the lodge not only to help get publicity before the sale but to help Jeff's dad with his franchise...and help Mike's own client by having Riley host it.

While Luke had been apprehensive about holding a Christmas Camp at the lodge, Mike had suggested that instead of a week-long event like the one's Jeff's dad did, they could just do a Christmas Camp weekend so it wouldn't be as much work to put on, especially since it was so last minute. Even just a weekend would still generate some great publicity.

But for Luke, it had really been his mom's enthusiasm that had been the deciding factor to hold the event. She loved the idea of a Christmas Camp. She adored all things Christmas and thought it was the perfect way to have one last memorable event at the lodge before they sold it. She'd said this way they could honor their family's history of hosting other people's families during the Christmas holiday for over the last century.

From the moment Luke had said yes, it felt like things had been going sideways. His mom had broken her ankle when she was in Florida with her sister looking at new potential places to live for when after they'd sold the lodge. Her injury made it really hard to travel, and Luke hadn't wanted her to risk it, or even to come back to Christmas Lake where there was so much snow on the ground. So while his mom was sitting by the pool in sunny Florida recovering, Luke had been left with having to figure out the Christmas Camp on his own.

Right now, Mike's favorite promise of a win-win was feeling more like a lose-lose to Luke as he faced doing a live TV interview he was completely unprepared for and talking about working with an author he didn't know, who had just run out on her own interview.

"So what's it going to be?" the anxious producer asked Mike.

Mike looked at Luke. "Well, buddy, it's your call," he said.

Luke hated it when Mike made it sound like he had a choice when they both knew he didn't. His family's lodge was already part of this story. They'd just shown a video of it. He knew it would be a PR nightmare if someone didn't finish the interview, and then this whole mess could end up hurting the lodge's reputation.

He knew he couldn't just bail on this interview the way Riley had. He didn't know what he was going to do about Christmas Camp, but he knew he needed time to figure out how to do damage control. So that meant he was going to have to go on live TV and *wing it.*

The host, Joe looked annoyed as he stood up. "I need to know what's going on here. Who am I talking to?"

Luke clenched his jaw. "Me. You're talking to me."

He didn't miss Mike's satisfied smile as they rushed to get him seated. Typical Mike, always getting people to do what he wanted one way or another. Luke knew Mike was only trying to help him and his mom get the best price for the lodge, but this little stunt today wasn't cool. It wasn't cool at all, and he really only blamed one person—best-selling author Riley Reynolds.

This was her interview. She should be doing it.

As the producer rushed to get Luke settled on the set, he hoped Mike knew what he was doing because his mom's future depended on it.

"Hi, I'm Luke Larchmont from the Christmas Lake Lodge." Luke held out his hand to Joe, but the host was too busy riffling through his notes to pay attention.

"Look," Joe said without looking up. "We have three minutes to fill. I have no idea who you are so I'll just ask you to tell us how you're going to be working with Riley Reynolds, the romance novelist who will never be on this show again. Got it?"

Luke forced a smile. "Got it," he said, but inside he was thinking, *What a jerk.*

When he looked over at Mike, who gave him an enthusiastic thumbs-up, all Luke could do was shake his head and hope he didn't make a complete fool of himself on national TV. He told himself he'd be fine as long as he was talking about the lodge.

He'd grown up working at the lodge. He could remember his first job when he was eight, gathering kindling for the fireplaces in the guest rooms. Many of the guests returned year after year, making them feel more like family. Luke had always believed that the Christmas Lake Lodge was special because of all the people who stayed there.

Raised in Colorado's breathtaking Rocky Mountains, Luke always knew he wanted to find a job where he could combine his love of hotels and resorts with his passion for protecting the environment, and he'd done just that.

After graduating from college in the top of his class, with a double major in hospitality and environmental design, he'd started working for a world-class company in Germany that was a leader in helping to create sustainable businesses. Over the years, he'd continued to exceed expectations. He'd been about to be named vice president when a year ago, his mom called saying his dad was sick and he'd rushed right home.

His dad had died shortly after, so Luke had stayed at the lodge to help his mom. He was an only child, and she needed him. That's when he learned just how much the lodge was struggling financially. His parents hadn't wanted to worry him, but after he saw the books, he was worried. Really worried.

Before he'd gone off to college, they'd talked about if he might someday like to run the lodge and keep it in the family. It had been hard, but he had been honest with his parents, saying he didn't want to stay in Colorado for the rest of his life. He wanted more. He wanted to travel and learn from people around the world who were spearheading Green initiatives for businesses of all kinds, including hotels and resorts.

They had all agreed that when it was time for his parents to retire, they would sell the lodge. It would be the end of an era, but a positive change and a new start for all of them. This way they could hopefully give another family a chance to make their own history at the lodge.

But when the city next to Christmas Lake, Forest Hills, had changed its rules it had allowed a huge hotel chain to build the Skyline Resort, a monster property with close to 1,500 rooms. The lodge, its thirty rooms, had quickly started losing customers. Before the Skyline Resort, no hotels or resorts over a hundred rooms had been allowed in an effort to protect the environment and maintain the charm and authenticity the area was beloved for. Now the Skyline Resort, with all the fancy amenities the area had never had before, including an award-winning spa, a giant gym with fitness classes, a year-round heated swimming pool, a 1,000-capacity theater, and a teen room with video games and all the latest technology, was getting all the publicity and bookings.

The lodge's drop-in business concerned Luke because he wanted to do everything he could to help his mom retire in Florida the way she had hoped to, but that all counted on them being able to get a good price when they sold the lodge. So, if that meant going on live TV to get the lodge some much-needed publicity, that's what he'd do. But he didn't have to like it.

Chapter Five

Later that same day, as the snow continued to blanket New York City, Riley, now wearing her much more practical power boots, rushed toward Café Lola. It was her favorite cozy little Upper West Side wine bar. She breathed a sigh of relief as she pulled open the door.

"I made it," she said under her breath with a thankful smile. As soon as she set foot inside, she could feel her stress start to ease. She was in her happy place. Her favorite escape when she'd lived in the neighborhood and had wanted to relax and have a glass of wine.

Café Lola was tiny, but what it lacked in space it more than made up for with its menu, which included authentic Spanish tapas and unique European wines. But the real reason she came was to talk to the bartender and owner, Alejandro— Alex for short.

Even though he was in his late sixties, Alex worked six days a week behind the bar, sometimes seven, and always during happy hour. He insisted it was his customers who kept him young. Riley could personally vouch for the fact that Alex had as much energy and enthusiasm as any twenty-year-old, and he always had a way of making everyone feel like they were his favorite customer.

It was no secret that Riley adored him. The truth was, Alex

was far more than just her favorite bartender. He'd been like a surrogate father to her when she had first moved to Manhattan and hadn't known a soul.

As she looked around the bar, she laughed. Alex had put up even more Christmas decorations than she'd remembered.

While the bar always had white twinkle lights up year-round to give it a romantic feel, at Christmastime, Alex went all-out, adding more lights anywhere he could find space. Whether it was over the bar, dangling from the ceiling, hanging down the wall, or lining the windows, there were lights everywhere, and there was always Christmas music playing.

Riley also wasn't surprised to see Alex was still putting up an impressive eight-foot Christmas tree that was decorated with hundreds of wine corks attached to red ribbon. She walked over to the tree and smiled when she looked closer at the corks where you could see people's names written on them. It was one of Café Lola's traditions. When you ordered a bottle of wine, you got to write your name and date on the cork, and it would be made into an ornament to be displayed on the tree. She smiled remembering how she'd contributed more than a few corks to the tree over the years.

At first, she'd been surprised when Alex had started decorating for Christmas right after Halloween, but he'd happily told her that Christmas decorations just gave you one more thing to be thankful for at Thanksgiving. Riley loved that Alex was always coming up with sayings like that.

He also said Christmas decorations were a wonderful way to show your Christmas spirit and that the amount of decorations you put up was a direct correlation to how much Christmas spirit you had in your heart. If this was true, then Riley didn't know anyone who had as much Christmas spirit as Alex.

Her first Christmas in New York he'd tried to recruit her

to help decorate. When she had passed, telling him she wasn't a Christmassy person he'd made it his personal goal to get her to embrace the holiday. But try as he might over the years, the only thing she'd ever embraced was Grandma Lola's mulled wine.

Riley was just taking off her coat when Alex came rushing over.

"I thought I might see you for happy hour," he said as he embraced her with a heartfelt hug and then took her coat.

Seeing Alex instantly made her feel better. She knew she'd made the right choice to head uptown in a snowstorm just to come see him.

He took both her hands and stood back. "Let me look at you."

When he looked into her eyes, Riley suddenly felt a little self-conscious because she knew Alex always saw her, really saw her, and she wondered for the zillionth time if he could actually look into her soul.

"Alex, it's so good to see you," she said and meant it with all her heart.

Alex smiled. "Do you know what I think?"

Riley smiled back. "What?"

"I think you need some of our mulled wine," Alex answered with confidence. "Your favorite. I made a fresh batch and saved your seat for you."

Alex motioned to a barstool in the corner. Riley laughed at the little reserved sign had been put up. She had never seen him put a reserved sign up anywhere in the bar.

She shook her head in wonder. "How did you know I was going to be here?"

Alex glanced up at the TV on the wall.

Riley signed. "You saw the interview this morning?"

Alex put his arm around her and walked her over to her

reserved seat. "*Mi tesoro…everyone* saw the interview."

It took some of the sting out of knowing everyone else had seen her TV meltdown when Alex called her *mi tesoro,* a Spanish term of endearment that meant "my treasure."

As if sensing her embarrassment, he took her hand again and gave it a little squeeze. "The first drink is on me. Some of my grandma's magic mulled wine coming right up."

Riley laughed. "When did it become *magic* mulled wine?"

Alex grinned back at her. "It's Christmas. Everything's always magical at Christmas."

Riley laughed as she took her reserved seat over in the bar's cozy corner. "I don't know about the magic part, but I have missed Grandma Lola's mulled wine and I've missed you."

"I have missed you more, *mi tesoro,*" Alex said as he stirred the mulled wine simmering in a giant Crock-Pot on the counter.

Riley let herself close her eyes for a moment as she blissfully inhaled the familiar scent of cloves and cinnamon.

"I've dreamed of this," Riley almost whispered in a soft voice. "I don't get this back in Arizona."

Alex nodded. "I always love making it for you. No one else appreciates my grandma's recipe like you do."

"Well, they don't know what they are missing," Riley said.

"That's what I always tell them," Alex said emphatically.

Riley laughed as she settled into her favorite spot. She loved leaning up against the brick wall and having full view of the entire bar.

She could still remember her first time coming into Café Lola on a cold winter night, her first night in New York City. It had been about this same time of year, just a few weeks before Christmas. She had flown in from her mom's place in Florida and had arrived in the city with only a carry-on suitcase, a laptop, and a dream. Her dream was to finally be the author she'd always hoped to be.

The path she'd taken to come to New York had been kind of like Dorothy's yellow brick road in *The Wizard of Oz*, filled with twists and turns and lots of drama.

She'd gone from working as an Emmy Award-winning TV news reporter and anchor, covering crime and corruption as an investigative reporter, to being a war correspondent in Iraq and Afghanistan, before doing a one-eighty and working as a freelance luxury travel writer, visiting some of the most glamorous places on the planet. The problem was her fabulous travel writer job didn't even come close to paying her bills because she was basically only paid in free travel, nothing more. She had tried to make it work, living off her savings, but when her money ran out, luckily, her mom had let her move home while she figured out what to do next. It was during this incredibly challenging time that she'd landed her first book deal to write a romance novel.

Knowing this was her chance for a new start, she'd decided that if she was going to reinvent herself from a tough crime and war reporter to a romance author who wrote uplifting and heartfelt stories, then Manhattan was the perfect place to do it. There, she could be anyone she wanted to be. So she had taken her small book advance, sold her car, and moved to the city determined to write the kind of love stories that would hopefully help inspire readers to find their own happily-ever-afters.

She'd ended up at Café Lola her first night in town. After taking one look at her ridiculously tiny studio apartment, she'd grabbed her computer and charger and had quickly headed downstairs to the bar. She'd met Alex as she was looking for a place to plug in her computer, which had run out of battery during her flight. She must have looked freaked out because Alex had asked her if she was okay. That's when she had babbled her life story and told him that she'd just moved to New York and didn't know anyone, and how she was convinced her apartment was smaller than a jail cell.

Alex had found her the corner seat at the bar, the same one she was sitting in now, where there was an outlet. He'd also brought her some mulled wine, on the house, as he welcomed her to the city, and promised her that his grandma Lola's secret recipe would warm her heart and that everything was going to be okay. That night had started their friendship and her tradition of using the cozy corner at Café Lola like her office. It was where she had written her first novel.

She was jarred back to the present when a steaming mug of mulled wine was put down in front of her. She looked up to see Alex's smiling face.

"Here you go," he said. "Just like you like it. With extra cinnamon."

"Cinnamon is the wonder spice," Riley said as she took the mug from Alex. When she got a closer look at the mug, she couldn't help but laugh.

It was a Santa mug.

"Not *you* again," she said to Santa's smiling face.

Alex gave her a knowing look. "I know it's your favorite mug, even though you pretend not to like it. You can't fool me."

Riley laughed loudly. "Oh, Alex. I really have missed you!"

"And I've never given up hope that you'll find your Christmas spirit," Alex said. He pointed at his heart. "It lives in here. It never goes away."

Since she couldn't remember what Christmas spirit felt like, she had no answer for him. Instead, she concentrated on her drink, waving the steam from her mulled wine toward her and inhaling blissfully.

"This smells like heaven." Riley said as she carefully picked up her mug.

"It smells like *Christmas*," Alex said proudly. "That's what Grandma Lola used to always say."

Riley took her first sip, and it didn't disappoint. As always, it was the perfect blend of red wine, brandy, and spices like nutmeg, cinnamon, and cloves, which pulled it all together and made you feel all warm inside. Despite her asking year after year, Alex had refused to share his grandma's secret recipe, insisting it could only be passed down to family members.

"This is delicious, as always," she said as she held up her Santa mug to Alex. "Cheers to Grandma Lola."

Alex quickly poured some mulled wine into another Santa mug and clinked it against hers. "Cheers to Grandma Lola and to Christmas."

Riley laughed. "You never give up…"

Alex gave her a determined look. "On you? Never. I have faith."

"In me?" Riley asked as she took another sip and smiled as it warmed her all the way down to her toes. She wiggled them around in her power boots.

"And in Christmas," he said with a confident smile.

She could only shake her head, but she was smiling. She always enjoyed banter with Alex, even if it was about Christmas.

When he took some more cork ornaments over to the Christmas tree and started adding them to the already overloaded branches, he looked around the bar and frowned.

Riley knew what he was thinking. "It looks like it's going to be a slow night," she said.

Alex nodded. "Probably all the snow, but you know what that means?"

Riley shook her head. "No, what?"

Alex came over and sat down on the barstool next to her.

"It means we have time for a little talk."

Riley laughed. "Uh, that's what I thought we've been doing."

Alex gave her a look. "I mean a talk about this next book you're doing. A *Christmas* book? Did I hear that right this morning on TV? How is this possible for Miss I Don't Do Christmas? And who is this great love of your life? How have I missed all this? What haven't you told me? You have a lot of explaining to do, so start talking."

She made a face as she put down her Santa mug. "You saw the *whole* interview?"

"All of it," he said. "Including the part after the commercial break when you weren't there. You walked out, didn't you?"

Riley nodded. "I did. I felt like I was being attacked."

"You *were* being attacked," Alex said.

Riley loved him for that.

"I know, but I really needed that interview. My last book didn't do so great, and this Christmas books is my last shot. I could lose my publishing deal."

"Your publisher can do that?" Alex asked, concerned.

"My publisher *will* do that if I don't write a new book that will win back my readers." She took another sip of wine.

"And that's supposed to be this Christmas book?" he asked. "So, they don't know—"

"What? That I don't do Christmas?" Riley sighed. "That I'm the last person that should be writing a Christmas book? No, they don't know any of that. How could I tell them that? If they think writing a Christmas book is the only way to save my career, and I tell them I don't have a clue about what kind of story to write, they're going to drop me right now."

Alex got up, took her mug, and went to get her a refill. She waited for him to say something, anything, but he remained silent as he handed her back the now full Santa mug.

"It's a mess," Riley said. "I know."

"I don't see this as a mess," Alex said. "I see this as an opportunity."

"What do you mean?" Riley asked.

He smiled at her. "You know what they say..."

Riley laughed. "No, but I know you're about to tell me."

"Even in the darkest moments a new day will bring light. You just need to find the light. You need to find Christmas," Alex said.

"You make it sound so easy," Riley replied.

"It shouldn't be that hard," Alex said. "But now I have to ask what all of America is asking right now."

Riley arched one eyebrow. "What's that?"

Alex locked eyes with her. "Who were you talking about that inspired all your romance books? Who is the love of your life that got away? It's not Tyler, is it? I just didn't see that with the two of you when you came in here."

Alex shook her head. "No, I wasn't talking about Tyler."

"Okay, then your boyfriend in Utah. The one you said you lived with. What was his name? Brandon?" Alex asked.

"Brendan," Riley corrected him. "And no, I wasn't talking about Brendan."

Alex's eyes lit up. "Oh, then it had to be your old college boyfriend from Los Angeles, the movie producer. Didn't you always say he was your first love?"

Riley looked impressed. "You're talking about Colin. I can't believe you remember all this. But then again, I can't believe I *told* you all this."

"Bartenders," Alex said. "We get told a lot."

Riley reached out and took his hand. "And so do friends.

Thank you for always listening to me and all my stories."

"You're welcome," Alex said as one of the waiters walked over carrying a huge plate of parmesan truffle fries and put them in front of Riley. She gave Alex a questioning look.

"You always say my truffle fries make everything better," Alex said.

Riley nodded, smiled. "I do say that."

"So I ordered you a double," Alex said.

Riley laughed. "Well, it has been that kind of day."

Just as she went to pick up a fry, he pulled the plate toward him, out of her reach.

"Hey," she said. "What's going on?" But she already knew. Whenever Alex wanted to get information out of her, withholding her favorite fries was one of his tactics.

"So what great love of your life were you talking about on TV?" Alex pressed. "If it wasn't your last boyfriend, Tyler, the hot-shot lawyer, and it wasn't Brandon, the guy you traveled the world..."

"Brendan," Riley corrected again.

"And it wasn't your college sweetheart, then who were you talking about in that interview? Those are the only three real boyfriends you ever told me about. Unless you left someone out..."

Riley shook her head. "I didn't." She picked up her cinnamon stir stick to swirl her mulled wine around. "There isn't anyone else. At least not anyone I was really invested in."

Alex, looking perplexed, leaned back and crossed his arms in front of his chest. "Then who is this mystery guy?"

"That's just it," Riley said. "There's no mystery guy. What I should have said was that I have had great loves in my life, *plural*, and that those loves have all inspired the stories in my romance novels. There isn't one true love that got away."

"Well, that's not what it sounded like," Alex said.

Riley picked up her drink. "I know."

She took a sip and was just putting down her Santa mug when a blast of cold air hit her full force, as someone came in the front door.

Riley shivered, but not from the cold. Because standing in the doorway was Margo, her agent, and her expression was as icy as the weather.

"Oh boy," Riley said underneath her breath and then met Margo's frosty stare. "You found me."

Chapter Six

R iley sat up even straighter as Margo marched toward her.

"It wasn't too hard," Margo said, her tone matching her demeanor. "You always come here." She turned to Alex. "Hello, Alejandro."

Alex smiled. "Margo, good to see you. It's been a while."

Margo looked at Riley. "Yes, it has. Some of my authors have been keeping me a little too busy."

Alex chucked. "Understood. Can I get you anything?"

Margo never took her eyes off Riley. "Yes, you can get me an author that doesn't disappear on me after she's just walked out on a national TV interview."

"So that's a no?" Alex asked.

"That's a no," Margo confirmed. "I won't be staying."

Alex gave Riley a sympathetic look and moved the plate of fries back in front of her before retreating to give them some privacy.

Riley picked up a fry, took a big bite, and slid the plate over to Margo. "You sure you don't want to stay and have some fries, order a drink?" Riley asked. "These fries are amazing."

Instead of a fry, Margo picked up Riley's phone from the bar and flipped it over so she could see the screen. There were dozens of missed messages. She held the phone up to Riley.

"I've been trying to call you. Mike's been trying to call you," Margo said, exasperated. She looked at Riley's phone again. "Apparently, everyone's been trying to call you. You need to answer your phone."

Riley rarely saw Margo this upset. One of the things that made Margot such a great agent was how calm and unflappable she usually was. But when she finally did get mad, it wasn't pretty. They'd become friends over the years, but Riley knew and respected that Margo never let that fact get in the way of being her agent first.

Margo pushed the fries out of Riley's reach. "I don't have time to sit here and have a drink, and neither do you," she said. She dug inside her tote bag and slapped an envelope on the bar in front of Riley.

"What's this?" Riley eyed the envelope. "A Christmas bonus?" she joked. She never got a Christmas bonus…

When Margo smiled, it made Riley nervous. She knew that smile, and it always meant Margo was up to something.

"I guess you could call it a *bonus*," Margo said sweetly—too sweetly. "It's your boarding pass. Your ticket to Colorado. You leave first thing in the morning."

"In the morning?" Riley asked as she grabbed the envelope, opened it, and took out the printed boarding pass. "How can I leave in the morning? I still have a whole day of interviews to do tomorrow that you and Mike have planned for me to promote this Christmas Camp and my novel."

Margo shook her head. "Not anymore. All your interviews have been canceled."

Riley's jaw dropped. "Everyone called off my interviews? I can't believe they would do that."

"They didn't. Your publisher did," Margo said without blinking.

"Wait? What? Why?" Riley asked, giving Margo her full attention. "I thought you said I needed all this publicity if we were going to save my career."

"I did say that, and we do," Margo answered. "That was the plan until your little stunt of running out on your live interview. Now everyone's doing damage control. They've canceled all interviews until they can figure out what they want to do."

Riley's heart beat faster as she fought to stay calm. "What do you mean, while they figure out what to do? What is there to figure out?"

Margo met her stare and didn't blink. "They're trying to figure out if they still want you as their author after you walked out on a national television interview this morning. An interview most authors would kill to have the opportunity to do."

"Margo, come on," Riley said. "What did you want me to do? I wasn't going to sit there and let that guy tear my personal life apart on national TV."

"He was a jerk," Margo said. "There's no doubt about it. And honestly, I would have probably done the same thing."

Riley looked relieved.

"But," Margo went on.

Riley didn't like the sound of that.

"There are consequences for your actions," Margo said. "I've been trying to call you, to explain, as maybe this could have been avoided, but…"

Riley shook her head, disbelieving. "But now all my interviews are canceled."

"That's not even the worst of it," Margo said. "The guy running the place where you're supposed to be doing this Christmas Camp is upset."

"What's he upset about?" Riley asked. "He got a lot of great coverage in that interview. They rolled video of the place and everything."

"Haven't you watched the segment?" Margo asked. "It's online everywhere. It's gone viral."

Riley shook her head vehemently. "Are you kidding? I don't want to watch how I was humiliated on national TV. It was bad enough that I had to live through it once."

"Then let me enlighten you," Margo said. "After you stormed out, they had to fill the time somehow, so the guy who runs the lodge had to go on in your place at the last minute."

Now Riley looked even more confused. "What do you mean he had to go on in my place? He's in Colorado."

"No, he came to the TV station to meet you," Margo corrected her. "He apparently had to be in town for some other business, so Mike set up a meeting for you after the segment. Anyway, the point is, this guy had to go on national television totally unprepared and talk about what you're going to be doing at the Christmas Camp."

"What?" Riley exclaimed. "I don't even know what I'm going to be doing at Christmas Camp."

"Exactly," Margo said. "So imagine how this guy felt when he was thrown on national TV to cover *for you* after you ran out. Mike says he doesn't like public speaking in the first place. So bottom line, he's not happy about any of this, and he's ready to cancel the whole author event."

Riley gave Margo an incredulous look. "Can he even do that? We're supposed to do this Christmas Camp in just a few days…"

"Yes!" Margo said, obviously losing the little patience she had left. "It's his family's lodge, and his reputation is on the line, too. He can do whatever he wants. Mike called in a favor to set this whole thing up, but now this Colorado guy doesn't think it's a good idea, doesn't think you're the right fit for the lodge."

Riley frowned. "What do you mean? The right *fit?*"

"Riley, it doesn't matter what he means," Margo said. "If this guy cancels, can you imagine all the bad publicity? We've already selected the Christmas Campers from the thousands of applicants. People have already bought their airfare. Your fans have made plans to come see you as part of their Christmas celebration. If this gets canceled, you'll be the Grinch who stole their Christmas."

Riley frowned. While she wasn't a Christmas person, she certainly didn't want to be known as a Grinch.

Margo wagged Riley's phone in front of her. "Mike and I have been trying to call you so you could meet with the guy while he was still in town, try to smooth things over, but you haven't answered your phone."

Riley jump up from her seat. "Okay, so let's go meet this guy and I'll explain. I'll win him over. It'll be fine."

Margo put Riley's phone down and crossed her arms in front of her. "It's too late."

"What do you mean 'it's too late'?" Riley asked.

"When we couldn't reach you, he wasn't about to wait around," Margo said. "He's already heading back to Colorado."

"So you're saying…" Riley started.

"I'm saying," Margo replied, "this could cost you."

"Cost me the Christmas Camp event?"

Margo shook her head and locked eyes with Riley again. "No, this could cost you your publishing *career.* Like I told you, you can't afford any more bad publicity, Riley. This isn't a game. This Christmas Camp was supposed to save your career, without it…"

"I'm done," Riley finished for her.

Margo nodded. "I'm afraid so."

Riley picked up the boarding pass again. "So this is…"

Margo took a deep breath. "Your last chance. Mike says you need to go to Colorado and talk to this guy, show him you're not the hotheaded prima donna he thinks you are."

Riley put her hands on her hips and looked part-insulted and part-hurt. "A prima donna? Seriously? Me?"

"Mike's words, not mine," Margo added. "Apparently, it was what the guy said after you stormed off the set."

Riley shook her head, annoyed. "I had every right to leave that interview…"

Margo held up her hands. "You need to get over the interview and who was right and who was wrong. What's done is done, and now you need to decide if you still want a publishing deal or not. If you do, you need to go to Colorado and make this right with this guy. You need to persuade him to reconsider holding the Christmas Camp for you. We're running out of time," she said. "If you're going to do damage control, you have to do it *right now*. You need to be on that plane first thing tomorrow morning."

Riley gave Margo an incredulous look. "This whole thing is impossible."

Margo's eyes flashed a warning. "If you care about being an author, you better find a way to make it possible. You're not going to get another chance. This is your only shot."

"Margo—"

But Margo cut her off. "Riley, I'm doing the best I can to try to help you here. So what's it going to be? I need to let Mike and everyone know. This is your call, your career. What do you want to do?"

Riley looked over to Alex for moral support. When he looked into her eyes and nodded, she picked up the boarding pass again.

Margo checked her phone. "I just got another text from Mike," Margo said. "Are you in or not?"

Riley felt a rush of adrenalin mixed with determination. It fueled her forward. "I'm in," Riley said with conviction. "I'll go apologize to this guy and make this Christmas Camp thing work. Whatever it takes to get my career back on track. I mean, how hard can it be? I'm sure once I talk to this guy, he'll understand what happened. Right?"

When Riley saw a flash of concern cross Margo's face, she tilted her head to one side. Riley tried again. "Right?"

Margo merely nodded as she started to head for the door. "I'll let Mike know you'll be on that flight to Denver."

She was halfway out the door when Riley called out to her. "Margo!"

Margo turned around.

"Thank you," Riley said. Her voice was softer, filled with sincerity. "I mean it. I'm sorry I let you down today, and I know you're just trying to help me. I'll fix this. You'll see. It's going to be okay."

When Margo just nodded again, Riley saw something in her eyes that made her feel like there was something Margo wasn't telling her. But before she could say anything more, Margo disappeared out the door.

Riley looked over at Alex. "I better go."

Alex had already gotten her coat for her and held it out so she could put it on. He then handed her a brown takeout bag.

"What's this?" Riley asked.

"Your favorite dessert," Alex said proudly.

Riley's eyes lit up. "Your homemade churros?"

"With extra sugar, just like you like them," Alex said. "I added red and green sugar to make them extra festive."

Riley laughed. "Of course you did." She gave him a heart-felt hug. "Thank you, Alex."

He put his arm around her as he walked her to the door. "It's going to be okay. Just go find Christmas. Find your story.

You can do this. I know you can."

Riley looked into his eyes and took a deep breath. "I hope so."

"Merry Christmas, *mi tesoro.*"

Riley gave him another quick hug. "Thank you for everything."

Chapter Seven

The next day, when Riley landed at the Denver airport, she was thankful Mike had hired her a driver, one that actually showed up this time. Originally, she'd planned to get a rental car. She didn't like the idea of being stuck anywhere without a car. But Mike had told her the drive to Christmas Lake, the community that the Christmas Lake Lodge called home, was about three hours up the mountain and that the roads could get tricky, especially with snow in the forecast, so she'd agreed to having someone pick her up.

But as they left Denver, Riley wished she'd had more time in the Mile High City. She'd wanted to do some shopping and pick up a few things for her trip to the Colorado Rockies. When she'd moved to Arizona, she'd happily donated all her winter clothes, embracing a new warmer climate and lifestyle. Her original plan had been to buy some basics in New York before going to Colorado, but that plan had flown out the window when Margo had only given her a few hours to catch her flight.

What she had packed was based on what Mike had told her, that all she needed to do at Christmas Camp was to host a welcome reception, some author chats, and join everyone for the meals. So she'd brought a couple pairs of black pants—one leather and one suede—and some lightweight designer sweaters, along with a couple of cute professional dresses and a cocktail dress for the reception.

When she'd asked Mike if there were any other activities she needed to know about for Christmas Camp, he said he'd check with the owner and send her a list if needed. When he never sent her anything, and she'd followed up again, he told her not to worry saying he's sure if there was anything more it would just be "regular Christmas stuff."

Her plan B—because she always had a plan B—was that if she did finally get her schedule from Mike and something else was needed, she could quickly do the necessary shopping in Denver before heading up to Christmas Lake. But that plan had also backfired when her driver, Harry, a kind, soft-spoken man in his late sixties, told her a storm was coming and it was best for them to get on the road as soon as they could before things got really bad.

When Riley had looked outside the icy car window, all she could see was a whiteout. She had thought the weather they were already experiencing was "really bad," but Harry had told her this was nothing, just a few flurries, and assured her they would get to the lodge safely. As they climbed up the mountain, the SUV's wheels kept spinning as they hit random patches of ice. She didn't even want to think about what Harry would consider bad weather.

She was thankful when he had slowed down enough that it felt like they were barely crawling as he expertly navigated the narrow, winding road. He had turned up the Christmas music and was humming along to it. The song playing was, "Walking in a Winter Wonderland."

As she peered out the window, she was glad she wasn't *walking* anywhere. Still, she had to admit the scenery, or what she could see of it through the whirling snowflakes, was breathtaking. The mountain pass was truly a winter wonderland. All the evergreens were draped in a thick blanket of snow, and all the waterfalls were frozen in time, surrounded by sparkling icicles.

Riley leaned forward so she could talk to Harry. "I don't know how you can drive in this. I can barely see."

Harry kept his eyes on the road and smiled. "I've driven Glacier Pass hundreds of times. I know every bend in this road. We'll be fine."

But when their SUV hit a patch of ice and fishtailed, Riley shrieked and grabbed the front seat. "Holy crap!" She exclaimed. "This is getting worse."

Harry just chuckled as they continued on their way. "That's just Shadow Corner. There's always ice there because the sun never hits it. Don't worry. We're safe. You can sit back and relax. Enjoy the ride."

He turned up the Christmas music.

As Riley sat back and checked her seat belt, making sure it was on as tight as it could go, she caught Harry watching her in his rearview mirror.

"Everything is going to be okay, Miss Reynolds," he said in the most confident of voices. "I will have you there in no time. You just have to believe."

Riley caught the twinkle in Harry's eyes.

Great, Riley thought, *now this driver thinks he's Santa Claus, too.*

"This is your first time to Christmas Lake?" Harry asked.

Riley nodded. "It is. I've been to a few ski resorts here in Colorado but nothing in this area."

"That's the beauty of Christmas Lake," Harry said. "They keep things pretty quiet and laid back here."

"Are you from the area?" Riley asked. "Or are you based in Denver?"

"I move around," Harry answered. "I go wherever the work

needs to be done."

Riley wasn't sure what he meant by that, but before she could ask any more questions, her phone rang. It was Mike. She let out a deep breath before answering.

Here we go, she thought as she braced for whatever drama Mike was about to bring.

"This is Riley."

"Where are you?" Mike jumped right in.

Riley could hardly hear him. "I'm in the SUV," she said.

"What?" he asked, shouting now.

Riley checked the bars on the phone. She barely had a signal.

"As soon as we go around this corner, you're going to lose the signal all together," Harry warned her.

Riley nodded. "Mike, can you hear me? I'm about to lose you. I'll call you when I get to the lodge."

"I need to tell you—" Mike started, but then the call dropped.

"Mike? Are you there? Hello?" She held up her phone trying to get a signal back but didn't have any luck.

"Is everything okay?" Harry asked.

Riley shrugged. "I hope so. He said he needed to tell me something, but then again, Mike always needs to tell me something. It will just have to wait until I get there."

Riley stared out the window. All the whirling snow was making her sleepy. She'd only gotten a few hours of sleep the night before, and she could never sleep on a plane or in a car. The last thing she remembered was letting her head fall back against the cool leather seat and thinking she would just rest her eyes for a few minutes...

"Miss Reynolds? Miss Reynolds?"

Riley heard her name faintly, as if it were coming from far, far away. Until it got louder and sounded closer.

"Miss Reynolds?"

Riley awoke with a start, sitting straight up. She couldn't believe she'd actually fallen asleep.

"What? I mean, yes?" She rubbed her blurry eyes.

Harry turned around in his seat and smiled at her. "We've arrived."

Chapter Eight

S till groggy, Riley looked out of the frosted SUV's window and blinked several times. She rubbed her eyes again as if not believing what she was seeing. For a second, she actually wondered if she were still asleep and dreaming because what she saw in front of her looked like a Christmas fairy tale.

It was that special time, right before dark, that everyone called "magic hour" and tonight the magic was turning the Colorado winter sky different shades of violet that were reflecting on what Riley guessed was Christmas Lake. The pristine frozen lake was covered with fresh snow and tucked up against the majestic mountains. All along the water's edge there were spectacular evergreens decorated with white twinkling Christmas lights.

But what really caught Riley's attention was the one beautiful Christmas tree standing all alone right in the middle of the lake. It was the only tree that had multicolored lights of bright red, green, gold, and silver.

"Welcome to Christmas Lake Lodge," Harry said proudly, as if he owned the lodge himself.

"Wow," Riley said softly. "Now I see why they call it Christmas Lake."

"It's really something," Harry said, smiling. "This lodge always reminds me of what Christmas should be like."

Riley gave Harry a curious look. "How's that?" she asked.

"You'll see," Harry said cheerfully as he got out of the car and went to open her door.

Riley was still taking it all in as she stepped out of the SUV.

Immediately, the lodge itself had her full attention. It was even more magical than the video she'd seen during her interview. The entire lodge was outlined in white Christmas lights, giving it a whimsical charm like something straight out of a Christmas fairy tale. It was two stories, and there was garland with more white lights draped all along a wraparound balcony. In every window there was a gorgeous giant wreath with a huge red velvet bow. The same style wreath, with an even bigger bow, hung on the front door.

It all looked so…welcoming.

This was a home that knew love. She could already feel it.

"You go on into the lodge," Harry said, bringing her back to reality. "Get out of the snow. I'll bring in your luggage."

"Thank you," she called back to him as she looked up at the sky and could only see a blur of whirling snowflakes all around her. "And thank you for getting us here safely. Are you're going to be able to get back down the mountain tonight? It looks like this snow isn't letting up anytime soon."

"This isn't anything to worry about," Harry said with a chuckle as he continued to get her luggage out of the trunk. "I've been in a lot worse." He held up her small carry-on suitcase and garment bag. "This is all you have?" he asked, sounding impressed. "I wish you'd teach my wife how to pack."

Riley laughed. "I do a lot of author events, so I've gotten pretty good at planning my professional attire for these things and keeping it simple."

Harry paused. "Professional attire? You need *professional attire* for a Christmas Camp?"

"Of course," Riley said as she made her way down the walkway to the lodge's front door. She inhaled, enjoying the fragrant

Douglas firs that lined the path. Each tree had its own set of white twinkle lights.

She was almost to the front door when she passed an impressive five-foot-tall wood carving of a bear. As soon as she did, music started playing.

> *"We wish you a BEARy Christmas…*
> *We wish you a BEARy Christmas…*
> *We wish you a BEARy Christmas…*
> *And a happy BEAR year!"*

She jumped back, startled.

The music stopped.

When she started walking again, it started back up.

> *"We wish you a BEARy Christmas…"*

She froze and looked around, but there was no one.

"Okay, who is messing with me?" she asked out loud.

Silence.

She suspiciously eyed the bear. She took a step toward it.

Silence.

She took another step.

Nothing.

Relieved, she continued toward the front door. Instantly, the song came back on.

> *"We wish you a BEARy Christmas…*
> *We wish you a BEARy Christmas…*
> *And a happy BEAR year!"*

A little freaked out, she ran the rest of the way and yanked the door open and dashed inside, shutting the door quickly behind her.

She looked out the window at the bear. She laughed to herself. "Okay, that was just weird."

When a dog barked, she whirled around.

Directly in front of her, staring up at her with dark-brown soulful eyes, was a Bernese Mountain Dog who stood almost three feet tall. Riley guessed he looked like he weighed at least seventy pounds. He was mostly black with some touches of chocolate brown, and the breed's characteristic white stripe down the middle of his face that continued on to circle his nose. He had little tufts of brown above his eyes that looked like eyebrows.

He barked again. But it wasn't a threatening, scary kind of bark. It was more of a welcoming bark, especially because he was also wagging his tail.

"Well, hello to you, too," Riley said with a smile. "Aren't you the great guard dog?"

He gave her a curious look, then turned around and trotted off, plopping himself down next to a spectacular stone fireplace where a roaring fire crackled away.

Riley laughed, watching him. "Or not."

As she walked farther into the room, she turned around, slowly taking it all in. It was enchanting.

The lobby looked like a giant cozy living room. Every inch, from top to bottom, was beautifully furnished with charming Christmas decorations. The stone fireplace reached up to the soaring beamed ceiling. Draped across its mantel was a gorgeous garland that was lit up with white lights and covered with pine cones, red berries, and red-and-green plaid bows outlined in a gold trim that glittered in the light.

On a bookcase next to the fireplace, there was a collection of colorful nutcrackers of all shapes and sizes, ranging from just five inches tall to more than two feet tall. They all wore military outfits, and most of them also had crowns and carried swords. They looked fierce, ready for battle. But it was the nutcracker on the far right that captured Riley's attention. It was a little different from the rest. It was about twelve inches high and wore a tall black hat instead of a crown. The hat looked like it was made of fur, and there was also fur around its jacket. It looked older than then the rest of them, and something about it was familiar...

The next thing that caught Riley's attention was the wall of floor-to-ceiling windows, showcasing a postcard-perfect view of the mountains and Christmas Lake. Even with the snow falling, she could catch a glimpse of the one lone tree lit up on the lake.

Inside the lodge, right in front of the window, there was another festive Christmas tree planted in a big, red ceramic pot that was rimmed with pine cones. The tree was decorated with red velvet bows and dozens of hand-carved wooden ornaments.

Riley walked over to the tree to get a closer look. She smiled as she carefully touched a little ornament. It was a cute pair of wooden skies. When she accidently knocked it off the branch, she caught it just before it hit the floor.

"Nice save," a husky male voice said from behind her.

Startled, Riley whirled around and then did a double take when she recognized the guy who had rescued her from falling outside the TV station the day before.

"You?!" they both said at the same time.

Riley recovered first. "You're the guy who helped me outside the TV station in New York. What are you doing here?"

The guy looked equally confused. "What are *you* doing here?"

Riley stood up straighter. "I'm hosting the Christmas Boot Camp. Are you one of the guests? What are the odds?"

The guy didn't look amused.

"No, I'm not a guest, and it's a Christmas *Camp*, not a *boot camp*."

"That's right, sorry," Riley said with a guilty smile. "I keep getting that mixed up."

The dog came over and sat down next to the guy, keeping an eye on Riley.

"I'm Luke. Luke Larchmont. My family owns this lodge," the man said with authority.

Riley's eyes grew huge. She shook her head, trying to make sense of what she was hearing. "Your family owns the lodge?"

"That's right," Luke said.

Riley, still processing, forced a smile and quickly held out her hand. "Hi, I'm Riley—"

"Yes, I know who you are," Luke shot back. "You're the author who ran out on a live interview on national TV, an interview I had finish, something I was completely unprepared to do."

Riley could see how upset he was. She bit down hard on her lower lip. "About that, I am so sorry that happened. None of that, of course, was planned and—"

"What are you doing here?" Luke asked, cutting her off again. He folded his arms in front of his chest. Nothing about his tone was welcoming.

The dog was looking back and forth between Riley and Luke as if he were following the conversation.

Riley took a deep breath and continued, choosing her words carefully. "I'm here to apologize and explain. I really appreciate you giving me this second chance to come here and talk to you and..."

But Riley was cut off yet again when Luke held up his hand.

"What do you mean a second chance?" he asked. "I certainly never invited you here. I told Mike I was done with his crazy plan. I'm canceling the Christmas Camp."

Riley shook her head, more confused. "But Mike said I needed to come here to talk to you so we could work this out."

"And he said I invited you here?" Luke asked.

Riley felt her stomach twist into a knot. "You didn't?" She

didn't know what was going on, but one thing she did know was that she was going to kill Mike.

Riley realized by the look on Luke's face that he obviously had no clue she was coming, and she knew this had to be another one of Mike's schemes.

Beyond embarrassed, Riley started for the door. "I am so sorry," she said. "I think there has been a huge miscommunication. I'll go right now."

But right when she got to the door, it opened and Harry entered.

"No one is going anywhere in this weather," Harry said, brushing the snow off him.

"What?" Riley asked as she hurried over to Harry. She needed to get out of there as fast as possible. "I thought you said everything was fine, that you drive in this snow all the time."

"Snow, yes," Harry said. "But now it's a blizzard. I don't drive in blizzards."

Riley's pulse quickened as she started to panic.

"It can't be that bad," she said as she flung open the door. An icy gust of wind and whirling snow instantly blasted her. She couldn't see even a few inches in front of her.

"Whoa!" She quickly shut the door. She was trapped. She shut her eyes and took a deep breath before she turned back around to face Luke.

Their eyes locked.

The dog barked.

"It's okay, Comet," Luke said, never taking his eyes off Riley.

But all Riley could think was that all this, being trapped at a lodge where she wasn't wanted, was anything but *okay*.

Chapter Nine

L uke turned his attention to Harry.

"You're right," Luke said. "No one should be driving in this weather. You are more than welcome to stay. We have plenty of rooms."

Harry gave Luke a grateful smile.

"Thank you. I appreciate that," Harry said. "Actually, I've always heard great things about this lodge. My wife and I always wanted to come here, but we just never made it happen." Harry looked around, impressed. "She would have loved all these Christmas decorations. She loved everything about Christmas. She passed several years ago, but she is with me more than ever this time of year." Harry smiled as he walked over to the bookcase and admired a nutcracker from the collection.

"That's wonderful that you have so many special memories of your time with her," Riley said.

Harry smiled and nodded. "Especially at Christmas."

When Harry walked over to the big picture window, Riley joined him.

"It's beautiful, isn't it?" Harry asked, looking out the window.

She gave him a funny look. "The blizzard? Beautiful? More like a menace since it's keeping us trapped here."

"I can think of worse places to be *trapped*," Harry said with a chuckle.

When Riley turned around, she found Luke staring at her. His expression was impossible to read.

"I really am sorry about this," she said. "I'm going to call Mike and get this all straightened out."

But when Riley got out her cell phone, she barely had a signal. She started walking around the lobby holding up her phone, hoping to find a better connection.

Comet, the dog, was following her.

She looked down at him. "So what's the secret here? Where is the good signal?" She walked over to the fireplace but still didn't have any luck. She looked back at Luke. "Where's the best place to get a strong signal?"

Luke shrugged. "Depends, but right now you're not going to get anything with the storm blowing through here." He looked over at Harry. "Please sit, make yourself comfortable. You must be worn out after that drive up here in this weather."

When Harry sat down on the couch, Riley picked a big overstuffed comfy chair to sit down in, too. It was just close enough to the fire that she could feel the warmth from the flickering flames.

As soon as she sat down, Comet came over to her.

She smiled at him. "Sit."

"Oh, he doesn't do that," Luke said. "Only for my mom."

Comet instantly sat and looked up at Riley with adoring eyes.

Luke shook his head, surprised. "Well, that's a first. Come here, Comet."

Comet quickly trotted over to Luke.

"Sit," Luke said.

Comet didn't move. He just stared back at him.

Luke pointed to the floor. "Sit, Comet. Sit."

Comet just kept standing and wagging his tail.

Riley patted her leg. "Come here, Comet,"

When Comet ran over to her, Riley leaned down and gave him a hug. "You're a good boy, aren't you?"

Comet barked and wagged his tail some more.

"Sit," Riley said.

Comet sat perfectly on cue.

"Seriously?" Luke asked Comet. "That's how it's going to be?"

Comet barked again, looking quite pleased with himself.

Riley tried to hide her laugh. "Why is he named Comet?"

"After the reindeer, right?" Harry asked.

Luke nodded and smiled. "Exactly. Comet is my mom's dog. She named him."

"Reindeer?" Riley asked, confused.

Luke raised an eyebrow at her. "You know, Santa's reindeer. I thought you would have gotten that right away, you being Miss Christmas and all."

Riley laughed loudly. "Miss Christmas? Where did you get that crazy idea from?"

"Mike," Luke said, but he didn't look amused. "And what's so crazy about it? I thought that's why you were doing this Christmas Camp thing and writing a Christmas novel."

Riley's smile quickly faded while she tried to comprehend what Mike had done now. The question that hit her full force was, why she was paying him so much when all he'd done lately was wreak havoc on her life? She could have done that on her own for free.

She forced herself to smile. "What exactly did Mike say?"

"When he was pitching me to have you do this Christmas Camp, he told me you'd be perfect because you loved all things Christmas and were Christmas twenty-four seven,"

Luke said, starting to look concerned. "Are you saying it isn't true?"

Riley knew she had to choose her words carefully. She cleared her throat. "I'm saying Mike definitely has a way with words, that's for sure."

She was saved from having to say anything more, though, when Harry jumped in. "What's this Christmas Camp you're talking about?" he asked, intrigued.

"Oh, it was just something we were going to do—a weekend of special Christmas activities here at the lodge to help people really embrace their Christmas spirit," Luke said.

"That sounds great," Harry said. "But now you're not going to do it?"

Luke looked into Riley's eyes. "No. The plans have changed."

"Well, that's too bad," Harry said. "I like the sound of this Christmas Camp. I bet it would have been really popular."

"We had literally thousands of people who wanted to come," Riley said.

Harry laughed. "Well, I don't think you're going to fit them all here. How many rooms do you have here, Luke? Fifty?"

"Thirty," Luke answered. "But we were only going to have about a dozen people to keep the experience intimate so Riley here could interact with everyone personally. Everyone else was going to follow along online and send in their questions and ideas that way."

"Ideas?" Harry asked.

Riley nodded. "Yes, for my first Christmas book. We're asking my readers what they want to see in the story so they can feel like they're part of the creative process."

"Well, I know what I'd want to see in the story," Harry said.

"What?" Riley and Luke asked him at the same time.

"Santa Claus, of course," Harry said.

Comet barked and wagged his tail. They all laughed.

"I'm good with that as long as he brings everyone presents," Riley said.

"What kind of presents would you want?" Harry asked, putting her on the spot.

Luke also gave her his full attention.

She scrambled for an answer because she'd never done the whole Christmas gift-giving thing. She decided to tell them the same thing she always told her friends at Christmas.

"I don't really believe in giving gifts just because it's Christmas. I think if there's something you see that reminds you of someone, or you see something you think someone would want, you get it for them no matter what time of year it is. Plus, who says it has to be a gift? Maybe just doing something together is the best gift of all."

Luke looked surprised.

"What?" Riley asked him.

"I just… Well, I agree," Luke said.

Riley laughed. "And that surprises you?"

Luke was smiling as he nodded, and she couldn't help but smile back at him. Maybe she had a shot at winning him over after all.

"You know," she said, "we could make that a part of Christmas Camp. We could challenge everyone to find a gift that really means something to someone in their life."

"I like that," Harry said. "I think this Christmas Camp is a wonderful idea. We could all use a reminder now and then of what Christmas is really about. I know my Annie would have been first in line to sign up for this kind of camp."

"I agree the idea's great, but it has to be done right," Luke said. When he gave Riley a skeptical look, it stung.

Comet made her feel a little better when he came and sat next to her. As she reached down to pet him, Comet wagged his tail.

"It was going to be the last event we did here at the lodge before we sell it," Luke added.

"You're selling the lodge?" Harry asked, sounding both surprised and disappointed. "Didn't I read that it's been in your family for a hundred years?"

Luke nodded. "This will be our ninety-ninth year to be exact. We've had a good run, but now it's time for another family to take over."

"You have a buyer?" Harry asked.

"We've had some interest," Luke said. "We just haven't found the right fit yet."

Riley listened, taking in all the information in case there was something she could use to try to persuade Luke not to cancel the Christmas Camp.

Luke stood up. "I'm sorry, Harry. I should have asked if you wanted something to eat or drink after your long drive up here. We have a special hot chocolate the lodge is known for."

Riley felt like waving her hand in the air and saying, *Hello, I'm here, too. Remember me?*

Harry smiled at Luke. "Thanks, but I was actually thinking I might just go up to my room and relax a little bit, if that's possible?"

"Of course," Luke said.

Harry got up and started heading for the door. "I'm just going to grab my bag from the SUV. I always keep one for emergencies like this."

"No, I'll get that for you, Harry. Don't worry about it," Luke said. "Let me show you your room."

Harry gave Luke a grateful smile. "Thank you. And thank you for taking me in tonight."

Luke nodded. "Not a problem at all."

As they started to walk off, Harry looked back at Riley. "Good night, Miss Reynolds."

"Please, call me Riley." She smiled at Harry. "And thank you again for getting me here safely."

"My pleasure," Harry said. "I'm glad it worked out. It looks like you've picked the perfect place to celebrate Christmas."

Riley didn't have a chance to respond before Luke jumped in. "Actually, Miss Reynolds will be going back to Denver with you in the morning, Harry."

"Oh," Harry said, sounding surprised.

As Luke and Harry left the lobby, Riley smiled down at Comet and whispered, "We'll just see about that."

While Luke couldn't have made it any clearer that he didn't want her there, he hadn't planned on one thing. She didn't give up easily, especially when her entire publishing career was on the line.

She wasn't going anywhere.

Chapter Ten

While she waited for Luke to return, Riley walked over to a table full of framed family pictures to take a closer look. She picked up a wooden frame and studied the picture inside. It was of Luke with who she guessed to be his mom and dad, standing down by the lake next to all the lit-up Christmas trees.

She took the picture and walked over to the window to try to find the spot where the pictures had been taken. She could just barely see some of the tree lights twinkling through the falling snow.

"Wow, the snow's really coming down now," she said to herself, leaning even closer to the window.

"But it's supposed to let up by morning," Luke said from behind her. "So you should have no trouble getting back to Denver with Harry."

Riley took a breath, then forced a smile before she turned around to face him. "About that. Can we talk?"

Luke crossed his arms as he studied her. "About?"

When he noticed the picture she was holding, he came over and held out his hand. When she placed it in his hand, she looked up into his eyes.

"Are these your parents?" she asked.

"Yes." He walked back over to the table and carefully put

the picture back exactly where she'd found it. "If you're tired, I can show you your room," he offered. "You're just down the hall from Harry."

Riley smiled at him. "Actually, I'd love to take you up on your offer of a cup of the lodge's famous hot chocolate."

For a moment, Luke just stared back at her, then he started walking out of the room. "Follow me," he said, not sounding very enthusiastic.

Comet ran after him, and Riley, smiling a victorious smile, followed Comet.

There was no way she was turning in early. She had work to do. And she was hoping this special hot chocolate would put him in a better mood.

As she followed Luke and Comet toward the kitchen, her mind was going a million miles an hour. All her original ideas of how to apologize and win him over would never work now. She'd come up to the lodge thinking he'd invited her so they could talk things over. Now that she knew she was basically an uninvited and unwanted guest, she needed a whole new plan—and fast!

When they walked into the kitchen, Riley checked her cell phone. Still no signal.

Luke looked over at her. "If you're trying to get cell service tonight you can forget it."

Riley frowned at her phone. "Because of the snowstorm."

"That's certainly not helping," Luke said as he took two reindeer mugs from the cupboard.

Riley laughed when she saw them. "So I'm starting to get the feeling that there's a real reindeer theme around here? First Comet and now the mugs."

When Luke nodded, Riley could almost see a smile. "My mom does pride herself on her reindeer collection."

"Where is your mom? And for that matter, everyone else?" Riley asked. "It's like we're the only ones here…"

"Because we are," Luke was quick to answer back.

"What?" Riley asked, amazed. "You're saying it's just us in this whole lodge?"

Luke opened the refrigerator and grabbed some milk. "That's what I'm saying."

Riley waited for him to explain, but when he didn't, she tried again. "Where are all the guests?"

"We didn't book December because we were hoping to have the lodge sold by now. Plus, December always books almost a year in advance. That's why when Mike had this Christmas Camp idea at the last minute, we were able to do it."

"And your mom and dad?" Riley asked. "Where are they?"

Luke hesitated a moment before answering. "My dad passed away, and my mom is in Florida with her sister looking for a condo. Trust me, she'd be here if she could, but she just broke her ankle and can't travel. She was the one who was really excited about having this Christmas Camp."

Riley watched him put a saucepan of milk on the stove and get out some of the ingredients for the hot chocolate. There was dark cocoa powder, a bar of dark chocolate, cinnamon, and nutmeg.

"So this hot chocolate looks like the real deal," she said, impressed. "You're making it old-school, from scratch."

"That's right," Luke said proudly. "My mom wouldn't have it any other way. Actually, this is my great-grandma's original recipe with a few tweaks from my mom."

"Tweaks?" Riley asked, walking over to join him. She picked up a jar of nutmeg. "What kind of tweaks are we talking about exactly?"

Luke smiled when he picked up a shiny vanilla bean. "This vanilla bean, for one. My mom puts some in every batch."

"Really?" Riley asked, intrigued. She picked up the vanilla bean and studied it, lightly running a fingertip over it. She held it up to her nose and inhaled. "Well it certainly smells good."

"That's how you know it *is* good," Luke said.

"Wow, pretty fancy," Riley said.

Luke laughed. "Not really. My mom just likes the idea of every generation adding something new to the recipe, so we're honoring an old tradition and creating a new one at the same time."

"That's pretty cool," Riley said as she watched him skillfully combine all the ingredients. "So what have you added to the recipe?"

When Luke looked back at her, she was surprised by the childlike look on his face, not to mention how handsome he was when he gave a genuine smile.

"My ingredient…is a secret," Luke said.

Riley laughed. "Seriously? Come on."

Luke gave her a look that said he was dead serious.

"Really?" Riley asked. "You really have a 'secret ingredient'?" She made air quotes when she said the words *secret ingredient*.

"I do," Luke said proudly. "And no, because I know you're going to ask, I'm not telling you."

Riley quickly scanned all the ingredients.

"You're not going to find it there," Luke said.

Riley looked around the kitchen.

"Or anywhere in sight," Luke said, laughing. "It wouldn't be much of a secret if it was that easy to find."

When Riley walked over and opened up a Santa cookie jar and peered inside, Luke laughed. "Boy, you really don't give up, do you?"

Riley smiled back at him sweetly. "Never."

She took a little brown cookie out of the jar. It had a Hershey's Kiss on the top. "What are these?" she asked. "Another secret family recipe?"

Luke laughed.

"Well, they *are* a family recipe, but they aren't a secret. We call them Christmas Lake's Gingerbread XOXO's. It's another adaption of my great-grandma's favorite gingerbread recipe. One year my mom said they were too busy to make the traditional gingerbread boys, so they created these and just put the chocolate on top to dress it up a little. The guests have really loved them. Try it."

Riley didn't need to be asked twice. She bit into the cookie. It was soft and chewy, and the gingerbread went perfectly with the chocolate. She happily she took another big bite. "This *is* good."

"I'll let her know you approve," Luke said. "She makes a ton of Christmas cookies. You might be *Miss Christmas,* but my mom is definitely the *Christmas Queen.*"

Riley's smile faltered as she put the cookie down. "About that," she started but was interrupted when the alarm went off on Luke's cell phone.

"Okay, just a few more minutes and this will be ready," he said, taking the saucepan off the stove.

"Do you run the lodge with your mom?" Riley asked, changing the subject.

"No," Luke answered quickly. "This was always my parents' passion, not mine. I just came home to help my mom when my dad got sick. Now I'm here to sell the place and make sure we get the best price so I can get my mom settled in Florida and she can retire without worrying about anything."

"So what do you do when you're not here playing real-estate agent?" she asked.

"I've been working and living in Europe," he said. "I help different hospitality groups, hotels and resorts, develop eco-friendly business practices and implement new Green programs to protect the environment."

Luke looked both exited and proud when he talked about his work. It was clear he was very passionate about what he did.

Riley wanted to know more. "What got you into that field?"

"Growing up here in Colorado, in the mountains, at the lodge," Luke said, "I've always been concerned about the environment. I thought this kind of work could combine the two things I really care about the most."

"What have you done here at the lodge that's eco-friendly?" Riley asked. "I noticed the Christmas tree in the living room was in a pot, so it's still living?"

Luke smiled. "It is. We've always used live trees inside the lodge. We decorate them for the holidays, but then after Christmas, we have a special area down by the lake where we plant them so they can keep living."

"Are those the trees lit up with white lights?" Riley asked, intrigued.

He nodded. "They are."

"That's a lot of trees," she said.

Luke nodded and smiled. "They represent a lot of Christmases. You figure one per year for almost a hundred years, and we usually have several around the lodge, so you do the math."

"That's pretty awesome."

"I think so, too," he said. "It's like my ancestors were helping to protect the environment even before it was the thing to do."

"What else have you done with the lodge?" Riley asked.

Luke continued to stir the hot chocolate. "Unfortunately, not much. My parents had a way they liked to run things, and they followed the way my dad's dad and his dad before him ran things. They were all about honoring old traditions, and that's something the guests loved. They knew exactly what they were getting when they came back year after year."

"So you didn't implement any of your ideas here?" Riley asked, surprised.

"I had some ideas when I was in college, but my dad always resisted any big changes. He would say that *someday* we'd talk more about it. But then he got sick and that certainly wasn't the time to be talking about any new business ideas."

"So *someday* never came," Riley said.

Regret swept across his face. "No, it didn't."

"I'm sorry," Riley said in a soft voice.

"Me too," Luke said. "Thank you." He held up the saucepan. "Could you grab those two mugs for me, please?"

Riley quickly picked up the reindeer mugs he'd gotten out of the cupboard earlier. She studied the reindeers. "I bet Alex would love these."

"Alex?" Luke asked. "Your boyfriend?"

Riley laughed as she put down the mugs next to him. "No. Oh, no. Alex isn't my boyfriend. He's my bartender and a friend. I don't have a boyfriend." Riley snapped her mouth shut, wondering why she had offered up that information. She obviously was more tired than she'd realized.

"So that Tom guy who interviewed you yesterday was right?" Luke asked.

Riley's guard was instantly back up. Just hearing the name *Tom* made her entire body tense. "What do you mean?" Her voice was sharper than she'd meant it to be.

"Didn't he say something like you weren't married and didn't have anyone in your life so how could you write romance novels?" Luke asked, very nearly quoting Tom.

Hearing Luke say the words again made her cringe.

"That guy was an idiot," Riley shot back, not able to help herself. "He had no idea what he was talking about."

"You do have someone in your life, then." Luke said it as a statement, not a question, as he filled both mugs with the steaming hot chocolate. He handed her one.

Riley decided the less that was said, the better, and she needed to get the conversation back on track to Christmas Camp.

She held up her reindeer mug. "Should we toast?"

"To what," Luke asked.

"How about to Christmas Camp," Riley said and clinked her mug to his before he could protest. "And following your family's tradition by continuing to make new Christmas memories." She felt like her best hope of winning Luke over was focusing on the lodge's legacy of celebrating Christmas.

She took a sip of her hot chocolate and closed her eyes in ecstasy. It was smooth and creamy and bursting with a rich chocolate flavor. There was also a hint of peppermint. She let out a content sigh.

When she opened her eyes, she found Luke was watching her and actually *smiling*.

She smiled back at him, and she knew this was her chance—her likely one and only chance to persuade Luke to hold the Christmas Camp.

Chapter Eleven

R iley took her hot chocolate with her as she strolled around the kitchen, taking in all the beautiful Christmas decorations that somehow made even the kitchen look like a postcard. There were fresh garlands with white twinkle lights above the cupboards and wreaths with those same plaid ribbons in all the windows.

On the counter was another collection of vintage nutcrackers, along with some pretty poinsettias. There was even another potted Christmas tree in the corner decorated with all kinds of different holiday cookie cutters. Some were tucked inside the branches while others were hanging from red ribbon. There were snowman, gingerbread boys, stars, Christmas trees, and angels. Riley could tell it had been decorated with love.

Riley picked up a snow globe off the kitchen table. Inside was a winter wonderland. She shook it so the snow spun around.

"This is just like it looks outside," she said, holding the snow globe up to the light.

Luke nodded. "That's one of my mom's favorites. She always says it reminds her of Christmas Lake."

Riley carefully put the snow globe back down. "You must have a lot of wonderful memories here."

"We do," Luke said, his voice softening a little. "And we have a lot of loyal guests who have come year after year, especially at Christmas, that have made their own memories."

"Are any of your regulars coming to Christmas Camp?" Riley asked.

Luke nodded. "Yes, one couple was selected. I put in a good word for them. They actually got married here on Christmas twenty-five years ago, so I thought they'd be a good fit. Plus, Beva loves your books."

"I like her already," Riley said with a smile. This was her opening. "You know, I'm sure Beva and the rest of the Christmas Campers would be very disappointed if you had to cancel all of a sudden, with only a few days before the camp is scheduled to start."

Luke frowned. "I know. I've thought about that. But the only thing worse than canceling on our guests is having them come for an experience that disappoints them."

"Disappoints them? What do you mean?" Riley asked, confused. "This place is amazing. I've never seen anything like it before. Almost every room is incredibly decorated. Anyone who loves Christmas will fall in love with this place."

"I'm not talking about being disappointed in the lodge," Luke said.

Riley bristled. "So then you're talking about the guests being disappointed in...*me*."

Silence.

Riley quickly covered her hurt with annoyance. "I'll have you know," she said, marching right up to him until they were toe to toe, "your Christmas Camp sold out because my readers are coming to see *me*. They are *my* fans..."

Luke met her challenging stare. "And they were promised an experience where they could relax and reboot and embrace the true meaning and magic of Christmas, and to connect with one another and with you."

"So?" Riley demanded, warning herself to stay calm but not able to help herself when her voice became louder. "I'm here. What's the problem?"

"Frankly," Luke said, "your attitude. That's the problem. How do I know if everyone shows up here for Christmas Camp that you won't get upset about something and just storm off again?"

"That's not fair," Riley said. "You can't just judge me by what happened with that one interview. That was a unique situation. You don't really know me."

"You're right," Luke said. "And that's the real problem here. I don't know you, and that means I don't know how you'll act. After almost a hundred years of taking such good care of our guests, I don't want anyone's last experience here to be a negative one and ruin our legacy. I take full responsibility for this being on me. I should have never agreed to do this without knowing more about you first. Mike insisted that it would be easy and…"

"Let me guess," Riley jumped in, "a win-win for everyone."

"Exactly," Luke said.

"Look. I get it," Riley said. "I would be nervous, too, but I can promise you I'm a very reliable person. I love my readers. I would never take off and leave something I was hosting."

Luke gave her a skeptical look.

Riley held up her hands in her defense. "Again, you can't judge me on just that one incident. I've never walked out on an interview in my life before that. But that reporter…he just went too far."

"Agreed," Luke said. "What he did was wrong. I would have been furious, too. But I have my family's legacy to worry about. Especially now that we're looking to sell the lodge. We were doing this Christmas Camp as a last positive event for the lodge, something for our guests to always remember..."

Riley nodded, excited, and smiled back at him. "And I think that's an amazing idea. Honestly, I do. This place is obviously the perfect location to host any event that has to do with Christmas. If you cancel now, not only are you going to be disappointing a lot of people but it's going to be a PR nightmare for both of us, and that's not going to help you sell this place."

"Or help you sell any of your books," Luke added.

"Exactly," Riley agreed. "So, as much as I hate to agree with Mike right now, I think he's right. I really do think this can work for both of us. Your guests will be able to have one last special memory at the lodge, and for the people who have never been here, they'll have a chance to experience how special it is before you sell. Wouldn't your mom want that?"

Luke walked over to the kitchen window and looked out, even though it was too dark and snowy to see anything.

Riley joined him there. She took a deep breath. She knew this was it, that her only hope was just to be completely honest with him.

"Luke," she said in a voice that, for the first time, sounded the way she felt...scared. "I need this. I really need to do this Christmas Camp."

When he turned around, he gave her his full attention.

She looked into his eyes. "The truth is my last book isn't selling well." She looked away as she crossed her arms in front of her chest, hugging herself for comfort. "If I don't do this Christmas Camp, I'm done. My publishing career is over. So this Christmas Camp means everything to me."

When she looked back at him, she couldn't read his expression. "Please, Luke, I promise I won't disappoint you or the people who come to Christmas Camp. I care about them, too.

I'm just asking that you give me another chance."

She held her breath as she continued to hold Luke's gaze.

Comet had come over to join then and was now sitting at Luke's feet. His big brown eyes gazed up at Riley when he barked.

Riley glanced from Comet to Luke and then waited for what felt like an eternity for Luke to stay something.

"I think you need to go," Luke finally said.

Riley's heart sank. "Really?" her voice cracked.

Luke nodded. "Yeah. You need to go get some rest because if we're going to do this Christmas Camp together, we have a lot of ground to cover in the next two days."

When Riley let out a huge sigh of relief, she felt her heart start beating again.

"Thank you so much!" she exclaimed, and without thinking, she gave Luke a heartfelt hug. "I promise you won't be sorry."

When Luke didn't hug her back, she quickly backed away and laughed nervously. "And I promise you I won't do *that* again. I'm just really grateful. You're literally saving my career, which is basically my life."

"Well, don't thank me yet. Let's see how this goes," Luke said. "I've never run a Christmas Camp before, but Mike says you're Miss Christmas so I'm looking forward to hearing all of your great ideas about what you want to do. He was supposed to send me your list, but he never did. You can just give it to me tomorrow morning, and we'll get started."

"A list of activities?" Riley asked, confused. "Do you mean the activities you've set up for us to do that I need to approve?"

Now it was Luke's turn to look confused. "No, the other way around. Mike said *you* had a list of all the activities set up for *me* to approve."

When her eyes grew huge, he gave her a sharp look. "Is everything okay?" he asked.

Riley quickly recovered. "Yes, of course. Everything's great," she lied. Her mind was whirling. None of this was adding up. Mike had told her everything would be taken care of and all she had to do was show up at Christmas Camp and interact with the guests, but now Luke was saying he was waiting for *her* to give *him* a list? She didn't have a Christmas clue as to what kind of holiday activities they should do.

When she absentmindedly rubbed her throbbing temple, Luke looked concerned. "You're sure everything is okay?"

Riley forced a smile. "Yes, all good," she said. "I was just thinking that you're right. I need to get some rest so we can start bright and early tomorrow morning."

"Great," he said. "I'll look forward to hearing all your ideas tomorrow. I know we got off on the wrong foot, but if we're going to do this right, we really need to work together."

"Agreed," Riley said, having no clue what she was truly agreeing to.

"I can show you to your room if you're ready," Luke offered.

Riley could only nod and then follow him out of the kitchen.

When Comet looked up at her she mouthed the word, *Help!*

She just needed to stay calm, she could figure this out. She was an award-winning reporter. She could certainly hop on Google, do a little research, and figure out some Christmas activities for the weekend.

But when Luke opened the door to her guestroom, she didn't even pretend to be okay.

"Whoa!" she blurted out without realizing it.

Inside her room were dozens of Santas. From a life-sized Santa cardboard cutout in the corner, to a collection of figurines on the dresser, to all the pillows on the bed, there were Santas *everywhere*. There was even an elaborate eight foot red-and-gold velvet Santa chair next to a real Christmas tree with Santa ornaments and a quaint stone fireplace. Hanging from the wooden mantle above the fireplace was just one red felt stocking that had Riley's name embroidered on it.

But it was the bed that Riley couldn't stop staring at.

It was a red Santa sleigh—an actual sleigh—that had been converted into a bed. And above the bed was a sign that read, *Always believe.*

Still in shock, Riley instantly covered her mouth with her hand to keep herself from blurting out anything she'd regret, because the only thing she *believed* right now was that if she had to sleep in that bed, she would go Christmas crazy.

"It's really something, isn't it?" Luke asked, walking over to the giant Santa chair.

Riley was relieved that he'd apparently taken her horror for wonder.

"It is…something," Riley said, forcing a smile that made her cheeks hurt.

Luke sat down in the Santa chair and smiled back at her. "When my mom, who is a huge fan of all your books, heard you were going to host the Christmas Camp and that you were Miss Christmas she insisted on redecorating this room just for you."

"Wow," Riley replied. She didn't know what else to say.

Luke stood up from the chair, walked over, and picked up one of the Santa figurines. It was about six inches tall, ceramic, and had an old-world charm about it. The Santa was holding a Christmas tree.

"She even included some of her own favorite Santas, like this one here, that my dad gave her. She wanted to make sure you were surrounded by…What did she say? Oh yeah, *lots of*

Christmas love. She said you're going to be like Santa Claus bringing our guests so much joy and making their wishes come true, so you needed your own special room."

"Well, this is…special. That's for sure," Riley said. "But it's so special, if you want to save it for one of your favorite guests, I completely understand…"

"My mom would never hear of it," Luke said. "She was so excited to do this room for you. She knows you're writing your first Christmas novel, and she wanted you to have lots of inspiration. That's why she even made you your own stocking."

When Riley walked over to the fireplace and touched her name on the stocking, her Grinch-like mood softened a little. "I've never had a stocking with my name on it. This was very thoughtful of her." She didn't add that she hadn't had any kind of Christmas stocking in a long time. "Please thank your mom for me."

Luke nodded and smiled. "I will be sure to do that."

As Riley continued to look around, even though all the Santa's were freaking her out, she could appreciate all the work it took to create the room. However, she wondered was how hard it was going be to stuff that huge cardboard cutout under the bed.

"Do the other rooms have themes, as well?" she asked.

Luke laughed. "No. They're decorated for Christmas, of course, but we don't have themed rooms. Just this special one for you."

"Yay, me," Riley said, feigning enthusiasm.

When Comet looked at her and tilted his head, she felt like he knew exactly how she felt.

"I'll go bring up your luggage," Luke said as he turned to leave. "Then you can make yourself at home. Do you have more in the car? I didn't see Harry bring in very much."

"Nope, that's it," Riley said. "I travel light."

"Great," Luke said. "As long as you packed a lot of warm clothes to wear outside, you'll be good to go. Like I told Mike, we'll want to be sure to plan a lot of outside activities. That's what the lodge is known for."

"Of course," Riley said. She didn't have the energy right now to get in the conversation about her lack of winter clothing.

When Luke left, she fell back onto her sleigh bed, grabbed a Santa pillow, covered her face, and screamed. The sound was muffled and strangled.

When Riley sat back up, the first thing she saw was the life-sized cardboard Santa staring at her. She threw her pillow at him and hit him in the stomach. But instead of falling over, the Santa started laughing.

"Ho! Ho! Ho!" the cardboard Santa said.

And then Santa got louder.

"Ho! Ho! Ho!"

"Oh, no, you don't," Riley said as she ran over to the still-laughing Santa.

"Ho! Ho! Ho!"

"No! No! No!" Riley answered back as she tried to figure out how to turn it off.

She had Santa upside down when Luke returned with her bags. He stopped dead in his tracks when he saw her.

"Problem?" he asked.

Riley scrambled to get Santa right side up again, but this only made him start laughing again.

"Ho! Ho! Ho!" Santa said, getting louder with each *Ho.*

Luke came to her rescue and flipped the switch under Santa's bag of toys. "Is this what you wanted?" he asked.

"Yes," she answered. "Thank you. I must have accidently set him off somehow. I didn't want him disturbing Harry.

You said he was right down the hall."

Luke nodded. "No problem." He pointed at her luggage. "You should have everything now. Let me know if there's anything more you need." He picked up the Santa pillow she had thrown to the floor and handed it back to her.

Riley took the pillow and carefully put it back on the bed. "I'm all set. Thank you for everything and for giving me another chance."

"You're welcome," Luke said. "It's Christmas. A time of forgiveness, right?"

She laughed a little. "Right."

"Well, good night then," he said as he left her room.

"Good night," Riley called out after him.

As soon as he was gone, she marched over to the cardboard Santa. "Look, Santa," she said with her hands on her hips. "You being here staring at me isn't going to work." She pointed at him. "So it's time for you to go night night."

She picked up the Santa and struggled to get it over to the bed. It wasn't heavy. It was just huge and awkward.

After she set the Santa flat on the floor, she got on her hands and knees and victoriously lifted up the red bed skirt so she could stuff Santa under the bed.

Only, the sleigh bed was on a platform. There was no space to hide the Santa.

"Oh no," she groaned as she looked at Santa's grinning face.

With a huff, she got back up, grabbed Santa, and put him back in his original spot in the corner. But this time he faced the wall.

"Looks like you're getting a time out," Riley said with a satisfied smile.

When she turned around, she saw Comet was watching her from the doorway.

She felt as if she had just been caught red-handed.

"Santa's fine. I'm just giving him a different view," she told Comet.

Comet looked like he wasn't buying her Santa story before he disappeared down the hall.

A minute later, Riley heard a phone ring downstairs. It was one of those old-fashioned rings, a strange tone for Luke to pick for his cell phone. But it meant one thing. Cell service was working again!

She grabbed her phone and tried to get a signal but still nothing.

When she started pacing around the room, she felt as though the Santas were all laughing at her efforts. Frustrated, she finally gave up.

"I'll just deal with it in the morning," she said to herself. "I need to start researching Christmas activities."

She grabbed her laptop and sat cross-legged on the bed. She wanted to write down her first impressions of the lodge in case they helped inspire ideas for her novel. While she'd meant to take notes about the lodge and Christmas Lake, instead, she found herself writing about Luke, using adjectives like *headstrong, stubborn,* and *determined.* She then added *good son, loyal,* and *cares about the environment.*

As she sat back and read back what she'd written so far, she couldn't decide what she really thought about Luke. All she knew for sure was that if he needed her to be Miss Christmas, that's what she'd be. He didn't know about her past, and she wanted to make sure it stayed that way.

Now more than ever, she needed to keep her personal life personal, because the less Luke knew about her, the better.

Chapter Twelve

L uke answered the phone in the lobby on the third ring. With the cell service always going down, he was thankful his parents had insisted on keeping their landline.

As he picked up the handset of the black 1930s antique phone, he smiled. They'd also insisted on using his great grandparents' original phone. He used to make fun of it when he was a kid, but now he appreciated it.

"Christmas Lake Lodge," he answered, sitting down in the chair next to the phone because the phone cord didn't stretch far enough for him to stand.

"Hello, Merry Christmas," the male voice on the other end of the phone said cheerfully. "My name is Colin, and I'm calling to talk to the owner or whoever is in charge of the upcoming Christmas Camp."

Luke sat back in the chair. "That would be me, Luke. I'm the owner's son. How can I help you?"

"I was hoping to get a reservation," Colin said. "I went on your website and saw that you're already sold out, but I know Riley and was hoping there was a way to still make this happen?"

Comet trotted into the room and sat down next to Luke.

"Oh, so you're a friend of Riley's?" Luke asked.

"Yes," Colin said. "We go way back to college. I saw her

interview on TV, and I knew I had to come see her."

"Well, we do have a few rooms available. We are trying to keep the group small, but if you're a friend of Riley's, I'm sure we can make an exception..."

"That would be great," Colin said. "Thank you so much."

"Sure, no problem," Luke said. "You can just go back on our website and send all your information through the contact form. I'll process your reservation in the morning. How long did you want to stay?"

"The whole time," Colin said. "Whatever that is. The weekend, right? If that works for you?"

"That works," Luke said. "I'll put you down for the whole weekend and let Riley know.

"No!" Colin pleaded. "Please don't tell her I'm coming. I want it to be a surprise."

"Oh, okay," Luke said. "I won't say anything. Your secret is safe with me."

"Perfect," Colin said. "And when I get there maybe you can help me plan some special activities with Riley."

Luke gave Comet a confused look. "Well, you know she's hosting all the Christmas Camp activities?"

"Yes, I heard, but I'm talking about when she has free time. Some special romantic dates. I have some ideas, but I might need some help in making them happen."

"Romantic dates?" Luke asked, surprised.

"The more romantic the better," Colin said. "You know how Riley loves romance."

"Yeah," Luke said, thinking he didn't really know Riley at all. "Whatever you need."

"Great," Colin said, sounding relieved. "I'll send you that information right now, and I'll see you soon."

"Safe travels," Luke said before hanging up the phone.

He had no sooner hung up when the phone rang again.

He instantly picked up and laughed. "Did you forget something?"

"Hello? Is this the Christmas Lake Lodge?" a different male voice asked.

Surprised, Luke shifted in the chair. "It is. I'm sorry. I was just talking to someone else, and I thought they were calling back. How can I help you?"

"My name is Brendan, and I'm calling about your Christmas Camp…"

"I'm sorry. We've completely sold out," Luke said.

"But I know Riley," Brendan said.

Luke lifted his eyebrows. "Really?"

"Yeah," Brendan said. "We go way back. We dated. We used to live together."

"Got it," Luke said, even though he had no clue to what was going on. "What can I do for you?"

"I'm actually living here in Colorado," Brendan said. "I work at the Mountain View Ski Resort. After I saw Riley on the news and found out she'd be up here hosting the Christmas Camp, I knew I had to come see her. I tried to reserve the weekend on the website, but it said you were sold out. Is there someone I could talk to a manager or the owner so I can explain why it's so important for me to be there?"

"That would be me," Luke said. "I'm running the camp."

"Great!" Brendan said enthusiastically. "Then I'm talking to the right person. So can you help me make this happen? Do you have room for one more? I know Riley will be really happy to see me."

"So she asked you to come?" Luke asked.

"In a way, yes," Brendan said. "If you saw her TV interview, I'm the guy she was talking about. That's why I want to surprise her."

Luke laughed. "Oh, I bet she'll be surprised."

"So we can make this happen?" Brendan asked, sounding hopeful.

"Yes, I think we can," Luke said. "Just go on the website and send me your contact information and how long you want to stay, and I'll confirm your reservation in the morning. Our Wi-Fi is down right now, but it should be back up tomorrow."

"Oh, I know how that goes." Brendan laughed. "The Wi-Fi woes of living in the Rockies."

"Exactly," Luke said. "Thanks for understanding. We'll look forward to seeing you soon."

"And please, don't tell Riley," Brendan said. "I want to surprise her. This is going to be epic."

"Got it," Luke said. "I won't say a word. Have a great night."

"You too," Brendan said before hanging up.

After Luke hung up the phone, he looked over at Comet. "That was weird. Two guys both wanting to surprise Riley? I sure hope she likes surprises."

Luke had just stood up and was walking over to check the fire when the phone rang again. He paused and looked at Comet. "Seriously? Please, tell me this isn't another someone wanting to *surprise* our star author."

Comet trotted over to the phone and stared at it as it rang again.

"Just hold on," Luke said to the ringing phone as he walked over and picked up the handset.

"Christmas Lake Lodge, may I help you?" he asked.

"I hope so," another male voice replied in a commanding tone. "I'm Tyler Caldwell. I'm an entertainment attorney from Manhattan, and I'm calling to reserve a space at your Christmas Camp. I know you're full, but..."

"Let me guess," Luke cut in. "You know Riley?"

"Yes," Tyler said, sounding surprised. "How did you know?

Did she tell you about me?"

Luke hid a laugh. "Uh, no. Let's just say I had a hunch."

"I'm hoping to surprise her," Tyler said.

Luke couldn't help but laugh. "She must really love surprises."

"She's always loved surprises from me," Tyler said, his voice full of confidence.

"You can just fill out the reservation request online," Luke explained for the third time.

"Thank you, and I'll see you soon."

"See you soon," Luke said back before he hung up the phone and looked at Comet again.

"I don't know what is going," he told Comet. "Riley said she's not dating anyone, but there are three guys coming up here to see her."

Comet lay down and put his head between his paws as if he could see trouble coming. Luke laughed.

The phone rang again.

"Oh, come on!" he said. "There can't be another one..."

But this time, it was his mom.

"Mom, I'm so glad it's you," Luke said.

His mom laughed. "Why do you sound so relieved? Is everything okay at the lodge? With Comet? I'm sorry I missed your call yesterday. I didn't even realize my phone battery had died."

"Mom, everything is fine—the lodge, Comet, we're all good. And I told you, you have to remember to plug in your phone every night before you go to bed," Luke said.

"I know. I know," she said, still laughing. "I just forgot. Blame it on my ankle."

"Is everything okay?" Now it was Luke's turn to sound concerned. "How is your ankle doing? Do you need anything?"

"I'm fine," his mom said. "The doctor says everything is

healing well. I just need to stay off it and take it easy, but I'm worried about you. I wish I were there at the lodge with you for Christmas Camp. I can't believe I'm missing this. And you sounded stressed when you picked up the phone. What's going on?"

Luke rushed to reassure her. "Don't worry. Everything's great. We're just getting some last-minute reservations that I wasn't expecting—friends of the author's or something like that. They all want to surprise her."

"Well that sounds lovely. What's she like? Riley Reynolds," Mom asked. "I loved all her books, and I'm about to read her most recent one, *Heart of Summer*. I'm finally getting a chance to catch up on my reading now that I'm being forced to spend so much time sitting around."

"But you're sitting around by the pool, right?" Luke asked with a laugh. "Aunt Mary sent me a picture."

She laughed, too. "Well, that is one of the perks of hurting yourself in Florida. It has been sunny and seventy here almost every day. No wonder everyone retires down here."

"Well, I'm just happy you're recovering. That's the most important thing," he said. "Don't worry about anything here. I have everything under control."

"And Riley?" she asked. "What's she like?"

He had hoped he'd successfully avoided the question, but apparently not. "She's okay," he said.

"Just okay? I'm going to need a little bit more than that." She chuckled.

Luke shrugged. "I don't know what you want me to say."

"I've seen her picture in her books. She's very pretty, don't you think?" his mom asked.

He rolled his eyes. He knew exactly where she was going with this, and he needed to shut her down fast.

"Yes, Mom, she's pretty, but no, Mom, I'm not interested, so don't even go there. And those friends of Riley's who are all coming to Christmas Camp? They're *all* guys."

"So?" she said. "You said they were just *friends.*"

"Honestly, I don't know what they are," Luke said. "Besides, I have way too much going on in my life to worry about dating."

"There's a thing called work-life balance, and you need to find it," his mom said.

Luke laughed. "Mom, you're watching way too many of those daytime talk shows. My life is great just the way it is. As soon as we sell the lodge and get you settled in Florida, I need to head back to Europe and my job, as planned."

"Well, sometimes life is what happens to you while you're busy making other plans," she said.

Luke laughed again. "And now you're quoting John Lennon?"

"Whatever it takes," his mom said sweetly. "I love you, son, and I just want you to be happy. I don't want you to miss out on any opportunities that are right in front of you."

"Mom, if you're thinking Riley is one of those *opportunities,* I told you she's already taken. But I promise I'll work more on that balance you're talking about if that would make you happy."

"That would make me very happy," she said. "Oh, sorry, your aunt is calling me. I better go. But keep me updated. I don't want to miss anything. I have a really good feeling about this Christmas Camp."

"I hope you're right," Luke said. "You take it easy and let me know if there's anything you need."

"I will," Mom said. "And don't forget…"

"Forget what?"

"Keep your heart open because anything is possible at Christmas," his mom said happily.

Luke laughed. "I love you, Mom."

"I love you, too," she said.

Chapter Thirteen

The next morning Riley woke up to a Santa alarm clock calling out, "Ho! Ho! Ho! Time to get up and go! Ho! Ho! Ho! Let's go! Go! Go!"

Still groggy and struggling to make sense of what she was hearing, Riley sat up in her sleigh bed, and looked around her room.

"Ho! Ho! Ho! Time to get up and go! Ho! Ho! Ho! Let's go! Go! Go!"

Her eyes landed on a stuffed Santa sitting on her night-stand. Only this was no ordinary stuffed toy. This was a Santa alarm clock, and it was getting louder and louder with each *Ho! Ho! Ho!*

"Ho! Ho! Ho! Time to get up and go! Ho! Ho! Ho! Let's go! Go! Go!"

"You have got to be kidding me," she said, grabbing the Santa and shaking it, trying to get it to stop.

"Ho! Ho! Ho! Let's go! Go! Go!"

"No! No! No!" Riley said back to the Santa and then finally found where the batteries were hiding in Santa's black boots.

"Ho! H—"

The Santa finally stopped when she yanked all the batteries out.

"Ha! Take that, Santa!"

As she victoriously set the Santa back on the nightstand, she noticed her laptop, phone, and iPad were surrounding her on her bed.

It all came rushing back to her.

She'd stayed up late trying to do some research on traditional Christmas activities so she'd have some ideas to give to Luke this morning, only she couldn't get the Wi-Fi password to work to get online. After she'd unpacked, she'd gone back downstairs to see if Luke could help her with the Wi-Fi, but the lobby and kitchen had been empty. She'd followed another hallway and found a charming library with floor-to-ceiling bookcases on each side of a vintage fireplace, but still no Luke.

She'd finally given up and gone back to her room, where she'd continued to try to get at least one of her devices online. She must have fallen asleep trying.

When she heard Comet bark from outside her door, she grabbed her phone to see what time it was. She was shocked when she saw it was already eight in the morning. She usually got up at six.

When she heard Comet bark again, she rushed to the door in her black silk pajamas, flung the door open, and laughed.

Comet was sitting there wearing a Santa hat. "Very funny, my friend," she said, still laughing.

As Comet trotted off, she grabbed the first thing she saw in her closet, dressed quickly, and headed downstairs.

She found Luke and Harry in the lobby. Both men did a double take when they saw her.

"Good morning," she said, as she smiled back at them, wondering what they looked so surprised about.

"Good morning," Harry said.

The way Luke was still staring at her with a perplexed look on his face made her glance down at her outfit.

She wondered what was wrong. *Am I wearing two different shoes? Is my top on backward?*

Nope. Everything looked good to her.

She was wearing black leather pants with one of her favorite black silk blouses, along with her black leather pumps and a simple pearl bracelet and earrings.

"What?" she finally asked when Luke just continued to stare.

"Sorry," he said. "I was just trying to figure out where you were going all dressed up like that."

Riley laughed. "This isn't dressed up. This is one of my casual outfits. For Christmas Camp."

When both Harry and Luke looked at each other and back to her, she put her hands on her hips. "Okay, guys. What is it? What's wrong?"

Harry was the first one to speak. "I don't think anything's really *wrong*..."

"Right," Luke added. "I think that outfit is...very nice."

Riley arched an eyebrow. "Very nice? Why do you say that like *very nice* is not so nice at all?"

Harry tried to cover up a laugh but didn't do a very good job. "I think what he's trying to say is that, around here, we're pretty casual."

Riley frowned. "I get it. I live in Arizona where we're really casual too—jeans, T-shirts, flipflops—but if I'm hosting an event, I have to dress the part. So that's what I'm doing—or at least trying to do."

"But this is a Christmas event," Luke said. "You're wearing all black like you're about to step into a board meeting."

Riley laughed. "What is it with everyone being against black?"

"It's fine," Harry said. "It's just not very, well, you know, Christmassy."

But Riley didn't know. She stared back at both of them.

"And up here, we host events wearing jeans, not black suits," Luke said.

Riley gave him a look. "This isn't a *suit*. Sheesh. What do you want me to wear?"

"Jeans would be better," Luke said.

"What?" Riley asked, and she didn't even try and hide her confusion. "You're saying I'm supposed to host this Christmas Camp in jeans? You're kidding, right? How is that professional?"

"Well, I don't know about professional, but I know jeans are a lot more practical for the kinds of activities we usually do around here," Luke said. "Or ski pants would work."

Riley's eyes grew wider. "Ski pants? We're going skiing?"

"No, but you know, with all the outdoor activities we're going to be doing, some kind of winter pants for the snow would be the best, whatever kind you have."

Riley looked down at her outfit again and then back up at Luke. "This is the warmest thing I have. I was going to pick up some things in New York, but I didn't have a chance…"

"And she wanted to stop in Denver to get something yesterday, but we had to get going because of the weather," Harry offered.

"I get it. Don't worry," Luke said. "We have a shop in town where you can get some stuff. You'll be all set."

Riley breathed a sigh of relief. "That would be great. Thanks."

"Well, I better get going," Harry said as he headed for the door. "I have some more airport pickups this afternoon, and then I think I'm scheduled to bring several of your Christmas Campers up here on Friday. So I'll probably see you both again in a few days." Harry shook Luke's hand. "Thank you again for your hospitality."

"It was my pleasure," Luke said and smiled back at him. "Anytime. We'll look forward to seeing you back here soon."

"Thank you again, Harry, for getting me here safely," Riley said with a grateful smile.

"I was happy to be of service," Harry said, smiling back. "Good luck to you both planning your Christmas Camp."

"Thanks," Riley answered quickly. "We're going to need it."

"We are?" Luke asked.

Riley scrambled to recover. "I just mean we have a lot to do."

"Then I better be on my way so you can get started," Harry said. He waved as he went out the door. "Merry Christmas!"

"Merry Christmas," Luke called back to him.

"Have a safe trip," Riley said.

Even Comet, who was still wearing the Santa hat, barked his goodbye.

As soon as Harry left, Luke turned to Riley. "Okay, let's get started," he said in a no-nonsense voice.

"With breakfast?" Riley asked hopefully.

"We can do that, too, but I was talking about finalizing our Christmas Camp activities. Do you have a list for me?"

Riley's heart sank. She hadn't been able to google anything because she couldn't get online. She got her phone out of her pocket and held it up. Still no cell signal or Wi-Fi. She tried to think of a response beyond, *Sorry, I don't do Christmas and have no ideas.*

"I e-mailed myself the list, but I haven't been able to get on Wi-Fi," Riley finally said, pleased with her quick thinking.

"It can just be finicky sometimes," Luke said.

"Finicky, as in not working?" Riley asked. She was almost

afraid to hear the answer.

Luke nodded. "Exactly."

"And let me guess," Riley said. "This would be one of those times?"

"Right again," Luke said with a smile. "I think we might just need a new router."

"Well, we definitely need to get that fixed before the guests arrive," Riley said.

"About that," Luke said. "Do you have any friends or family without a reservation who are planning to come to Christmas Camp that I need to know about?"

Riley was walking around, holding up her phone, trying to still get a cell signal. "No one told me I could invite anyone. Was I supposed to?" She glanced up at Luke.

For a moment, he looked confused, and then he shook his head. "No, I mean, if you wanted to you could have, but Mike didn't say you were bringing anyone."

"And I'm not," Riley said, looking back at her phone. "Hey, if we don't have Wi-Fi and the cell service isn't working, how do you get ahold of anyone?"

Luke walked over to a side table and picked up the handset from the antique phone. "If you need to call anyone you can use this."

Riley laughed as she walked over. "Seriously? That really works? I thought that was just a decoration."

Luke handed her the phone. "Nope, it works just fine."

It all suddenly made sense. "That's what I heard last night when the phone kept ringing! I thought that was the tone you'd set on your cell phone."

"No," Luke said. "Even I'm not that old-school."

Riley laughed.

"Do you need to make a call?" Luke asked.

Riley looked doubtfully at the handset. "Yes, I do. But…"

"Don't worry. It works just fine," Luke said. "I'll give you some privacy. I'll be in the kitchen. I put a fresh pot of coffee on, if you're interested."

Riley's eyes lit up. "Oh, I'm always interested in caffeine in the morning. I'll be right there. Thanks."

As soon as Luke left the room, Riley studied the phone again and had to laugh a little. "This thing's older than I am," she said out loud to herself. For a minute, she just stared at it as she realized she had no idea what Mike's number was. She didn't know anyone's number by heart.

She quickly got out her phone, looked up Mike's number in her contacts list, and started to dial the old-fashioned way.

"You better work," she said to the phone.

She sat in the chair next to the phone because the cord didn't reach very far.

After three rings, Mike finally picked up. "Hello?"

"Mike!" Riley held the phone closer to her ear so she could hear better. "It's Riley," she said louder, then realized she was practically shouting into the phone.

Silence.

"Mike?!" she said even louder, so loud that it had Comet, who was lying down by the fire, come trotting over to her. "Mike, it's Riley."

"I know," Mike said impatiently. "I heard you the first time. What phone are you calling from? I almost didn't pick up."

"I'm using the phone at the lodge," she answered quickly.

"So you made it," he said. "Good."

She held out the phone and gave it an incredulous look. "Seriously? All you have to say is *good*?"

Silence.

"Mike?" Riley held the phone closer. "Are you still there?"

"I'm here," Mike said. "What's the problem?"

Incredulous, Riley jumped up. "What's my problem? What's my problem?!" When she almost pulled the phone out of the wall, she quickly sat back down, now even more agitated. The problem is you didn't tell me Luke had already canceled the Christmas Camp. You told me to come here because he wanted to talk about it so we could work things out. Imagine this guy's surprise when I showed up." Her voice was getting louder. "Mike, you knew he didn't want me here. You totally threw me under the bus."

Comet sat down next to her and barked. He obviously could tell something was wrong.

Riley gave him an apologetic look. "Sorry, Comet. It's okay."

"Who's Comet?" Mike asked.

"It doesn't matter," Riley snapped.

"Look," Mike said, "you're there now, so it's all good."

"No, Mike. Everything is not *all good.*" She lowered her voice and looked around to make sure Luke wasn't nearby. "You apparently also told this guy that I was *Miss Christmas* and that I had a list of activities that we could do for this Christmas Camp, when you know that's just one big fat lie."

When Comet tilted his head and stood up, Riley lowered her voice again. "You've totally set me up to fail."

"Look, Riley, I can't do everything for you," Mike said. "I created this opportunity for you to help save your career. Now it's up to you to do whatever you need to do to make that happen. It's not like coming up with some Christmas activities is brain surgery. Bake some cookies, sing some songs, figure it out. I have another call coming in. I have to go. You're welcome."

"Mike, wait—"

But it was too late. Mike had already hung up.

Riley stared at the phone for a good ten seconds before putting the handset back down. "Unbelievable..."

Chapter Fourteen

When Comet sat down next to her again, she started petting him and found herself talking to him to make herself feel better.

"Mike is out of control," she told Comet. "I should fire him, but I can't right now and he knows it. This latest stunt he's pulled…this is not okay. This is *so* not okay."

Comet continued to look up at her with his compassionate dark-brown eyes, as if he were understanding every word she was saying.

"What am I going to do?" Riley asked Comet.

Comet got up and started heading out of the room. He stopped and looked back at her, like he was waiting for her to follow.

She reluctantly stood up. "Okay, I'm coming."

I must be losing it, she thought. She was not only talking to a dog but she was also asking it for advice.

There was one thing she knew for sure. Those Christmas miracles she'd never believed in? She was going to need one, and fast.

When Comet barked, she walked a little faster. "I'm coming, Comet," she said. "Take me to my miracle."

As she followed Comet into the kitchen, she could smell fresh coffee brewing and decided she would just take things one step at a time. She knew she needed a plan, but right now, she also desperately needed a big jolt of caffeine for inspiration.

Luke looked up and smiled when she and Comet entered the kitchen.

"Coffee is ready," he said, holding up a mug. This time the mug had the face of an elf on it. The elf had pointy pink ears.

Riley didn't even try to hide her laugh. "Let me guess. Your mom also collects elves?"

"No," Luke said. "That was my dad. He loved the elves. He believed they were the ones that brought the Christmas magic. Of course, my mom always insisted it was Santa who did that. They would have quite the debate."

Riley was still smiling as she sat down at the kitchen table. "That had to be some debate."

"Oh, you have no idea," Luke said. "When I was little, I thought they were just doing it to entertain me."

"But…?" Riley asked.

"Well, when the annual debate continued every Christmas, I realized they were doing it for themselves as much as they were doing it for me. Call it one of our crazy family traditions."

"That must be nice," Riley said, not realizing she'd said the words out loud until Luke answered her.

"The debates or the traditions?" he asked.

Riley answered honestly. "Both."

Luke nodded. "It was. How would you like your coffee? Do you want cream or sugar?"

"Actually," Riley said, "I'd love some cinnamon if you have any? Or I can just take it black."

Luke opened the cupboard, took out some cinnamon, and held it out to her. "Your Christmas wish has just come true," he said, smiling.

Riley laughed. "Well, I don't know if I'd call it a Christmas wish. It's more like a habit I've had since college."

Luke gave her a curious look as she took the cinnamon and added a heaping spoonful of it to her coffee.

Luke laughed. "Okay, that's a lot of cinnamon. Why so much?"

Riley smiled as she happily inhaled the scent and then stirred the cinnamon into her coffee until it disappeared.

"My college roommate, Kim, was studying to be a nutritionist and said she'd read that cinnamon in your coffee is supposed to help kickstart your brain in the morning. Even the scent alone is supposed to help you concentrate more."

Luke gave her a doubtful look. "Cinnamon can do all that?"

Riley laughed. "That's what she said, so I tried it and I've been hooked ever since. Do you want to try it?" She held out her elf cup.

Luke laughed. "No, I'm good. I'm a purist. I drink mine black. I feel like if the coffee's good, you don't need anything else." He held his mug out to hers. "Merry Christmas."

Riley hesitated only a moment before clinking her cup to his.

As she took a sip of her coffee, she thought about how *Merry Christmas* were two words she rarely used. Usually, if people wished her a Merry Christmas, she would answer with something like *Have a great day,* or *You too,* or something like that. But there was something about actually saying those two words, *Merry Christmas,* that tugged at her memories of when she was a little girl and the last time she'd celebrated Christmas with her dad. She was lost in thought when she realized Luke was talking to her.

She gave him an apologetic smile. "I'm sorry. You were saying?"

Luke smiled back at her. "I was just asking what some of your family Christmas traditions are. Maybe we could use some at Christmas Camp. Were you planning to put any in your book?"

Riley instantly stiffened. Over the years, she'd always avoided the topic of Christmas traditions because whenever she'd told people she didn't have any traditions, they always thought something was wrong with her. So early on she'd come up with an answer that she always used, and she decided to use the same one now with Luke.

"Oh, you know," she said, staring into her coffee, "the usual stuff like everyone else. We didn't do anything really unique or special."

"Really?" Luke asked.

Without looking up, she could sense him studying her.

"I would have thought Miss Christmas had all kinds of interesting family traditions."

Riley put her coffee cup down and met Luke's stare. "About that name," she started.

Luke smiled. "Miss Christmas?"

Riley tried to smile, but it was forced. "Yeah. I think Mike has been exaggerating a little."

Luke laughed. "Mike? Exaggerate? Never!"

Luke's response had Riley relaxing a little bit. "So you know how Mike likes to—"

"Embellish the truth," Luke finished for her.

"Yes," Riley said. "That's a nice way to put it."

Luke laughed. "Oh, trust me. I know Mike well. Ever since we were roommates in college, Mike has been spinning stories. I think he should have been a writer, the way he likes to make things up."

Riley put both hands on the kitchen table and leaned toward Luke. "That's exactly what I always say."

"The thing is," Luke continued, "I think he actually believes his own made-up stories. He just doesn't sell other people on them, he starts believing them. That's why he's so insistent and just goes full speed ahead when he gets one of his ideas."

Riley leaned back in her chair and gave Luke an impressed look. "I think you just summed him up perfectly."

"In his defense," Luke started.

Riley held up her hands. "Wait, just when I thought we were going to agree on Mike."

Luke laughed. "I was just going to say that I don't think Mike's a bad guy."

Riley gave Luke a skeptical look.

"Hear me out," Luke said.

Riley crossed her arms in front of her chest. She doubted there was anything Luke could say that would redeem Mike in her eyes, not after his latest stunts. "Go ahead. I'm listening."

"Mike has always seen the best in people," Luke said.

"What do you mean?" Riley asked.

"I mean, he sees people's potential often before they even see it," Luke said. "It's like his mind jumps ahead to the future and what could be possible, and then he sets out to actually make it possible. He's been like that since college. That's why he makes a great publicist. He really believes in the people he's representing. So if he's saying your Miss Christmas, that's likely how he sees you."

Riley burst out laughing. "I'm sorry, but on this one, he's way off base."

"Then maybe he sees your *potential* to be Miss Christmas," Luke said.

Riley was still laughing. "Well, I don't know how he's seeing that."

"Aren't you getting ready to write your first Christmas novel, and that's why you're hosting this Christmas Camp?" Luke asked.

"Yes," Riley said slowly, being careful not to talk herself into a trap.

"Mike must think you have Miss Christmas potential, or he wouldn't have suggested you host this camp."

Riley didn't even know how to answer that, so she picked her coffee back up and took another slow sip. She was waiting for the caffeine to kick in. She knew she needed her mind to be sharp to figure out how she was going to handle all this. Maybe she needed to add some more cinnamon.

Luke stood up and grabbed a glossy red folder off the counter and sat back down at the table. He put the folder down in front of her.

"What's this?" Riley opened the folder with curiosity.

"It's our Christmas Camp agenda—or at least what I have down so far while I was waiting to get your list."

Riley opened the folder and fought to keep smiling when she saw all the blank spaces on the Christmas Camp calendar of scheduled events. Trying to stay positive, she pointed to some of the activities that were already scheduled.

"It looks like you have a lot of great things planned," she said. "Christmas cookie decorating, Christmas Camp cocktail making, stargazing with s'mores, and Christmas movie watching."

Luke nodded. "Those were the easy ones. They came from Jeff and his dad, Ben, at the Holly Peak Inn. They are the traditions they want everyone to do at every Christmas Camp, and it's part of the franchise agreement. We even get to use the Jacoby family's special sugar cookie recipe."

"Well, that sounds like a delicious rule I can get behind," Riley said.

They shared a smile.

"So if we have all these original Christmas Camp activities, then we're all set, right?" Riley asked.

Luke laughed. "Not quite. The idea is that everyone who holds a Christmas Camp will also bring in some of their favorite traditions to share with their guests, tailoring the Christmas activities to the area so that they can be unique to that camp experience. That's why I've been waiting to fill in these blanks to include some Christmas activities that would fit up here in the Rockies but that would also fit in with what you might want to include in your book."

Riley forced a smile and nodded, telling herself not to panic.

"So what are you thinking for Christmas activities?" Luke asked.

As she shut the Christmas Camp folder, she saw Comet was staring at her. No pressure.

Riley knew this was the moment of truth. This was her chance to come clean and tell Luke that not only did she not have any Christmas activities to offer up, but that she was the last person he should be asking because she didn't even celebrate Christmas. She knew she could blame the whole misunderstanding on Mike. Clearly, Luke knew how Mike was.

But she also knew that as soon as she told Luke that she didn't have a Christmas clue he would see her differently. What kind of person didn't celebrate Christmas? People had judged her before, and it had never gone well. She had learned her lesson in the past, and that's why she never talked about how she really felt about Christmas anymore. She didn't want Luke or anyone else judging her or, worse, feeling sorry for her. Christmas was part of her past, a past she was perfectly happy never to think or talk about again. So she decided to do what she always did—pretend and deflect as much as she could.

She looked up at Luke with a new confident smile. "You know, now that I'm here, I think that the best way to start would be to get ideas from you. This is your family's lodge. You know what would work best here."

Luke looked surprised. "You'd be okay with that? With me picking some of the activities? I mean, you could have veto power, of course."

"Of course," Riley said, relieved her plan appeared to be working.

Luke smiled back at her. "Thank you. That would be great. I do have some ideas I'd love to run by you. Some things I think that would work really well here at the lodge."

"Great," Riley smiled back at him. "Go ahead. I'm all ears."

"Well, actually, it would be easier to show you," Luke said.

Riley gave him a curious look. "Okay..."

Luke held out her chair. "But we have to change."

Riley looked down at her outfit and frowned. "Really, I'm fine wearing this. It's comfortable..."

"We're going outside," Luke said. He pointed at her three-inch heels. "And you're not going to get very far in those shoes,"

"I have some riding boots I can put on," Riley offered.

Luke laughed. "We have about a foot of fresh snow out there. The only boots that are going to work are snow boots. What size are you? A seven?"

Riley gave him a surprised look. "Good guess. Seven and a half."

"Perfect. My mom is about that size, and she has several pair you can try on. I'm sure one will fit. She also has some ski gear—hats, gloves, the works—whatever you need. Come on."

Luke was already heading out of the kitchen.

Riley stood up but hesitated. "Luke, I can't wear your mom's clothes. Can't we just run into town and I can buy something there?"

"You're not even going to make it out the door in those shoes you're wearing. I'll just grab you some stuff of my mom's. You wouldn't believe how much stuff she has, and she loans it out to the guests all the time. It's like her own store of winter clothes. She would insist, and so do I. I can't have you going out in that," he said, pointing at her outfit, "and breaking your neck or getting frostbite. Then who would host the Christmas Camp?"

When Comet barked and wagged his tail, she saw that she was outnumbered.

"Okay," she said reluctantly. "But I'm only going to borrow the boots. I'm fine with this outfit to get us to town."

Luke shook his head. "You're going to need a good coat, hat, and gloves, at least. Trust me. I know what I'm talking about."

As he started to leave the kitchen, Riley doubted she would ever trust him. She wasn't exactly the trusting type. She preferred to rely on herself.

He turned around and saw her still standing there. "You coming?"

She took a deep breath. "Coming."

Chapter Fifteen

A few minutes later, wearing Luke's mom's borrowed winter gear, Riley stood in her room, staring at herself in the mirror.

"You've got to be kidding me…" was all she could say.

When she looked over at Comet, who had followed her into her room, even he appeared to be laughing at her.

He was lying down on the floor by the fireplace and had covered his face with his paws.

"Even you can't look at me," she said, exasperated.

When she turned back to the mirror, her mind tried to process what she was seeing.

Luke had brought her a box of his mom's clothes and two pairs of boots to choose from.

Riley had been stunned to find that the items inside the box looked like his mom had raided a Christmas-themed store. Every single thing she had to choose from screamed Christmas.

She took everything out and decided there wasn't one thing she could possibly wear. She was putting everything back inside the box to give back to Luke when he knocked on her door.

"Everything okay in there?" he asked.

Riley had no words…"Uh, I'm fine."

Fine. She laughed at her own words. *Fine* if she were in a Christmas insane asylum. *Fine* if she were ten years old in a Christmas play. *Fine* if she were in an episode of *Christmas Horror Stories.* She didn't know if *Christmas Horror Stories* was a real thing, but if it was, she was sure she could star in the show.

"Is there anything else you need?" Luke asked, interrupting her pity party. "My mom has everything."

"I can see that." Riley cringed as she picked up a red scarf that had snowmen on it. "Does she have anything that's not Christmas themed?" she asked hopefully.

She could hear Luke's deep, rich laugh though the door.

"Christmas Camp is Christmas-themed, so you want to look the part, right?"

"Right," Riley said as she picked up a Christmas sweater that would have won any ugly sweater contest. It had a giant reindeer face on it. Its antlers had long tufts of fur sticking out of them and the reindeer's pink tongue moved from side to side. The rest of the sweater was covered in reindeer tails that were hanging off the front, the back, and even the sleeves.

"Okay, great," Luke said. "I'll go start the truck so it's warmed up when you're ready."

"Thanks," Riley said, realizing she was no closer to deciding what to wear.

She picked up a red-and-white stocking cap that had elf ears attached to it and whispered to herself, "Kill me now."

When Comet barked at her, she quickly put the hat down. "I agree," she said. "We're definitely *not* wearing this one. So what's it's going to be? What won't get me arrested for looking Christmas crazy?"

Comet put his nose in the box and came out with a red hat in his mouth. He dropped it at her feet.

"This is your pick?" she asked Comet, laughing.

She grabbed the hat and checked it out. Actually, she thought, it wasn't that bad. It was a red knit hat with a white faux-fur snowball on the top. The snowball was pretty huge, but thankfully, there were no elf ears.

She gave Comet an appreciative look. "Okay. What else ya got?"

Comet trotted over to an emerald-green sweater that had fallen to the floor, grabbed it, and brought it over to her.

Riley laughed as she gently took the sweater from him. It had a Santa Claus on the front who was going down a chimney with a bag of toys. A teddy bear and a tiny toy soldier were dangling from the bag.

Riley laughed. It was another contender for the ugly sweater contest, but at least it wasn't covered in reindeer tails. She didn't even want to know what the little brown specks were underneath all the reindeer tails.

"You're right, Comet," Riley said, holding the sweater up. "This appears to be the best of the worst."

When Comet barked his approval, Riley knew she had a winner.

"Now, which boots?" she asked.

She modeled her left foot, where she was wearing all-white, furry, knee-high boot that looked like it belonged to the Abominable Snowman.

Comet barked.

"Or this one?" she asked. This time she held up her right foot, where she was wearing another knee-high snow boot, only this one was all black and looked suspiciously like something Santa would wear—a stylish Santa because it had a white fur trim and sparkling gold, crisscrossing shoelaces that had big, white. furry snowball puffs at the end of them.

Comet barked again.

She gave Comet a look. "Seriously? A tie? You're no help at

all." When she looked around the room and saw all the Santa's staring at her, she grabbed the other Abominable Snowman-looking boot and pulled off the Santa boot.

"I've had enough of Santa Claus. This one will have to do."

When she looked out her window and saw Luke pacing around waiting for her, she picked up her pace.

"Okay," she said. "I'm as ready as I'll ever be."

Comet barked again when she quickly grabbed her own black scarf and black leather jacket and zipped out the bedroom door.

By the time she got outside, Luke was shoveling all the fresh snow off the walkway to the lodge.

"Sorry," she said. "It took me a few minutes to figure out what would…fit."

She stopped in her tracks when she saw the one lone Christmas tree in the middle of the lake still had all its lights turned on, even though it was daylight. Scanning the edge of the lake, she noticed it was the only tree that was still lit up.

She turned to Luke. "What's with that one tree? Why are the lights still on?"

"They're always on." Luke followed her gaze. "I'll show you around down by the lake later. It's always a favorite place for our guests."

Riley held up one foot and wiggled it, all the white fur from the Abominable Snowman boot swaying back and forth. "Okay, I'm ready. I'm wearing your mom's boots, even though I'm pretty sure a yeti called and wants his feet back."

Luke laughed for a moment but then looked at what else she was wearing and frowned.

"What's wrong?" Riley asked, checking out her outfit.

"The boots are great, but where's your coat? Why didn't you wear one of my mom's?"

Riley tried to think fast. How could she tell him that the

only thing worse than the ugly sweater and the yeti boots were his mom's huge puffy coats that were way too big on her? She figured her leather coat would be just fine for a quick trip into town where she could buy herself a winter coat that didn't make her feel like the Stay Puft Marshmallow Man.

"I'm good," was all she came up with to say. "Let's go."

As she made her way to the truck, she had to laugh. This wasn't just any ordinary truck. The vintage pickup truck was painted bright red and had a huge wreath on the front grill that matched the wreaths on the house. There were even blinking, white LED lights on the dashboard.

"Wow, you guys really go all-out at Christmas here," Riley said before climbing into the truck.

Luke headed back to the lodge. "I'll be right back."

"Okay," she said. She was thankful the truck was running because her hands were freezing. As she tried to warm her hands by the dashboard heat vents, she accidently knocked down a strand of twinkling Christmas lights.

"Oops," she muttered as she quickly bent over to pick the lights up. One end got tangled around the gear stick, its lights still blinking. She had just gotten the one end free when the other end got wrapped around one of her boots. When she tried to lift up her boot in the limited space, it only made things worse. Now the lights were caught up in her other boot and getting stuck in all the fur.

She was still struggling to free herself from the stubborn Christmas lights when Luke returned.

He laughed loudly. "Well, what happened here?"

Riley gave him a frustrated look. "Seriously, help me out here. Every time I move, I get more tangled up in these lights. They're grabbing on to my boots and not letting go."

Luke laughed again. "You make it sound like they're out to get you."

"Aren't they?" Riley asked, sounding serious.

"They're Christmas lights," Luke said as he got in and tried to help her lift up one boot. "They're supposed to make you happy."

Riley laughed. "Well, I'll be happy when I'm not in Christmas-light jail anymore."

As Luke continued to help with her boot, she fell back onto the seat, sending her one boot sticking straight up in the air.

It was not a dignified position.

Embarrassed, she tried to sit up but only made things worse when she accidently smacked Luke's shoulder with her sky-high boot.

"Oh no!" Riley gasped. "I am so sorry..."

Luckily, Luke just laughed. He seemed completely amused by her whole tangled mess.

Finally, Riley gave in to the sheer ridiculousness of the situation and started laughing, too. "I give up," she said. "These crazy lights win. I should have worn the Santa boots."

"Okay, don't move. I got this," Luke said as he leaned down to get a closer look at her boots. They were both now back on the floor. A second later, he sat back up, holding the string of lights above his head victoriously. "Ta-da!" He chuckled. "You just needed to have the right touch."

"No way!" Riley gave the lights an incredulous look. "How did you do that?"

"Christmas magic," Luke said as he tossed the lights back onto the dashboard.

"Of course." Riley laughed.

As Luke started to pull out of the long driveway, Riley glanced around the vintage truck. Hanging from the rearview mirror was a collection of dangling silver stars.

"You even decorate your truck," she said.

Luke smiled back at her. "Oh, no. This little beauty is my mom's, not mine. She uses this truck all year long. She says it's one of the ways she likes to keep the Christmas spirit alive."

"Even in the summer?" Riley asked, her voice filled with disbelief.

"Especially in the summer. Haven't you heard of Christmas in July?"

"You're kidding me," Riley said, convinced he was just messing with her.

"No way. Christmas in July is a thing," Luke said.

"If you say so," she said. "So how far is it to town?"

"Only about two miles," Luke said. "It's so close you can cross-country ski or snowshoe into town."

Luke pulled the truck over.

"Why are we stopping?" Riley asked, confused.

Luke opened his door and pulled some snowshoes out of the back of the truck. "You wanted to get to town." He held up the snowshoes.

Riley's eyes grew huge. She looked at him like he was nuts. "You can't be serious?"

"As serious as Santa's sleigh," he said before shutting his door.

"Why do people keep saying that?" Riley shook her head. "That's not a real thing, you know."

"Are you sure about that?" Luke asked with a twinkle in his eyes. He opened her door for her. "Coming?" He held up the pair of snowshoes.

"We don't have time for this," Riley insisted. "Don't the Christmas Campers start showing up the day after tomorrow? We still have so much to do, don't we?"

"Are you asking me or telling me?" Luke asked, laughing.

"I guess I'm asking," Riley said.

"Well, then the answer is we have time," Luke said. "Don't worry. I have people coming in to help. We'll make it work. You just have to have a little faith."

"I'm trying," Riley said and meant it.

"Okay, great," Luke said. "Then let's go."

Riley didn't budge. "I can't," she said stubbornly. "I don't have snowshoes."

Luke waved the snowshoes at her. "Yes, you do. Right here. They're my mom's, and they work great with those boots."

Riley's eyes shot down to her borrowed yeti boots. It was like they were mocking her.

When a cold blast of air blew into the truck, she shivered and pulled her leather jacket around her tighter. "And," she said, almost cheerfully, "I'm not dressed to go snowshoeing. I didn't wear the right coat, or gloves, or anything."

Luke pulled a bag out of the back of the truck. "Then lucky for you, I brought all you need," he said. "That's why I went back into the lodge. You'd apparently forgotten a few things." He gave her coat a pathetic look. "That might work great for high fashion, but it's not going to work in this mile-high winter weather."

Riley rolled her eyes. "Dare I ask what will?"

Luke whipped out one of his mom's huge puffy coats from the bag and tossed it to Riley. It was made of red patches of down and had a white-fur collar and matching white fur around the sleeves."

Riley could only shake her head in disbelief. "Why is someone bound and determined that I dress up like Santa Claus?"

"Well, you are in the Santa room," Luke offered with a grin.

"Seriously?" Riley shot back.

When Luke laughed again, it looked like he was enjoying this way too much.

Another gust of icy wind had her entire body shivering.

"So what's it going to be?" Luke asked.

Riley locked eyes with him. She knew this was a test. She

just didn't know if she was going to pass it, but one thing she did know was that she was going to freeze if she didn't put on some warmer clothes.

"Did you put some ski pants in there?" she asked, already knowing he had because he apparently thought of everything. "Because I can't go out there in these pants."

"That's what I tried to tell you," Luke said. "And yes, there are some ski pants, along with some good gloves, a hat, and a better scarf—everything you need."

Riley grabbed the door handle and shut the door, leaving Luke standing there watching her. She rolled down her window and waved him off with her hand. "Well, turn around. I can't get changed with you staring at me like that."

She caught Luke laughing as he turned around.

It was more than a little challenging getting changed in the truck, especially getting off her form-fitting leather pants. She'd been grateful to see that besides his mom's bright-red ski pants, Luke had also tossed in some black leggings. She put those on first and then tackled the ski pants. As she wiggled trying to get everything on, she was already feeling toasty warm.

When she pulled the hat out of the bag Luke had brought her, she shook her head. "Is this some kind of joke?" The hat was a dead ringer for Santa's red stocking cap. It made her wish she'd taken Comet's suggestion and worn the other hat.

After she reluctantly put it on and wrapped a matching red scarf around her neck several times, she moved the rearview mirror over so she could see how she looked. "Yup, it's official," she said. "Forget Miss Christmas. I look like Mrs. Claus!"

When Luke tapped on her window and held up the snowshoes, she yelled back at him, "Hold your reindeer. I'm coming!"

"Ho! Ho! Ho!" Luke said, holding his belly and laughing.

She took some small satisfaction in pretending she couldn't hear him and then opened the door.

Chapter Sixteen

S tepping out of the truck, Riley had to admit she didn't feel cold at all. Apparently, Luke's mom's gear, while Christmas crazy, was Colorado Rockies–proof. She joined Luke, who was standing a few feet away laying out two pairs of what looked like vintage wooden snowshoes.

He nodded his approval when he looked up and saw her. "Much better."

"I'm not sure if I should take that as a compliment or not," Riley said, adjusting her Santa hat. She eyed the snowshoes with trepidation. "Exactly how far are we going to go?"

Luke gave her a surprised look. "Into town. Isn't that what you wanted?"

Riley laughed. "What I *wanted* to do was drive into town."

"What fun would that be?" Luke asked. "Besides, I thought you'd want to check this out because it's one of the activities I was going to suggest for the Christmas Campers. Are you ready?"

She took a deep breath. "Ready as I'll ever be."

"I thought you liked outdoor sports," Luke said with a frown.

Riley laughed. "Let me guess…"

"Mike," they said at the same time and shared a laugh.

"What else did Mike tell you about me?" Riley asked. "You might as well tell me now. I don't like surprises."

"Really?" Luke laughed. "You don't like surprises?"

Riley gave him an odd look. "No. And why are you laughing like that?"

"No reason," Luke said.

But by the look on his face, Riley felt like he was hiding something.

"Well," she said, "I actually do like outdoor sports, but I've been living in Arizona. So my idea of outdoor sports is more like running, hiking, swimming, kayaking, and boating. You know, things like that."

Luke nodded. "So snowshoeing isn't on your list?"

"Nope. But I'm game to try," Riley said, moving closer to the snowshoes.

"Great. I was thinking for the Christmas Campers, we could just do some of the trails right outside the lodge and down by the lake, or maybe I could give some guided walks and offer some different times, like at sunrise or sunset. What do you think?"

Riley was impressed by this enthusiasm. "I think that sounds great. So just pretend I'm one of the Christmas Campers and give me a quick lesson."

"Done!" Luke held up one of the snowshoes. "Lesson number one: how to get into the bindings." When he put the snowshoe back down in the powder-soft snow, he motioned for her to come toward him. He picked up some trekking poles and handed them to her. "Use these for balance. They should already be adjusted for your height."

Riley tried the poles out. "Perfect."

"Now just put your foot right here," Luke said, holding the snowshoe for her. But when she went to put her furry boot into the binding, some of the fur got caught and she lost her balance.

"Whoa!" As she started to fall, she reached out for Luke and grabbed his arm.

He was caught off guard, and they both fell at the same time, landing practically on top of each other.

"Are you okay?" he asked, sounding genuinely worried.

She was covered in snow. For a moment, she just lay there and then…

She started laughing.

It was the kind of laugh that once you started, you couldn't stop.

When Luke also joined in, they both lay back on the snow and looked up at the sky. They looked at each other, they just laughed louder.

"It was the boots again," Riley said. "I swear it's revenge of the yeti."

This had Luke cracking up even more. "You and those boots."

Riley was about to sit up when Luke stopped her. "Wait," he said. "Don't get up. We're not done."

"We're not?" Riley gave him an incredulous look. "What now?"

"Uh, snow angels, of course," Luke said and started moving his arms and legs, making a snow angel.

Riley threw some snow at him. "You're nuts," she said. But as she began to sit up, he took her hand and pulled her back down.

"Hey," she said. "That's not very angel-like of you."

"You can't get up without making your snow angel," Luke said.

"Is that some kind of Christmas Lake rule?" Riley asked.

"No," Luke said, smiling back at her. "It's one of my rules." He watched her and waited. "Go ahead. You act like you've never made a snow angel before."

Riley wasn't about to tell him that he was exactly right. There had been no snow angels in her past, not one.

When she realized she was still holding Luke's hand, she let go, embarrassed, and quickly started moving her arms and legs as Luke had done.

"There you go," he said. "You're an angel expert."

"Hardly,' Riley said but couldn't help but smile as she continued flapping her arms. Satisfied, she looked up at Luke, who was already standing. "How do I get up without wrecking the angel?" she asked.

Luke held out his hand. She hesitated a moment but then took it, and he instantly pulled her up. This time she let go of his hand right away.

"Thanks," she said. When she turned around her, face lit up when she saw the snow angel she'd just made.

"I did it," she said, excited. "I really did it. That's so cool. It really looks like an angel."

"And our wings are touching," Luke said, pointing at his angel right next to hers. Sure enough, their angel wings were, in fact, touching.

"Does that mean something?" Riley asked.

"You're the romance author, you tell me."

"So it has to mean something *romantic*?" she teased.

Luke gave her a look. "Uh, yeah. Come on. It's Christmastime, there are two angels, and their wings are touching. It has to mean something special."

"Well, when I figure it out, I'll be sure to let you know," Riley said.

"Does that mean I'll be reading about this in your next book?" Luke asked.

"The snow angels or us?" Riley started brushing the snow off her.

Luke caught and kept her gaze. "Both."

For a second, Riley forgot everything else except how blue Luke's eyes were.

He looked away first and then up into the sky. It was starting to snow. "We better get going," he said.

Riley stretched out her arms and shook out her legs. "I'm ready to try again. Let's go." Her voice was full of determination.

"Snowshoeing is going to have to wait," Luke said. "I don't trust this weather. Let's just drive into town."

He was already grabbing the snowshoes and putting them in the truck. "We can try again tomorrow, but right now we need to get moving."

Disappointed, she followed him to the truck. Who knew she'd like snowshoeing so much? Or at least trying to snowshoe.

But deep down, she knew it wasn't the snowshoeing she liked as much as the company. She couldn't remember the last time she'd laughed so hard or had so much fun. Luke was turning out to really surprise her in more ways than one.

As they drove into town, the first thing Riley saw was a charming hand-painted wooden Christmas Lake welcome sign in the shape of a Christmas tree alongside the road. The next thing she noticed was that there was only one main road, Lake Street, and it was lined with about a dozen mom-and-pop shops and businesses that had gone all-out to decorate for the holidays.

There was garland with big red velvet bows wrapped around all the antique black streetlights. In front of every business there was a lit-up and decorated Christmas tree in the theme of that business and beautiful wreaths on the front doors that had real pine cones and holly berries and gorgeous glittering gold bows.

Looking around, Riley thought the little town, with its

Bavarian feel, looked like something you'd find inside a Christmas snow globe, and she couldn't help but be charmed.

"This doesn't even look real," she said as they pulled up to a store called Merry and Bright.

Luke smiled at her. "It's not. It's better than real."

Riley returned his smile as they got out of the truck. She liked that. *Better than real.* She'd have to write that phrase down and find a way to use it in her book.

"This is our one clothing store in town, but Lisa has a little bit of everything. She should be able to help you out," Luke said as he continued walking down the street.

"Wait." Riley stopped walking. "Aren't you coming with me?"

Luke laughed. "You really want *me* to go shopping with *you?*"

Riley, embarrassed, continued quickly. "No. Of course not, but where will I find you?"

"I'm going to go talk to Brianna. She's the local realtor. Her office is the last one on the right. Just come meet me there when you're done."

"Got it," Riley said as she headed into Merry and Bright. But as soon as she walked in the door, she froze. Every inch of the store was decorated for Christmas. There were giant Santas and reindeer and snowmen and Christmas trees, wreaths, and garland, and the song "We Wish You a Merry Christmas" was playing.

Riley laughed. "Not this song again…"

"Not a fan of the song?" a cheerful woman asked as she walked toward her. Riley guessed she was probably in her mid-sixties. Before Riley had a chance to respond, the woman gave her a candy cane.

"Merry Christmas! This is for the little girl inside you," the woman added with a twinkle in her eye. "I'm Lisa. Welcome to Merry and Bright."

As Riley took the candy cane and looked around, she wondered if she was in the wrong shop. She didn't see any clothes. All she saw were Christmas decorations. *Lots* of Christmas decorations. There were so many bright and blinking, sparkling things it was starting to make her dizzy.

"I'm Riley." She held out her hand.

Instead, Lisa gave her a warm, welcoming hug. "I'm a hugger, and I know just who you are, my dear. You're one of my favorite authors." Lisa pointed over to a giant Fraser fir Christmas tree in the corner. "See?"

Riley did a double take. The tree was decorated with *her books*. Every book she had ever written was expertly tucked away in the tree branches, spotlighted with Christmas lights so you could still read every cover.

Blown away, Riley walked over to the tree. "Wow, I've never seen anything like this. All my books are here."

"And some book reviews," Lisa pointed out by taking a cut-out paper heart ornament off the tree. The review was written in the middle. Lisa started reading it out loud. *"Get ready to fall in love all over again with Reynolds's latest novel,* A Summer's Heartbeat, *which shows the power of true love."*

Riley didn't know what to say. She was so touched. She looked back at Lisa. "This is truly amazing. This must have taken you so long to do."

Lisa smiled proudly. "I was honored to do it. I feel like your writing is such a gift to us all, and isn't that what Christmas is all about? Giving to others? All your books are about love, Christmas is about that, too, so they needed their own special place, and I thought this Christmas tree would be perfect. I hope you like it?"

Riley touched her heart. She was still in awe. "I love it." She gave Lisa a grateful hug. "Thank you."

"You're very welcome." Lisa smiled. "We are so happy to have you here at Christmas Lake. I just know this is going to be the perfect place for you to write your first Christmas novel. You must be so excited."

"I'm actually not going to be writing it here. I'll be getting ideas from the people who come to Christmas Camp and then hopefully using some of those ideas when I do start writing it later."

Lisa's eyes lit up. "Well, maybe you'll come back when it's time to write it. I'm sure you're going to find lots of inspiration here."

Riley nodded. "I'm sure I am. Although, right now I think I might be in the wrong place. I was looking to buy some clothes."

Lisa linked arms with Riley. "No, you are just where you are meant to be. What are you looking for?"

"A jacket, some winter clothes," Riley said hopefully.

Lisa led her to the back of the store where there were some winter clothes in the corner on racks that were covered with white twinkle lights.

Riley couldn't believe it when she even recognized several designers.

"Will this work?" Lisa asked, giving Riley a friendly wink.

Riley, impressed, smiled and nodded. "This will work!"

A half hour later, Riley was happily strolling down the street in one of her new outfits on her way to find Luke.

She was surprised that she'd actually found some really cute things that were all Colorado Rockies approved. Right now, she was wearing a stylish pair of black ski pants that hugged her figure in all the right places and a pretty red ski coat with a black faux-fur-lined hood. Lisa had insisted she buy the red coat instead of the black one she'd been eyeing and had promised her that with the chic black fur trim, she didn't look anything like Mrs. Claus.

She'd also picked up some really nice wool sweaters in bright and cheerful holiday colors and a red fleece with matching red gloves and a hat. The only place she'd struck out was finding some new boots in her size. Lisa was all sold out. So for now she was going to have to keep wearing her yeti feet and hope they didn't get her in anymore trouble.

She was just reaching the end of the street where the realtor's office was when, through a window, she saw Luke hugging a very attractive woman. After the hug, Luke held both the woman's hands. Riley couldn't see Luke's face, but by the way the woman was smiling at him, it made her think theirs was definitely more than a professional relationship.

Riley frowned. She turned back around and started walking quickly in the opposite direction.

She had no idea where she was going. She just knew she didn't want to interrupt Luke in what looked like a private moment.

When she ended up back inside Merry and Bright, Lisa came hurrying over. "Did you forget something?"

Riley shook her head. "Uh, no, but I thought I'd just look around some more if that's okay. Maybe get some inspiration for my Christmas novel like you were saying."

"Of course," Lisa said. "I would love that. You know a lot of the things we have are made by local artists." She picked up a beautiful ceramic Christmas platter that was white with blue snowflakes. It was big enough to fit a whole turkey. "Emily, one of our young artists made this."

Lisa put the platter back down and walked over to a shelf where there was a collection of all white glossy ceramic angles that were about six inches tall. "And these angels," she said proudly, "are a Christmas tradition here at Christmas Lake."

"How so?" Riley asked.

Lisa carefully picked up an angel and brought it over to show Riley. "They're made by the Harrison family. The family has been making these special angels for almost a hundred years."

"Why are they so special?" Riley asked.

Lisa smiled as she led Riley over to a cozy sitting area by a crackling fire. They both took a seat before Lisa continued.

"As the story goes, Thomas Harrison was a struggling artist," Lisa said. "Pottery was his specialty, but he was barely making enough to live on. That's when he fell in love with our local railroad tycoon's only daughter, Cynthia. It was a Romeo-and-Juliet love story from the start."

Riley frowned. "Cynthia's parents didn't approve of Thomas?"

Lisa shook her head. "Tom was pretty much penniless, and they wanted more for their daughter, so right before Christmas, Cynthia's parents forbid them from seeing each other."

"But they saw each other anyway," Riley said confidently.

"No," Lisa said with a sigh. "Sadly, they didn't. Thomas thought Cynthia's parents were right, that she deserved much better than him. He loved her and wanted the best for her. Cynthia, being the spirited girl that she was, was very angry at Thomas for not fighting for their love. They argued and broke up, just as Cynthia's parents had hoped."

Riley leaned forward. "What happened next?"

"Thomas was, of course, heartbroken," Lisa continued. "He went back to his workshop, and to try to take his mind off Cynthia, he started working on one of his ceramic bowls. That's when a flash of bright white light blinded him for a

moment and the bowl slipped from his fingers and crashed to the floor, breaking into pieces."

Lisa paused.

"And?" Riley pressed. She was totally invested in the story.

Lisa smiled an all-knowing smile. "And when Thomas went to pick up the pieces, one of the pieces was in the shape of an angel."

Riley's gaze flew to the angel figurines, then back to Lisa. "What happened next?"

Chapter Seventeen

Lisa smiled a knowing smile. "Some say what happened next was a Christmas miracle. The broken piece of pottery gave Thomas an idea. He decided he would try to make his first angel and give it to Cynthia for a Christmas present. Even if they couldn't be together, he wanted her to know that he would never stop loving her. So he worked night and day for the next two days, putting his whole heart and soul into making that angel. He finally finishing it just as the sun was coming up on Christmas morning. He quickly wrapped it in the only thing he could find, an old gunny sack, and he persuaded one of housekeepers that worked for Cynthia's family to hide his gift underneath the family's Christmas tree."

Riley, barely able to stand the suspense, reached out and took Lisa's hand. "Please tell me Cynthia got the angel and that her parents didn't find it first and throw it away,"

Lisa gave Riley's hand a reassuring squeeze. "The housekeeper was apparently thinking the same way you are. So she tucked the burlap sack way behind all the family's beautifully wrapped presents."

"So Cynthia found it?" Riley asked.

Lisa smiled and nodded. "She did, but only because once she was done opening all her extravagant gifts, a ray of light beamed through the window, illuminating the hidden present. When Cynthia opened the sack and took out the angel, it glowed in the light, and there was also a note from Thomas."

"What did it say?" Riley asked breathlessly.

Lisa's smile grew. "It said, '*Cynthia, you will always be my angel. You will always have my heart. I love you now and always. Merry Christmas, Thomas.*'"

Riley didn't realize her eyes had filled with tears until she felt one tear slowly slide down her cheek. Embarrassed, she quickly brushed it away. Then she noticed Lisa also had tears in her eyes.

"I always cry when I tell this story because it's so beautiful," Lisa said as she gently wiped a tear away.

"What did Cynthia do?" Riley asked.

"Cynthia took her angel and went to find Thomas," Lisa answered. "She told her parents that she didn't care if they cut her off from the family fortune like they had threatened to. She said she didn't need their money, that she and Thomas would be just fine on their own because they had what really mattered. She had love."

"Wow," Riley said softly.

Lisa nodded. "You see, she had faith in Thomas and faith in their love. When she went to the pottery shop to find Thomas, she took out the beautiful angel he had made for her and set it on the table by the window. She told Thomas how much she loved the angel and how much she loved him. She told him she wasn't going back to her family, that he was her family now."

"What happened?" Riley asked.

"Thomas, of course, was overjoyed," Lisa said. "They were just about to kiss when someone came into the shop."

"On Christmas Day?" Riley asked.

Lisa smiled. "Yes, it was someone who was passing through

Christmas Lake on their way to visit family, and they stopped when they saw the angel in the window. They thought it would make a wonderful Christmas gift."

"No!" Riley exclaimed. "Tell me they didn't sell it?"

Lisa laughed. "Of course not, but it did give them the idea that maybe Thomas could make more angels and try to sell them."

Riley nodded. "And of course the angels became a big hit."

"More than anyone could have imagined, especially after the story of how the first angel was made got around. I think everyone really connected with how out of something broken, Thomas's relationship and that piece of pottery, came something beautiful. After the story was covered in the local newspaper, people came from all over the region to buy Thomas's special angels. He called them the Christmas Lake Angels, and he would only sell them right here in Christmas Lake. He wanted people to come and see how special it is here. These angels have become a symbol of true love and always having faith in love."

"What an amazing story," Riley said.

Lisa nodded. "For decades now, it has been a tradition for people to buy them and give them to the people they love most at Christmas, just like Thomas gave his first angel to Cynthia. They are only sold at around the holidays, starting on December first and ending on Christmas Eve."

Riley walked over to the display of angels. She picked up a little framed saying that said, *Give the gift of love to your one true love.*

"They sell out fast. This is all I have left. If you'd like to get one, I would do it now," Lisa offered as she joined her.

Riley shook her head. "Thanks, that's okay. I don't need one."

Lisa gave her a curious look. "But in the TV interview you

talked about your one true love. I thought maybe—"

"No," Riley said. "That whole interview was taken out of context. Trust me, I have no one to give an angel like this to."

Lisa put her arm around Riley. "Don't worry, dear. You still have lots of time to meet 'the one.'"

Riley laughed. "Oh, trust me, that's the last thing I need. The only 'one' I care about right now is my next novel. That's what I need to focus on and give all my love to."

"But a book can't love you back," Lisa said.

Riley laughed. "I don't know about that. I've felt a lot of love from some of the books I've read."

They shared a smile.

"Well, I'm sure you know what you're doing," Lisa added. "I mean, after all, you're the one writing best-selling love stories."

Riley smiled, but she couldn't help thinking that she hadn't been writing best-selling love stories lately. She'd never thought she had to be *in love* to write about love. She'd always just used all the inspiration from her past relationships. But had that all finally dried up? Was she out of material? If that was the case, she was in big, big trouble.

Lisa had started walking away. "I will leave you to look around," she said. "Enjoy yourself, and hopefully you'll find something that speaks to you."

As Lisa left her to browse, all Riley could think was that if anything in this store started *speaking* to her, she was going to run—fast.

She was just passing a wall of wreaths when one of her shopping bags hit the shelf of Christmas Lake Angels. One angel teetered back and forth, looking as if it was about to topple over. Riley quickly reached out to steady it.

"Oh, no, you don't. You're not going anywhere," she said to the little angel. After making sure it was safe, she continued around the corner.

That's when she heard Luke call out her name. "Riley? Are you still in here?"

"I'm over here," she answered. "By the angels."

Luke appeared quickly. "I should have known I'd find you by a good story," he said, picking up one of the angels. "Did Lisa tell you about our Christmas Lake Angels?"

"Oh, yes, she did," Riley said. "I heard the whole story."

"And what did you think?"

"That it's a brilliant marketing plan," Riley answered.

Luke laughed as he gently set the angel back down. "And I thought you were a romance author. That's not a very romantic way to look at it."

Riley shrugged. "What do *you* think of the story?"

"I grew up hearing it," Luke said. "It's part of my Christmas tradition."

Riley gave him a thoughtful look. "So, you believe in…"

"Love," Luke finished for her, looking into her eyes. "I do. Don't you? I mean, you have to, right? It's all you write about."

"First, it's not *all* I write about," Riley corrected.

"So your answer is?" Luke asked.

When Riley realized he wasn't going to let her off the hook, she knew the only answer she could give him was that yes, she believed in love. What kind of romance writer would she be if she didn't believe in love? As all these thoughts raced through her head, she couldn't help wondering who she was trying to convince—him or herself.

She met his stare. "Yes, of course, I believe in love," Riley said. "Happy?"

Luke kept staring at her. "Yes. Are you?"

She laughed to hide her discomfort. The way he was looking at her made her feel as if he could see right through her.

"I guess what I mean is…you must believe in love for other

people because you write love stories about other people," Luke said. "But what about you? Do you believe in love for *you*?"

Riley hadn't seen that question coming, and because she wasn't sure how she felt, she covered her confusion with annoyance. "Now you sound like Tom."

"Tom?" Luke asked. "Who's Tom?"

"The talk show host who asked me how I could write romance novels when I still haven't found 'the one.'"

Luke held up his hands. "Slow down. I wasn't asking you why you didn't have someone. I was just asking if you *believe* in love for yourself—that's all."

Riley locked eyes with him. "How do you know I don't have someone?" Riley demanded.

Luke opened his mouth to say something but then apparently changed his mind and shut it. "You know what," he said. "Forget I asked the question. I didn't mean to upset you."

"I'm not upset," Riley shot back, but her tone told a different story. She picked up a snow globe off the shelf and shook it hard. She was done talking about her love life or lack thereof.

"So how's the weather out there?" she asked, changing the topic. She held the snow globe up to him. "Better or worse than this?"

When Luke took the snow globe from her, their hands touched and their eyes met. Riley looked away quickly. The way Luke was looking at her, like he was trying to figure her out, made her feel even more antsy.

"I'm ready to go," she said and headed for the door.

"Thank you, Lisa," Luke called out as they passed the register.

"You're welcome, Luke." Lisa smiled at them both. "Great

to meet you, Riley. Come back soon. Merry Christmas."

"Merry Christmas," Luke replied.

"Thanks again," Riley chimed in.

As they walked back to the truck, Riley studied Luke. He seemed happy. He was humming "Deck the Halls." It was the first time she'd heard him hum a Christmas song.

"How did your meeting go?" she asked, unable to help herself, remembering how she'd seen him with the pretty girl in the window.

Luke's eyes lit up. "It was a great meeting. Couldn't have been better."

Riley couldn't help wondering if Luke had ever bought a Christmas Lake Angel for someone he cared about. She shook herself mentally. She was annoyed that she'd let her mind even go there. What Luke did or didn't do was no concern of hers. She didn't know what was wrong with her. Her emotions were all over the place, and she blamed one thing... Christmas.

Chapter Eighteen

When they pulled up to the Christmas Lake Lodge, Riley saw a gray SUV parked out front.

"Were you expecting company?" Riley asked.

"That's not company. That's Maryanne," Luke answered.

Riley didn't have time to ask who Maryanne before he rolled down his window and hollered a hello to a woman who was unloading boxes of groceries from the SUV's trunk.

"Maryanne, don't worry about that. I got it," Luke said as he pulled up to the SUV.

The truck had barely stopped when he got out and swept Maryanne up into a big hug. "Merry Christmas! I'm so glad you're here."

Riley frowned. Here was another pretty woman that Luke seemed enamored with. When she hovered in the background, Luke called her over. "Riley, come meet Maryanne, our chef extraordinaire."

Riley barely noticed Maryanne because she was too busy watching Luke put his arm around her. "Nice to meet you," Riley said.

"Great to meet you," Maryanne said in the sincerest of voices.

When a gust of wind whipped by them, Luke took a box of

groceries out of the SUV. "You girls get inside. I'll get this."

"Are you sure?" Maryanne asked, already heading for the door.

Luke laughed. "Yes. Go. Both of you."

When Luke smiled at Riley, she smiled back, and then she quickly grabbed a box of groceries before she headed for the door, sidestepping the bear as Maryanne had just done. She was relieved to see it worked and no "We Wish You a BEARy Christmas" had begun.

Just as Riley got to the door, another gust of wind almost took her box of groceries with it. She flew through the front door, almost running over Comet, who was eagerly waiting for her.

"Sorry, boy," she said, practically leaping over him.

She heard Maryanne laugh before she saw her. "Oh, he loves to wait right by the door. No one is coming or going without him knowing it, right, Comet?"

Comet went running over to Maryanne, who happily petted him.

As Riley brushed the snow off herself, she smiled at Maryanne. "So you're the chef?" Riley asked. "I'm impressed and very jealous of anyone who can cook."

Maryanne came over and held out her hand to shake. "And you're Riley Reynolds, one of my favorite authors."

Riley was flattered. "Thank you. That's high praise, indeed."

"And well deserved," Maryanne said.

After talking to Maryanne for just a few minutes, Riley could tell she was passionate about her cooking. She guessed Maryanne was around the same age as she was. Even in her jeans and oversized fleece, wearing no makeup and her hair in messy ponytail, Maryanne was beautiful. She had the kind of classic features—high cheekbones, flawless skin, large almond-shaped eyes with long, dark, natural eyelashes—that any model would die for.

The best part was that it seemed like Maryanne didn't even know how pretty she was. Either that or she just didn't care. That made Riley like her even more.

Of course, it didn't hurt that besides just bringing groceries, Maryanne had also brought a new Wi-Fi router. That had sealed the deal for Riley. If they could get the Wi-Fi working, Maryanne would be her new BFF.

Maryanne started telling Riley about all the different holiday dishes she was planning and some of the culinary classes she was going to teach during Christmas Camp. Her enthusiasm was contagious. Riley's idea of cooking was warming up something in the microwave, but she was open to learning a few tricks from Maryanne.

Riley still wasn't sure what the relationship was between Maryanne and Luke, but Maryanne clearly adored him. Apparently, Luke was one popular guy. First the realtor and now Maryanne.

When Riley looked out the window, she frowned seeing how fast the snow was still coming down.

"What's wrong?" he asked as he came up next to her.

"I'm just hoping all this snow doesn't hurt the travel plans for our Christmas Campers."

"Don't worry," Luke said. "They'll get here. Even if I have to go get them from the airport myself. Okay?"

Riley gave a soldier's salute. "Yes, sir."

She still had her hand up to her forehead when the front door flung open, and a pretty girl in her twenties rushed inside. When the girl saw the end of Riley's salute, she laughed a little. Riley instantly put her hand down, feeling foolish because the girl standing in front of her was wearing an Army combat uniform.

But the girl quickly forgot about Riley when she saw Luke and went rushing toward him. "Luke!" the girl exclaimed with the kind of smile that would light up any room.

As soon as Luke saw her his eyes lit up. "Caylee!"

As Caylee threw herself into Luke's arms, he exuberantly picked her up and spun her around. There was laughter and tears of joy. Riley felt like she was intruding on a special moment.

By the time Luke put Caylee down they were both breathless.

Comet, who had joined them, was equally excited, barking and wagging his tail.

"You made it!" Luke said, holding both her hands and looking into her eyes.

"Barely," Caylee said, looking up at Luke.

He instantly looked concerned. "Trouble getting out of Afghanistan?"

Caylee laughed as she slung her duffel bag off her shoulder. "No, trouble trying to get into the Denver airport. Flights are being canceled all over the place because of some snowstorm. I wasn't sure if I was going to make it."

Luke gave her a heartfelt hug. "But you're here now, and you're safe, thank God."

"I had to come, right?" Caylee laughed. "There was no way I'd ever miss you doing a Christmas Camp at the lodge. I love this idea. It's brilliant. I don't know why we haven't done something like this before."

"My mom was saying the same thing," Luke said. "She sends her love from Florida."

"I've missed her so much," Caylee said.

When Maryanne entered the room, Caylee rushed over and gave her a hug, too. "And I've missed you, too, Maryanne. All those cookies you sent me in Afghanistan, I swear you made me the most popular soldier at the base. Every time I got a package everyone would gather around and hope it was from you."

Maryanne smiled and looked pleased. "That's why I always sent you an extra-large box. I knew you'd share."

"Only with my favorite people," Caylee said with a teasing twinkle in her eye. "But seriously, the cookies and the letters from home mean more than you know." She turned to Luke. "And thank you for all the updates on what's happening here at the lodge. I can't wait to hear more about this Christmas Camp!"

When Caylee gave Riley a curious look, Luke looked apologetic. "I am so sorry," he said, looking right at Riley. "Riley, please forgive me for being so rude. I just haven't seen Caylee in more than a year, and…"

Riley smiled back. "Please, don't apologize. I completely understand." She walked over to Caylee and offered her hand to shake.

"I'm Riley," she said to Caylee. "Thank you so much for your service."

Caylee smiled back at Riley, but instead of taking her hand, she gave her a hug, too. "I'm a hugger," she explained. "And I know exactly who you are. I'm a huge fan of your books. When Luke told me you were hosting this Christmas Camp, I knew I had to come."

Luke pretended to look hurt. "And here I thought you came home to see me."

They all laughed.

When Luke led everyone over to the couch to sit down, Comet took his favorite spot by the fire where he could watch them all. Caylee sat on the floor next to him and started petting him, then turned her attention back to Riley. "I really do love your books. There's a group of us girls on the base who share them whenever we can get them."

Riley was surprised and flattered. "Really?"

"Oh, yeah!" Caylee continued. "One of the other soldiers in my unit gets your books from her mom, and I trade cookies for books. It's totally the barter system, and thanks to Maryanne's amazing cookies, I can get some really good stuff for them."

Everyone laughed, and Maryanne stood up from the couch. "And that's my cue to get back to the kitchen. I need to start making some cookies for our Christmas Campers." Before she left, Maryanne leaned down and gave Caylee another hug. "I'm so glad you're home safe. We've all missed you so much."

"I can't believe I'm actually home." Caylee took a deep breath and smiled. "I love you guys."

Comet barked and wagged his tail. "Especially you, Comet," Caylee said and gave him a hug.

As Maryanne left the room, Luke turned to Caylee. "So you've really read some of Riley's books?"

Riley was glad he asked the question because she was curious herself. She had never heard of her books being read by any soldiers in war zones.

"I have," Caylee said proudly and smiled at Riley. "I haven't read the latest ones, we're a bit behind, but your first book, *Loving the Dream,* was amazing."

Riley was touched. "Thank you. That's one of my favorites, too. And thank you for taking the time to read them while you're in Afghanistan. You're obviously incredibly busy with much more important things."

Caylee smiled. "That's the thing that's so great about your

books. They're the perfect escape when I want to forget where I am for a while. They also always give me hope that I'll find my own love story someday."

Luke looked surprised. "What about that guy, Terry? Larry? The one you were seeing?"

"Gary," Caylee laughed. "Didn't work out."

Caylee turned to Riley. "He was another soldier. Good guy, but at the end of the day, it turned out the only thing we really had in common was being in Afghanistan and being in the army. There was no spark."

"Well, you have to have the spark," Riley said emphatically.

"Exactly," Caylee agreed.

When Luke shook his head like he wasn't following, Riley and Caylee shared a laugh.

Caylee jumped up. "If you guys don't mind, I haven't slept in, like, forever. I was going to go upstairs and crash for a few hours."

Luke stood up, too. "Of course. Your regular room is waiting for you."

Caylee gave Luke another hug. "Love you!"

"Love you more," Luke said, and Riley could tell he meant it.

As Caylee started to leave the room, she smiled back at Riley. "So great to meet you, Riley. I can't wait to do this Christmas Camp with you. The girls back at the base are going to be so jealous!"

"Great to meet you, too," Riley said. "Get some rest."

Riley and Luke both watched Caylee leave the room. Then Luke let out a deep sigh of relief and sat down for the first time. "I'm so glad she's home and okay," he said. "I feel like I'm holding my breath the whole time she's gone."

"And you said she'd been gone a year?" Riley asked, sitting down next to him.

He nodded. "And a year is a long time to hold your breath."

They shared a smiled. Riley could tell from the first moment Luke saw Caylee that she was someone special to him. When he talked to her, his eyes lit up and his voice softened.

"Does she live here at the lodge?" Riley asked.

Luke laughed a little. "No, though don't try telling her that. She still calls this *home*."

When Riley looked confused, he continued as he got up and put a few more logs on the fire. "Caylee's mom, Sue, used to work here at the lodge. She did a little bit of everything from housekeeping to organizing events and activities for our guests. Caylee's dad was in the military so he was gone a lot, and Sue would bring Caylee to work with her. My parents insisted and loved having Caylee here. My mom always said having an energetic little girl at the lodge kept them all on their toes and kept them young."

Riley laughed. "I bet it did. Caylee has so much energy now I can only imagine her when she was little."

Luke nodded and smiled. "Oh, Caylee was something all right. She has always been full of life. I'm an only child, and when I went off to college and moved to Europe, I think my parents missed having me here so having Caylee around was great for them. She got her first job here at the lodge when she was ten—the same job I was given."

"What was that?" Riley asked, intrigued.

"Collecting firewood for the fireplaces in the guest rooms," Luke answered. "Actually, it was more like kindling, picking up little sticks around the property, but it was something to do that kept us out of trouble and gave us some responsibility."

Riley nodded. "Smart parents."

"Right?" Luke smiled. When he paused for a moment and looked away, his smile faded. He took a deep breath before continuing.

"When Caylee was eighteen, her parents were killed in a car accident. It happened just a few miles from here. A car, someone not from the area, was coming the other way and hit a patch of ice and lost control…"

Riley touched her heart. "I'm so sorry. That's terrible."

"It was rough," Luke said as he stared into the fire.

She couldn't see his expression, but she could hear the pain in his voice.

"My parents decided to take Caylee in," he continued. "She was getting ready to graduate from high school. Legally, she was an adult…"

"But emotionally…"

When Luke turned to face her, his own pain was clear. "Emotionally, she was lost and scared, and this was the only other home she'd ever known."

"That was wonderful of your parents to take her in," Riley said.

"There was never really a question," Luke said. "She came back here the night of the accident and never left. No one ever talked about it. She just stayed here. This is where she belonged."

Riley nodded.

"She wanted to follow in her father's footsteps and serve her country," Luke continued. "She'd already been accepted into a military academy, where she graduated top of her class. She graduated almost two years ago and was almost immediately deployed to Afghanistan. She works in Army intelligence. I'm not even sure doing what." Luke smiled a little. "Whenever I ask, she always jokes saying that line about how if she told me she'd have to kill me or whatever it is. She really is something."

"And you love her very much," Riley finished for him.

Luke nodded. "Like a little sister, and I worry about her

every single day."

"But now she's home," Riley said.

Luke nodded. "And now she's home. But I don't know for how long. Her tour is almost up, but she's talking about re-enlisting. She's always saying we need to be thankful for the time we have together because tomorrow is never guaranteed."

"And she's right," Riley said, thinking about the last Christmas she'd had with her dad.

"Caylee is going to be a great help to us during Christmas Camp," Luke said. "She can do just about anything around here, and the guests always love her."

"Then I'm really glad she's here," Riley said. "For a lot of reasons."

"Me too," Luke said.

They shared a smile.

"And you know what," Luke said, "I'm glad she's not with that Harry, Larry guy."

"Gary," Riley corrected him.

"Whatever," Luke said. "I didn't like the sound of him."

Riley laughed. "Now you sound like a true big brother."

"Well, didn't you agree that without the *spark,* forget about it?" Luke asked, locking eyes with her.

For a moment, Riley had to remind herself they were still talking about Caylee. She looked away as she stood up from the couch. "That's right. I did. Having a spark is everything."

As if on cue, some embers from the fire sparked and cracked. When Riley looked into the flames, she told herself it was the fire that was making her all warm and tingly, *not* the way Luke was still looking at her.

Chapter Nineteen

Needing to get her mind off Luke, she took her phone out of her pocket and held it up. Still no signal.

"How long do you think the cell service will be out?" she asked.

Luke shrugged. "You never know. It's a good thing one of Christmas Camp's mottos is, 'Disconnect to reconnect with what matters most at Christmas.'"

"Well, right now, what matters most to me is getting ahold of my agent," Riley said. "I'm supposed to be checking in with updates so we can get some posts on social media"

Luke walked over and picked up the old-fashioned phone and held the handset out for her. "Here you go," he said, smiling. "Call anyone you'd like. I'll go see if I can hook up the new router and get our Wi-Fi back up."

"That would be great," Riley said. She eyed the phone. "But in the meantime, I'll just use this relic again."

"Be thankful we have it," Luke said.

"Oh, believe me, I am," she replied. "I bet we're already getting tons of people saying what they want me to write about in this Christmas novel. I want to start writing everything down and see if anything inspires me."

"So basically you're going to let our Christmas Campers write your story for you?" Luke asked.

Riley tilted her head while she studied him. "Why do you make it sound like I'm doing something wrong when we're trying to include what my fans want to read?"

"No judgment here," Luke said.

Riley put her hands on her hips. "Really, because right now you're sounding pretty judgy to me."

Luke laughed. "Then I'm out of here. Good luck with your call."

"Thanks." Riley watched Comet start to follow Luke out of the room. "Alone at last," she said quietly to herself as she sat down to make her call. But apparently, she had spoken too soon because when she looked up, she saw Comet hadn't actually left the room yet. He was standing in the doorway watching her.

"What?" she asked, feeling guilty for some reason. "I'm only making a call. That's it. Nothing fun. You're not missing anything. Trust me. It's just a call to Margo."

When Comet heard Margo's name, it did the trick and he trotted out of the room. Riley couldn't help but laugh.

Margo's phone rang four times before she picked up. Riley had almost hung up.

"Margo Meyers," Margo answered.

When Margo's voice sounded a little off, Riley wasn't sure if it was Margo or the connection. She tapped the headset several times.

"Margo? It's Riley. Is everything okay? Can you hear me all right?"

"Clear as a bell," Margo said with a bite to her tone. "What number is this? Where have you been? You were supposed to call last night."

So far, Riley thought, this was shaping up to be a typical Margo call where she shot a lot of questions at her but never gave her a chance to answer any of them. When she tried to sit back in the chair and get comfortable, the phone cord pulled taut and the entire phone almost fell to the floor.

"You stupid thing," Riley muttered, scrambling to save the phone.

"What did you just call me?" Margo snapped.

Riley's eyes grew huge. "Sorry! Margo, I wasn't talking to you."

"Then who are you calling stupid?" Margo asked. "I hope not one of your Christmas Campers."

Riley stared at the handset, annoyed. "Like I would ever do that. I was talking to the phone." She took a deep breath to regroup. "Never mind. It doesn't matter. I'm calling from a landline at the lodge. The cell service isn't working."

"Good to see you're taking this whole disconnect-to-reconnect Christmas Camp theme to heart," Margo said.

Riley knew if she heard that phrase one more time she was going to lose it. She fought to keep her cool. "Look, Margo, I'm calling to see if you have any social media feedback for me yet? Has anyone sent in ideas yet of what they'd want to see in this Christmas book? I haven't been able to get online since I got here."

Margo laughed. "Do we have feedback yet? It's been incredible. We've gotten more than thirty-two thousand responses so far with all kinds of ideas. They're all using the hashtag we created, #ChristmasCamp. I'm having a couple of my interns pulling everything together, getting rid of the duplicates, and then we'll send you a list."

"Wow," Riley said, stunned. "And we haven't even started the camp yet."

"I know," Margo said. "The response has been amazing, and your publisher team is calling Mike a genius."

"Oh, great, just what we need, for him to have an even bigger ego," Riley said.

"If that ego ends up saving your career, then I'm all for it," Margo said. "How far are you on your outline?"

"What outline?" Riley asked. "If you're talking about the outline for this Christmas book, I haven't even started. I've been waiting to see what kind of feedback we get and what people want to read about."

There was silence on the other end of the line.

"Margo? Are you still there?"

"I'm here," Margo said, her voice icy. "I'm just trying to figure out why in what world you think it's okay that you haven't even started on an outline that's due in a just a few weeks."

"I told you," Riley said, getting frustrated. "I'm waiting to get the fan feedback. That's what you wanted. That's why I'm here, right?"

"You're there for the publicity, for some positive press. You still need to create your own original Christmas story. Sure, you can use a few generic ideas from people, like including a snowball fight or making a snowman, things like that, so when people read it they'll think it was their idea, but it's up to you to figure out how all these Christmas activities tie in to your characters falling in love. You should have already started on that."

Riley didn't know how to respond. She didn't have a clue what she wanted to write about, and she had been hoping that something would inspire her at Christmas Camp. She didn't want to panic Margo, so she just decided to play along.

"Sounds good," she told Margo.

Silence.

"Margo?" Riley asked.

"Yes, I'm still here," Margo said. "It's just so rare that you simply agree with me without putting up a fight."

"Well, when you're right, you're right," Riley said, hoping

Margo would buy it.

Margo laughed a genuine laugh. "Who are you and what have you done with my author?"

Riley laughed, too. "Seriously, Margo, everything's going to be great. I appreciate what everyone's doing on your end. Is there anything you need me to do from here?"

"Yes," Margo said. "Find your Christmas spirit."

Riley rolled her eyes. When reindeer fly, she thought.

"I'm serious about this, Riley," Margo said as if reading her mind. "Don't think you're fooling me. I've known you for seven years, and in that time, you've never once talked about celebrating Christmas or talked about Christmas at all, for that matter. And," she continued, "when it was first brought up that you needed to do a Christmas story for your next book, I saw the look on your fa—"

"What look?" Riley interrupted.

"Like you'd rather chew broken glass," Margo said.

Riley winced. Margo always had a way with words.

Silence again. But this time It was from Riley.

"Are you going to say something?" Margo asked.

"Nope," Riley said. She wasn't about to incriminate herself, and she knew Margo could read her like a book, pun intended. "Look, Margo, I really need to go. Luke is waiting for me to finalize the Christmas Camp plans."

"Okay," Margo said. "But there's one more thing."

"What?" Riley asked. "Whatever you need."

"I need a Christmas picture of you with your family—something when you were little or one of those pictures kids get every year with Santa. A couple of the online outlets are requesting them since Mike is promoting you as 'Miss Christmas.' You know how everyone loves to see childhood photos."

Riley shook her head as she stared up at the ceiling, thinking Margo may as well have been asking for all the snow in the North Pole. She didn't have any childhood Christmas pictures, and this was something Google couldn't help her with.

"Riley? Are you still there? Did you hear me?" Margo asked. "I swear we have a terrible phone connection."

"Yes," Riley said in a voice that sounded far away, even to her own ears. "I heard you."

"Great," Margo shot back. "So it won't be a problem to get me something right away?"

Riley looked over at Comet and mouthed the word, *Help*.

She then answered Margo with a lie that rivaled Mike's. "No, Margo, it won't be any problem at all."

Chapter Twenty

Riley stared at the phone for several seconds after she hung up with Margo. She looked over at Comet. "Now what am I going to do?"

When Comet looked up at her, Riley thought his big brown eyes almost looked sympathetic. It was like he understood exactly what was going on. She loved him for that. She kissed the top of his head and gave him a hug.

Riley blamed all of this on Mike and his pitching her to media outlets as "Miss Christmas." If there really was a Naughty or Nice List, Mike would be at the top of the Naughty List, and instead of a lump of coal in his stocking, he'd get an entire coal mine. All the stories he was spinning about her were spinning *out of control,* and right now, *naughty* was about the nicest word that came to mind when she thought of Mike.

Riley knew she only had one last hope.

She picked up the phone and dialed her mom. She dreaded asking her about this. She didn't want to upset her by bringing up any painful Christmas memories. Ever since they had started going to Hawaii for Christmas, they never talked about how the holiday had been when her dad was still alive. It was like Christmas had never happened.

They had just moved on, into the future, with their fun-filled, beach-themed Hawaii trips that had made them both happy. Yet, now here she was, about to bring up the past.

She was halfway through dialing the last number when she stopped. She stared at the phone. She couldn't do it. She was about to hang up when Comet barked.

Her attention flew to him. "What's wrong?" she asked.

Comet barked again.

And then she heard another sound. It was her mom on the other end of the line.

"Hello? Hello? Is anyone there?"

Surprised, Riley looked at the phone and realized she must have accidently dialed the last number when Comet distracted her with his bark. When she gave him a look, Comet was wagging his tail.

"Hello?" she heard her mom ask again.

She looked at the phone and steeled herself. "Mom? It's me. Can you hear me?"

Her mom laughed. "I can now. I thought I heard a dog barking."

Riley eyed Comet, who put his head down on his paws and continued watching her. "You did, that was Comet."

Her mom laughed. "Like the reindeer?"

"That's the idea," Riley said.

"What kind of dog is he?" her mom asked.

"A crafty one," Riley answered without hesitation, but she smiled as she looked over at him. "He's really smart. He's a Bernese mountain dog. They're from Switzerland, from the town of Bern. Remember when I visited there when I was doing my travel writing? That's the first time I ever saw one. They were raised to heard cattle, and I think some of them even pulled farm carts. Comet looks strong enough to do that."

Comet lifted his head up when he heard his name.

"I've read about them," Riley's mom said. "They're supposed to be great watchdogs and very loyal companions."

Riley nodded and smiled. "I can totally see that."

"So where are you right now?" her mom asked. "You didn't get a dog, did you?"

Riley laughed. "Me? A dog? Come on, Mom, you know me better than that. I don't have time to talk care of a dog. I'm in Colorado…"

Riley hesitated. She hadn't told her mom much about the Christmas Camp. As a matter of fact, she'd left the word *Christmas* out entirely, just telling her that she was hosting a writing event to promote her next book. She also knew her mom wasn't on social media and rarely watched the news, so Riley had avoided telling her anything about writing a Christmas novel. But she knew she couldn't hide it forever. She just wasn't sure what to say.

"Riley? Are you still there?" her mom asked.

Riley sat up straighter. "Sorry. Yes, I'm here."

"So you're in Colorado for that author event you were telling me about? How is it going?"

"It hasn't started yet," Riley answered. "It's actually starting the day after tomorrow. And that's one of the things I was calling to talk to you about."

"About your Christmas book," Riley's mom said.

Riley's heart stopped. "You know about that?"

"Honey, I saw you on the news. All my friends here in Florida are on social media, and they all follow you. They read all your books. They told me about everything about the Christmas Camp and how you're writing a Christmas book…"

"Mom, I'm sorry. I was going to tell you." Riley felt terrible that her mom had found out this way.

Her mom laughed. "What are you sorry about? I know

you're busy."

Riley took a deep breath. "About the whole Christmas thing. Trust me, this isn't something I wanted to do. I really didn't have a choice. Everything happened so fast. Margo says this is my last shot at keeping my publishing deal. I thought I only had to show up and host a reception or something, but now it looks like I have to do a lot more," Riley said, talking faster and faster.

Now that she was finally telling her mom what was going on, she felt a huge sense of relief. She always told her mom everything, but this was Christmas and they never talked about Christmas.

"Honey, take a breath," her mom said in a soothing voice. "Everything's going to be okay."

Tears started to well up in Riley's eyes. She quickly brushed them away. "I'm just sorry I didn't tell you sooner. I didn't want to upset you."

"Upset me?" Riley's mom asked. "How in the world would you upset me? I'm so proud of you and everything you do. Everyone, especially me, is so excited for your next novel."

"A Christmas novel," Riley said in a small, faint voice. "Mom, I'm writing about *Christmas*."

"I know," her mom said in a soft voice. "And you're going to do great."

Riley fought back more tears. "I thought you'd be upset…"

"Why would I be upset?"

"Because I'm writing about *Christmas*." Riley put extra emphasis on the word *Christmas* again. "And we don't celebrate Christmas. We don't even talk about Christmas."

"That's because you never wanted to talk about it," her mom said gently.

"What? Me? But you're the one who didn't want to celebrate since…Dad…"

Just saying it out loud made Riley start choking up again as a wave of emotion washed over her.

"Riley, honey, I'm so sorry. We should have talked about this a long time ago. I just didn't want to upset you, and if I'm being one-hundred-percent honest, I've felt guilty for the way I've handled things for a long time."

"Handled what?" Riley asked, confused.

"Christmas."

Riley shut her eyes as her mom continued talking.

"That first Christmas after your dad passed, you were so little and so heartbroken," her mom said. "I hated seeing you that way. So I took you to Hawaii. I thought it would help get your mind off things."

"And it did," Riley jumped in. "We had a wonderful time. We didn't need Christmas. We had each other. Even though I was so young, I knew how sad you were, but in Hawaii, it was different. We were different. There was no Christmas to make us sad."

"But, honey, I never planned for us to forget about Christmas. That first one I knew was going to be tough so we went to Hawaii, but after that, you wanted to go ever year. You were so excited about it, and I just wanted you to be happy. Anytime I tried to bring up Christmas, you would get so upset. I even talked to a child psychologist about it, and they told me to give you time and that you would let me know when you were ready to celebrate Christmas again."

Riley, stunned, sat back in her chair. "You did Hawaii all those years for me?"

"Of course," her mom said. "You know I would do anything for you, and we had a wonderful time, didn't we?"

"Yes, but I always thought you didn't want to celebrate Christmas because it was too hard without Dad. I thought Hawaii was what we *both* wanted," Riley said.

"I wanted what was best for you. That's all I wanted."

"And we never celebrated Christmas again," Riley said, trying to take it all in.

"Because you weren't ready," her mom said. "But now it looks like you are, and when I heard about this Christmas Camp and your next novel, I couldn't have been happier for you. I always prayed you would find your way back to Christmas, and now you have."

Riley struggled to process everything. Her mom sounded so happy, she didn't have the heart to tell her that she wasn't embracing Christmas—far from it—and that she was only doing all this to save her career. Nothing had changed for her when it came to Christmas.

"I'm glad we've talked about this," Riley said because she didn't know what else to say. "Actually, I'm calling because Margo asked if I had any Christmas pictures from when I was little. I guess some online magazines are asking for them for some feature stories they're doing. There's no problem if you don't have any. I don't remember any. I just thought I should ask before I tell her we don't know where they are or that they're buried somewhere in storage or something like tha—"

"I have some," Riley's mom said, interrupting her. "I have some really adorable ones I think would work great."

Riley instantly stopped talking. "You do?" Her voice sounded faint.

Riley's mom laughed. "Yes, of course. One of my favorites is a picture you took with Santa when you were eight. I also have some where you're decorating the Christmas tree with Dad and—"

"The one with Santa," she said quickly, cutting her mom off. "That should be fine." She didn't want to hear anymore. She couldn't hear anymore. She didn't want to remember. "Do you think you could just take a picture of it and e-mail it to me?"

"Sure," her mom said. "How soon do you need it?"

"As soon as you can send it," Riley said. "You know how Margo and Mike are. They want everything yesterday."

"And you're sure you just want the one picture?"

"I'm sure," Riley said emphatically. "One is all I want to see."

"Consider it done," Riley's mom said. "I should be able to get it to you in the next hour."

"Thanks, Mom," Riley said, feeling conflicted.

She knew she should feel grateful that she'd found a picture, but she didn't know how she felt about seeing that picture or sharing it with the world.

"Oh, and Mom, I forgot to tell you—our internet and cell service have been down here. Luke was going to get it back up and running, so why don't you wait and I'll let you know when I can get the e-mail."

"That sounds great, honey," Riley's mom said. "And who is Luke? Is this a new boyfriend you've also forgotten to tell me about?"

"Ha! No," Riley said. "Who has time for a boyfriend? Luke is just the guy who is holding this Christmas Camp. It's at his family's lodge."

"Well, I know you're busy, but you're never too busy to find love."

Riley laughed loudly. "Mom, you must be reading too many of my romance novels."

"Never." Her mom replied. "And I can't wait to read this next one. I think this Christmas novel of yours is going to be very special."

"I hope so," Riley said. "I really do."

"Oh, wait. I have a quick question. I know you're busy and have to get back to work, but I have to ask you…"

"What, Mom? Ask me anything."

"Which old boyfriend were you talking about on the news

yesterday? Colin from college, Brendan, or Tyler the lawyer?"

"Mom, I wasn't talking about just one of them. When I said that in the interview, I meant my old boyfriends, plural. I was talking about all three of them in general," Riley said. "There's no big secret I've been hiding. I don't have one person who was the love of my life."

"That's not what it sounded like on TV," her mom said.

Riley groaned. "I know. Thanks to that wannabe host."

"Well, I think everyone's asking the same question I am. Maybe all the mystery will help with the publicity for your Christmas book."

Riley laughed. "Okay, now you sound like Mike. I'm going to tell him your gunning for his job."

Her mom laughed. "You know I only want you to be happy." Riley nodded. "I know, Mom."

"And I hope you do find your one true love," Riley's mom said. "It's time."

"Actually, Mom," Riley said, "you're wrong about the timing. Even if the perfect guy showed up here at Christmas Camp, I would be too busy right now to even notice."

"Just remember you can't see the forest for the trees," her mom said.

Riley laughed. "Oh no. Is this another one of those sayings you've made up?"

"Oh, I can't claim this one," Riley's mom said. "*You can't see the forest for the trees* is an old, famous saying your dad always used to say."

"What does that even mean?" Riley asked.

"It means," her mom answered, "Don't let your emotions in the moment prevent you from losing sight of what's really important—the big picture, what will make us happy in the long run."

Riley still looked confused.

Riley's mom chuckled. "It's just something to think about."

When Riley looked out the window, all she saw were snow-covered trees. She couldn't see the entire forest.

"I'll think about it," Riley promised. "But right now, I have to see if our Wi-Fi is working so you can send me that picture and make Margo and Mike happy. I'll e-mail you as soon as I know."

"Sounds good," Riley's mom said. "And, Riley..."

"Yes, Mom?"

"I'm glad we had this talk...about Christmas. I love you. Merry Christmas."

Riley abruptly stood up and almost knocked over the phone again. She saved it just before it crashed to the floor.

"I love you, Mom. I'll talk to you again soon."

Chapter Twenty-One

As soon as Riley hung up with her mom, she checked her cell phone. The Wi-Fi still wasn't working.

"Okay, where's Luke?" she asked Comet.

As if understanding, Comet ran for the front door. Riley gave him a suspicious look. "Is Luke really outside, or do you just want to go for a walk?"

At the sound of the word *walk,* Comet barked twice and wagged his tail.

Maryanne came into the room, laughing. "Oh, now you've done it," she said. "You said the magic word."

"*Walk?*" Riley asked.

When Comet barked again, Riley understood. "Let me guess," she said. "Anyone who says *walk*—"

Comet barked again but this time louder

"—has to take Comet for a *w-a-l-k,*" Maryanne finished, spelling out the word. "See?" She smiled at Comet. "I've learned my lesson."

Comet wagged his tail and then expectantly looked back at Riley.

"Okay, okay," Riley said. "You win. We can go. But I need to find Luke."

"Oh, he's down by the lake," Maryanne said. "And that's Comet favorite place to go."

"Perfect," Riley said.

"The leash is in the hall closet, and you better bundle up. It's still snowing out there," Maryanne said.

"No problem," Riley said cheerfully. "I bought some new clothes in town."

"At Merry and Bright?" Maryanne asked.

Riley nodded. "I found some really great things."

"Did Lisa tell you about the Christmas Lake Angels?" Maryanne asked.

"Oh yes," Riley said. "I got the full story."

"Isn't it an amazing love story?" Maryanne asked. "Even though I haven't met my own Prince Charming yet, but I still have hope someone will give me a Christmas Lake Angel someday."

"Or you'll give them one," Riley said.

Maryanne smiled at her. "Exactly!"

When a timer went off in the kitchen, Maryanne headed that way. "Ah, that's my cue. You two have fun!"

"We will!" Riley said. "Ready for that walk?"

Comet barked and ran to the front of the door.

Less than five minutes later, after Riley had taken Maryanne's advice and bundled up in some of her new winter gear, Comet was leading her down a snow-covered path to the lake.

The snow had stopped falling, but there was still an icy chill in the air that made her thankful she'd also bought some silk long johns at Lisa's insistence.

As she followed Comet, she had to navigate several inches of fresh powder. She was thankful for her yeti boots.

When they'd first left the lodge, she'd thought she spotted Luke down by the Christmas trees along the lakefront. He'd looked like he was stringing some new Christmas lights—or taking some down, it was hard to tell—but as she'd gotten closer, he'd disappeared.

"Where did Luke go?" she asked Comet.

Comet picked up his pace and pulled on the leash so hard she almost had to run to keep up with him. By the time she got down to the lake, she was breathless and laughing. That's when she finally saw Luke. He was actually *on* the lake, out in the middle where the one Christmas tree was lit up.

"Good boy," she praised Comet. "You found him."

She walked to the edge of the lake and stopped. The only time she'd been on a frozen lake was when she'd worked as a news reporter in Minnesota and was sent to cover a story of a car that had gone partially through the ice.

Her not-so-brilliant cameraman had decided to drive their super heavy live van out on the lake so they could get closer for the best video. Even though she'd told him it wasn't a good idea, he'd insisted he'd grown up on frozen lakes and knew what he was doing. He hadn't, and when the van's front wheel had broken through a layer of ice and she had heard the cracking of ice all around her, she had never been more afraid in her life. They'd called for help, and luckily, a rescue crew had gotten them safely off the ice.

She shuddered just thinking about it.

When Comet trotted out onto the lake, Riley let his leash go taut. He turned around and gave her a look.

"Sorry, Comet," she said, eyeing the lake. "I'm not going out there."

When Comet barked his displeasure, Luke looked over and waved.

Riley shouted out to him. "Luke, I need to talk to you!"

Luke motioned for her to join him.

She shook her head. There was no way she was going out on that ice. Giving up, she turned around and started walking away from the lake. When she saw a wooden bench over by the Christmas trees, she headed that way and sat down.

Comet sat down next to her and barked.

"Sorry, Comet. No can do," she said.

Soon, she saw Luke walking their way. "Here he comes," she said happily to Comet. While she waited, she inhaled a deep cleansing breath, enjoying the scent of the evergreens. For a moment, she shut her eyes and let herself relax.

The only things she could hear were Comet panting and a few birds chirping. When she heard the crunch of boots on the fresh snow, she opened her eyes and saw Luke heading straight for them. He was smiling.

"It looks like you two found one of my favorite spots," Luke said.

Riley stood up as he approached. "I can see why," she said, smiling back. "It's beautiful here. This is a million-dollar view."

"Don't say that too loud," Luke said. "The developers who built the big Skyline Resort over in the next town have already been sniffing around."

"But I thought you wanted to sell the place, so that should be good, right?" Riley asked.

Luke shook his head. "Not exactly. It's complicated."

She sat back down on the bench and motioned to the seat next to her. "Why?"

Luke laughed a little as he sat down. "If you're looking for something for your Christmas story, this won't be it. Unless you plan to have a Scrooge in your book."

"And in this case the Scrooge would be…?" Riley asked.

Luke looked out over the lake. "The big developers who just want to cut down all these trees and build huge buildings. There was even talk of filling in the lake."

Riley's jaw dropped. "They could do that?

Luke nodded. "It would be incredibly expensive, but if they

bought the land, they could do whatever they wanted. So I need to make sure that doesn't happen. I promised my dad I would make sure the property stays as it is. Christmas Lake is part of my family's history, not to mention the town's."

Riley shook her head. "I can't believe anyone would do that. I mean, the town is called Christmas Lake. What would Christmas Lake be without the lake?"

"They'd probably just try to rename the town," Luke said.

Riley's eyes grew wide. "They could do that, too?"

He nodded. "With enough money, you can do anything." Luke stood up. "You know what, let's not talk about it. Right now, I'm just taking it one day at a time and trying to concentrate on making this Christmas Camp special for our guests. So what are you two doing down here?"

"Actually, looking for you," Riley answered.

Luke held out his hand to take Comet's leash. "Here, I'll take him."

"Okay." Riley handed over Comet.

"So what do you need?" he asked.

She gave him a hopeful look. "I was checking to see when you think we'll have Wi-Fi. I need to send some stuff to my agent for some media that's covering Christmas Camp, and she's waiting for it…"

Luke nodded. "Got it. So you need it now."

"That would be ideal," Riley said. "When you have a chance."

"Okay, then let's go."

When Luke held out his hand, Riley took it. They shared a smile before Riley looked back at the lake and the one lone Christmas tree in the middle of it.

"I've been trying to figure out how all those lights are working on that one tree. Battery operated?" Riley asked. "But I'd think in this snowy cold weather batteries would just go dead.

Luke followed her gaze to the Christmas tree.

"Actually, that's what I was doing—making sure all the tree's lights stay on," he said. "You're right about the lights being run by batteries. Only, to make it work out here we use a special battery pack that's insulted against the cold. But I still like to check it a couple times a day to make sure it's working."

"I know you said you keep them on twenty-four-seven, but you didn't say why," Riley said.

"Because it's our Christmas Lake Christmas tree," Luke said with pride. "Back during World War I, some families in town had sons fighting in the war, including my family, and when Christmas came around it was hard on everyone having their loved ones in harm's way. So, one Christmas, on December first, a Sunday, the town pastor and my great-grandfather invited everyone to come down to the lake after the service. The pastor had put up a Christmas tree right in the middle of the lake, like we have it now. Of course, back then, they didn't have battery-operated lights so he handed out candles. Everyone circled the tree and prayed for their loved ones who were serving in the military and for their families. The pastor said the light from the candles represented everyone keeping the soldiers in their hearts at Christmas and always."

"That's really beautiful," Riley said. She was genuinely touched by the story.

"There's more," Luke said. "After that Sunday, some people asked my great-grandfather if they could continue coming down on their own, during the day and at night, with candles to honor and pray for the soldiers. That started a tradition here at Christmas Lake that continued during World War II, the Korean War, Vietnam, and now Iraq and Afghanistan. Eventually, with technology, we were able to use battery-powered lights to make sure the Christmas tree is always lit up, day and night, starting December first until the new year, to honor our military service members and remember those who have made the ultimate sacrifice. So in December these lights are always on, a reminder of how we're holding them in our hearts always, especially this time of year, at Christmas."

When Riley looked at the Christmas Lake Christmas tree again, she now saw more than just the tree with lights. She saw a symbol of love, hope, and faith.

"That's an amazing story," she said softly, almost to herself. She was trying to think about how she could possibly work something like that into her Christmas book.

"Are you ready to go?" Luke asked as he started heading for the lodge. Comet was already leading the way.

"Yeah," Riley said. She was still thinking about the Christmas tree. "You know, first the Christmas Lake Angel and now the Christmas Lake Christmas tree...you have some really great stories here."

"We do," Luke agreed. "Christmas Lake is full of Christmas stories like this. I haven't even told you about our famous Christmas Lake Ugly Sweater Pageant."

Riley burst out laughing. "What? Now you're giving me a hard time."

Luke crisscrossed his hand over his heart. "Scout's honor. The Ugly Sweater Pageant is a real thing."

Riley narrowed her eyes at him. "Are you even a scout?"

Luke grinned. "It's practically required when you grow up here. If you're nice, I'll even let you borrow one of my mom's sweaters for the pageant."

They shared a laugh. Then Riley gave him a thoughtful look. "You know, I bet the Christmas Campers would love to hear these stories. Maybe you could do a Christmas Lake tour and tell them about the angel and the special Christmas tree. We could even do a ceremony down by the lake with candles the way it was originally done."

Luke nodded, looking impressed. "I think that's a great idea. Let's finalize the schedule when we get back to the lodge. I've filled in all the blanks, and I want to make sure you're good with everything. Maryanne also wanted to meet with us about the menu she's planning and what she's looking to do for tomorrow's welcome cocktail party."

"Sounds great." Riley grinned at him.

Luke arched his eyebrows.

"What?" she asked.

"I just thought you'd be harder to work with," Luke said. "Mike said you had some very specific ideas on what kind of activities you'd want to do, but so far, you've let me plan everything. Honestly, I'm just surprised."

Riley laughed. "I hope in a good way."

Luke looked into her eyes when he smiled back at her. "In a very good way."

Riley's pulse quickened until she remembered that Luke probably had this same effect on the pretty realtor and even Maryanne. Clearly, he could be charming when he wanted to be. This made her even more determined to stay focused on why she'd come to Christmas Camp. She couldn't afford to let anyone distract her. She was here to save her career. Period.

Chapter Twenty-Two

As soon as they got back to the lodge, Luke, as promised, set up the new Wi-Fi router, and the internet was back up and running.

Back in her room, Riley was sitting cross-legged on her Santa sleigh bed. She couldn't wait to get back on her computer. But when she finally got online and found hundreds of new e-mails in her inbox, she almost wished the Wi-Fi wasn't working.

Especially when she saw she had more than twenty *urgent* e-mails from Mike alone.

Margo was a close second in how many e-mails she'd sent.

Riley quickly fired off an e-mail to everyone on her publishing team to let them know she was back online and then e-mailed her mom letting her know it was okay to send the Christmas picture now.

Staring at her e-mail inbox, Riley's head started to spin. There were so many e-mails she needed to read, but right now, she knew it was more important to finalize the Christmas Camp itinerary with Luke and Maryanne since their Christmas Campers would be showing up in less than twenty-four hours.

"I'll deal with all you later," she said to the e-mails as she closed her laptop and carried it downstairs.

Luke was standing by the fire waiting for her. "Ready?" he asked.

Riley held up her computer. "Ready. I'm waiting for my mom to send me a picture that Margo and Mike are waiting for, but we can still get started."

"A picture of you?" Luke asked.

Riley rolled her eyes. "Yes, unfortunately. It's of me when I was a kid with Santa."

Luke smiled at her. "I bet that's a cute picture."

"I have no idea," Riley said truthfully. "I've never seen it."

Luke's brow furrowed. "What do you mean?"

Riley realized her mistake instantly and scrambled. "I just mean my mom has a zillion pictures, and she found some old ones that aren't in the...album."

"Well, I definitely want to see it," Luke said.

Riley shook her head. "Trust me, you don't."

Luke laughed. "Well, mine will be on the Christmas Camp memory board with the rest of them."

Riley was confused. "Memory board?"

"I'll tell you all about it," Luke said. "It's actually one of the activities on our list. Should we get started? Maryanne and Caylee are waiting in the kitchen. We figured we could go over everything there. This way Maryanne can show you some of her ideas for the menu. She's right in the middle of making the Christmas Camp Popcorn."

Riley's eyes lit up. "Christmas Camp Popcorn? What's that?"

"You'll see," Luke said, leading the way to the kitchen. "It's for Christmas movie night, of course."

Riley laughed. "Of course. But I still get some even if I don't watch Christmas movies, right?"

Luke turned and tilted his head. "What do you mean you don't watch Christmas movies? Isn't that a prerequisite of being Miss Christmas?"

Riley kept walking toward the kitchen. She didn't want

Luke to see how she cringed when he called her Miss Christmas. "I can't wait to see this popcorn," Riley said, sidestepping his Christmas-movie question.

By the end of the day, even though she'd OD'd on Christmas Camp Popcorn, Christmas Camp cookies, and all sorts of other Christmas Camp–themed food Maryanne had whipped up and insisted she try, Riley knew the Christmas Campers were going to be in great hands when it came to holiday treats.

The next thing Riley learned about was the Christmas Camp memory board that had actually been Caylee's idea. The way it worked was everyone who had signed up for Christmas Camp was asked to bring their favorite Christmas picture from when they were growing up. Then they could put their pictures on the board so it could remind everyone of the joy and wonder they'd felt at Christmas when they were children. The memory board itself was very festive. It was lined in fresh garland and lit up with white twinkle lights.

When Riley saw that Luke, Caylee, and Maryanne had already put up their adorable Christmas pictures to get things started, she knew the memory board was going to be a huge hit. She caught herself smiling as she stared at Luke's photo. He'd probably been around six years old when it was taken, and he was standing by a snowman looking as proud as he could be. The snowman was lopsided with a crooked hat and branches for arms, and Luke's smile was ear to ear as he put his arm around the snowman.

"What do you think?" Luke asked, coming up behind her. "I make a pretty mean snowman, right?"

Embarrassed to be caught looking at his picture, Riley quickly turned around. "You definitely have some skills."

"So are you going to add your picture up there with ours?"

Luke asked. "I'm sure the Christmas Campers would love it."

"I don't know," Riley said, because she honestly didn't know how she felt about even seeing this picture her mom was sending, much less sharing it with the rest of the world. "But that reminds me, I need to see if my mom has sent my picture yet."

Riley went over to where she'd left her laptop open on the table and checked her e-mail. She quickly found her mom's e-mail with an attachment. "It's here," she said.

As she clicked on the attachment, she suddenly felt very nervous. She didn't even realize Caylee had come over and was looking over her shoulder until the picture filled up her screen.

"Oh my gosh, this is the cutest thing I've ever seen!" Caylee exclaimed.

But Riley barely heard her as she stared at herself as a little girl sitting on Santa's lap. For a moment, it took her breath away. She looked so...happy.

It all came rushing back to her. She'd been eight years old. It was the last Christmas before her dad had passed away. She was wearing a pretty, red velvet dress with a big, white satin bow with white tights and black patent leather shoes. She was smiling at Santa like he was her entire world.

She didn't realize her eyes were filling with tears until Luke gently touched her arm.

"Riley, are you okay?" he asked.

She nodded. She couldn't take her eyes off the picture. "I'm sorry," she said, wiping her tears away. "I don't know what's wrong with me."

"Nothing's wrong with you," Luke said. "Pictures always bring back so many memories, and this looks like it was a very happy one. It looks like you started being Miss Christmas at a very early age."

"Clearly, you loved Santa," Caylee said. "Just look at that smile on your face. You are so adorable."

A rush of so many different emotions flooded Riley—joy and sadness all mixed together. By avoiding all her Christmas memories all these years, she had never really dealt with them, and now they were back to haunt her like the Ghost of Christmas Past.

"You need to send the picture to your agent, right?" Luke asked.

Riley nodded, thankful Luke had helped her refocus. "Yes, right away." She *needed* to concentrate on work. Right now she couldn't deal with any more Christmas memories.

She quickly e-mailed Margo and attached the photo and felt instant relief when she pushed send.

She turned back to Luke. "Okay, done. Now let's finish finalizing the activities for Christmas Camp."

"Sounds good to me," Luke said. "But before we start, I want to run one thing by you."

"Sure," Riley said.

"What do you think about doing a Christmas Camp dance on our last night? We could play Christmas music, and everyone could get dressed up, and we could invite people from town. We used host a dance every year, but when money got tight after the economy crashed, my parents stopped. I thought it might be nice to do one more time before we sell the place."

"I think it sounds great, but if we're inviting people from town, where would we do it? I don't think you have enough room," Riley said.

Luke chuckled. "Let me show you."

Five minutes later, they had walked to a part of the lodge

Riley hadn't seen yet. When they got to the end of a long hallway, Luke opened two massive French doors to reveal a beautiful ballroom.

"This is where we have the dance," he said.

Riley's jaw dropped as she stepped inside and looked around the beautiful ballroom. It had vaulted, beamed ceilings and a wall of windows looking out over Christmas Lake. "This is amazing," she said. "Why haven't you been using this?"

Luke shrugged. "There's been no reason to."

Riley gave him an incredulous look. "Are you kidding? This space is spectacular. You could have weddings here, parties, corporate events—everything, anything. This view is priceless."

"It's the best view in town," Luke said proudly.

"I believe it," Riley said.

"So is that a yes to having a Christmas Camp dance?" Luke asked.

Riley grinned back at him. "That's a huge, yes. Yes, please."

After they made their way back to the lobby and sat down by the fire, Riley actually started getting excited listening to all of Luke's ideas.

"We've planned everything from your traditional, and always a favorite, baking and decorating cookies and making Christmas crafts to cocktail mixology classes, movie watching, and a special Christmas Camp Bingo," Luke said. "We'd already posted some of the activities on the website so the Christmas Campers and the media would know what to expect, but we saved spots for any activities you thought would be a good fit."

"I think this all sounds great," Riley said. "You've done a fantastic job."

Luke smiled back at her. "Thanks. I appreciate that. When

it comes to the outdoor activities, it will depend on the weather, so we'll play that by ear."

Riley nodded. "Sounds good."

"But on the list of potential activities we have snowshoeing, ice-skating, cross-country skiing, and even a snowman-building contest. We also added daily 'Miss Christmas Author Chats' so you can talk with the Christmas Campers about the kinds of things they want to see in your book. That was Mike's idea."

Riley laughed. "Of course, it was."

"We also made sure to put free time so the Christmas Campers have a chance to relax and do whatever they wanted to do, and the same for you, in case you need to get some work done," Luke added.

"I appreciate that," Riley said. "I have a book outline I need to be working on so this should work out great."

Luke looked pleased. "Okay, so we have a plan. Tomorrow's the big day. The first Christmas Campers should start arriving around three o'clock and the cocktail party welcome reception is scheduled for six o'clock."

Riley nodded. "Okay."

"And Caylee had an idea about the cocktail party...and you," Luke continued. She thinks, and Maryanne and I agree, that you should make a grand entrance..."

Riley's smile quickly turned into a frown.

Luke laughed. "Just hear me out. We know the Christmas Campers are going to start showing up at different times, and everyone is going to want to talk to you. It could get a little chaotic. This way, you can be in your room, relaxing, and then we'll introduce you at the party and everyone will see you at the same time. Caylee thinks it will create a little anticipation and excitement, too."

"You're serious?" Riley asked.

Luke nodded.

She shrugged. "Okay, if you think it's a good idea, sure."

"Great! Thank you," Luke said.

Caylee and Maryanne entered the room at the same time as there was a knock at the door. They all looked at one another, confused.

"Are we expecting anyone?" Caylee asked.

"No," Luke said as he got up and headed for the door. "Comet, it's okay."

Comet instantly stopped barking but didn't leave Luke's side.

"Maybe it's one of the Christmas Campers checking in early," Maryanne said.

Riley gave Maryanne a worried look. "I hope not. We're not ready. *I'm* not ready…"

They were all standing up, looking concerned, when Luke returned holding a big box.

"It was just Fred, the postman," Luke said, holding up a big two-foot-by-three-foot package. "He apologized for the late delivery but said it was express mail and needed to get here right away."

Riley collapsed back on the couch, relieved. "Thank goodness."

Luke walked over and held the box out to her. "And it's for you."

"Me?" Riley took the box and looked confused. "Who'd be sending me anything?" She set the box on the couch.

Caylee, excited, rushed over. "Open it. See what's inside."

Luke laughed. "Some things never change. You should see Caylee at Christmas. If you don't open your gifts right away, she'll come over and open them for you."

"People always take too long to open their gifts!" Caylee said, defending herself. "So come on, Riley, open it."

Everyone laughed at Caylee.

"Hold on," Riley said, fighting with the packing tape. "I'm trying."

Caylee leaned in and grabbed a piece of tape and dramatically ripped it off for her. "I can do the rest if you want."

Luke chuckled. "See?" he said as he pulled Caylee back. "Let Riley open it."

When Riley saw Caylee's disappointed face, she pushed the box toward her. "It's okay. Go for it, Caylee."

It only took a second for Caylee to tear into the box and another second to open it up to find another box. This one was only a little bit smaller than the first, and it was white and glossy with a big, red satin bow.

"This looks fancy." Caylee took out the new box and handed it to Riley. "You should open this one."

Riley took the smaller box out and set it on her lap. When she took the top of the box off, the first thing she saw was a bunch of gold tissue paper.

"Yup, it's fancy, all right," Caylee said as she leaned in closer.

Riley laughed, knowing if she didn't hurry, Caylee would rip the tissue paper off for her. As Riley pulled the tissue back, Caylee gasped. Inside the box was a spectacular dress covered with red sparkling sequins.

"Wow!" Caylee said, taking the words right out of Riley's mouth. But they were both speechless when Riley held up the dress and they realized the box was filled with more clothes.

There were two more sparkling dresses and three sequin tops, and almost everything was the same color—Christmas red—except for one stunning white dress at the very bottom and a silver sequin top.

Riley picked up the note card and read it out loud.

"Making sure you have something festive to wear for Christmas Camp. I'm sending a photographer to cover it. We need good pictures. Mike."

Luke laughed. This must be because you wore black for that TV interview."

"What's wrong with black?" Riley asked.

Luke and Caylee exchanged a look.

"It's not very Christmassy," Caylee said.

Luke nodded. "What she said."

Riley playfully rolled her eyes as she held up another spectacular sparkling red dress. "Wow, Mike really went overboard. This is too much."

"What?!" Caylee said, taking a sequin top out of the box. "I'd say this is just right." She happily held it up to her chest. "I want to know who is this Mike and where can I get one?"

Everyone laughed.

"What happened to the tomboy I knew who would have never been caught dead in a dress, much less sequins?" Luke asked as he took the top from Caylee and handed it back to Riley.

Caylee never took her eyes off the top. "She grew up. I might be a soldier, but come on, every girl loves a little sparkle, right?" She looked over to Riley and Maryanne for support.

Maryanne nodded but Riley didn't.

"Honestly, I don't think I've ever worn anything sparkly in my life," Riley said as she closed the box and set it on the couch. "None of this is my style."

Luke laughed. "Then it's a good thing Mike sent all this because you're going to need to look the part."

"What part?" Riley asked, confused.

"Miss Christmas," Luke answered. "Everyone's going to

want to take pictures with you, and Mike said they're sending a photographer so..."

"So you have to look Christmassy," Caylee finished for him as she grinned at Riley.

"Exactly," Luke said.

Riley gave them both a skeptical look. "I brought clothes that will be just fine."

Caylee frowned. "Well, *fine* doesn't sound very Christmassy. Fine sounds...boring."

When Luke gave Caylee a look, she shrugged and looked back at Riley. "Sorry."

Riley smiled back at her as she stood up. It was impossible to be mad at Caylee. "That's okay. Everyone has different taste. These clothes just aren't mine. I'm going to go have a little chat with Mike, set a few things straight, and make sure he doesn't have any other surprises for me. I don't like surprises."

When Riley saw Luke and Caylee exchange a look, she frowned. "What was that look?"

Luke feigned innocence. "What look? There was no look."

"No look at all," Caylee chimed in.

Riley's eyes narrowed as she studied Caylee's grinning face. She knew something was up and just hoped that Luke and Caylee weren't planning any surprises for her. She really didn't like surprises. All she wanted to do was follow the plan and get through the weekend.

"I'll see you guys later," Riley said as she left the room, reluctantly taking the box of clothes with her.

"See you later, Miss Christmas," Caylee cheerfully called after her.

"Bah humbug," Riley said under her breath.

Comet barked. When she looked over her shoulder, she

saw he was right on her heels. She knew he'd heard her *bah humbug,* and she felt like her new, furry, four-legged friend was doubling as the Christmas police.

She couldn't help but laugh a little as she thought about how Comet was a watchdog all right. He was watching her like a hawk, making sure she had Christmas spirit. But then her smile faded.

If I can't fool a dog, how am I going to fool the Christmas-loving Christmas Campers?

When she got to her room, she immediately called Mike on FaceTime.

He picked up almost instantly. "Riley? He shouted over all the noise. "Where are you?" He laughed. "You look like you're in Santa's workshop."

Riley, embarrassed, looked behind her and saw all the Santa figurines were in the shot. She quickly moved over, but this only got her bed and all the Santa pillows in the frame.

She gave up. The Santas were everywhere. There was no avoiding them. "I'm in my room at the lodge," she said.

He laughed. "Nice background. We'll have to get some shots of you in that room. That's gold! Did you get the clothes?"

"Uh, yeah, that's why I'm calling," Riley said as she started to pace the room. "Look, while I appreciate you trying to help me with my wardrobe, I brought some really nice things to wear during Christmas Camp."

Mike put his face close to the screen. "Christmas things? You have a red cocktail dress?"

Riley struggled to keep her patience. "No, I don't have a *red* cocktail dress, but my black one is designer. I just bought it, and it's great."

Mike shook his head. "Nope. Won't work. We need you in red. Red is the best for photographs. Red is Christmas. I told you I've set up for a photographer to be there, and we have to sell you as Miss Christmas, and that means you have to look the part."

Frustrated, Riley picked up one of the red sequin tops. "I did not agree to this. I'm not a Vegas showgirl."

When she looked down at Comet for support, he wagged his tail as he gazed up at her. Riley smiled at him.

"You're a romance author that's about to write her first Christmas novel," Mike said. "You need to look the part. You need to sparkle, glitter, dazzle, all that stuff. You need to bring the romance."

Riley picked up another top. "You're trying to tell me wearing sequins is...romantic?"

"I'm trying to tell you it's *Christmas,*" Mike said impatiently. "Besides, you have to wear it. A friend of mine is the designer. She gave me the clothes as a trade-off for the publicity you'll get her. So you're welcome, and I have to go."

"Wait, Mike!" Riley shouted.

But it was too late. He'd already hung up.

"Unbelievable," she said as she continued to pace. Everywhere she looked the Santas were staring at her. She ran around and turned all the Santa pillows upside down so she couldn't see the grinning Santa faces, then felt foolish.

"What? Am I twelve?" she asked herself. "I need to go for walk."

At the mention of the word *walk,* Comet ran over and sat almost on top of her feet. He barked.

"Oh boy, now I've done it," Riley said. "I said *walk.*"

Comet barked again.

"Shh! Comet. Okay, fine. You win. We'll go for a wa—"

When Comet looked like he was about to bark again, she stopped herself.

"See? I'm learning," she said as she grabbed her coat.

He ran to the door and waited for her.

An icy gust of wind swirled around them as she and Comet stepped outside. That's when she realized she'd forgotten to wear her hat. For a moment, she debated going back upstairs to get it but she wasn't going to be outside for very long. She'd be fine.

Before she knew what was happening, Comet was leading her down to the lake. Not that she really needed any encouragement. She was mesmerized by the Christmas Lake Christmas tree lit up in all its glory. It was even more magical in the moonlight.

She stopped to get out her phone and take a picture, but the photo didn't even come close to capturing the dreamlike image. She frowned and tried to take several more pictures.

"I see Comet has talked you into to another *w-a-l-k*," Luke said, coming up behind her.

Startled, Riley jumped. Her hand flew to her heart. "You scared me." She had been concentrating so hard that she hadn't heard him approach.

"Sorry, I didn't want to disturb your picture-taking," Luke said. "Get any good ones?"

Riley frowned again as she scrolled through her photos. "No, not really. Nothing that captures how special it really is." She looked back up at Luke. "What are you doing down here?"

Luke reached into his own coat and pulled out a red-and-white-striped stocking cap that had a big, red puff ball at the end. "You forgot your hat."

When he held it out to her, she laughed and backed away. "Oh, that's not my hat. That's gotta be one of your mom's."

"I'll tell you what this is," Luke said as he looked into her eyes and walked toward her. Riley held her breath as Luke got so close to her that she could see his breath turn into a white cloud.

"It's going on your head," Luke added with a smile as he carefully put the hat on her and "We can't have our star author catching a cold before her Christmas Camp."

When their eyes met, her heart beat faster. For a moment, it seemed like he was going to kiss her. She leaned in.

And that's when it happened...

Chapter Twenty-Three

A giant snowball hit Luke in the arm, sending snow flying everywhere. When they both spun around and saw Caylee about to fire another snowball at them, Luke instantly sprang into action.

"Get her!" He laughed, scooping up a bunch of snow and making an even bigger snowball to hurl at Caylee. She jumped to one side just in time to dodge the hit.

Riley was still standing there watching, laughing.

"Come on," Luke said to her. "I could use a little help here."

Riley hesitated. She'd never been in a snowball fight before, but when one of Caylee's snowballs hit her on the leg, she followed Luke's lead and started making her own snowballs to hurl at Caylee.

When her second snowball surprised her by hitting its mark, tagging Caylee on the arm, Riley jumped for joy. "I did it!"

Luke gave her an enthusiastic high five. "Nice job!"

"Thanks!" Riley laughed. "I learn from the best."

Luke gave her a funny look. "What? You've never thrown a snowball before?"

Riley was saved from answering when Caylee ran up behind Luke.

"Watch out!" Riley shouted, trying to warn him.

But it was too late. Caylee had already stuffed some snow down the back of Luke's coat.

He grabbed Caylee before she could escape. "Now, that's just playing dirty," he said as he lifted Caylee up and spun her around. "Looks like it's time for a reindeer bath."

Caylee was kicking and screaming. "You wouldn't dare!" Caylee shouted while still laughing. "Luke, you put me down right now! I mean it! I'm not a kid anymore."

"Really?" Luke laughed. "Because you sure act like one."

Seconds later, Luke was dumping Caylee in the snow and covering her with more snow.

"No!" Caylee shrieked, but you could tell by the huge grin on her face that she was loving every minute of it. "Riley, help me!"

Riley ran over, and Caylee reached out her hand. "Help me up, please…"

Luke was on the other side of Caylee, down on his knees, still trying to bury Caylee in the snow—or as he'd called it, giving her a reindeer bath.

But as soon as Riley gave her hand to Caylee, Caylee grabbed it and pulled Riley down into the snow with her.

Luke laughed even harder now. "Riley, I can't believe you fell for the oldest trick in the book!"

"Totally," Caylee said as they both lay flat on their backs looking up at the sky.

But Riley didn't mind. She was laughing the kind of laugh that reached all the way down to her toes. When Comet came over and started licking her face, she tried to wiggle away from him.

"Comet, stop it." Riley laughed.

"Comet's just giving you Christmas kisses," Caylee said.

"Lucky me," Riley said but was smiling.

When Luke laughed and held out his hand to help Riley up, Caylee held up her hand, too.

"Don't forget me," Caylee said sweetly—too sweetly.

It had Riley giving her a curious look wondering what she was up to. When Riley saw the mischievous gleam in Caylee's eyes, she had to fight off a laugh.

"Okay, you two, come on," Luke said, holding out a hand to each of them.

Caylee looked at Riley. Riley nodded, getting it. They took Luke's hands at the same time and pulled him down into the snow with them.

He landed right in the middle of them, and now all three of them couldn't stop laughing.

"Again, the oldest trick in the book, and you fell for it," Caylee said as she jumped up. "Now who's getting a reindeer bath?" Caylee started tossing snow on Luke. "You're totally off your game, Luke. Last one to the lodge makes the hot cocoa!"

When Caylee raced off with Comet, Luke didn't move. He continued to lie on his back staring up at the stars.

Riley had already sat up. "Aren't you coming?"

Luke shook his head. "Nope."

"But then you're going to have to make the hot cocoa," Riley said.

"Yup," Luke said. "But I'm the only one who ever makes it because I'm the only one who knows the secret recipe besides my mom."

Riley laughed.

Luke kept looking up into the sky. "So I'm just going to lie here for a minute and enjoy the peace and quiet."

Without thinking about it, Riley lay back down. "Me too."

When Luke looked over to her, they shared a smile. In

that moment, she felt happier than she had in a long time. She didn't feel the freezing snow or the biting wind. All she felt was alive. Suddenly self-conscious, she turned away from Luke and studied the sky, but she could sense him still watching her.

She didn't know exactly what was happening between them, but there was something happening—at least for her—and that scared her for a lot of different reasons. As she watched the stars twinkle in the sky, she told herself that anything she was feeling for Luke was likely just the result of the crazy romantic setting and her imagination working overtime.

She laughed a little, thinking how she was lying in the snow, stargazing, beside a handsome guy in a place that looked like a Christmas fairy tale. It was no wonder she thought she felt something for Luke. Anyone would feel something in this kind of magical setting. It would be impossible not to.

She got up quickly.

"You're going?" Luke asked, still not moving.

Riley nodded. "Yeah, I still have some work to do tonight. I want to go over all the activities again and make sure I'm not missing anything."

Luke sat up and held out his hand for her to help him up.

Riley hesitated. "You think I'm going to fall for the oldest trick in the book again?"

Luke's eyes flashed mischievously. "A guy can hope, can't he?"

Riley laughed, shaking her head. "You're impossible."

Luke smiled. "And I'm also the only one who can make the hot chocolate, so what's it's going to be?" He waved his hand at her, and the look in his eyes was like a challenge.

Riley never had been one to back away from a challenge.

"You're not going to pull me down?" Riley asked.

"You're just going to have trust me," Luke said.

For a moment, they just stared at each other. When neither blinked, Riley finally took Luke's hand, but not before bracing herself just in case. She didn't want to risk ending up back in the snow with him for many reasons.

After Luke took her hand, he stood up immediately, without her help.

But when Riley tried to take her hand away from him, he resisted for a moment and looked into her eyes.

"I told you, you could trust me," he said with a smile that could melt any girl's heart.

Riley nervously pulled her hand away. "Okay, let's go," Riley said. "I'm thirsty."

Together, they walked side by side and followed a moonlit path back to the lodge.

They were all sitting by the fire finishing the famous Christmas Lake hot chocolate that Luke had made and eating some of Maryanne's famous Gingerbread XOXO cookies. Riley savored the taste as the sweet chocolate mixed perfectly with the spicy gingerbread. They were fresh from the oven and still warm and chewy.

Riley studied the final printout of the Christmas Camp activities. "You guys did a really great job. The Christmas Campers are going to love it. Thank you for all the hard work you've done pulling all this together at the last minute. When Mike first told me about this weekend, I had no idea what would be involved. But everything you've planned has far surpassed my expectations. This is great."

"Thank you for coming and making it possible," Luke said. "After all, everyone's coming to see you."

"Their favorite author," Caylee added.

"This is all about you," Maryanne chimed in. "At the end of the day, you're what everyone cares about."

Comet barked and wagged his tail.

"No pressure," Riley said with a laugh. "You know, this is pretty unique. Usually an author will do a reading and a book signing, or maybe speak at an event, but to be here like this and interact with the people who read my books, hosting several days of activities where we're all going to be together is really different."

"I think that's what people are so excited about," Luke said. "To have this kind of access to you and the chance to help give you some ideas for your next book. I know that's already getting a lot of buzz on social media."

Riley gave him a surprised look. "You've been following?"

"Of course," Luke said. "I'm all in for hashtag Christmas Camp."

"Me too," Maryanne chimed in. "So, Riley, how does it all feel knowing this is all happening tomorrow?"

Riley took a deep breath. "It's exciting, but also, honestly, I'm a little nervous. I don't know what people are expecting from me. I don't want to let anyone down..."

"You won't," Luke said. "All you need to do is be yourself. They just want to share their favorite Christmas traditions and make some new traditions with you."

"About that," Caylee said. "If you could just look at the list and highlight any of the traditions that you do with your family, then we can share those as your own traditions. I'm sure the Christmas Campers will love that."

That familiar feeling of dread that happened anytime someone asked her about her Christmas traditions washed over Riley. There wasn't one thing on the list that she ever remembered doing, but she knew she couldn't tell anyone that.

"Can I let you know in the morning?" she offered instead.

"Of course," Caylee said.

"And then just be ready to have some fun stories to tell, some Christmas memories that you have, Riley. People always love hearing that personal stuff. I know I'm looking forward to it," Maryanne said.

Don't panic, Riley told herself. *You're a best-selling author, you can just make something up.*

"No problem," Riley said, hoping that if she said it, it would help her believe it. She realized one of the things that was making her so nervous about hosting this Christmas Camp was being caught off guard with a ton of questions she couldn't answer about her own Christmas traditions. Over the years, she'd been able to dodge the occasional Christmas question, but with being branded as Miss Christmas and with the new novel, she knew she needed to be ready, and that meant coming up with a Christmas story she could tell people. Something simple. Something believable. Something that would help her relate and fit in with the kind of Christmas lovers who would be reading her book. She needed to get to work.

She abruptly stood up. "I'm going to head up to my room and finish up some work I need to do before tomorrow."

Luke stood up, too. "Is there anything we can do for you or help you with?"

Riley smiled at them. "No, you guys have been great. This is just some…author stuff I need to do." That was going to be her new go-to phrase. Anytime she couldn't explain what she was really doing, like researching the heck out of Christmas hoping Google could save her, she would just call it "author stuff."

"See you in the morning," Caylee said. "Our first day of Christmas Camp—I can't wait!"

"Me too," Riley said, trying to match Caylee's enthusiasm. "Good night everyone. See you in the morning."

When Riley got to her room, she immediately turned on her computer and went to work googling the activities on the Christmas Camp list. The time flew by and before she knew it, it was already midnight.

Comet had joined her on the bed. His head was resting on one of the Santa pillows, and he was watching her.

As she petted him, she was thankful for his company. "Okay, Comet. I think I have a great start here, don't you?"

Comet lifted his head.

Riley smiled back at him and turned her laptop around to show him the spreadsheet she was creating. She was making two lists of Christmas traditions. One list was filled with all the different Christmas traditions she'd been able to find in the last few hours. This list was huge with more than fifty traditions listed.

The other list, however, only had two entries so far. This was the list she was creating to make part of her fictional Christmas past. That way, when anyone asked her what her favorite Christmas traditions were, she wouldn't have to panic. She would be ready with some practiced answers. Doing research, making lists, and being organized always made her feel calmer and in control.

Her plan was not to actually claim the traditions as her own, but to talk about them and share what she liked about them and then get the Christmas Campers to say what they liked, shifting the attention off her as fast as she could.

The more she researched and prepared, the more confident she felt.

When Comet lifted his head and looked at her, she smiled.

"I know, Comet. I need to get to work." She turned the computer back toward her and studied the two things she'd added so far to her own personal Christmas traditions list.

She'd tried to pick things that were easy, things that everyone did. First on her list was making Christmas cookies. While she didn't remember ever baking Christmas cookies specifically, she had made other cookies with her mom so she could use some of those memories.

Next, she added making a snowman, inspired by Luke's picture on the Christmas Camp memory board. She figured making a snowman would be easy enough to talk about.

"What else?" she asked Comet. Then it hit her, just like Caylee's snowball. She could add a snowball fight to her Christmas traditions list! Thanks to Caylee's sneak attack, she'd actually done that activity. She could even talk about Luke's reindeer bath revenge, attributing it to him, because she thought that was pretty funny. Still, she needed to google it as she did everything else.

When she did, she found that there were actually tricks to making the perfect snowball. When making a snowball for a snowball fight, apparently the wetter the snow, the better, so you needed to find some warmer, melted snow that was closer to a building that was giving off heat or that was in the sun. Another technique was standing in one place and stomping up and down and then using the snow under your boots where it had been warmed up. Another pro tip was to pack the snowball as tightly as possible and, of course, always look for clean snow and avoid the yellow snow at all costs.

She looked over at Comet when she wrote down that tip and laughed.

She smiled, satisfied. "I think I got the snowball fight thing down."

Comet gave her an adoring look and wagged his tail.

As she studied her list, she felt it was all believable and something she could have done growing up in Washington state. For a favorite Christmas cookie, she was also going to play it safe and say any sugar cookie that had frosting on it. She knew she couldn't go wrong there.

"What else?" she asked herself as sat back against her Santa pillows and looked at the huge list of activities in the other column.

She started at the top.

"Caroling? Absolutely not," she said, remembering the carolers from her hotel lobby. Plus, she couldn't sing, so that was definitely out. Next on the list was decorating a Christmas tree. She nodded as she added that to her personal list. "This is easy. Everyone does this." She scrolled the bottom of the list. "Watching Christmas movies?"

She shook her head. "Nope. Not going there."

When Comet gave her a look, Riley shook her head. "Comet, I can't fake seeing a movie I've never watched. Christmas-movie watching is a whole big thing. I don't dare touch that world. I'll just tell people I'm too busy writing my books to watch movies."

When Comet laid his head back down on the Santa pillow and closed his eyes, she nodded her head and shut her laptop. "You're right," she said softly as she gave him a hug. "It's time to get some sleep."

After she put all her work away and turned out her light, she snuggled underneath her covers. She petted Comet one more time as she let out a deep breath, finally relaxing.

Much of the stress she'd been battling earlier was gone. She had done all that she possibly could, under the circumstances, to prepare for Christmas Camp. She had studied ever last detail of the schedule, and she knew the program inside and out.

She was ready.

As long as there were no surprises, she would be just fine.

The last thing she saw before she closed her eyes was the jolly, happy face of one of the charming Santa figurines lit up in the moonlight.

As she drifted off to sleep, she thought she must have been already dreaming because she could of swore, she heard the Santa say, "Ho! Ho! Ho!"

Chapter Twenty-Four

R iley woke up with the sunrise and, for a moment, couldn't remember where she was. But when she looked around and saw all the Santas illuminated by a ray of sunshine, it all came rushing back to her.

"Are we ready for this?" she asked the life-sized cardboard Santa she'd moved so he was now looking out the window instead of facing the wall like before, doing a "time out."

She let out a deep breath. "It's the first day of Christmas Camp." With determination, she flung off her covers and jumped out of bed.

"Let's do this!"

After joining everyone for breakfast and having a last-minute strategy session, Riley felt like she was as ready as she was ever going to be, and the next five hours flew by so fast she didn't have time to be nervous.

Even though they'd finalized all the activities the night before, the list of things that still needed to be done before the Christmas Campers arrived seemed to keep growing, not shrinking, as the day went on.

Still, all around the Christmas Lake Lodge there was a festive feeling as the final Christmas decorations were put up and classic Christmas music played.

While Luke was outside making sure all the Christmas

lights on the house, the trees by the lake, and the Christmas Lake Christmas tree were working, Riley and Caylee were inside making sure all the Christmas trees had fresh water in their pots, and they misted down all the evergreens to make sure the garlands and wreaths stayed fresh and fragrant.

"We sure don't have anything like this in Afghanistan," Caylee said as she put her nose up to a garland that was framing the front window and inhaled blissfully. "This smell of fresh-cut pine and balsam fir always reminds me of home... and of Christmas."

Riley smiled watching her and then turned her attention back to the wreath she was misting. It hung high above the fireplace, and she had to keep jumping up to try to reach it.

"We don't want you drying out being so close to the fire," she said, talking to the wreath, as she tried to spray the very top of the wreath.

When Caylee laughed at her, Riley gave Caylee a look. "What? You were talking to the Christmas trees earlier."

"Oh, I'm not laughing about that," Caylee said. "I'm laughing at you jumping up and down. You know we have a stepladder you could use."

Riley shook her head. "What fun would that be? Plus, I need to burn off some calories from all of the treats Maryanne keeps making."

"I know. They're impossible to resist," Caylee said. "Maryanne's up for a head pastry chef job in Los Angeles. They'd be crazy not to take her. I'm excited for her, but I'd hate for her leave Christmas Lake."

Caylee joined her and started jumping up and misting the wreath with her. "I need the exercise, too."

Riley laughed as she looked at Caylee's fit physique. "You have nothing to worry about. You look great."

"I agree," a male voice said as it walked into the lobby.

Both of them spun around to see who it was. Riley smiled

but Caylee did not. A good-looking guy in his early twenties walked toward them holding a poinsettia.

"Merry Christmas," he said cheerfully.

Riley noticed instantly that he only had eyes for Caylee.

"Paul, what are you doing here?" Caylee asked sharply. "Are you the local florist now?"

The way Caylee said *florist* made it sound like a bad thing.

Riley was surprised by Caylee's tone, but it didn't faze Paul at all. In fact, he was grinning as he walked over to Caylee and handed her the poinsettia.

"It's great to see you, too, Caylee," Paul said. "I saw the florist when I pulled up and thought I'd help bring something in."

"Still doesn't explain why you're here," Caylee said, her expression was impossible to read as she put the plant down on the table.

Paul held out his hand to Riley. "Hello, I'm Paul Harrison. You must be Riley Reynolds, the author everyone's talking about."

Riley nodded. "I am," she answered, but she was still much more interested in why Caylee was acting so strange. "And if you're not the florist—"

Paul answered her question before she could finish by holding up a camera that was slung over his shoulder.

"I'm the photographer your publicist hired to cover the Christmas Camp."

"No!" Caylee blurted out.

Riley gave Caylee a confused look.

Paul just smiled. "Small world, right?"

Caylee, hands on her hips, stared back at him and didn't blink. "Clearly, not small enough."

Riley looked from Caylee to Paul. "So I'm guessing you two already know each other?"

"We do," Paul said. "Caylee and I go way back. We both

grew up here in Christmas Lake. Caylee was my first girl-friend."

"When we were six years old," Caylee shot back.

"Still counts," Paul said as he smiled at her.

Caylee rolled her eyes. "Don't listen to him, Riley."

"So you still live here?" Riley asked.

Paul laughed. "No, I moved to Denver. I've been freelanc-ing there for the past five years. I do photography and a lot of different social media, so I'll basically just be here to follow you around and document everything you're doing."

Riley raised her eyebrows. "Follow me around? I know Mike said someone was coming to take some photographs, but—"

"Exactly," Paul cut in. "That's what I meant."

"But you're not staying here," Caylee said. It was a state-ment, not a question. "We don't have any room."

Riley gave Caylee a curious look because she knew the lodge was far from full.

"Don't worry, I'm staying with my parents in town," Paul said. "They love having me here for Christmas."

Caylee stood there staring at Paul and then finally turned to leave. "I need to go check with Maryanne to make sure everything's good with the...cookies."

Paul laughed. "You're making cookies now? When did you start cooking?"

Caylee clearly didn't appreciate his question. When she smiled a sweet smile, Riley could tell it was forced.

"First of all, it's *baking*," Caylee corrected him. "And a lot of things have changed since I saw you last."

"I look forward to catching up, then," Paul said with a confident smile.

"Can't wait," Caylee said, her voice dripping with sarcasm, as she left the room.

Paul laughed as Caylee disappeared. "Same ole Caylee," he said, smiling.

"I'm guessing there's some history there?" Riley asked.

Paul nodded. "Oh yeah, we've got history, but I'll let her tell you about it. I don't want to get on her bad side since I'm going to be here all weekend."

Riley couldn't help but laugh. "Smart man."

"I saw Luke down by the lake. I'm going to head down and talk to him," Paul said. "I'll get the lay of the land and see where some of my best shots will be. What's your schedule like? I'd like to get some pictures before the party tonight, after you're all dressed up. Mike told me to make sure you were wearing a red dress."

"Seriously?" Riley said, shaking her head. "That guy is out of control."

"Or just being a good publicist," Paul offered.

When Riley gave him a warning look, he rushed on. "I mean, the guy hired me so what else am I going to say," he said. "Don't worry. We're going to have a great time this weekend. You'll barely know I'm here."

Riley wasn't sure she believed him. "I'll be upstairs in my room before our guests arrive. Luke and everyone want me to make my first appearance at the party tonight."

"A grand entrance," Paul said. "Smart. Adds to the drama."

Riley laughed. "I don't know about the drama part, but that's the plan."

"Is it okay if I get some shots of you in your room once you're ready? Mike told me you have a very Christmassy room."

Riley rolled her eyes. "Of course he did."

"So is that a yes?" Paul asked hopefully.

Riley took a deep breath. "Sure, whatever you need."

"Great!" Paul said as he headed back out the front door. "I

think it will be cool to see the room that Miss Christmas is staying in. See ya later."

"See ya," Riley responded while wondering how many ways she could hit Mike with a snowball.

Paul passed the real florist who was coming in holding two more poinsettias.

"Where do you want these?" the florist asked. "I have two dozen coming in."

Riley looked around. "You know, I'm not sure, but I'll find someone who knows. Hold on."

When she got into the kitchen, she found Caylee telling Maryanne about Paul's arrival.

Riley was surprised to see the usually chipper Caylee frowning with her arms crossed defensively in front of her chest.

Riley walked over to her. "Okay, you have to tell me what's going on. What's the story with you and Paul?" She was dying to know. The sparks flying between those two had been Fourth of July–worthy.

"It's nothing," Caylee said, then viciously bit the head off a gingerbread boy cookie.

Riley raised an eyebrow. "Well, it doesn't look like nothing by the way you're attacking that cookie."

Caylee, annoyed, broke the gingerbread leg off next. "Did Paul say something?"

"No," Riley said. "He didn't tell me anything, but come on, I write romance novels for a living. The sparks between you two would fit perfectly in one of my books. What happened?"

"Caylee broke his heart," Maryanne offered.

Caylee shot Maryanne a frustrated look. "It wasn't that simple."

"Yet, you still broke his heart," Maryanne said.

"And that wasn't my fault," Caylee said stubbornly. "Can

we not talk about my personal life, please?"

"Really?" Maryanne looked at Caylee. "Because you're always talking about mine and everyone else's."

Caylee was saved from answering anymore questions when an alert went off on her phone.

Riley stared at it. "Cell service is working?"

"It is today," Caylee said and checked her text. "Some of the Christmas Campers are heading this way. They'll be here an hour."

Riley felt a rush of nerves. She grabbed a gingerbread cookie and bit off its arm.

"Okay, no more talk about Paul," Caylee said, finding a smile. "I'm not going to let anything ruin our first day of Christmas Camp. We have work to do, including finishing up the lobby."

"And we need to make sure Riley's in her room before anyone shows up and sees her," Maryanne said.

"Exactly," Caylee agreed.

Riley tried to jump in. "I really don't think we need to do that…" But she was quickly shut down by look on Caylee and Maryanne's faces.

Maryanne looked almost giddy. "I can't believe this is about to happen."

Riley swallowed her cookie. "Me neither."

When they walked back into the lobby, the two dozen poinsettias were lined up on the floor.

"Oops," Riley said, looking guilty. "I meant to tell you guys the florist was bringing these in. I wasn't sure where you wanted them?"

"Luke thought it would be nice to have one in each guestroom," Caylee said.

Riley nodded. "I can do that."

"Are you sure?" Caylee asked.

"Of course," Riley said. "It will give me a chance to check out all the rooms now that the final decorations are up."

"And then you'll go to your room and get ready," Caylee said.

Riley laughed. "Whatever you say, Mom."

They all shared a laugh.

Caylee picked up a poinsettia and gave it to Riley. "Perfect! Then here you go. Thanks."

Riley picked up another poinsettia. You could barely see her face. "You're welcome," she said through the red leaves.

When Riley got to the first guestroom, she turned on the light and looked around. Not only was the room beautifully decorated in a style similar to the downstairs area with wreaths and garland over the fireplace and some nutcrackers and snow globes on the mantel but strung all across the ceiling were white twinkle lights.

Riley put the poinsettias down and looked up. "Wow," she said. "So cool."

When she looked up, she felt like she was looking up at the stars in the sky.

When she finished delivering all the poinsettias and got to her own room, she saw that Luke had somehow found the time to even add the white twinkle lights to her ceiling. She had to admit, it was a happy surprise, and that was saying a lot coming from the *I don't do Christmas* girl who never liked surprises.

Chapter Twenty-Five

After shoveling the snow off the entrance one more time, Luke stood in front of the lodge making sure all the Christmas lights were working. He wanted everything to be perfect. He'd already been down to the lake and the Christmas Lake Christmas tree was shining bright. The lights on all the other Christmas trees along the lake were also on and twinkling.

It was one of Luke's favorite times of day, golden hour, just before sunset, when the clouds could change colors quickly and dramatically before darkness falls.

He looked down at Comet, who was by his side. "Well, Comet, we're as ready as we're ever going to be. Are you nervous?"

When Comet barked and wagged his tail, Luke bent down to affectionately scratch the top of his head. "Yeah, I feel the same way."

But as Luke looked back at his family's lodge, he felt a sense of pride knowing he'd done everything he could to get ready for this Christmas Camp. He was glad he'd decided not to cancel it. He trusted that Riley wouldn't let him or the Christmas Campers down. He knew she had just as much riding on this event being a success as he did.

As he looked up at Riley's window, he couldn't help but

think that even though he'd spent a lot of time with her the last two days, she was still a mystery to him.

At times she could be funny, smart, and playful, and at other times she was no-nonsense, serious, and driven. These were all traits he admired and understood. But it was when she became very quiet, distant, and guarded that he couldn't figure her out.

The only thing he knew for sure was that somehow talking about her Christmas past triggered her to withdraw, and that didn't make any sense for someone who was known as Miss Christmas.

He wanted to get to know her better, but he was afraid she wouldn't let him in. The few times he'd tried to get closer, she'd put up her walls so fast he knew he didn't have a chance. The last thing he had planned was to have any kind of feelings for her, but there was something about her that made him want to know more. At times he'd felt that maybe she was feeling something, too, but then as quickly as the moment came, it disappeared.

Maybe he was imagining all of it. Or maybe he was just interested in her *because* he couldn't figure her out. Whatever it was, it made him nervous. He couldn't afford to let himself get emotionally involved with someone who might not be emotionally available. He had to remind himself that there were three different guys coming to see Riley, and he needed to get back to Europe soon. He didn't need any complications, and he had a gut feeling that Riley could, if he let her, be one very big complication.

He was heading back toward the lodge when he saw an SUV making its way up the long, winding driveway to the front entrance.

"Here we go," he said to Comet.

Comet barked and wagged his tail again.

Luke met the SUV where it stopped. There was only one man inside—the driver.

The driver got out and looked around, taking it all in. "Hi, I'm Colin," the man said, walking right up to Luke and offering his hand.

"Welcome to Christmas Camp," Luke said as they shook hands. "Can I help you with your bags?"

"Thanks, but I'm good. I travel light." Colin grabbed a small suitcase out of the back. "I know I'm early, but I was hoping to see Riley before the reception tonight."

Luke had already recognized Colin's name, knowing he was one of Riley's *friends*. "Actually, she's doing some work and won't be coming down until the party tonight," Luke said.

Colin looked disappointed as they both made their way to the front door.

"But you'll have lots of time to see her tonight and this whole weekend," Luke offered, opening the front door.

Colin nodded. "I hope so. That's why I'm here. You didn't tell her I was coming, did you?"

Luke shook his head. "Nope, you said to keep it surprise."

Colin looked relieved. "Thank you. I appreciate that. It's not every day you get a second chance with the one who got away."

"The one who got away?" Luke asked.

Colin smiled back at him as he put down his luggage. "You heard Riley in her TV interview, right?

"Oh, yeah, I heard her," Luke answered.

Colin proudly pointed to himself. "I was the one she was talking about. The one that got away..."

Luke gave Colin a curious look. "Really?"

Colin nodded. "What was it she said exactly? Her *one true love?*"

Luke was thankful Colin had walked over to the nutcracker collection to get a closer look. It gave him a moment to collect himself. Now he knew why Riley didn't seem emotionally available. Her emotions and her heart already belonged to someone else. They belonged to Colin.

"So you and Riley…" Luke started to ask before he could help himself.

Colin turned to face him. "We were in love for years, and I'm hoping, if this weekend goes as I plan, we will be again. I'm counting on you to help me with that."

Luke fought to keep a smile on his face. "Me?"

"Yeah," Colin said. "I was hoping you could help me plan some of the most romantic Christmas dates you've ever seen. I have some ideas for tonight." Colin walked back over and picked up his suitcase. "But right now, if I could get to my room, I have a few calls to make."

"Of course," Luke said and was relieved when Caylee came into the room.

"I thought I heard someone," Caylee said cheerfully. "Are you our first Christmas Camper?"

Colin smiled at her. "I am."

"He's a…friend of Riley's," Luke said. "This is Colin. He's here to surprise her."

"So please don't tell her I'm here," Colin said.

Caylee gave Luke a questioning look but quickly covered. "Of course not. Your secret is safe with us."

"Thank you," Colin said as he continued to look around. "Your place here is really something. All the Christmas decorations are great. It looks like a movie set. I'd know because I work in the industry."

"Thank you," Luke said. "We appreciate that. Some of these decorations we've had for generations, and every year my mom keeps adding more. We're glad you like it."

Colin looked back at Luke. "It's great, but... Are you sure there's no way to see Riley before the party tonight?"

Luke shook his head. "It's what she asked for, so we want to respect that."

Colin held up his hands. "Right, of course. I don't mean to push. It's just when you finally find the person you want to spend the rest of your life with, you want that time to start right now."

Caylee tilted her head to one side as she studied Colin. "Isn't that a line from a famous rom-com?"

Colin nodded, excited. "That's right. One of Riley's favorites, *When Harry Met Sally*. It's a classic."

Luke had heard enough. "Caylee, why don't you show Colin to his room? I think I see someone else driving up."

"You got it," Caylee said. "Colin, if you just want to follow me."

As Luke watched them go, he was still trying to wrap his head around Colin being Riley's "one true love" when the front door open and another handsome guy entered.

"Welcome to Christmas Camp," Luke said.

"Thanks. Hi, I'm Brendan." He held out his hand and shook Luke's hand. "I'm here for Riley."

Now this is getting more interesting by the second, Luke thought.

"Welcome to Christmas Lake Lodge," Luke offered.

Brendan looked around, impressed. "This place is so cool. It reminds me of somewhere we stayed when Riley and I took a ski trip to Zermatt, Switzerland. We went spring skiing, though, so we didn't have all these great Christmas decorations."

"You and Riley traveled together?" Luke asked.

Brendan smiled. "All the time. When we lived together, we traveled the world. Did she tell you about it?"

"No," Luke said, trying to keep the surprise out of his voice as he walked over to the fireplace. He put another log on the fire as his brain struggled to process this latest information.

"Well, we went to some of the coolest places," Brendan said. "She was great to travel with. I've missed that. And her. That's why I'm here."

"And you're here to…"

"Surprise Riley," Brendan said with a boyish grin. "I already have some great dates planned—just the kind she loves."

Luke had no words.

"Don't worry. I know she's here to work," Brendan rushed on. "I know she's hosting this Christmas Camp, but when she does have time off, I plan to spend as much time with her as possible because I'm not leaving here without her."

"You're not?" Luke asked, masking his surprise as best he could.

Brendan shook his head. "No way. I lost her once, and now that I know she still thinks of me as the one, I'm not going to lose her again."

Luke was saved from commenting when Caylee walked back into the room and smiled brightly at Brendan.

"Another Christmas Camper," she said happily.

Luke faked his own cheerfulness. "And another…friend of Riley's."

The way Luke said *friend* had Caylee giving Brendan a curious look before she glanced back at Luke.

"Well, I'm Caylee, and it's nice to meet you. So, let me guess, you're surprising Riley?"

Brendan smiled and nodded. "That's right. Where is she now? I can't wait to see her…"

Caylee jumped in before Luke could say anything. "Riley's

upstairs getting ready for the party tonight. You'll be able to see her then. She wants to make an entrance, you know?"

"Yeah, sure," Brendan said. "That will give me a chance to plan something special."

"Like…?" Luke asked. He hadn't meant his voice to sound so sharp. He hurried to continue in a better tone. "We just have a pretty full night scheduled to kick off our Christmas Camp."

"I totally get it," Brendan said. "Don't worry, I won't steal the spotlight. This is Riley's night. I was just talking about planning something for later tonight, after she's done working."

Caylee jumped in when Luke struggled to find his words. His felt like his brain was about to explode trying to process what was going on with these two guys and Riley.

"Brendan, why don't I show you your room so you can get settled in?" she offered.

Luke gave Caylee a grateful look.

Brendan smiled at her. "Thanks, Caylee, that would be great. Then turned to Luke. "And thanks, Luke, for making room for me when I know you were sold out. This is going to be one epic weekend."

"It sure is," Luke said. "Well, see you down here later. The final schedule of activities is in your room. The cocktail party starts tonight at six."

Caylee was already heading out of the room. Brendan followed her. "See you then."

When Caylee let Brendan go upstairs ahead of her, she turned back to give Luke an incredulous look and mouthed the words, *What is going on?*

Luke shrugged because he didn't have a clue. He felt like he was on some kind of crazy dating reality show with both Colin and Brendan showing up for Riley. A reality show that got even more insane when a third guy came through the front door next.

Only this guy looked like he belonged on Wall Street, not in the mountains. He was totally different from Colin and Brendan, who seemed pretty laid back. They'd come dressed in jeans and winter hiking boots, but this guy was wearing a black overcoat and what looked like Gucci loafers. His scarf screamed fashion, not function.

When he smiled at Luke, Luke guessed the guy's million-dollar smile had also been bought. He looked like something out of a magazine. He was that perfect.

"Welcome to Christmas Camp," Luke said. "I'm Luke. I'll be one of your hosts this weekend."

The guy frowned. "I'm here to see Riley? Riley Reynolds? She's supposed to be hosting this."

Luke nodded. "And she is. She will be. And you are?"

"Tyler, Tyler Caldwell. I called earlier. You found me a room last minute…"

Luke nodded. "Yes. You're a friend of Riley's."

"From New York City," Tyler said with pride. When he took off his coat and carefully draped it over his arm, Luke could see Tyler was wearing an immaculately cut gray designer suit with a matching classic gray tie.

Luke made the snap judgment that there was nothing casual about this guy.

When Caylee entered the room, she smiled at Tyler. "Welcome," she said warmly. "I'm Caylee."

"Thank you. I'm Tyler."

"Can I take your coat for you?" Caylee offered.

"I'm fine," Tyler said. "Where can I find Riley?" Tyler's tone was all business.

"She'll be at the party tonight," Caylee said happily. "We have quite the weekend planned. We're really happy to have you at Christmas Camp."

"Honestly, I'm only here to see Riley," Tyler said. "I won't be doing any of the activities. The only thing I want to do is get Riley and me back on track."

Luke couldn't help but laugh a little. "Back on track?"

"Our relationship," Tyler responded quickly. "And I don't have a lot of time, so the sooner I can talk to Riley, the better. I really need to get back to the city for work."

Caylee looked even more confused. "Do you work with Riley? Are you on her publishing team?"

Tyler laughed. "No, I'm a lawyer. Riley isn't my colleague. She's my girlfriend."

"Wait, what?" Caylee asked, not even trying to hide her confusion as she looked over at Luke.

Luke just kept smiling, because what else was he going to do?

Tyler shifted his coat to his other arm. "More accurately, she *was* my girlfriend, but clearly after seeing the interview on TV and hearing her talking about me, I know she wants to get back together, so here I am."

"Here you are," Luke said, pretending not to see the shocked look Caylee was giving him.

"Let me guess," Caylee said flatly. "You're surprising her."

Tyler nodded. "I know she's not really into surprises, but I didn't want to distract her from her job doing this camp. Riley always puts work first, just like I do, and that's why we're such a good match. We're both career driven, and we both understand that about each other."

Caylee was frowning. "That sounds…"

Luke jumped in, knowing whatever Caylee was going to say wasn't going to be positive.

"It *sounds*," Luke said, giving Caylee a warning look that Tyler couldn't see, "like you have this all planned out."

Tyler smiled a confident smile. "I do, and this time it's going to work."

Good luck with that, Luke thought to himself.

"Caylee, why don't you show Mr. Caldwell to his room and explain the schedule and what we're doing tonight," Luke said.

"I would be happy to," Caylee said. "Right this way, Mr. Caldwell."

"Thank you," Tyler said. "And Riley? Where would she be right now?"

"Don't worry. I'll explain everything," Caylee answered as they left the room.

When Tyler walked in front of Caylee up the stairs, she turned back again and looked at Luke. She put both of her hands against her head and then pulled them away, spreading out her fingers as if she was saying, *Mind blown.*

Luke laughed because it was exactly how he felt.

Three guys had just shown up, and all three guys thought Riley was talking about them during her TV interview when she'd talked about her one true love. Now all three guys were all here to surprise her, and they all planned to win her back.

Even for a dating reality show this was next-level crazy, Luke thought. He looked down at Comet, who had left his spot by the fire and was now sitting by his side. "Well, Comet, it looks like this is about to get *very* interesting."

When Comet heard his name, he barked and wagged his tail.

Luke didn't know what was going on, but he knew one thing for certain. Any feelings he thought he was starting to have for Riley were pointless. She already had three guys fighting for her, and apparently one of them was her *one* true love.

He never stood a chance.

Chapter Twenty-Six

Riley felt overwhelmed as she stood in her room, looking down at her bed. It was covered with all the glittering and sparkling clothes Mike had sent her. She blinked several times, trying to take it all in.

Reluctantly, she picked up a red cocktail dress. It was sleeveless with a halter neckline, and every inch was covered with red sequins. She knew this was the dress Mike wanted her to wear for the party. He'd said it would look perfect in the photographs. But holding it out in front of her, Riley could only cringe. She felt like the dress screamed *Look at me!* and she wasn't the kind of person who liked to draw attention to herself.

A knock on her door had her tossing the dress back on the bed.

When she opened the door, she found Caylee standing there. "I thought you might need some help getting ready," Caylee said. "And I brought reinforcements."

When Caylee moved to one side, Comet came trotting into the room. He headed straight for the bed, but when he saw it was covered with clothes, he barked. He didn't look happy about it.

Riley laughed. "I know, Comet. I hear you. I'm not happy about all this, either." She gave Caylee a grateful look. "Thank you for coming. I'm not sure what I'm doing here."

Caylee laughed as she entered the room and picked up a pretty sequin top off the bed. "I swear you're the only girl I know who complains about a guy sending her a box of designer clothes."

"Well, when that guy is your publicist and that publicist is as demanding and controlling as Mike, trust me, you wouldn't like it, either."

Caylee picked up the red cocktail dress Riley had been looking at. "I don't know. He has great taste. All of this is pretty awesome, if you ask me."

"Then you wear it," Riley said, meaning it.

Caylee laughed and handed back the cocktail dress. "Nope, this is meant for *you*. This is your big night. You're Miss Christmas. You need to look the part." She paused. "Trust me, you want to look your best."

Riley laughed. "You say that like you know something I don't."

Caylee turned her back on Riley as she picked up a silver sequin halter top. "I'm just saying, our Christmas Campers are expecting a star, and you need to sparkle like one." Caylee held the halter top up to herself and turned around to face Riley.

"I love this one," Caylee said in a wistful voice.

"Wear it," Riley said.

When Caylee laughed and put it back down on the bed, Riley came over, picked it back up, and gave it back to her.

"I'm serious," Riley said. "If I need to look the part so do you."

When Caylee held the top up again, it caught the light and sent sparkles shooting across the room. "I couldn't…"

Riley looked Caylee in the eye. "You can, and you will. I'll make you a deal. If I wear this—" Riley picked up the red sequin cocktail dress "—then you wear the top. We all have to look festive for this Christmas Camp. Go get Maryanne. She can wear something, too."

Caylee's face lit up. "Are you serious?"

"Of course," Riley said. "We're all in this together. If I have to wear sequins, we all have to wear sequins. It's a new Christmas Camp rule I'm making up right now. Everyone must wear sequins."

Caylee laughed. "Well, I can't wait to see Luke in sequins!"

Riley laughed loudly imagining it.

"Are you really serious?" Caylee asked. "About me and Maryanne wearing something?"

"As Santa's sleigh," Riley responded quickly, then laughed at herself. "I can't believe I just said that. All this sparkle is going to my brain."

Caylee was already heading for the door. "If you're sure about this, I'm going to go get Maryanne right now…"

Riley waved her off. "Do it. Go get her. There are enough clothes here for all of us."

"This is amazing!" Caylee said, not even trying to hide her excitement. "I'll be right back."

As Caylee raced out the door, Riley turned her attention to Comet. "Now what about you?"

Comet sat down at her feet and gazed up at her lovingly.

When Riley looked around the room, her focus landed on the pretty red satin ribbon that had been on the gift box.

She eyed it, then Comet, and smiled.

About an hour later, after a Christmas makeover session that would have fit perfectly in any romantic comedy, Riley, Caylee, Maryanne, and Comet were all ready for the party. Riley barely recognized herself when she looked in the mirror.

Maryanne had helped do Riley's hair and makeup so it was festive but classy. Still, for Riley, seeing herself with extra coats of shiny black mascara on her already long thick lashes and a soft dusting of gold shimmer on her eyelids and cheekbones, along with a luscious red lip gloss, made her feel like she was staring back at a stranger. Not to mention the form-fitting red sequin dress made her feel like she was going to an awards show.

Caylee joined her in the mirror. "You look amazing. You're the perfect Miss Christmas."

"I still don't know about this dress," Riley said, feeling nervous. "It's a lot."

Caylee modeled her silver sequin top. "A deal's a deal."

Caylee had paired the top with a pair of black leather pants she'd also borrowed from Riley. Her usual casual ponytail had been exchanged for a sleek blowout, and she was wearing just a touch of gold shimmer on her cheeks and eyelids, too.

Caylee, thrilled, did a little spin. "I feel like a princess. No one in my unit would ever believe this is me."

"Wait, we need some pictures of you," Riley said, grabbing her phone. "Stand over by the bed. The light's a little better."

Caylee practically skipped over to the bed. "Right here?" she asked, striking a pose.

Riley framed up her shot. "A little to right."

Caylee took a few steps as instructed.

"A little more. Stop. Perfect," Riley said and started snapping pictures of Caylee. "You are literally sparkling."

They all laughed.

"Wait, now get some pictures of Maryanne," Caylee said, going over and grabbing Maryanne's hand. "Talk about rockin' the sequins. Maryanne is killing it."

"Agreed," Riley said and started snapping more pictures, this time of Maryanne.

Maryanne looked phenomenal. She was wearing one of the other tops Mike had sent like she owned the world of glitter and glam.

In awe, Maryanne, gently touched the fabulous red top that was a sensational mix of satin and sequins. She looked over at Riley. "I've never worn anything this beautiful. "This pretty much blows my usual red Christmas sweater out of the water. Thank you, Riley. Thank you so much for sharing all this with us."

"Of course," Riley said. "I feel like you're both doing *me* the favor. If I have to wear this stuff, at least I'm not alone. Check out the pictures. You guys look great."

When she showed Caylee and Maryanne the photos, they both loved them.

"But wait," Caylee said, taking Riley's phone from her. "We need one of the three of us." Caylee held her arm out. "Selfie time! Say Christmas Camp!"

They all said "Christmas Camp" at the same time and then started laughing. Even Comet got in on the action by barking and wagging his tail.

Riley got her phone back from Caylee and kneeled down in front of Comet. "Okay, it's your turn, Comet. Smile." Riley snapped several adorable pictures.

"He looks so cute," Caylee said. "Great idea with the red bow."

"Right?" Riley said. "Thanks. I felt like he needed to get dressed up, too."

"Absolutely," Maryanne agreed.

"You're the best," Caylee said, giving Riley a spontaneous hug. "The guys downstairs are going to flip when they see you."

Riley laughed. "What guys?"

Caylee snapped her mouth shut as if she'd just said something she wasn't supposed to say. "The guys, you know. Any guy who might be here."

Caylee was saved from saying anything else when there was a knock on the door. "Riley, it's me, Paul. Are you ready for some quick pictures before the party?"

Caylee's eyes flew open wide. She touched her hair, her face. She ran to the window. "He can't see me like this. I have to get out of here."

Maryanne laughed. "What are you going to do? Jump out the window?"

Caylee looked at the window. "I would if I could." She ran back over to Riley and whispered, "Please, just tell him to go away. Say you need more time, say anything, just let me get out of here first."

"What is it with you two?" Riley whispered back to her.

"Riley?" Paul called out again.

Caylee gave Riley a pleading look and put her hands together like she was praying.

Riley laughed. "Paul, can you come back in five minutes? I'm just finishing up."

"Sure," Paul said.

They all waited in silence until they heard him walk away.

Caylee fell back onto the bed and grabbed a Santa pillow and covered her face.

Riley wasn't letting her get off the hook that easy. "Caylee, you need to tell me what's going on." She took the pillow away from Caylee's face.

"Oh, boy," Maryanne said. "We could be here all night."

As Caylee sat up, she snagged another Santa pillow and threw it at Maryanne.

Riley crossed her arms. "I'm waiting."

Caylee jumped up from the bed, ran over to the door, and cracked it open just enough so she could peer out. "And

I promise to tell you," she said. "We just don't have time tonight, and I need to get out of here before he comes back."

"You do know he's going to be here for the party," Riley said. "So Paul *is* going to see you."

Caylee took a deep breath. "I know. I just freaked out for second. I'll be fine. I just need to be prepared and ready when he does see me. I wasn't ready."

"I'm so confused," Riley said.

"I'll explain later, but tonight is your night," Caylee said as she headed for the door. "I'll see you guys downstairs." She turned around and smiled. "Riley, you really do look beautiful. Any guy would be lucky to have you. Whatever guy that might be."

Riley laughed. "Thanks, but right now, I don't need a guy. I just need to be the best host I can be for this Christmas Camp. My entire future is riding on this."

Caylee gave her a knowing look. "And you know what they say… 'Life is what happens to you when you're making other plans.'"

"John Lennon," Riley said.

"Is that who said it?" Caylee asked, but she didn't wait for an answer as she disappeared out the door.

Maryanne was right on her heels. "I need to go down and make sure the food and drinks and everything else are all set." She was halfway out the door when an attack of nerves suddenly hit Riley.

"Maryanne?" Riley called out, her voice shaking.

Maryanne instantly turned back around. "What's wrong?"

Riley rung her hands together. "I'm nervous."

Maryanne smiled at her. "You have nothing to be nervous about. You've gone over the plan a dozen times. Everything is ready. Everyone downstairs is wonderful, and they're all here because they're excited to see *you*. Just be yourself because who you are is pretty great."

Riley took a deep breath and gave Maryanne a grateful look. "Thank you. That's very sweet of you to say."

"And I mean it," Maryanne said. "I'll see you downstairs."

As Riley watched Maryanne leave, Comet also head for the door. "You, too?" Riley asked. "You're just going to leave me? What happened to you being my emotional support animal? You know that's a real thing, right?"

Comet barked and wagged his tail, then trotted out the door.

Riley looked around her room at all the Santas staring at her. "I guess it's just you and me, Santas."

Paul laughed as he appeared in the doorway and snapped a candid photo of her.

Startled, she spun around and faced him. "I'm going to get photo approval of these pictures, right?"

Paul put the camera down. "Actually, Mike said he'd be doing that."

Riley laughed, but it was the kind of laugh that held a warning. She smiled sweetly at Paul. It was *too* sweet. She walked over and locked eyes with him. "Paul, there's one thing you need to do if I'm going to let you take my picture."

Paul shifted his weight from one foot to another. "What's that?" he asked, looking a little uncomfortable.

Riley didn't blink. "You need to stop listening to Mike. He might have hired you, but I'm the one who hired him, so I have the final say on everything. That means photo approval of *every* photo before it's posted anywhere. If you have a problem with that, then we can just shut this down right now." She paused for a beat. "So what's it going to be?"

Paul turned his camera around and showed her the picture he just took of her where she was talking to the Santas. She leaned in closer, saw how the picture make her look like a crazy person, and pushed "delete."

Then she smiled back at Paul. "Glad we're on the same page. Now tell me what you need and I'll try to help you get some good pictures that are *on brand* for who I am as an author, as well as show off the lodge. This place is special, and Luke's family and friends have worked really hard to get this ready for Christmas Camp so I want to make sure these pictures help them sell this place. Okay?"

Paul nodded "Okay. No problem. I get it." He held up his camera. "And I'm ready if you are."

Riley smiled. "I'm as ready as I'll ever be. Let's get started because I have a party to get to."

She was grateful that it didn't take long for Paul to snap a few quick pictures of her in her Santa room. He'd just wanted to show her working on her Christmas novel, so she'd set her laptop on the desk that was lined with Santa figurines and sat down. He had told her she could write anything because he wouldn't be showing it. He just wanted to see her working. So she started writing down the first things that came to her mind…

> *Christmas Lake Christmas tree*
> *Christmas Lake Angel*
> *Christmas Lake cookies*
> *Christmas Lake famous hot chocolate*
> *Luke*

Her fingers froze after she had typed *Luke*. Embarrassed, she quickly erased it, not wanting Paul to see it, and typed *Comet* in its place.

A little flustered, she looked up at Paul. "Do you have what you need yet?"

Paul checked the pictures and nodded. "We're good. Want

to see?"

"Sure," she said. When she'd looked at the pictures and saw all the Santas lined up like some kind of Santa army watching over her as she wrote, she had to laugh. "You don't think that looks a little Christmas crazy? All those Santas staring at me?" she asked.

Paul shook his head as he looked at the pictures. "I think it's perfect. Those Santas look like they're inspiring you to write your Christmas book."

"If you say so," Riley said, even though she wasn't so sure.

Paul headed for the door. "I'm going to head downstairs so I can set up for your big entrance."

"Great," Riley said. "No pressure."

Paul laughed. "Don't worry. Everyone's really excited to see you. They've all come for you."

Riley playfully swatted him. "Thanks a lot. Now I feel even more nervous."

"You're going to kill it," Paul said as he left the room. "I'll see you down there soon."

After he was gone, Riley took a deep breath and started pacing around the room. When she rubbed her palms together, they were sweaty and damp. Her stomach was twisting into a knot. This was it. This was her moment of truth.

But when she thought about the phrase *moment of truth,* she felt her guilt grow even more, because *truth* wasn't a word she could use right now. She was being so dishonest with everyone about being Miss Christmas.

She forced herself to smile. She only had to get through one weekend.

How hard could it be? she thought. *Everything's planned. I just need to focus on the future. No one needs to know about my past.*

Chapter Twenty-Seven

When Riley first opened her door to go downstairs, she heard the Christmas song "The Twelve Days of Christmas."

> *"On the first day of Christmas*
> *My true love gave to me*
> *A partridge in a pear tree..."*

When she apprehensively looked down at her sparkling red dress, Comet came to stand by her, making her feel better. He looked even more lovable wearing his bright-red bow.

As she bent down to pet him, he gazed up at her with his adoring dark-brown eyes.

"This is it, Comet," Riley said. "Are you ready for Christmas Camp?"

Comet wagged his tail, barked, and ran for the stairs.

"Wait for me." Riley laughed, following him. "I'm coming."

As she started walking down the stairs the Christmas music got louder...

> *"On the third day of Christmas*
> *My true love gave to me*

Three French hens
Two turtle doves
And a partridge in a pear tree..."

She heard people laughing. Everyone sounded like they were having a great time. That made her relax a little. She felt even better when she saw Luke waiting for her at the bottom of the stairs.

In that instant, she forgot about everything else and kept walking toward him. He looked incredibly handsome wearing a perfectly tailored, black designer suit with a crisp white shirt and a red tie the same shade as her dress.

They were a perfect match.

When he smiled up at her, her heart beat faster. The way he was looking at her made her feel...beautiful.

Feeling weak in her knees, she reached out for the staircase railing as she finished her descent. When she got to the bottom, Luke held out his hand to help her down the last step. She put her hand in his, and their eyes met.

"You're shaking," he said in a low, rich voice.

"I am?" she asked, not recognizing her own voice. It sounded silky soft, almost like a whisper.

"Doesn't she look amazing?" Caylee said, interrupting the moment as she rushed over to them.

"She does," Luke agreed, never taking his eyes off Riley.

When a flash went off and Riley caught Paul taking pictures of them. She quickly let go of Luke's hand.

"You really do look beautiful," Luke said.

Riley smiled at him. "You clean up pretty well yourself."

Luke laughed. "Thank you. I think?"

They shared a little laugh.

"Everyone's waiting, Riley," Caylee said. "Are you ready?"

Riley nodded, though she didn't feel ready. "Uh-huh."

Luke reached out and took her hand. "You're going to be great. You got this. Everyone's here to see you because they love you. Just enjoy the moment. You've earned this."

Riley gave him a grateful look. "Thank you."

"Come on!" Caylee said, nearly bursting with excitement.

As she took Riley's hand free hand, Riley reluctantly had to let go of Luke's hand. Caylee led her over to the fireplace where they'd set up a special display of Riley's books surrounded by white twinkle lights.

As the flash from Paul's camera went off, Riley blinked several times. But then everything was a blur, and she didn't see any of faces of the people who were starting to gather around.

Riley kept her attention on one person, Luke, and the only thing she heard was the "Twelve Days of Christmas" still playing...

"On the twelfth day of Christmas
My true love gave to me
Twelve drummers drumming..."

Luke smiled as he looked over to Riley. "You ready?" he whispered.

She nodded and smiled back at him.

"Everyone, if I can have your attention please," Luke announced, his deep voice booming.

Like a ship seeking shelter in a storm, Riley kept her focus on Luke as she clasped and unclasped her hands together. She wasn't usually this nervous to talk in front of people. She actually did a lot of public speaking and enjoyed it. But this was different. This time she was pretending to be something she wasn't, and she certainly wasn't an actress.

A potential title for her book popped into her head—*The*

Runaway Christmas Author.

In that brief moment of panic, she would have run if she could. For years, she'd avoided all the Christmas hoopla, and now she was about to be a part of it.

"Thank you, everyone," Luke said, interrupting her getaway plans. "First, I want to welcome you all again to Christmas Camp. I believe I've met all of you, but I know I'm not the one you've come to see…"

Riley smiled when she heard the laughter but kept looking at Luke. She was impressed by and a bit envious of how calm and relaxed he looked.

Luke continued, "When I was first approached to put on this Christmas Camp for an author to host at my family's lodge, I'll admit I thought there was no way we could pull it off with just a few weeks before Christmas. But as my mom likes to say, anything is possible at Christmas. With the help of some of our family friends, who you've met and will meet more of this weekend, and the community of Christmas Lake, and most of all author Riley Reynolds, we've put together a one-of-a-kind holiday experience that's going to knock your Christmas socks off."

Everyone, including Riley, laughed and clapped.

"But before I pass this over to Riley, I wanted to make sure you all had a chance to make your Christmas wish." Luke pointed to the three-foot-tall Santa next to the fireplace.

Riley did a double take. The Santa hadn't been there before. They must have put him out when she was upstairs getting ready.

"You should have found a little scroll and a red ribbon in your room when you checked in," Luke continued, "There were also instructions to write your Christmas wish on the scroll and then roll it up, tie it with the red ribbon, and put it in Santa's gift bag here."

Luke walked over, peered in the bag, and smiled as he picked out one little scroll. "Looks like we have a lot of Christmas wishes in here. Has everyone had a chance to make their wish?"

When everyone either said yes or nodded, Luke turned to Riley and handed her a little piece of paper, a pen, and red ribbon. "So that just leaves you, Riley."

"You want me to do it now?" she asked, trying not to look as uncomfortable as she felt. *Please say no, please say no, please say no,* was all that kept going through her head.

"What do you think, guys?" Luke asked the crowd.

When everyone shouted yes and clapped, Riley had no choice but to laugh along with them.

"Okay," she said. She knew this wasn't the time to tell everyone she didn't believe in Christmas wishes, so instead, she turned toward the fireplace and used the mantel as a flat place to write, quickly jotting down her wish.

To write a wonderful Christmas love story.

She turned back to face everyone. "Okay, done!"

"You have to put it in Santa's bag," Caylee said.

"But first tie the red ribbon around it," Maryanne added.

"That *is* how it works," Luke agreed.

Everyone laughed.

Riley laughed, too, as she tied the ribbon around it and headed over to the Santa. As she was putting her wish into his bag, she did another double take when it looked like Santa winked at her. She let out a sigh of relief when she realized it was just the reflection from the Christmas lights on the mantel.

She quickly returned to Luke's side.

"Okay," Luke said, "without further ado, let me officially introduce the host of our Christmas Camp, best-selling

author Riley Reynolds!"

As everyone clapped, Luke stepped aside so all the focus was on Riley. Paul snapped several more pictures.

The flash was making her see stars. She blinked several times as she looked around trying to take everyone in for the first time.

Riley cleared her throat. "Thank you all for being here." She motioned to Luke. "Can we please give Luke and his family and friends a huge round of applause for making this weekend possible? I think you'll agree that Christmas Lake and the Christmas Lake Lodge is right out of a fairy tale. Thank you for having us, Luke."

As everyone clapped, Riley gave Luke a grateful smile. He nodded and smiled back at her.

"Is this going to be the setting for your book?" a girl standing just a few feet from Riley eagerly asked.

It was the first time Riley made eye contact with one of the Christmas Campers. For a moment she thought she was seeing double, but it was actually two identical twin sisters in their early twenties. They were wearing matching gold sequin dresses and cute, fuzzy reindeer antler headbands.

The twins grinned back at her. "I'm Carrie," the twin who had asked the question said.

"And I'm Terrie," the other twin chimed in.

"We're from Florida, and we love your books!" they said in perfect unison.

Riley laughed. "And I already love you both. Thank you!"

When there was more laugher from the group, Riley felt herself start to unwind. She smiled at the twins. "And about having Christmas Lake in my next book, that's a really good question, one I'm hoping you'll all can help me with as we go through the weekend. I can't wait to hear what kind of Christmas story you want to read."

"We love all your books, Riley," a woman called out.

Riley smiled back at her.

The woman looked to be in her mid-sixties and was standing to the right of the twins. "My name's Barbara, from Charlotte, North Carolina. I'm here with my husband, Larry. I love all your books, *and* I watch every Christmas movie every year. You can ask my husband. It drives him crazy."

"She's not kidding," Larry said. "She watches every single one."

"See, told you," Barbara said. "And I love Christmas novels, too. I'm so glad you're finally writing one. I've been hoping you would. Haven't I, Larry?"

"Yup," Larry said and nodded. "She has."

"Anyway," Barbara continued with even more enthusiasm, "I've been talking to everyone tonight—"

"Everyone," Larry emphasized. "Trust me, *everyone*."

People laughed.

Barbara kept going without missing a beat. "Anyway, as I was saying, I've been talking to everyone, and I think I can speak for all of us when I say a heartfelt thank-you to *you* for hosting this Christmas Camp, and to Luke and everyone and honoring this very special time of year."

When there was more applause and cheers, Riley touched her heart. The energy in the room was already so welcoming. She felt very relieved and blessed.

She smiled back at the people who had gathered around her. "Well, I am truly looking forward to getting to know all of you this weekend."

"Do you already know what kind of guy your heroine is going to fall in love with?" Terri asked.

"Is he going to be a Scrooge and she has to help him find his Christmas spirit?" Carrie jumped in.

Terrie waved her hands excitedly. "Or maybe *she's* the

Scrooge, and he has to help her embrace the magic of Christmas."

Riley laughed, impressed the twins had thought this out more than she had. "Honestly," she said, "I haven't decided yet."

"What about an old boyfriend who comes back into the picture to win her back?" a man asked from the very back of the room.

Riley shrugged and smiled, looking around for the man who'd spoken. "Anything's possible."

When Colin took a step forward out of the shadows, he smiled his most winning smile. "That's good to know."

Riley gasped and rubbed her eyes. She couldn't believe what she was seeing.

"Colin?" she whispered. *It couldn't be,* she thought, but this guy looked just like her college boyfriend.

Before Colin could answer, another guy from the back of the room spoke up. "That *is* good to know," the guy said, also stepping into the light.

Riley's jaw dropped. It was Brendan.

"Very good," another guy added, as he too stepped into the light from the back of the room.

It was Tyler.

Riley covered her mouth with both hands. She couldn't even begin to process what she was seeing.

The three men she had loved in her life—Colin, Brendan, and Tyler—where all there smiling back at her.

Chapter Twenty-Eight

"Surprise!" Colin said.

Brendan and Tyler quickly followed. "Surprise!" they said in unison.

The twins spoke before Riley could. "Who are they?" Carrie asked her, excited, as if she were unraveling the plot of one of Riley's novels.

When Riley just kept staring at the guys, Terrie took over, looking back at them. "Who are you guys?" she called out to them. She gave her twin a look. "Whoever they are, they're hot."

At the same time, all three guys answered, "Riley's boyfriend."

The twins' eyes grew huge, and their shocked expressions matched everyone else's in the room. Including the three guys who were now looking at each other, sizing each other up.

Barbara, fascinated, swatted her husband's arm. "I told you this was going to be amazing!"

Tyler was the first to make his way to the front of the room, but the other two guys were right on his Gucci heels.

Riley watched everything happen in slow motion. She still couldn't believe what was happening, even when they all stood broad shoulder to broad shoulder in front of her.

"Riley, you look beautiful," Colin said.

"You really do…" Brendan agreed.

"Stunning," Tyler added.

When the three men looked at one another, it wasn't a friendly look.

When Riley started laughing, it was one of those high-pitched laughs you'd hear someone let out before they totally lost it.

"What is going on?" she asked. "How can you all be here? Did Mike set this up?" She knew she was babbling, but she couldn't help it. She spun around to look at Paul, who was taking pictures as fast as he could.

"Paul, did you know about this?"

He shook his head. "No, but this is great. Can I get a picture of the four of you together?"

Riley glared at him. "No!"

When Riley also noticed the twins taking video, she gave them a pleading look. "Guys, can you please not post any video or pictures of this until I figure out what's going on?"

The twins looked disappointed but put their phones down.

Riley looked back at Colin, Brendan, and Tyler. "I'm not sure what's happening here," she said to them, "but I'm right in the middle of this party. Can we all talk later?"

"Absolutely," Colin said.

"Of course," Brendan agreed.

"Whatever you want," Tyler added.

Riley started to laugh again. Now she was losing it.

Thankfully, Luke came to her rescue. "All right, everyone, you'll have lots of time to ask Riley questions this weekend, but right now we're going to get ready to do a special Christmas Camp toast. So if you'll just give us a few minutes to get the bubbly flowing, we'll continue this celebration."

When Riley, still in shock, looked up at Luke, he put his hand on her back and guided her toward the kitchen. Caylee and Maryanne quickly followed.

"Just breathe," Caylee whispered to Riley, taking her hand. "You're as white as a ghost. Just keep breathing."

Riley's head was spinning. At least she knew why she was as white as a ghost. Because she had just seen three ghosts. The ghosts of boyfriends past were all at her Christmas Camp, and she had no idea why.

When they reached the kitchen, Maryanne hurried to bring Riley a glass of water.

"Thank you," Riley said, taking the glass with shaking fingers. She took a sip and a deep breath, and then looked over at Luke.

"This had to be Mike," she said. Her shock was starting to wear off, and it was quickly being replaced by anger. She started pacing around the kitchen like a wild animal in a cage. "This must all be a publicity stunt. I can't believe he would go this far and humiliate me like this. I hope Paul got some great pictures because that's obviously what Mike was banking on."

"I don't think Mike did this," Luke said.

Riley whirled around and looked at him. "Why not? Who else would have done this? Someone had to do it. All three of my ex-boyfriends are out there. What are they doing here? Someone had to know they were coming. They didn't just show up like...*poof!* Santa didn't bring them. Who did this? Who knew about this?"

Riley knew she was spiraling out of control, but she couldn't stop herself. She needed answers, and she wanted them now.

Caylee and Maryanne both looked at Luke.

Riley felt like the wind was being knocked out of her. She shook her head in disbelief. "Luke? Did you do this? How—"

"No, I didn't do this," Luke rushed to correct her. "How could I have done this? I don't know these guys or your past."

Riley watched him loosen his tie. He looked uncomfortable.

"But you knew about it, didn't you." It was a statement, not a question.

Silence.

Riley marched over to him until they were toe to toe. "Luke, did you know about this?"

"Just tell her, Luke," Caylee said.

Riley spun around and faced Caylee. "And you knew, too?" Now her voice sounded more hurt than angry. When she looked over at Maryanne, Maryanne looked down at the floor.

Riley felt like a knife was twisting in her back.

They'd all known. They'd all been in on this.

She'd thought these girls were her friends, and Luke... Well, she didn't know what she thought about him, but she certainly didn't think he'd ever do something like this. This was all just one big joke to them.

When she felt tears well up in her eyes, she knew she had to get away from them before they saw her cry. She was already humiliated enough.

With her head held high, she started to leave the kitchen.

"Riley, wait," Luke called after her, "I can explain. It's not how it looks. You can't just leave."

Riley froze. So that's what he was worried about. That she was going to take off again, like she'd done during her live TV interview. He didn't trust her to stick around, and that hurt more than she liked to admit.

Her pride had her pulling herself together. She was here for a job, to host Christmas Camp. That was the only thing Luke cared about. She never should have let herself think otherwise. She needed to focus on what really mattered, and that was saving her career.

She took a deep breath. She had people out there who were waiting for a Champagne toast, and she wasn't going to let them down.

She turned around and walked back into the kitchen on a mission. Avoiding Luke, she grabbed a bottle of Champagne and looked at Caylee and Maryanne.

"Well, are we doing this or not?" she asked in a voice that meant business. "We promised everyone a Champagne toast."

She grabbed the cork on the bottle she was holding and yanked it off. After the loud *pop!*, Riley held up the bottle. "So let's give them a Champagne toast." She turned to Luke. "You can go. We can do this." Her voice was flat, emotionless.

"Riley," Luke started, but Caylee stepped between them.

"She's right, Luke," Caylee said. "You go entertain the guests, and we'll be right there with the Champagne."

When Luke looked at Riley, she had nothing left to say to him. She was in crisis mode. Right now, she needed to try to find a way to go back out there and face the Christmas Campers, who all thought she was Miss Christmas. She also had to face her three ex-boyfriends who had all crazily claimed they were her *current* boyfriend. In her wildest author imagination, she never could have made something like this up.

After Maryanne poured the first glass of Champagne, Riley picked it up and drank it. She didn't stop until the glass was empty. She put the glass down. "Who is ready for a party?"

Maryanne and Caylee quickly continued to fill up Champagne flutes and put them on a silver tray.

"We are," Caylee said.

"Great," Riley said, picking up the first full tray. "Then let's do this."

As Riley passed out Champagne, she introduced herself to each and every one of the Christmas Campers.

She was surprised to see such a variety of people, of all ages who had come from all over the country and all walks of life. There were people who had come from her home state of Washington, and others from California, Maine, and Florida, and still others from Mississippi, Tennessee, North Carolina, Texas, and a lot of places in between.

The youngest Christmas Campers were the twenty-two-year-old twins, Carrie and Terrie, from Clearwater, Florida. The eldest, Patricia, was almost ninety. She was from Dallas, Texas, and brought her daughter, Linda, and granddaughter, Renee, as a Christmas gift.

There was a young engaged couple in their late twenties, Carolyn and John, and several couples who were retired, including the couple that Luke had recommended be invited, Debbie and Bill. There was even a group of four girls in their thirties from Tennessee, Rachel, Madison, Kara, and Julie, who were doing a Christmas Camp girls' getaway weekend. Two of them had left husbands and babies at home, and two were single. When Riley got to Barbara and Larry, she could barely get away because Barbara wanted to keep taking pictures.

Then there were her exes, Colin, Brendan, and Tyler. At the moment, they had all picked different places to hang out in the back of the room and were staring at their phones.

Talk about awkward, Riley thought. She'd asked Caylee to give them their Champagne and let them each know she'd talk with them later. She just couldn't deal with them right now. It wouldn't be fair to her Christmas Campers.

After they'd finished passing out the Champagne, Riley saw Luke motioning for her to join him back at the fireplace. She forced a smile as she joined him, still hurt and angry that he'd been in on this ex-boyfriend fiasco.

"If I can have everyone's attention for a moment," Luke said, "we'd like to do a toast to officially start off our Christmas Camp."

When Riley saw the twins give each other a guilty look because they'd already drank their Champagne, she quickly grabbed a bottle and filled up their glasses.

"Thanks," both twins whispered to her at the same time. "You're the best."

"No problem," Riley whispered back. She then gave Caylee the Champagne bottle and then walked back to join Luke.

"Ready?" Luke asked her.

"Ready," she said and smiled, but the smile was for the benefit of the Christmas Campers. When she looked to the back of the room and saw Colin, Brendan, and Tyler raise their glasses to her, she just kept smiling, even though she was thinking, *Shoot me now.*

"I'm not sure if you all know this," Luke said to the group, "but the idea of Christmas Camp was actually the creation of my friend's dad, Ben. He owns the Holly Peak Inn in Massachusetts, and now he's working with other places, like my family's lodge, so we can host more Christmas Camp experiences like this one."

When everyone cheered, Luke smiled and then continued. "Part of the agreement to hold a Christmas Camp is to make sure we honor some of Ben's family's original Christmas Camp traditions like making their famous Christmas Camp cookies and doing a Christmas Camp cocktail mixology class…"

"Cheers to that," the twins said as they clinked their Champagne glasses together.

Everyone laughed, including Riley.

"So tonight's cocktail party is the beginning of the Christmas Camp journey we're all going to be taking together," Luke went on. "I know a lot of you have traveled a long way to get here, so after this cocktail party we have a simple but delicious buffet dinner that you can eat at your leisure, either in the dining room or in your own room. This is your time to settle in and relax before we start our first full day of Christmas Camp activities tomorrow that Riley will be hosting."

When everyone clapped, Riley lifted her glass and smiled. "And you'll definitely want to get your rest. We have a *big* day planned for you tomorrow."

"We can't wait," Carrie said.

"We are so excited," Terrie added.

"And now for our first toast," Luke said as he held up his glass. "Ben has a special toast his family always does at their Christmas Camp, and we'd like to continue that tradition and share that toast with all of you."

When Riley looked out at all the Christmas Campers, she saw that everyone was smiling and seemed excited. Even her exes in the back of the room had looked up from their phones.

"So, Riley," Luke said, turning to her, "would you like to do the toast?"

Riley gave him a surprised look. This had not been part of their plan.

"Oh, it's okay," she said. "I don't know it by heart. You go ahead."

The truth was, she didn't know the toast at all. This was the first time she was hearing about any Christmas Camp toast. Yet another surprise she wasn't prepared for. It made her wonder what else Luke was planning to spring on her.

When Luke looked back at her, he kept smiling. "Riley, you should do the toast. This is your Christmas Camp. Don't you agree, everyone?"

When Luke looked out into the group everyone started cheering.

"Riley! Riley!" the twins started chanting.

Luke picked up a 4x6 glossy red card from the table. "We've printed up a copy of the toast right here and have a copy for everyone else, too, in case they'd like to have it. So please, do us the honor of making this first toast to Christmas Camp at the Christmas Lake Lodge."

When everyone started clapping, Riley didn't feel like she had much choice. She forced herself to smile as she joined Luke. He handed her the card and stepped aside.

"Toast," Carrie said.

"Toast," Terrie echoed.

Everyone laughed.

"Okay," Riley said, holding up her Champagne glass in one hand and the note card in the other. "Here we go. The official Christmas Camp toast." She took a deep breath before she started to read.

"To our family, friends, and community...
To the people we've lost but will never forget..."

For a moment, Riley felt herself choke up as she thought about her dad, but kept going.

"To love everlasting..."

She couldn't help looking to the back of the room where she made eye contact with each of her exes before continuing.

"Merry Christmas... To Christmas Camp."

Everyone repeated back to her, "To Christmas Camp!"

Then they started clinking their Champagne glasses with their fellow Christmas Campers and wishing each other merry Christmas.

When Luke held out his glass, he looked into her eyes.

"Merry Christmas, Riley. I hope you get everything you wish for." He looked over at her three exes as he clinked his Champagne glass to hers, making his meaning clear.

She didn't have time to respond because he was already heading toward the front door where Brianna the realtor had just walked in.

Riley watched him smile as he took her coat. Riley couldn't help but notice how happy he looked to see her or how beautiful she looked in a backless, sexy, black cocktail dress. Riley was jealous that Brianna was wearing black and looked amazing.

She was so busy watching Luke with Brianna that she didn't even see Caylee come up to her.

"Wow, that's some dress," Caylee said, following Riley's gaze.

Riley nodded. "It sure is." She turned to Caylee. "So Luke and Brianna…"

"Yeah, they've been a thing on and off for years," Caylee said.

"Why on and off?" Riley asked.

"Luke travels so much for his job, I'm guessing the long-distance thing wasn't working for them." Caylee shrugged.

Riley glanced back over and saw Brianna take Luke's hand. "Well, it looks like right now they're back *on*." Riley said. She didn't know why it bothered her, but it did, which was crazy since she had three guys claiming to be her boyfriend.

"Riley? Did you hear me?" Caylee asked.

Riley quickly brought her attention back to Caylee. "Sorry, what?"

"I was saying you really hit the jackpot with the three guys in the back of the room. They're all hot and seem nice." Caylee whistled as she glanced back at the three guys. "I mean, seriously, Riley, leave some for the rest of us."

"It's not like that," Riley said. "It's not like that at all."

"I know," Caylee said. "Because I know why they're all here."

Riley's eyes grew huge. "What?! Tell me!"

Caylee looked around and saw the twins were eagerly listening. "Not here," she whispered. "Come on."

Chapter Twenty-Nine

A couple of minutes later, as soon as they were safely in Riley's room, Caylee pounced.

"Tell me *everything*," Caylee demanded.

"Wait," Riley said. "You tell *me* everything. You're the one who talked to my exes. What did they say? Why are they here?"

Caylee, with an all-knowing smile, walked over to the desk where the Santa figurines were lined up. She picked up one of the Santas, headed for the dresser, and put the Santa down in a new spot in front of the mirror.

Riley, baffled, threw up her hands. "Caylee, are you going to redecorate my room or tell me what's going on?" She was losing her patience. "We need to get back downstairs. I don't want people wondering where I've disappeared to."

"Hold on," Caylee said as she walked back to the desk and picked up two more Santas and had them join the other Santa on the dresser. So now there were three Santas lined up, facing the mirror.

"What are you doing?" Riley asked, exasperated.

Caylee put her hand on top of the first Santa she'd brought over to the dresser. "Colin, the guy with the great smile..." She moved her hand to the next Santa. "And Brendan, the ruggedly handsome guy. Now I understand that description from your books…" Her hand moved to the third Santa. "And Tyler, the high-society guy who looks like something out of *GQ* magazine. They are all here for one reason."

"Let me guess. Mike invited them," Riley said. She knew this had Mike's fingerprints all over it.

Caylee shook her head. "Nope. You did."

Riley's eyes grew huge. When Caylee laughed, Riley looked at her like she was fruitier than a fruitcake.

"Me? What are you talking about?" Riley asked, sounding incredulous. "I haven't talked to Colin since college, or Brendan since we broke up more than ten years ago, or Tyler since we broke up a few years ago. I haven't seen or talked to any of these guys, so I certainly didn't invite them here!"

"But they've all *seen* you," Caylee said, moving all three Santas closer to the mirror. "In the TV interview when you talked about how your novels are inspired by your *one* true love. Emphasis on *one*…"

Riley's jaw dropped. "No," she said, shaking her head. It was all starting to come together, and the reality was even worse than what she'd imagined.

Caylee nodded. "Yup. They all saw the interview and thought you were talking about them as your one true love, so they've all come here to win you back and rewrite their happily-ever-after with you!"

Riley collapsed on the bed and covered her face with a Santa pillow. "This can't be happening," she said into the pillow.

When Caylee sat down next to her, she took the pillow away from Riley's face. "Okay, now it's your turn. Spill. You have to tell me all about these guys. I'm dying to know!"

Riley sat up and gave Caylee a confused look. "Dying to know what?"

"Which one is it?" Caylee asked, excited. "Is it Colin,

Brendan, or Tyler? Which one was your one true love?"

"All of them," Riley answered honestly.

"What?" Caylee asked, confused.

"I loved them all when we dated," Riley said.

"Then who did you love the *most*?" Caylee asked, clearly not giving up.

Riley thought about the question. *What boyfriend did I love the most?*

She knew Caylee was waiting for an answer, but she also knew she couldn't give her the clear-cut one she wanted. She had loved Colin, Brendan, and Tyler in different ways, and they each represented a different time in her life.

Colin had been her first real true love. They had dated all through college and supported and encouraged each other. They'd made plans, and together, they'd dreamed of what they would do after graduation. She'd always felt safe dating Colin. She had known he would never hurt her and would always have her back. He was fiercely loyal and even protective of her at times, and at that time in her life, when she was basically on her own, having lost her dad and her mom moving to Florida and getting remarried. She had needed the security of Colin. He had become like her family, someone she trusted and counted on. He was reliable, the safe choice. He fit perfectly into the very specific plan she had made to create a stable future for herself.

But after graduating, when she'd landed her first reporting job and had to leave California and move to Idaho, Colin had been crushed. He, of course, had been proud of her, but he also didn't want to lose her. Unfortunately, to follow his career path as a movie producer, he needed to stay in Los Angeles.

They tried doing the long-distance thing for a little while, but when neither of them had much time off and they were both barely making any money, the months between their visits grew.

Looking back, Riley remembered how she had thrown herself into her work. She'd also quickly learned that to succeed as a TV reporter she'd have to move ever few years, going from one small market to the next, working her way up the ladder. This meant it would likely be years before she had enough experience to work where Colin lived, in Los Angeles, one of the top TV markets in the country.

Feeling it was best for them both, she'd decided to break things off with Colin so he could go after his dreams and she could go after hers.

It still hurt her remembering how heartbroken he'd been. He'd claimed she'd given up on them. While she'd wanted to stay friends, he'd insisted it would just be too hard. So he'd been the one to cut off all contact with her, and she hadn't heard from him since.

Breaking up with Colin and letting go of someone she loved so much had made her even more determined to make her sacrifice worth it by succeeding in her career.

More than ever, she'd volunteer to work overtime and on her days off. She had put all her heart and soul into every story she did, earning her the respect of her colleges and superiors. Over the next five years, she'd won awards and moved up to bigger TV markets. While she'd dated a few people casually along the way, she'd never had the time or desire to get too involved. Remembering what had happened with Colin, she had always wanted the freedom to move to the next TV job, wherever a promotion could take her, without feeling guilty about leaving someone behind again.

But then, about five years after dating Colin, Brendan came into her life when she was working as a reporter and anchor in Salt Lake City, Utah. She had just gotten the coveted promotion to the main anchor of the five, six, and ten o'clock news, and she was hosting a charity fundraising dance for a local ski resort when Brendan had literally swept her off her feet.

Brendan had been the opposite of Colin in many ways. He had never was the kind of guy to play anything safe. Where Colin had been solid and dependable, Brendan had been a free spirit and a risk-taker.

She smiled remembering how Brendan had boldly asked her to dance while she had been talking to two other men. He'd then grabbed a bottle of Champagne and two glasses from behind the bar, and had taken her outside where he wanted her to go with him and ride one of the ski gondolas up the mountain.

When she'd told him he was crazy, pointing out the obvious that she was wearing a cocktail dress and high heels, he'd assured her the gondola was heated and they'd just ride it up and down the mountain without getting out. When she'd hesitated, he'd asked her a question she'd never forget…

Are you going to always just report on other people's adventures or have your own?

When she had gotten on that gondola, that choice had changed her life. For the first time, she hadn't been worried about playing it safe and following the life plan that she'd mapped out when she was an overambitious thirteen-year-old. She had just lived in the moment. She still remembered how she felt going up that mountain. She'd felt free, free from her own expectations and pressure she'd put on herself.

Brendan had poured them both a glass of Champagne and had made a toast.

To a lifetime of adventures…

When their Champagne glasses touched, their eyes had met, and she'd known in that moment that her lifetime of adventures was just starting.

She'd dated Brendan for four years. From that first night, the spark between them had ignited something inside her that made her feel more alive than she'd ever felt in her life. Brendan was constantly challenging her, pushing her to take risks, to be daring, and to always go after what she wanted.

After six months, they'd moved in together. They were already together 24-7 so it had just seemed like the natural thing to do. Brendan was a ski instructor, and in the off-season, he worked as an outdoor guide, doing everything from white-water rafting to hiking and fishing adventures. Their schedules had worked well together. Even though she had been anchoring three shows a day, which meant she'd go to work in the afternoon and come home around midnight, they always found a way to spend quality time together.

Riley had always appreciated how Brendan had given her the freedom to do what she loved and never made her feel guilty for the long hours she worked. His hours had also been all over the place, and sometimes he'd be gone for several weeks as a guide on different tours.

When she'd fought hard for the opportunity to go to Afghanistan as an embedded TV reporter with a local Army Reserve unit, Brendan had supported her decision. He'd also stood by her when her boss had initially refused to send a female reporter into a war zone, and she'd threatened to quit her job over it. After she'd finally won that battle and gone to Afghanistan for several months, Brendan had understood how emotionally and physically challenging the assignment had been and had welcomed her home with open arms.

He had continued to support her when, after doing her first TV documentary, she decided she needed to go back to Afghanistan for a second story. This time, when her boss had refused to approve her trip, she'd made a life-changing career decision and quit her job. That's when she'd called her mom and said she hadn't just quit her job, she'd quit her career.

She'd seen the way news reporting was changing, favoring the more sensational, and she hadn't wanted to be a part of that change.

Within a week of. her quitting, Brendan had planned a trip for them to Switzerland, where he'd been asked to guide a two-week tour in the Swiss Alps. At first she had said there was no way she could go, she had to figure out what she was going to do for work, but when Brendan had said the outfitting company he worked for was looking for a freelance writer to go along and report on the story for a national travel magazine, she'd agreed to give it a try.

At the time, she'd only ever covered hard news stories. She'd never written a travel story, but with Brendan's encouragement, she gave it a shot. When it turned out she not only loved it but was also really good at telling inspiring, uplifting stories, they'd started traveling the world together. She had never been happier, telling stories she loved with the person she loved. It was a dream come true. Until the dream didn't pay the rent...

While they had gotten to travel for free, living a million-dollar lifestyle with all their amazing trips, they were getting paid hardly anything. To make ends meet, she started dipping into her 401K retirement fund, which everyone warned her not to touch. When all her savings were almost gone, that's when she came face-to-face with her financial reality.

It's not as if she had planned for it to happen. She was always searching for new ways to monetize her travel writing, but this was before the world of influencers and travel writers getting paid to post their content on social media. Her only outlets were print and online magazines, and they had started paying less and less, barely making it themselves.

So where she'd started in high school always doing every-thing right financially, making sure she'd have a secure future, she now found herself living the life of Peter Pan, traveling the world, having an amazing time, but not acting like a real grown-up.

When her savings had almost run out, she had known she'd come to the end of this adventure. She'd needed a new plan, and to come up with one, she had to stop traveling and put in the work. But this time, Brendan hadn't understood or sup-ported her decision. He'd loved their lifestyle, and he'd had no intention of giving it up. He'd kept telling her it would work out, she just had to have some faith.

As the tension between them continued to grow, Riley no longer saw Brendan as her great adventure. Instead, she saw him as her great *distraction*. It had been clear that to truly move forward with her life, she would have to let him go.

The breakup hadn't been as hard as she'd thought it would be.

He'd already come to the same conclusion that they no longer wanted the same things in life. But since their apart-ment technically had been his, she'd had nowhere to go and an empty bank account, she'd had to move in with her mom and stepdad for the summer. She had been so embarrassed to ask them for help, but they'd welcomed her without judgment.

When she'd first gotten to her mom's, she hadn't had any idea what she was going to do to make a living, so she did the only thing she knew how to do...write.

She'd started out by writing about her life with Brendan and all their travels because she'd found it therapeutic. She'd missed Brendan a lot. Even though she'd known they'd made the right decision, it hadn't meant she had instantly stopped loving him.

She still could remember the day when one of the travel magazine editors she'd freelanced for had called asking if she had any travel content to sell. Riley had joked that the only thing she'd been writing lately was her own personal story about traveling with her ex-boyfriend.

The editor had been intrigued and asked her to send a sample. When she'd sent in a short story about one of her and Brendan's first trips, no one had been more surprised than Riley when the editor bought it for their online magazine and wanted more.

Looking back, Riley realized this was another one of those moments that had changed everything, where at the time she had no idea of what was to come.

The magazine editor had like Riley's stories so much she'd given Riley her own online column, which had led to a top New York City literary agent finding her and telling her that she needed to take the inspiration from traveling around the world with Brendan and start writing romance novels. That agent had been Margo, and this advice had led to her first publishing deal.

But while Brendan had inspired her first novel, her next novel had been inspired by Colin, and by novel number three, she was using the inspiration and love she had received from both Colin and Brendan to create handsome, sexy, interesting men that her heroines could eventually fall in love with, after learning how to truly open their own hearts and accept love.

This formula had won her awards until her last book, *Heart of Summer,* where she'd inadvertently let her last relationship with the third love of her life, Tyler, influence her writing—this time not in a good way.

Her relationship with Tyler had started with Riley's first trip to Manhattan to meet her new agent. They'd met at The

Royal, one of New York's hot spots for power lunches. They'd drunk ridiculously expensive wine and talked about what she'd wanted to do as an author. Riley had decided right then that if she was going to really make a run at a publishing career, she couldn't continue living with her mom in a sleepy little Florida beach town.

She also knew she'd still need to do some freelance writing to make ends meet, and the best place to network and pick up assignments was New York City, where all the top magazines, newspapers, and TV stations where.

Determined to make it work, she'd gone to New York with a positive attitude and a burning ambition to not only make her mark as an author but to find a way to make a good living. She was done with being broke and living the fly-by-the-seat-of-her-pants lifestyle she'd been living with Brendan.

Being surrounded by so many successful people in Manhattan had made Riley even more determined. She wanted power lunches at The Royal to be the norm, not the exception.

Margo had promised that she'd introduce Riley around when she relocated to New York, and Margo had kept her word. During Riley's first few months in Manhattan, she'd met some great guys through Margo, but when there had been no one special, she had decided the best relationship to invest in was with herself. So she focused on becoming a best-selling author.

When one of her books, *Summer Love Never Ends,* caught the eye of a Hollywood producer, that's when Margo had introduced her to Tyler, the third and last man she had ever truly loved.

She'd been attending a charity event with Margo at a posh Manhattan penthouse when Margo had insisted that they add a sharp entertainment attorney to their team to help handle any Hollywood inquiries. Of course, Margo already knew who she wanted, and he was at the party.

Tyler Caldwell, of the Bridgeport Caldwells, had just been featured in *Manhattan Magazine* as one of the "Top Forty Under Forty" New York City entertainment attorneys to watch. And people were watching, especially single women, because Tyler was as handsome as he was talented, and he quickly became one of Manhattan's most eligible bachelors.

When Riley had met him at the cocktail party, she'd been impressed with his professional resume, but she hadn't been so sure about his personality. She'd always liked confident men, but Tyler took confidence to a whole new level. Still, with Margo's urging, Riley had agreed to take a meeting with Tyler, which he'd ironically set up at The Royal.

As she had sat across from him during their power lunch, she'd discovered that they had more in common than she'd originally thought. He'd also grown up in Oregon, had gone to college in California, and had passion for travel. He was fascinated by some of the more exotic places she had visited like Burma, Thailand, Cambodia, and Bali.

They'd also talked about being single in the city that never sleeps, and Riley had been surprised to learn that despite what was written about him in the press, he rarely dated with his crazy busy work schedule. He'd told her he'd barely had time to make himself dinner, much less actually go out on a dinner date. He'd said that the women he'd dated sadly didn't have much tolerance of the fact that he always put work first and that an eighty-hour work week was his norm.

Of course, this lack of work-life balance had been something Riley could totally relate to.

Before Riley even knew how it happened, she had found herself totally relaxed and enjoying her time with Tyler. Neither of them had believed it when two hours had flown by and they hadn't even talked shop yet.

So when Tyler had asked her for a favor, to be his plus-one to a fancy cocktail party one of his clients was hosting, she'd agreed to go without a second thought. They'd even laughed about how they could help each other out and be each other's plus-ones when they had to attend these kinds of functions. That way they could avoid all those awkward questions about being single when they showed up alone.

And that's how it had all started. She had never intended to actually date Tyler, and she was fairly sure he'd say the same thing about her, but pretty soon they were being photographed together at all the most exclusive parties and being dubbed one of Manhattan's newest power couples.

She still laughed thinking about being part of any high-society power couple. She had gone from moving back in with her mom because she was flat broke, to living an opulent life in New York City, where power lunches, swanky cocktail parties, and elegant dinners were her new normal.

After Tyler had gotten promoted to partner at his law firm and upgraded to a penthouse apartment, she'd moved in with him, giving up her tiny studio and frugal lifestyle. At the time, her books had been selling better than ever, and Tyler had negotiated two Hollywood movie options for her, so she was making great money and living the life she thought she wanted.

Until it wasn't.

She honestly couldn't remember when things had taken a turn in their relationship. It hadn't been one big thing that happened. They had rarely argued, in large part because, in reality, they rarely saw each other. Tyler would leave for the gym at five in the morning and often not get home from work until almost midnight because he was always taking one client or another to dinner and drinks.

She hadn't minded. She'd understood that as an entertainment attorney a huge part of his job, with the kind of showbiz clients he had, was to entertain. At first, she'd gone to a lot of the dinners and parties with him. She'd had a blast living the kind of glamourous life she'd seen on reality TV shows. But when it had turned out the reality of her life had become very empty and superficial, Riley realized her perfect-on-paper relationship with Tyler was more like a business merger than a romantic relationship.

She'd also found her lavish lifestyle was impacting her writing. All the late-night parties meant she was sleeping in later, and her best time to write had always been the mornings. When she did finally carve out some time to write, it had felt forced and she hadn't been able to find her rhythm. She had tried to tell herself she was being too hard on herself and that what she was writing was fine. But deep down, she knew something had been missing. When she'd turned in her next first draft to her editor and her editor had questioned—for the first time—where the love was, where the passion was, Riley had known it was time she made some big changes and fast.

Her life with Tyler had run its course.

It had been an amazing ride. With Tyler, she had been accepted into the illusive and exclusive world of Manhattan's elite. It had opened a whole new world up to her, but with that world came at a price she was no longer willing to pay.

So she'd broken up with Tyler and moved to Scottsdale, Arizona, a place where she could reboot and refocus. She had gone there with Brendan once, on their way to a hiking trip in the Grand Canyon, and she had found Scottsdale to be incredibly peaceful. It was just what she'd needed at the time.

She'd actually been surprised by how much Tyler had resisted her decision at first. She'd figured he was already on the same page and that this breakup would be similar to the one with Brendan, but she'd been wrong. Tyler had argued, using all his lawyer skills, that they had a lifestyle most people would die for and that they were so compatible he couldn't imagine finding anyone else who would be such a great fit.

When she'd told him they both deserved more than just a great *fit* he still didn't get it. He'd been angry when she'd left for Arizona, and while he'd called several times trying to get her to reconsider, she'd known Tyler wasn't what she needed.

Instead, she'd thrown herself into rewriting the novel her editor hadn't been happy with at first and found new ways to add more heart into the story. Bu still, when *Heart of Summer* came out, it had bombed.

The readers who had written reviews were right. It was a love story that was missing the love, and for the first time she was scared, really scared, that she'd lost what had made her novels so special, and she didn't know how to get it back.

Riley was really counting on this Christmas Camp being the beginning of her comeback. The last thing she needed was the complication and confusion of her three exes showing up.

"I can't believe this is happening…" Riley didn't realize she'd said the words out loud until Caylee quickly responded.

"Oh, it's happening all right!" Caylee jumped in, not even trying to hide her enthusiasm. "So, of the three, there wasn't one you loved the most?"

Riley walked over to the dresser and picked up one of the Santas, then put it back down to join the other two.

"I don't know," Riley answered honestly. "They were all so different. They all brought something unique to my life when I needed it. Colin made me feel safe and loved, and I really needed that back then. But then Brendan brought out the daring side of me and taught me how to live in the moment."

"And with the last one? The lawyer?" Caylee asked.

Riley smiled and touched the neckline of her dress. "Tyler.

He loved dressing up like this. He showed me what it would be like to live a life of luxury where I didn't have to worry about money all the time. That gave me a different kind of freedom. With Tyler, I learned the power of success."

Caylee studied her. "Did you love the power or Tyler more?"

Riley gave Caylee a thoughtful look. "Good question. I know I should say Tyler, but if I'm honest, I really don't know."

"Well, it looks like you're going to have a chance to find out," Caylee said. "You're so lucky."

Riley shook her head, confused. "Lucky? How?"

"Think about it," Caylee said. "How many people get a second chance with someone they loved? You loved them all for a reason, but the timing wasn't right. Maybe now, for one of them, the timing is finally right, and your one true love is here. You just have to figure out which one of those guys could be your happily-ever-after."

Riley laughed a nervous laugh. "You make it all sound so easy."

"It shouldn't be that hard," Caylee countered. "It's Christmas. It's the time of year when everyone falls in love, and the three loves of your life are all here. Don't you think that's a sign? Don't you owe it to yourself to see if there's anything still there? You don't want to always wonder 'what if.'"

Riley knew Caylee was right about one thing. She didn't want to live with the dreaded "what if" hanging over her.

That meant she needed to talk to all three guys and see if there were still any sparks or if her ghosts of boyfriends past needed to stay right there—in the past.

Chapter Thirty

After Riley went back downstairs and rejoined the party, she spent about an hour making sure she talked to all the Christmas Campers. The whole time she could feel the eyes of Colin, Brendan, and Tyler on her.

Clearly, they weren't going anywhere.

When she spotted Luke talking with Brianna, laughing and having a great time, she looked away quickly. But apparently not fast enough because Luke caught her eye and walked over to her.

"Everything okay?" he asked. "Do you need anything?"

"No, everything's fine," Riley said. "I think everyone's having a great time."

"And what about your...*friends?*" Luke asked.

Riley looked over at Tyler, who was glued to his phone. "I think they're entertaining themselves. And about that, I really owe you an apology..."

Luke held up his hand. "It's okay."

"No," Riley said, "It's not okay. I totally jumped to conclusions in blaming you. You didn't deserve that. I was in shock and freaking out, but that's still no excuse. You've done nothing but work hard to make this event a success. I had no right to treat you like that. I hope you can forgive me?"

"Apology accepted," Luke said. "I would have freaked out,

too, if all my old girlfriends had showed up."

Riley arched one eyebrow. "Would they have filled the room?"

Luke laughed. "Maybe a corner or two."

They shared a smile.

"But seriously, Riley," Luke said, taking her hand and looking into her eyes. "It's Christmastime, and there's nothing I want more than this Christmas Camp to be a success for you."

Riley was touched. "And I want the same for you and your mom. We're in this together."

Luke gave her hand an encouraging squeeze. "We sure are."

The moment was interrupted when Brianna came over holding two glasses of Champagne and handed one to Luke.

"I got you a new glass," Brianna said, smiling up at Luke. "We have so much to celebrate."

When Luke let go of Riley's hand, it suddenly felt very cold.

"Thank you," he said as he took the glass. "Riley, I haven't had a chance to introduce you to Brianna yet. She's—"

"The realtor," Riley finished for him.

Brianna linked arms with Luke. "And a little more than that, but yes, I'm a realtor. Has Luke told you the good news?"

Riley fought to keep smiling. She didn't like the possessive tone of Brianna's voice.

"Not yet," Luke said. "This is her big night. I want to focus on that."

Riley looked from Brianna to Luke. "Well, don't keep me in suspense. What's the good news?"

"It looks like I found a buyer for the lodge," Brianna jumped in, unable to contain her excitement. "Isn't that amazing?"

Riley's eyes flew to Luke's but was surprised he didn't look half as excited at Brianna did.

"That *is* amazing," Riley agreed. "Isn't it?" She directed her question to Luke.

But Brianna answered. "We're getting full asking price, so yes, it's a very good thing." She clinked her Champagne glass to Luke's.

"Nothing is set in stone," he said. "I'm not going to jump the gun and start celebrating yet. There's a long way to go from interest to signing final paperwork, and right now, this weekend, I need to focus on Christmas Camp."

"It's already a success," Brianna said. "It's trending on social media after that picture was posted of Riley with her three ex-boyfriends."

"Wait, what?" Riley asked, almost choking on her words. "What picture?"

Brianna got out her phone and showed Riley a picture where Colin, Brendan, and Tyler were all standing in front of her and she had a look of pure shock on her face.

Riley felt blindsided. "Where did that picture come from?"

Then she knew. She whipped around, and her eyes zeroed in on Paul. He was drinking a glass of Champagne.

As she marched over to Paul, she didn't even pretend everything was okay.

"Hey, what's up?" he asked as she approached, but his smile quickly faded when he saw her expression.

"Why don't you tell me," Riley said, locking eyes with him. She pointed at his camera. "Did you get some good pictures tonight?"

"Yes," Paul said. His voice was hesitant.

"Good, because those are the only photos you'll be getting. You're fired," Riley said.

Paul put down his Champagne. "Look, Riley, if it's about the picture I sent Mike, I told him not to give it out to anyone until you approved it," he said. "I know, I know. I heard it's gone viral, but you need to talk to Mike about that."

"No," Riley said, stepping even closer to him until he took a step back. "I'm talking to you about it because we had an agreement that I would have photo approval, and you *know* I didn't approve this."

Paul held up his hand like he was trying to defend himself. "I know, but Mike texted and wanted to know how it was going, and I told him there was this huge surprise with your exes showing up and how it would be great for social media. But I also said we should *all* talk about how to handle the story. When he asked me to send a picture just to see the guys, I didn't know he'd run with it."

Riley laughed. "Really, Paul? You didn't know Mike would run with it? This is *Mike* we're talking about. Even if you've only worked with him for a second, you know how he is."

"Okay, yes, I know," Paul said. "But I also saw other Christmas Campers posting the same pictures, and I thought Mike was right that we should be the one to break the story before a news outlet saw one of the Christmas Campers' posts."

"You should have talked to me first," Riley said.

"I tried to find you, but you had disappeared with Caylee," Paul replied. "You know how fast this kind of thing blows up, so I thought by telling Mike I was doing my job and protecting you. Look, I was wrong. I get it. If you want me to leave, I will, but Mike will just send someone else who will do the exact same thing. Riley, I promise you, going forward, no matter what happens, I'll make sure I show you everything before I sent it to Mike."

Riley crossed her arms in front of her chest. "How do I know I can trust you?"

Caylee appeared. "Paul's a lot of things, but he's not a liar."

Riley and Paul both looked surprised.

"How much did you overhear?" Riley asked her.

"Most of it," Caylee answered.

"So you're saying I can trust him?" Riley asked Caylee.

Caylee locked eyes with Paul. "Yes, I believe you can trust him."

"Thank you, Caylee," Paul said.

"Don't thank me," she said. "Just don't let Riley down again, or I'll make sure you never freelance for anyone in this state again. Understood?"

Paul opened his mouth like he was going to say something but then closed it. Instead, he answered Caylee with nod.

Caylee linked arms with Riley. "Now, you need to come with me. Some Christmas Campers are asking for you."

As they walked off together, Riley gave Caylee a curious look. "Now, I really need to hear this story about you and Paul."

Caylee just keep her eyes straight ahead. "No. What you *need* is time with our Christmas Campers.

As Riley spent the next hour with their guests, she was amazed at how friendly and genuine everyone was. The Christmas Campers' excitement and enthusiasm was exactly what she needed to take her mind off her personal life being blasted all over the internet.

When everyone started calling it a night and going upstairs, Riley finally had the chance to gather her exes together over by the fireplace. Colin sat down on the couch, Brendan took a chair, and Tyler took another chair. When she remained standing, Comet came over and sat down next to her, looking up at her with his big brown eyes.

She took a deep breath. She everyone's full attention. Butterflies fluttered in her stomach when she saw her three handsome exes all staring back at her.

"Well, this is awkward," she said with a little laugh, hoping to break the ice.

When the guys didn't laugh, she rushed on. "I'm guessing by now you all have gotten to know each other?"

Tyler frowned. He clearly wasn't amused. "If you mean, do we all know we're your ex-boyfriends, yes. We figured that out."

Brendan laughed. "This is pretty crazy."

"In the TV interview you said you had one great love of your life," Colin said. "Apparently, we all thought you were talking about us."

Brendan laughed again. "So crazy."

No one else was laughing.

Tyler stood up. "So, Riley, we're all busy. We know you're busy with this publicity event, so just tell us which of us you were talking about, and the other two will leave. Right, guys?"

"We never meant to disrupt your Christmas Camp," Colin said, also standing up.

"Or stress you out," Brendan added as he stood, too.

"Just tell us," Tyler said, never taking his eyes of Riley's. "Who were you talking about?"

Riley sat down. "None of you," she said.

All the guys looked confused.

She took another deep breath. "And all of you."

All three guys sat back down.

"What do you mean?" Brendan asked.

Colin gave her a confused look. "How could you be talking about all three of us?"

Tyler locked eyes with Riley. "But you really were talking about all three of us, weren't you?"

Riley nodded. "I was so frazzled when that guy put me on the spot during the live interview. What I'd meant to say was that my novels were inspired by *all* the great loves in my life.

All, as in more than one, not just one person."

Brendan and Colin looked at each other, then they both looked at Tyler.

"So you really did mean all three of us?" Colin asked.

"Unless there are more than three of us," Brendan said. "Is anyone else going to be showing up?"

This had Riley laughing for the first time. "I sure hope not," she said. "You three are it."

"This is nuts," Colin said with a sigh.

Riley gave him a sympathetic look. "I know, and I'm really that the interview confused all three of you. I know it confused a lot of people…"

"You can say that again," Tyler said.

Riley rung her hands together. "So, now that you know about the mix-up you can all go back to your normal lives."

"But the three of us were the great loves of your life, right?" Colin asked.

"Yes." She smiled for the first time. It was a genuine smile. "I will always be thankful that I had each of you in my life."

Colin got up and walked over to her and took her hand and looked into her eyes.

"Riley, I'm here because when I saw that interview, I realized I've never truly stopped loving you, and if there was a chance to rekindle that love, I wanted to try," Colin said. "Yes, I thought you were talking about me, about us, in that interview, and I get that there are two other guys here, but I know what we had was real. The timing was just off back then, but I'm here now. So, I'd like to stay to see what could happen. I already planned a special date for us for tonight, if you're up for giving us another try."

At that moment, everything she had loved about Colin came rushing back. His sincerity, his kindness, his quiet confidence, his ability to always share his feelings. When she looked into his eyes, she remembered their love and how wonderful it had been.

But before she could answer, Brendan came over and surprised her by taking her other hand. "I'm in, too, Riley. I don't want to leave," Brendan said. He looked at Colin. "I don't have a date already planned for tonight, but I do have a special breakfast planned for us before you start your camp tomorrow. We had a good thing. I'd like to see if we could get that back."

"Hold on," Tyler said, joining them. He looked at Colin and Brendan, who were still holding Riley's hands, and frowned. "Look, you both are part of Riley's past. You dated a long time ago. Riley and I just dated."

"A few *years* ago," Riley corrected him.

"Yes," Tyler said, "but I'm not someone you dated in college when you didn't even know who you were or what you wanted yet." He looked at Colin. "No offense."

"Some taken," Colin said. He still wasn't letting go of Riley's hand.

Tyler looked into Riley's eyes. "Riley, what I mean is, I know who you are *now,* and we were good together. We made a great team. We had some things to work on, sure, but what couple doesn't? I still love you, and I think you still could love me."

"Wow, going big and throwing out the *L* word," Brendan said as he looked at Tyler.

"Tyler, what are you saying?" Riley asked, her head spinning.

Tyler gave Colin and Brendan a confident look. "I'm saying that I'm not going anywhere until I've had a chance to spend some time with you. I've also planned a special date for us and think it will show you that we're meant to be together."

Riley, dazed, looked from one guy to another. She gently let go of Colin's and Brendan's hands and rubbed her hands together. One at a time, she looked at each of them.

"Are you *all* saying you want to stay?" Riley asked thinking, *please tell me this is not happening...*

"Yes," Tyler said.

Brendan nodded. "Totally."

"Without a doubt," Colin said. "And our date can start right away. It's all set up."

Riley gave them a questioning look. "These dates you're all talking about, how did you even plan them? You all just got here."

"Luke," they all said at the same time.

Riley's eyes widened. "Luke?"

"He was great," Brendan said. "He helped with everything."

"He did," Colin agreed.

"Unbelievable," Riley said as her reality continued to spin out of control.

"I asked him to keep it a secret," Colin said. "I wanted to surprise you."

Brendan laughed. "Same."

Tyler just nodded.

Colin smiled his most charming smile. "So what do you say? I know this has all been a lot, but we're all here. We've all planned special dates for you. Why not go on the dates and see how you feel? See if there's still a spark with any of us. Think of it as if you're on *The Bachelorette* and we've all planned these one-on-one dates for you, and you can decide who to give the rose to at the end."

Riley could only laugh. *Leave it to Colin, the movie producer, to come with* The Bachelorette *reality TV analogy.*

She looked at Brendan and Tyler. "Are you guys still really

wanting to do this?"

"Sure," Brendan said.

When the two guys looked at Tyler, he flashed them a confident smile. "The dates are already planned," Tyler said. "I say we see this through."

Colin jumped back in. "Look, I know it's crazy, but the only thing crazier would be for all of us to go home and never know."

"You could let us know the last night of Christmas Camp, at the dance, after you've had some time to spend with each of us," Brendan said.

They were all staring at her.

When Riley looked down at Comet, he was gazing up at her, too.

She exhaled slowly. "Okay," she said, already wondering what in the world she was getting herself into. Speed dating with her three exes at Christmas Camp while working to save her career and pretending she's Miss Christmas when she didn't even celebrate the holiday… What could possibly go wrong except *everything?*

"Fantastic!" Colin said, giving her a big hug. "So my date's first. It's super casual as I knew you'd be tired tonight. So we're just going to relax. You can change into something comfortable—sweats, jeans, whatever you want—and meet me in my room, in say, a half hour. Does that work for you?"

"Your room?" Tyler questioned.

Colin laughed. "Come on, it's not like that. I just wanted somewhere private where we could talk."

"It's fine," Riley said. "I'll meet you in your room. Where are you?"

"The Alpine suite," Colin said.

Brendan stepped forward and gave Riley a hug. "And for our date, meet downstairs at six in the morning and be dressed for an adventure."

Riley laughed. "Why am I not surprised? You're always chasing an adventure."

"Always," he said. "And our best one together is yet to come."

Riley's heart beat a little faster as she remembered the adrenalin rush she'd get when spending time with Brendan. She'd loved that feeling, and she'd missed it over the years.

While Brendan and Colin were smiling, Tyler didn't look so pleased. He raked his fingers through his hair.

"Riley, are you sure you want to do this?" he asked. "You don't have to go through all this. I know you don't want to hurt anyone's feelings, but shouldn't you be focusing on your Christmas Camp and writing your next novel? You always told me your work had to come first."

"You're right, Tyler. I always did say that," Riley agreed, "because I thought it had to, but a lot has changed in the past few years and now I'm not so sure. I broke up with you to concentrate on my writing, but then I couldn't write and my next book crashed and burned. Everyone said it was missing its heart. I'm realizing that I've spent so much time writing other people's love stories that I haven't been living my own life, and that's showing up in my writing."

Tyler arched an eyebrow. "Are you saying…"

Brendan smiled and jumped in. "I think she's saying she's down for these dates, aren't you, Riley? Because maybe they'll help you with your writing, give you some new inspiration."

All three guys waited for her answer.

"So what do you say?" Colin asked hopefully.

"Honestly," Riley said, "I don't know. This is all a lot to take in. I don't know what I'm supposed to do. I just know I don't want to have any regrets, any 'what ifs.'"

"Exactly," Colin said. "Neither do I."

"None of us do," Tyler said.

"Okay, then it's settled," Riley said. "Colin, I have to make a quick call first, then I'll meet you in your room. Brendan, I'll see you in the morning, and Tyler, we'll have our date tomorrow night. I hope you all understand that the rest of the time, I really need to concentrate on my guests. They have to come first."

"We understand," Colin said. "We can stay out of the way, right, guys?"

"Sure," Brendan said.

"Not a problem," Tyler agreed.

"Great, then it's a plan," Riley said. She quickly hugged each of them. "I'll see you later."

Riley was still trying to wrap her head around everything that had happened when she got back to her room, but before she could do anything, she needed to make an important call.

She called Mike on FaceTime because she wanted him to see her face-to-face and know how serious she was. The call didn't take long.

From the moment Mike answered, she had been in charge. She'd told Mike that while she couldn't control what was already out there in social media, she could control what her own publicist covered, a publicist *she* paid. And if he wanted to keep his job, he would pass everything by her from now on, no matter how small, before ever posting a picture or facts about her personal life again.

Mike had pushed back at first but had finally backed down when she promised that when Christmas Camp was all over, if there was something *relevant* to share about her personal life, like if she got back together with one of her old boyfriends, *then* she would talk about it, but only in the way she saw fit. When he'd asked if she thought that was really possible, for her to get back together with one of her exes, she told him the truth. She honestly didn't know. But she should have an answer by the end of Christmas Camp.

She had only just hung up with Mike when Margo popped up on FaceTime. Before she could even say hello, Margo started in.

"Riley, is this true that all three of your exes showed up at Christmas Camp?" Margo asked, looking excited.

"You saw the picture," Riley said. It was statement not a question.

"Yes, but I also know Mike, so I didn't know exactly what I was seeing," Margo said. "That's why I'm calling. Tell me this is true because it would be amazing."

"Amazing for me," Riley asked, "or for publicity?"

"They're one in the same," Margo said quickly. "So it's true?"

Riley took a deep breath. "Yes, it's true."

Margo's smile lit up the screen. "Riley, why aren't you more excited about this?"

"Because this is my life we're talking about, not just some publicity stunt," Riley responded.

"Hey, you did this," Margo shot back. "Mike said these guys heard you talking on the news and all thought you were talking about them as being your one true love. I think this is going to be the best thing that's happened to you yet. You've been running on empty. That's why your books are falling flat. This way you can refuel your tank."

Riley leaned in closer to her computer screen and gave Margo a confused look. "What are you talking about, running on empty, refueling? I'm not a car."

"Okay, and I'm not the one who's good with words, you are. What I'm trying to say is that when you started writing romance novels, they were inspired by your travels with Brendan. Then you used him and your college boyfriend as inspiration for your next novels, and then eventually Tyler. But lately the love hasn't been in your love stories. You're running empty on love, and you need to refuel that tank to move forward. Like a car needs gas, you need love. There, did I explain it better this time?"

Riley cringed. "So now I'm an empty gas tank? Lovely visual."

"You know what I mean," Margo said.

Riley sat up straighter. "Yes, I know what you're trying to say. All this could be good for my writing."

"Exactly," Margo said, sounding pleased. "I just want what's best for you, professionally and personally."

"I gotta go," Riley said. "I have a date with Colin. I'll keep you posted."

"And keep an open heart," Margo said. "Just like in the stories you write. You always say you have to have an open heart to find love. Good luck."

When Riley hung up, she fell back onto her bed and stared up at the ceiling of white twinkling lights. She wondered if there were any fairy tales where the heroine got to have three Prince Charmings.

She sat back up again. She needed to go.

Colin was waiting for her, for their first date.

Chapter Thirty-One

It was almost midnight by the time she finished her date with Colin. She couldn't believe how fast the hours had flown by and how it easy it was to pick up right where they'd left off in college.

She was so touched by all the trouble he had gone to, to set up the perfect date down memory lane. It was just like the movie nights they always did in college together.

Beyond all the beautiful Christmas decorations that were already in the room, he'd added dozens of white candles, saying it was the perfect mood lighting to watch their movie. She'd been impressed, remembering how they use to do the same thing in college, only back then, having very little money, they'd used some cheap battery-operated imitation candles that were always breaking.

She loved that he'd planned a movie night. It brought back so many great memories of all the romantic comedy classics they'd watched together like *When Harry Met Sally, Sleepless in Seattle,* and *Notting Hill.* He'd reminded her that during their first year in college, she had talked about how cool it would be to write stories like that, and now here she was doing it.

However, one thing that had caught her off guard was the movies he'd selected. They were all Christmas movies.

While he'd remembered that she wasn't a Christmas movie

fan, he figured that now that she was hosting a Christmas Camp and writing a Christmas novel, they could finally celebrate Christmas together.

When he'd asked her to pick the movie, she didn't have a clue so she told him he could decide. He picked *It's a Wonderful Life,* telling her that the angel, Clarence, was one of his all-time favorite characters.

She'd also been touched and impressed that Colin had remembered all her favorite movie foods, from chocolate-covered peanuts to barbeque potato chips to gummy bears and Milk Duds. The only thing he'd changed was replacing the cheap wine they'd drunk in college with a top-rated bottle of Champagne. He'd even brought an old photo album he'd kept of them that highlighted their four years together.

The night had been filled with laughter as they relived old memories. They'd had such a great time talking and catching up that they'd never even gotten around to watching the movie.

Even when Riley had realized it was almost midnight, she hadn't wanted the night to end. With Colin, she felt like she could totally relax and be herself. He was everything she remembered loving and more. Now, instead of a college student talking about his dreams, he had made those dreams come true and was a successful movie producer who appeared to have found a way to still be genuine instead of getting caught up a world that usually rewarded the superficial.

"I have something for you," Colin said, surprising her. "A Christmas present."

"But it's not Christmas yet," Riley said with a laugh.

When he handed her a little white jewelry-sized box with a big, red satin bow, Riley became nervous.

"Colin, you really shouldn't have gotten me anything..."

"It's just something small. I promise," Colin said. "Open

it."

Riley tentatively opened the box and smiled when she saw what was inside. She held up a beautiful red, heart-shaped glass Christmas ornament. It was just like the one he'd given her in college their first Christmas together when she'd decided to stay at school and work but had encouraged him to go home and see his parents. He hadn't wanted to leave her. When he had given her the heart ornament, he'd told her that she would always have his heart at Christmas, whether they were together or not.

He really had thought of everything.

"Do you remember?" he asked.

When she looked into his eyes, what she remembered all the reasons she'd loved him. He was kind and thoughtful, romantic and caring. He was the kind of guy any girl would be lucky to have. She felt her own heart beat faster as she held the heart ornament up to the light.

"I remember."

When Colin leaned in to kiss her, she leaned in, too, until Comet started barking outside the door, interrupting the moment.

Flustered by her feelings, Riley got up quickly. "I'm sorry. I have to see what's wrong with Comet."

Colin stood up, too, and they both went to the door.

When Riley opened it, Comet took off running down the hall.

Riley gave Colin an apologetic look.

"Go." Colin laughed. "We have lots of time."

It was just another reason Riley remembered loving Colin. He always understood.

After she chased Comet downstairs, she found him waiting by the front door.

"You want go for a walk?" Riley asked, and as soon as she said *walk,* Comet barked.

"Shh," she whispered and leaned down to give him a hug. "My bad. I shouldn't have said the *W* word. But we don't want to wake anyone up so if I agree to this wa—" Riley caught herself just in time. "If I agree to take you out, then you have to be a good and not bark. Deal?"

Comet wagged his tail and spun around once.

Riley laughed. "Okay, just hold on. I have to get my coat."

A couple of minutes later, Riley felt invigorated as she breathed in the cool, crisp air and admired the frosty landscape as she walked Comet down to the lake. Actually, the truth was, Comet was walking her down to the lake, and he was in a hurry.

"Slow down," she told Comet. "It's slippery out here."

Comet somehow took that as a cue to speed up.

Riley laughed as she tried to keep up without falling.

They were just arriving down by the lake when Riley saw Luke and Caylee stringing up some more Christmas lights on one of the trees along the shoreline.

"Hey, guys. What's going on?" she called out. "You know it's past midnight? Even decorating elves have to sleep sometimes."

Surprised, they both turned around to look at her.

"What are you two doing down here?" Luke asked. "I thought you were on a date."

"I was," Riley said, "but Comet had other ideas."

Comet looked up at her and wagged his tail.

Riley looked around, taking in all the Christmas lights.

"What are you two, the Christmas light fairies who put up more lights while everyone sleeps?"

Caylee laughed. "I like that idea. You should use it in one of your books. Christmas light fairies."

Riley laughed. "Maybe I will."

"And will you use three ex-boyfriends showing up to try to win back their old girlfriend?" Caylee asked with a mischievous twinkle in her eyes.

"No, I will not be using that crazy storyline," Riley said.

"They say truth is stranger than fiction," Luke added.

"Well, I'll agree with the strange part," Riley said.

"Well, for what it's worth, I still think everything went great," Caylee said. "Everyone seemed to be having a fabulous time. The Christmas Campers all love you and love Christmas and seem really happy to be here."

Riley turned to Luke. "What did you think?" As she asked the question, she realized how much it mattered to her what Luke thought.

Luke nodded. "I think Caylee's right. Everyone seemed to enjoy themselves, and that's what matters most, right?"

Riley nodded. "Right."

"Are *you* okay, is the big question," Caylee said. "Are you going to be able to do this with your three boyfriends here?"

"*Ex*-boyfriends," Riley quickly corrected her. "I've just talked to them, and we're good. It's going to be fine. They're going to do their own thing, and I'm going to do Christmas Camp."

"Great," Caylee said as she handed Riley her lights and took Comet's leash. "Then you're now officially on lights duty. It looks like the snowstorm blew some of them off so we're just replacing them. I need to check with Maryanne to make sure everything's ready for tomorrow."

Before Riley could protest, Caylee was already heading

back to the lodge with Comet.

Riley held the tangle of lights up that Caylee had given her. "So what do you want me to do with these?" she asked Luke.

"Find a place that needs them and go for it," Luke said.

He'd already gone back to work putting up the lights he was holding.

When Riley stared at the tree and just stood there, Luke glanced back at her. "Anything wrong?" he asked.

Riley wasn't about to confess that she'd never put up lights before. "Nope. All good." Still, she didn't move.

"You can start on this side," Luke said, pointing out a spot that didn't have any lights yet.

"Got it," Riley said as she rushed over to the tree. She watched what Luke was doing and tried to copy him. *How hard can it be?* she asked herself.

When she was done, she proudly stood back to survey her work. "Nice," she said, excited.

Then a gust of wind blew all her lights off the tree.

Luke laughed.

Riley didn't. "What happened?"

"You did great," Luke said, "but with the wind out here, you really need to put them deeper into the tree and kind of hook the lights around the branches. Like this." Luke picked up her lights and started stringing them back on the tree.

"See?" Luke said. "This is what you do with the branches…"

At the same time as Riley leaned in to get a better look, Luke turned around to face her. They were so close Riley could feel his breath on her cheek. Their eyes locked.

The way her heart raced confused her even more than the lights did.

They both stepped back at the same time.

"You're obviously the pro," Riley said quickly as she

regrouped. "Maybe I should just let you do this."

She looked over to the Christmas Lake Christmas tree. Its sparkling lights were perfect. "So who is going to watch out for your tree on the lake when you sell this place?"

Luke stuffed his hands into his coat pocket as he followed her gaze.

"That's a good question," he said. "I hope the next person who buys it will keep up the tradition. It means a lot to a lot of people."

"Will you miss this?" Riley asked.

"Putting up lights?" Luke asked.

When Riley gave him a look, he smiled back at her. "You mean, will I miss this when we sell the lodge?" Luke said.

Riley nodded. "It seems like you really love it here."

When Luke sat down on the little bench by the trees, Riley joined him.

"I grew up here," Luke said. "I have so many good memories here, but I agree with my mom, it's too much for her to handle. It's time to sell."

"Have you ever thought about running it yourself?" Riley asked.

Luke laughed. "A long time ago, but so many things have changed, and with the Skyline Resort over in the next community, the lodge can't compete anymore. People want all the new fancy amenities, a swimming pool, an ice rink, a health club, a spa."

"Wait, they have a spa?" Riley asked, only half-kidding.

Luke laughed. "See what I mean?"

"But seriously, couldn't you turn this into one of your Green-friendly properties?" Riley asked. "You said this is where you were first inspired to do something to help protect the environment. Why not start right here at the lodge? That Skyline Resort might have a lot of bells and whistles, but if you could turn this into a Green property that would get a lot of attention. I know a lot of people who would come to stay just to support this kind of healthier living."

Luke gave her a surprised look.

"What?" Riley asked.

"Nothing," Luke said. "It's just that years ago I had thought about doing exactly what you're saying, even before the Skyline Resort was built, but at the time, my dad didn't want to make any changes."

"Maybe now is the time," Riley said. "It's never too late to follow a dream."

Luke laughed. "Did you write that in one of your books?"

Riley smiled back at him. "No, but maybe I should."

"Speaking of your books and your inspiration for your stories, where are your boyfriends?" Luke asked. "I'm surprised they let you out of their sight. They seem very…"

"Loyal?" Riley offered.

"*Determined* was the word I was looking for," Luke said.

"Oh, that's right," Riley said. "They told me you helped them plan all these special dates. Didn't you think it was weird that three guys wanted to plan dates with me?"

"The part about guys wanting to go on dates with you, I didn't think that was weird at all, Luke said. "You're great. Who wouldn't want to go on a date with you…?"

Riley's eyes flew to Luke's face to see if he was being sarcastic, but he looked sincere.

"But," Luke continued.

Riley knew there would be a *but*…

"The part about all three guys saying they were your boyfriend was a little weird," Luke said with a laugh. "But, hey, not my business how many boyfriends you have."

Riley gave him a look. "I don't have three boyfriends. They're all from my past."

"So you told them all to go home?" Luke asked.

Riley kept looking out at the Christmas tree on the lake. "Uh, no... They're staying."

"So you're going on the dates," Luke said. It was a statement not a question.

"I am," Riley said, "It's the only way I'll really know..."

"Know what?" Luke asked as he turned to face her.

Riley looked into his eyes. "If there's still something there. I loved them all once. They're all three great guys."

"So you're thinking you could love one of them again?" Luke's expression was impossible to read.

"Maybe?" Riley said. "I mean, do you ever really get over someone you loved? Now that the timing is different, maybe there's a chance. I write love stories about second chances all the time. Anything's possible..."

"Especially at Christmas," Luke finished for her.

When Riley looked back at the Christmas Lake Christmas tree all she could think about was that this Christmas had been full of nothing but surprises so far. She just wasn't sure yet if they were good surprises or not.

She shivered but not just from the cold.

Luke noticed, took off his scarf, and wrapped it around her. "We should go. The wind's picking up."

Riley looked into his eyes. "I'm fine. I don't need an extra scarf. I don't want you to get cold..."

Luke got up. "Don't worry about me. I can take care of myself. Let's go."

As they walked toward the lodge together, they walked in silence.

"You better get some rest," Luke said when they got closer. "You have a big day tomorrow."

"*We* have a big day tomorrow. It's our first full day of Christmas Camp," Riley said, smiling back at him.

"And you have a six o'clock adventure date," Luke reminded her. He checked his cell phone. "That's starting in less than six hours."

"So what am I going to be doing?" Riley asked. "Since you helped plan all these dates, you can give me a heads-up."

"Oh no. This was all supposed to be a surprise so you're on your own," Luke said.

"I don't like surprises," Riley said.

Luke laughed. "Well, maybe you should have told your boyfriend's that,"

"They're not my boyfriends," Riley said.

Luke laughed. "Yet they're all still here." He headed for the side of the lodge. "I'm just going to check a few more lights. I'll see you in the morning."

"Good night," Riley called out as she watched Luke disappear around the corner.

She was about to walk up to the front door when she remembered the singing bear and did a big detour around it.

The last thing she needed to do was wake up all the Christmas Campers with "We Wish You a BEARy Christmas."

Chapter Thirty-Two

It was still dark out when Riley woke up to the sound of Comet barking. Only this time, she quickly realized Comet wasn't outside her bedroom door. He was outside her window.

She threw off her covers and ran over to the window to see what was going on. When she looked outside and saw Brendan and Comet playing in the snow, she couldn't help but laugh. Brendan was throwing snowballs at Comet, and Comet was trying to catch them in his mouth.

When Brendan looked up and saw her, she waved. He smiled and he motioned for her to come down.

Riley checked the time on her phone. It was almost five thirty, and she had her date with Brendan at six. Even though she'd only gone to bed a few hours earlier, she was excited for her adventure with Brendan.

Twenty minutes and a quick shower later, she was ready to go. She remembered Brendan warning her to dress warmly and she'd seen him outside in his ski gear, so she was wearing her new ski pants and coat, along with her red hat and gloves. When she went to grab her scarf, too, Luke's white scarf was twisted up with it from when he'd put it on her last night. She smiled as she untangled the two scarves, and she brought Luke's scarf to her face where she'd inhaled the scent of his clean, earthy cologne.

As soon as she got downstairs, Comet came running over to her. She leaned down to give him a hug, and she brushed some snow off his nose.

"Well, you look like you've been having some fun," she said to Comet. "But you can't bark so early in the morning. You'll wake everyone up." Riley looked up at Brendan.

"I know," Brendan said. "It was my fault. I came downstairs to get everything ready for us, and Comet was sitting by the door. He's pretty impossible to say no to."

Riley laughed as she continued to pet him. "Yes, he is."

Brendan picked up a backpack off the couch. "So, I have everything we need, if you're ready to go."

Riley eyed the backpack. "I thought you said this was a breakfast date. I hope you have food in there. I'm starving."

Brendan laughed. "Don't worry. I know you need to eat breakfast or you get hangry."

Riley laughed. "Lucky that you remembered that. In that case, I'm ready."

"Let's do this," Brendan said as he slung the backpack over his shoulder.

For the next two hours, Brendan did exactly as he'd promised and took her on an adventure. He reminded her of what it had been like when they'd traveled the world together, how they'd always get up for the sunrise whenever they were in a new place.

For this sunrise, Brendan had planned a snowshoeing trip up to Christmas Lake Point. Riley laughed when Brendan told her that Luke had been the one to suggest snowshoeing, saying how much she loved it.

At least this time she was able to get the snowshoes on.

It was tricky getting up to the lookout with all the fresh powder, but by working together, they'd made it just in time to toast the sunrise with the mimosas Brendan had brought along. A sunrise toast was another one of their favorite travel traditions.

For breakfast, Brendan had packed her favorite granola bars and also some homemade croissants and fresh fruit Maryanne had put together for him. It was the perfect picnic. Riley smiled. It had been a long time since she'd done something like this—too long.

And Brendan was as fun-loving as she'd always remembered him. She liked that he also now had a more mature side, sharing with her how he'd turned his passion for traveling into a successful, profitable business. He now owned his own touring company, with almost a hundred tour guides that did tours all around the world.

As she listened to the amazing places he'd traveled to, she had to admit she was jealous. She'd put aside her love of travel to do what she thought was the right thing, to buckle down and be an adult and get a real job. Now, listening to how happy Brendan was, she wondered if she'd made the right decision in giving up one of her true passions and walking away from Brendan.

He also wanted to hear all about her life as an author and had asked a bunch of questions, seeming genuinely interested in her writing process. He'd admitted that he'd followed her over the years, keeping track of her success. He admired her gutsy move to start over and move to New York to be an author.

It had been funny hearing him say that because Riley had never thought it was gusty. She had just thought it was survival. She liked Brendan's version better.

After their sunrise toast and breakfast, Brendan had another surprise for her.

Riley watched with curiosity as he pulled a leather pouch from his backpack. When he unzipped it, Riley saw a folding saw, and she backed away a little.

"Uh, what are you planning to do with that? Tell me this date isn't going to have a bad ending," she joked.

Brendan laughed. "You and your imagination. No, actually, I thought this could help us start a new Christmas tradition."

Riley's eyebrows arched. "Really?"

"Yeah," Brendan said. "I was thinking about when we dated, and one of the things I regretted is that we never really celebrated Christmas together."

"We were together at Christmas," Riley said.

"We were together, but we didn't celebrate it," Brendan corrected her. "We were always traveling, and you said you weren't into Christmas so we never put up a Christmas tree or did anything like that." Brendan held up the saw. "So I thought we'd change that."

Riley gave him a skeptical look. "What are you thinking?"

"That we needed to get a Christmas tree together," Brendan answered with a grin.

Riley didn't even pretend that she thought it was a good idea.

"We can't do that," she said with conviction.

"Why not?" Brendan asked.

"We can't cut down any of these trees. They're Luke's family's."

Brendan laughed as he looked around. "And there are hundreds of them. I'm sure he won't mind."

Riley shook her head. "Actually, I think he would. He's all about conservation and protecting the environment, and they don't even cut down their own tree at Christmas. Did you see the one in the lodge? It's a live tree so it can be replanted."

Brendan looked impressed. "Okay, that's pretty cool." He looked around and walked over to small tree. "Then how about we get this one? I can come back later and dig it up, and it can be replanted later, too. Then we can still have our first Christmas tree together. What do you say?"

When Brendan smiled back at her, he was impossible to resist.

Riley laughed. "I would say that you haven't changed a bit. You still don't take no for an answer."

Brendan stepped closer to her and looked into her eyes. "Not when it's something I care about and want." He put the saw in his backpack and pulled out a small wooden box with a red bow on it. He handed it to her.

Riley felt her heart race. "What is it?" she asked in breathless voice.

"Open it." Brendan smiled at her.

Riley slowly opened the box and held up an antique bronze compass. She read the inscription on it...

So you can always find your way back to me...

The beautiful words brought tears to her eyes.

"Riley, I know our paths went different ways, but I've never stopped loving you," Brendan said. "When I saw that interview, it reminded me that true love deserves a second chance. I still think we could have a lifetime of adventures together. We could travel like we used to, only now you can write your novels using inspiration from all the amazing places we'd visit. Together, we could have it all—adventure, travel, successful careers, and most of all, love. I think we owe it to ourselves to try and find out if we could do this. What do you think?"

She responded by giving him a heartfelt hug, and at that

moment, she didn't want to ever let go. When she did finally, slowly, pull away, Brendan took her hands in his. He was about to kiss her when a huge pile of snow fell off a tree branch above them, making them both jump back in surprise.

They were laughing and brushing the snow off each other when Riley got a text from Luke checking to make sure they were on their way back. Some of the Christmas Campers were up early and asking about her.

"We have to go," Riley told Brendan.

"To be continued?" Brendan asked.

Riley smiled back at him and nodded. "To be continued."

When they got back to the lodge, Brendan reminded her of the compass and said he'd always be there for her no matter what she decided.

As she walked away from him, the only thing she knew was that she didn't want to lose him again. He added something to her life that she hadn't realized she truly missed until now.

For the rest of the day, Riley didn't have time to think about her incredible dates with Colin and Brendan because she was completely consumed with all things Christmas Camp.

She was thankful the guys had agreed to let her focus on her Christmas Campers and catch up with her later when she had free time.

After she'd gotten back to the lodge, she joined the Christmas Campers for their breakfast. Right after breakfast, they started their first activity with Luke giving a tour of the town of Christmas Lake. When he shared some of the town's history, including the story of the Christmas Lake Angel, every one of the Christmas Campers fell in love with the story and bought an angel. When Riley noticed Merry and Bright's supply of the angels was running low, she asked Lisa about it. Lisa told that they always sold out fast every Christmas, which was a good thing because that meant there was a lot of love to share.

The tour ended back at the lodge, down at the lake, where Luke told everyone the story of the Christmas Lake Christmas tree and how much it had meant to military families over the years. Luke had also found out ahead of time that there were several people in the Christmas Camp group that had connections to the military, either having served themselves, having lost someone, or having a family member that was currently serving, and he'd put together a special tribute to honor them.

Everyone, including Riley, had been touched by his thoughtfulness. Everyone also loved how one of the Christmas Camp activities for giving back, which they could do at their leisure, included writing letters for military members serving overseas, thanking them for their service. Thanks to Caylee helping, it was all set up so the letters could be delivered in time for Valentine's Day.

After everyone went inside to warm up with some of Luke's family's famous hot chocolate and Maryanne's famous Gingerbread XOXO cookies, Luke and Caylee started setting up the next Christmas Camp activity—making ornaments. Only these were no ordinary ornaments.

The ornaments they were for the Christmas trees outside and were edible. They'd be little Christmas gifts to the local birds that were braving the winter at Christmas Lake. The idea was a huge hit with the Christmas Campers. Riley was especially thrilled to see everyone so excited about the ornaments because this activity had actually been one of her ideas, inspired by Luke and his Green-friendly work to give back to the environment.

She'd found a couple of easy recipes online where you just combined birdseed with unflavored gelatin, corn syrup, and water. Then you used cookie cutters for your shapes, created a little hole in the middle with a reusable straw, threaded a piece of twine or ribbon through the hole for hanging, and voilà! You had a beautiful and ecofriendly Christmas tree ornament that birds would love.

For cookie cutters options, Riley had picked an angel to represent the Christmas Lake Angel story and a tree to represent the Christmas Lake Christmas tree. Luke had added a heart to the mix, saying it represented how the true heart of Christmas is all about giving back.

The birdseed ornaments were such a huge hit that Mary- anne suggested they also do pine cone ornaments for the birds. They were even easier to make. All you had to do was get a pine cone, cover it with peanut butter, and then roll it in birdseed. You attached a little hanger at the top and you were good to go.

The best part of this activity was it gave the Christmas Campers a chance to explore outside as they searched for their perfect pine cones.

After making the birds their treats and hanging all the ornaments on the Christmas trees down by the lake, and everyone taking a break for lunch, the next activity was learning how to make Maryanne's famous Christmas Lake Gingerbread XOXO cookies.

For this one, they broke up into several groups so they could all fit in the kitchen in shifts, but everyone got a chance to do their part, from mixing the dough to decorating. Riley floated around, joining all the different groups, and designated herself the official taste-tester. By the time their baking class was done, she must have eaten at least a dozen cookies and taken five dozen pictures with everyone.

During all their activities, Paul was also there taking photos, and he'd kept his promise to let Riley approve anything before he sent it to Mike. So far, everything that was being posted on social media was going viral.

Riley also couldn't believe how many great ideas for her book she was already getting from the Christmas Campers, even before the scheduled Author Chats, because everyone was so eager to share their own Christmas traditions. She had set up a special notes page in her phone to write everything down that inspired her, and it was already filling up fast.

By the end of the day, Riley realized that somewhere along the line she had stopped pretending to be enjoying the Christmas activities and had actually started to enjoy them. There was something so soothing about doing simple things like frosting cookies. Nothing they were doing at Christmas Camp was brain surgery. It was all just a way to relax and have fun, and despite herself, she had to admit she was having fun.

The next time she saw Colin, Brendan, and Tyler was after dinner when she was running upstairs to get ready for the Christmas Camp Ugly Sweater Pageant. The three of them had been coming in the front door.

Surprised, she stopped in her tracks. "Hey, guys. What are you doing...together?"

"We ran into one another in town," Tyler said.

"So we grabbed dinner," Colin added.

Riley's eyes widened. "Together?"

"Yeah," Brendan said. "These guys are pretty cool."

Brendan slapped Colin on the back. "Turns out we have more than just *you* in common."

Riley laughed. "Well, okay, that's great. I'm glad to see you're all getting along. Are you going to join us for our Ugly Sweater Pageant?"

"What about our date?" Tyler asked.

"We're still good," Riley said. "We should be wrapped up by eight. Can you give me a hint as to what we're doing so I know what to wear?"

"Don't worry. Everything you need will be delivered to your room later," Tyler said.

While Riley looked intrigued, Brendan and Colin frowned. "Okay, I gotta go, I'll see you guys later."

She was almost to the top of the stairs when Colin called out to her. "I'm up for this Ugly Sweater Pageant," he said. "Does the offer still stand?"

"Sure." Riley smiled. "The more the merrier."

"Then I'm in, too," Brendan piped up.

Tyler looked at both of the guys. "Seriously, you're both doing this?"

"Oh, yeah," Brendan said. "And I plan to win."

"Not if I have anything to say about it," Colin said. "There's a prize, right?"

Riley laughed. "Yes, but you'll need an ugly sweater to win it."

Luke appeared from around the corner. "If anyone needs to borrow a sweater, I have a whole box of them."

"Thanks, Luke," Colin said. "I'll take one."

"Me too," Brendan said. "What about you, Tyler?"

They all looked at Tyler. Riley could never imagine Tyler, Mr. Fashion, wearing an ugly sweater of any kind.

Tyler's jaw clenched but then he looked at Riley. "Sure, why not."

Riley's jaw dropped. "Really? Wow." She looked at her three exes. "I can't wait to see this."

Chapter Thirty-Three

A few minutes later, the first person Riley saw when she came back downstairs was Luke. They burst out laughing when they saw each other's sweaters.

Riley was wearing one of Luke's mom's sweaters. She'd picked the one with the giant reindeer face with its fuzzy antlers sticking out and flopping around. It also had at least two dozen reindeer tails hanging off it everywhere. Under each tail were brown specks that looked like reindeer droppings.

Luke had also gone all-out. His sweater looked like he'd rolled around in a thousand Christmas lights. The sweater was green, so Riley could only guess he was channeling the Christmas trees out front because there were even real ornaments hanging off the lights.

This was going to be the Ugly Sweater Pageant to end all Ugly Sweater Pageants.

"You look ridiculous," Riley told Luke.

He laughed. "And you're one to talk. You do know you're wearing a sweater that has reindeer poop on it."

Riley smiled sweetly back at him. "Whatever it takes to win."

As they entered the lobby, Riley had to laugh again when she heard the song that was playing...

"I'm too sexy for my ugly Christmas sweater..."

She looked at Luke. "Where did this song come from?"

"Caylee," Luke said with pride. "She put it together. It's great, right?"

"It is," Riley had to admit. As she scanned the room, taking in all the Christmas Campers, she was happy to see they were also taking this competition very seriously. They'd all brought their own holly-jolly-ugly-Christmas-sweater spirit to the pageant, wearing everything from sweaters that lit up and played Christmas music to ones covered in garland and tinsel.

By far the most creative sweater was a giant red sweater worn by the twins. Each twin had one arm in a sleeve and across the front it said *Christmas Camp* in huge white letters. Hanging off the front of the sweater were all Riley's book covers, lit up with LED lights.

"Okay, should I be offended by this?" Riley asked the twins in a teasing voice. She pointed at her book covers. "You're thinking you're going to win the ugly prize with my books? Ouch."

Everyone laughed loudly.

"No! We love your book covers," Carrie rushed to say.

"They're the best," Terrie added. "Carrie, I told you this was a bad idea."

Riley laughed. "I was just kidding, you guys. I think it's great! Extra points for creativity."

When Paul showed up eager to get some pictures, Riley stopped him.

"Aren't you missing something?" Riley asked him.

Paul checked his camera. "What?"

Riley tugged on her ugly sweater as a hint.

Luke joined them. "Don't worry, Paul. I can help you with that."

Riley laughed as she watched Luke lead Paul away. Caylee

joined her looking curious.

"Where's Paul going?" Caylee asked.

"He forgot something," Riley said with a smirk.

When Luke and Paul came back a few minutes later, both Riley and Caylee cracked up laughing. Paul was wearing what looked like an abominable snowman sweater that had more fur on it than the Riley's yeti boots.

Paul looked like he wanted to hide. "Happy now?"

Caylee burst out laughing again.

Riley fought to keep a straight face. "Very."

"Okay, so who is ready for the pageant to start?" Luke asked.

Riley and Caylee both eagerly raised their hands.

As Luke got everyone's attention and started explaining how the Christmas Camp Ugly Sweater Pageant was going to work, Caylee whispered to Riley. "Where are your exes?"

Riley looked around. "Good question. I haven't seen them yet. Maybe they chickened out."

Caylee shook her head. "No, none of them strike me as the kind of guy who gives up."

"We'll see," Riley said as she listened to Luke explain that everyone who was competing would need to strut their stuff down the runway, modeling their sweaters, and would then be judged on three key factors: creativity, uniqueness, and of course, owning the ugliness.

They'd even set up a mini red velvet runway down the middle of the lobby where the judges—Riley, Luke, and Caylee—waited at the end, holding up their scorecards. Contestants would be rated from one to ten, and the highest combined score would win.

They were getting near the end of the contestants when, all of a sudden, Riley saw Colin start making his way down the red carpet. She gasped before she started laughing. "No way!"

But Colin was owning every second of it. His red and white striped ugly sweater was covered in real candy canes, and he was wearing a sparkling red garland around his neck like a boa. As he spun around, modeling, several candy canes flew off him. The twins were ecstatic when they each caught one.

Everyone went crazy laughing and clapping.

When Colin went by Riley, he handed her a candy cane. "Sweets for my sweetheart."

When Riley laughed, Luke rolled his eyes.

Riley was just taking the candy cane from Colin when the next contestant stepped up to the carpet, and it was Brendan. He was wearing a Santa sweater that lit up and said, "Ho! Ho! Ho!" For added impact, he was also wearing a Santa hat and had snowshoes slung over his shoulder. When he went up to Riley, he stopped and put a matching hat on her head. Then he got down on one knee, kissed her hand, and asked her if she'd be his Mrs. Claus.

The Christmas Campers all started whistling and clapping even louder.

The twins started chanting, "Say yes! Say yes!"

Before Riley could answer Brendan's Santa proposal, Tyler appeared, and all the cheering and clapping turned to loud laughter.

Riley did a double take. The last guy she thought would ever be caught dead wearing an ugly Christmas sweater had totally committed from head to toe. Tyler was wearing a hilarious elf-themed sweater onesie that included a hoodie with elf ears and the green felt elf shoes. He looked absolutely ridiculous and proud of it.

Riley found it both hilarious and endearing.

As Tyler strutted down the runway, he never took his eyes of Riley.

Whoa! Riley thought. With that smoldering look, even in the elf onesie, she couldn't deny Tyler was heating up the competition in the best of ways.

"Wow," Caylee said, picking up on what Tyler was putting down for Riley.

Riley, laughing, just fanned her face with one of the score-cards.

When Tyler came over and held out his hand to Riley, still laughing, she stood up and played along, taking his hand. He quickly spun her around in a perfect dance move and dipped her, looking into her eyes. He brought her back up, he was about to kiss her when Comet barked and ran up to them.

Riley laughed as she let go of Tyler's hand. "Look at Comet, everyone. He's getting in on the competition."

Comet, perfectly on cue, trotted down the red runway, looking to the left, then the right as if he was making sure everyone was watching him. They were, and they loved him.

Because, of course, Comet was wearing an ugly sweater, too. It was all green and had the Grinch on it. Only the Grinch was a cat.

In the end, the winner didn't surprise anyone. It was Tyler in his outrageous onesie. For his prize, he got a *new* ugly Christmas sweater. It was brown with a huge gingerbread house on the front, and there were recipe cards attached every-where. There was also a pocket that ran across the bottom hem that had been stuffed with a wooden spoon and spatula. The final edition to the sweater came when Maryanne handed Tyler a giant gingerbread cookie that was wearing its own ugly sweater.

When everyone clapped, Tyler happily took a bite of his cookie.

Riley smiled watching him. She couldn't remember a time when he'd ever looked so relaxed and playful. He was even taking pictures with all the Christmas Campers. She really liked this goofy side of him. After all the pictures, Riley finally made her way over to him.

She did a silly little bow in front of him. "Congratulations, Tyler, for being the king of the ugly Christmas sweaters. You totally surprised me."

Tyler laughed. "In a good way, I hope."

Riley smiled at him. "In a very good way. Who knew you had this in you?" She pointed at his onesie.

"Well, you've just never seen me at Christmas," Tyler said. "We never celebrated it when we were together."

"I know," Riley said. "That was all me. I'm sorry for that."

Tyler put his arm around her. "Don't be. We're making up for it now. So, are you ready for my surprise?"

Riley laughed. "I don't know if I can handle another one."

Tyler laughed. "I mean our date."

"I know," Riley said. "I'm just kidding. But I'm guessing I should go change?"

"Good guess," Tyler said. "You should find something appropriate in your room."

"So you were serious about that?" Riley asked, intrigued.

"Riley, you know I'm always serious about fashion," Tyler said, hands on his hips.

She looked at him in his onesie and laughed.

"Okay, just go," Tyler said, also laughing. "Meet down here a half hour."

"Perfect," Riley said and found herself really looking forward to their date together.

As Tyler was walking out, Paul grabbed him. "One more photo," he said. "I need you, Colin, Brendan, and Riley."

Tyler looked at Riley. "That's up to the boss, not me."

"It's fine," Riley said. "We can do a quick picture."

After she gathered Colin and Brendan together, she also

got Luke and Comet to come over for the picture.

"Okay," she said to Paul. "I have all my favorite guys here, so let's do this. I have a date to go on."

When Riley looked back at the guys, the one person she locked eyes with was Luke. He was smiling at her as he tried to get Comet to sit next to him.

"Sit," Luke said.

Comet kept standing and wagged his tail.

"Sit," Luke tried again.

Nothing.

Riley came over and smiled down at Comet. "Comet, sit," she said, and Comet sat instantly. When she looked up at Luke, she laughed. "You're welcome."

Luke shook his head as he looked at Comet. "You've got to stop doing that. You're making me look bad."

After Paul got all the pictures he wanted, he called Riley over to quickly approve the ones he could send to Mike.

Riley laughed as Paul quickly scanned through the photos. Every one of them made her laugh. "Can I get copies these?"

"For social media?" Paul asked.

"No, just for me," Riley said, surprising herself as she said it.

"Sure," Paul said.

"Oh, and one more favor. Did you see the picture of me with Santa that Margo wanted?"

"Yeah, it's great," he said. "We got a lot of hits on that when we shared it on social media."

"Can you print me up a copy by tomorrow?" Riley asked.

Paul nodded. "Sure, no problem."

When she caught him looking around, she smiled. "She's in the kitchen."

"What?" Paul asked.

"Caylee, who you're looking for, she's in the kitchen," Riley said with a knowing grin.

"Oh, I wasn't looking for her," he rushed to say.

Riley crossed her arms. "Seriously, Paul, I wasn't born yesterday, and I write romance novels for a living. I know a love story when I see one, even if you both are too stubborn to see it. I don't know what happened between you guys, but my advice is, life is short. Fix it. If you care about her, don't waste any more time. She could be headed back to Afghanistan. Do you really want her to leave without her knowing how you really feel?"

"It's not like that..." Paul started, then stopped. "Okay, it *is* like that, but it doesn't matter. She's the one who broke up with me before she went to Afghanistan. I tried to stay in touch. I called, sent texts, e-mailed. She never responded. I didn't even know she was coming home."

Riley felt for him. She could see he was struggling. "Well, now you know she's here," she said in an encouraging voice. "Talk to her. Find a way to make it happen, because I think she really cares about you, too."

Paul looked surprised, then hopeful. "You really think so?"

"I do," she said. "I'm the romance expert, remember?"

Paul laughed. "Good point."

"Now, I need to go change for my date with Tyler," Riley said. "Why don't you go see if Caylee can't help you pick out some of the best pictures from tonight and you can show me them later. Tell her I asked her to help you."

"Great idea," he said. "And thanks...for the advice."

"Happy to try to help," Riley said with a smile. "Good luck."

As she headed for her room, she made a mental note to have a little chat with Caylee.

She needed a little push in the right direction—the direction of Paul. He was starting to grow on Riley, so if there was anything she could do to help the two of them finally talk about how they really felt for each other, she was ready, willing, and able.

She entered her room to find a big white box with a red bow on her bed. For a minute, she thought it was the same box Mike had sent her, but as she got closer, she saw this box was a little smaller, and when she picked it up, it wasn't nearly as heavy. Still, she knew what was inside because she knew Tyler. It had to be something to wear.

When they'd been dating, he'd always loved surprising her with a new outfit for some special party they were going to. She would always joke that he was way more into fashion than she was. Her tastes had always been more classic and simple, but she'd quickly learned that you needed to dress for success in New York City, and Tyler had been great at helping her with that.

She opened the box and her breath caught when she saw a beautiful, white couture cocktail dress. It was covered in white lace, making it look like it was made of tiny snowflakes. When she held it up to her, she knew it would make any girl feel like a princess.

But it was completely impractical. It was something she would never buy for herself, and for all those reasons, Riley loved it.

Also in the box were silver strappy heels and a matching cocktail purse.

She had no idea where she as going with Tyler, but she knew one thing. She was certainly going to be dressed like she belonged in a Christmas fairy tale.

Chapter Thirty-Four

When Riley was ready and came downstairs, she was surprised to see Luke was the only one in the lobby. He was stacking more wood for the fire.

"You're just a lumberjack at heart, aren't you?" Riley asked as she entered the room.

Luke turned around and almost dropped the piece of firewood he was carrying.

All of a sudden Riley felt very self-conscious in her dress.

"It's too much, isn't it," she asked, nervously smoothing her palms over her hips. "Tyler always says you have to go big or go home. But this might be too big…"

Luke never took his eyes off her. "You look…beautiful."

The sincerity in his voice made Riley blush, but before she could respond, Tyler entered the room looking incredibly handsome in a classic, clearly custom, black tuxedo.

"Riley, you look sensational," he said, taking her hand and stepping back to admire her. "I knew this dress would be perfect on you."

Riley smiled at him. "Thank you for the dress. I love it. And you look pretty sharp yourself." She adjusted the collar of his shirt. "But then you always do."

"We've always made a great pair," Tyler said proudly. He looked over at Luke. "Could you get a picture of us?" He held out his phone to Luke.

"No, he doesn't need to do that," Riley said, embarrassed.

She tried to take the phone from Tyler, but Luke got to it first. "It's no problem. You both look like you've stepped out of a magazine."

"That was the plan," Tyler said as he put his arm around Riley. She knew she should have been enjoying the moment, but instead, she felt awkward having Luke take their photo.

"Say 'Christmas Camp,'" Luke said as he held up Tyler's phone.

"Christmas Camp," Riley said, smiling the kind of smile that said, *Hurry up and take the picture.*

"Got it," Luke said and handed Tyler his phone.

"Thank you," Tyler said. He checked the picture and smiled. "We look great."

Riley frowned. "You look great. I look a little…constipated."

Tyler laughed. "You're always so critical of yourself. That dress looks fantastic on you. We need to get going. Are you ready?"

"I'm ready," Riley said.

"You two kids have fun," Luke said as he started to stack the firewood again.

When Riley glanced back at him, he had already turned away.

Tyler took her hand. "Let's go."

When Riley saw a shiny black stretch limo waiting in front of the lodge, she felt like Cinderella going to a Christmas ball.

Tyler held the door for her, and they got in. As the limo pulled out of the driveway, Tyler popped a bottle of Champagne and poured them each a glass.

"You got my favorite Champagne," Riley said. "You remembered..."

Tyler handed her a glass. "I remember everything. The time we spent together was the best time of my life."

"Really?" Riley asked. She didn't even try to hide her surprise. "You never told me that before."

Tyler held his Champagne up for a toast. "I realize I never told you a lot of things that I should have, but I'm hoping to change all that, starting with tonight. A toast, to new beginnings and happy endings."

When their glasses touched, their eyes met, and Riley felt like this really was the start of a new beginning for her and Tyler.

A half hour later, as the limo pulled up to a ritzy resort, guilt twisted in Riley's stomach. They were at the Skyline Resort, the new five-star resort Luke had told her about that was taking away all his customers.

Even from the limo, Riley could see how impressive the property was. By the size of it, she guessed there were well over a thousand rooms. The entrance to the resort was lavishly decorated with modern gold Christmas decorations. There was also a huge waterfall lit up with shimmering gold lights.

When they entered the lobby, they were immediately whisked away by one of the concierges to a penthouse suite Tyler had rented, where he had planned a private dinner for them.

The suite was decorated in the same gold theme as the rest of the resort and had its own magnificent Christmas tree and a wall of windows with a breathtaking view of the mountains. There was also a fire burning and dozens of candles, giving the suite a romantic glow.

There was more Champagne, as well as chocolate-covered

strawberries, when they arrived, followed by one of the most elaborate—and delicious—meals she'd ever had.

Tyler had ordered all her favorite foods, including fresh oysters and mussels flown in from Atlantic Canada to start, a local Colorado grass-fed T-bone steak and an Australian lobster-tail for their main course, and crème brûlée for dessert.

A string quartet played classical Christmas music during their meal, and when they played "Silent Night," Tyler got up and asked her to dance.

Riley hesitated.

"What's wrong?" Tyler asked. Then he remembered. "That's right. You don't love Christmas music. I can have them play something else…"

Riley quickly stood up and touched his arm. "No, this is fine, but maybe we can sit by the fire instead…"

"And have some port," Tyler finished for her. "I remember you like that."

Riley was impressed again. "Only because you introduced me to it. It's like a liquid dessert. Who wouldn't like it?"

"Consider it done."

Riley saw a waiter was already leaving the room and figured he was probably going to get the port.

As she sat down on the couch by the fire in the magical setting, she felt very spoiled.

When Tyler sat down next to her, she smiled at him. "Thank you for planning such a special evening."

Tyler looked into her eyes. "Thank you for saying yes."

Riley smiled back at him. "How is work? Busy as always?"

Tyler settled back and got comfortable. "Actually, I've been cutting back on my hours."

Riley raised her eyebrows. "Really? Why?"

"I want more time to travel and enjoy life," Tyler said.

"Wait, who are you and what have you done with Tyler?"

Riley asked. "You love your work."

Tyler nodded. "I do, but once I made partner, I realized I got the title and the money, but without having someone to share my success with, it all felt pretty empty. I've met all my goals. Now I want to set some new goal that have nothing to do with my career."

Riley nodded. "I'm happy for you. You deserve some downtime and to figure out what makes you happy and to do it."

Tyler took her hand. "I already know what makes me happy, and that's why I'm here. I know when we were dating I didn't make enough time for us, but if you'll give me a chance, I'll show you how things could be different. With my new schedule, I'll have more time to visit you in Arizona, and we could do some trips together, whatever you want. What are your plans for the future? What do you want?"

Riley stared into the fire. "That's a great question. I thought I had a plan with writing my books, but now everything is a little bit up in the air. A lot will depend on how this next book does."

"And how has it been living in Arizona?" Tyler asked. "Have you missed New York City at all?"

Riley nodded. "Yes, I have. Don't get me wrong, I've really enjoyed living in Arizona and the slower pace, but lately I've also felt a little isolated. I've missed the energy of the city. There's always something new and exciting going on to experience. I guess I didn't realize how much I missed Manhattan until I was back in the city again. I want to keep traveling and learning new things. That's what's going to make me a better writer and a better person."

"Well, I think you're already pretty spectacular just the way you are," Tyler said. "But of course, it would be great to have you back in New York where you belong."

When the waiter returned with their port, Riley realized

talking to Tyler was almost like a kind of therapy for her, and for the first time in a while, she realized what she *didn't* want. She didn't want to continue just living to work. She wanted to start working to live and making time to fall in love again.

To find out Tyler was on exactly the same page had her remembering all the amazing qualities that made her fall in love with him in the first place.

Like their date tonight. Tyler knew how to spoil her and make her feel special, to feel deserving of the finer things in life. While she knew she didn't need all the glitz and glam to be happy, she appreciated being able to experience a kind of luxury she otherwise could have only dreamed of. She always knew Tyler could give her that world, but now it looked like he could also give her his time, and that was the most important thing for Riley—and exactly what had been missing in their relationship before.

When the waiter handed Riley a pretty silver gift back with an extravagant silver bow, she gave Tyler a surprised look. "What is this?"

"Just a little something I hope you like," Tyler said. "Open it, please."

For a moment, Riley felt like she was in a Christmas *Groundhog Day,* with three ex-boyfriends all giving her gifts.

There were two presents inside the bag. The first was a lovely crystal star ornament. When she held it up to admire it, it caught the light from the fireplace and sparkled. "It's beautiful," Riley said. "Thank you."

"You're welcome," Tyler replied. "It's to always remind you that you're a rising star, no matter what you write, because you have a special light and talent inside you."

Riley was touched by how much Tyler believed in her. She looked into his eyes. "Thank you. This means a lot to me."

Tyler smiled back at her. "I was hoping we could put the

star on a Christmas tree together. Now open the other one. It's the best one."

When Riley pulled out her next present, she wasn't sure what to say. It came in a long, thin, red velvet jewelry box. When she opened it, she gasped. Inside was a dazzling diamond star pedant.

"Oh, Tyler, this is too much," Riley said. "You shouldn't have."

"Of course, I should have," Tyler said. "It's like I was saying, what is the point of working so hard if I can't share it with someone? Here, let me put it on for you."

Riley handed him the necklace, and she felt her heart skip a beat when his fingers touched the back of her neck.

"I got you this star necklace to always remind you that you're my bright and shining star," Tyler said. "Do you like it?" He sat at back so he could see how it looked on her.

As she touched the star gently and nodded, she smiled at him. "It's beautiful, but I like what it means even more. You've always believed in me."

"Always," Tyler said. He was leaning in for a kiss when Riley's cell phone rang.

"I'm sorry," Riley said. "I thought I turned this off." When she checked her phone, she frowned. "It's Margo. She needs me to call her back."

"This late?" Tyler asked.

"You know Margo. She doesn't sleep, and I really should be getting back, too. We have another big day planned for tomorrow."

Tyler stood up and held out his hand for Riley. "Then let's get you back to the lodge."

Back at the lodge as they were walking up to the front door, Tyler took her hand and told her how much he'd enjoyed spending time with her again and that he'd missed her in his life.

He was leaning in to try once again to kiss her when all of a sudden, the wood-carved bear out front started singing.

"We wish you a BEARy Christmas…
"We wish you a BEARy Christmas…"

Startled, they both turned around and stared at the bear.

Riley started laughing the same moment Caylee opened the door to find out why the bear was singing.

But the bear had stopped. There was no more "We Wish You a BEARy Christmas."

"Everything okay out here?" Caylee asked, giving them a curious look.

Riley and Tyler entered the lodge. "Everything's great," Tyler said as smiled at Riley.

Riley yawned. "Except that I'm suddenly exhausted. I'm going to call it a night, you two."

"Sleep well," Tyler said, kissing her on the cheek.

"You too," Riley said. She touched her star necklace. "And thank you again for a really special night."

"I hope the first of many," Tyler said, causing Caylee to arch her eyebrow.

After calling Margo and getting an update on how their social media campaign was doing, Riley happily crawled into bed with her laptop. Even though she was craving sleep, she knew she needed to write down some notes from her three different dates first. She didn't want to forget anything or how the dates had made her feel because she was hoping it would spark some inspiration and help her come up with a story idea for her Christmas novel. So far, she didn't like any of the storylines she had thought of, which meant she hadn't been able to start her outline, despite its looming deadline.

When she started writing, she found her fingers could barely keep up with her thoughts, and she couldn't stop smiling. The dates had all been so different—just like Colin, Brendan, and Tyler were so different. Yet, all the dates had all been special in their own way, reminding her why she had loved these three men so much.

But when she tried to pick one guy who stood out over the others, one guy she had the strongest connection with, one guy she could see herself starting over with, she couldn't choose. Right now, all three guys were on a level playing field. They all had impressed her, and they all had touched her heart.

What she did know was that she wanted to try to embrace love again. They had all reminded her what it was like to love and be loved. It was something she had been missing in her life, and she knew how lucky she was to be getting a second chance with three amazing guys.

But at this moment, she couldn't choose one over the other, and she knew her time was running out. Tomorrow night was the Christmas Camp dance when she'd promised to tell the guys her decision, and she didn't have a Christmas clue what that decision was going to be.

She hoped having one more day with them would give her the clarity she needed to make what could turn out to be one of the most important decisions of her life.

She had always tried to follow her heart, but the problem was, this time her heart was pulling her in three completely different directions with three completely different guys.

She picked up her cell and started scrolling through the pictures she'd taken on the three dates. All the guys looked so happy. But it was the picture of her and Luke, the selfie he had taken of them, where *she* looked the happiest.

When she glanced up from her phone, one of the Santa figurines, lit up in the moonlight, caught her eye. She shook her head emphatically. "No, I'm not going there," she said to the Santa. "He has a girlfriend. He doesn't have a reindeer in this race."

But when she turned out the light and shut her eyes, it was Luke's face she saw as she drifted off to sleep.

Chapter Thirty-Five

The next morning, Riley woke up to the Santa alarm clock.

"Ho! Ho! Ho! Time to get up and go! Ho! Ho! Ho! Let's go! Go! Go!"

"What? No. Stop it," she grumbled as she fumbled around trying to turn it off. The batteries she'd taken out were somehow now back in.

Santa continued, only getting louder and louder. "Ho! Ho! Ho! Time to get up and go! Ho! Ho! Ho! Let's go! Go! Go!"

"What's going on?" she demanded, yanking out the batteries. She looked over at the Santa figurines. "Who did this?"

But she didn't have time to obsess over the answer because when she saw the time was almost nine o'clock. She freaked out.

"Oh no. I overslept." She jumped out of bed. "My phone alarm didn't go off!"

Riley scrambled around her room and got ready in record time. She ran down to the kitchen, closely followed by Comet, and found Maryanne alone, cleaning up from breakfast.

"Have I missed everyone?" Riley asked. "I'm so sorry. I overslept. I swear I never do that. Why didn't you guys wake me up?" She looked down at Comet. "Even you didn't wake me up."

Comet barked and wagged his tail.

"Luke said to let you sleep, that you probably had a late night on your date with Tyler," Maryanne said. "How was it? Luke said Tyler took you to the Skyline Resort."

Riley nodded. "The resort was impressive."

Maryanne laughed. "I meant how was spending time with Tyler?"

"Oh, Tyler. He was pretty amazing, too," Riley said. "And it seems the things I always worried about with Tyler—him being a workaholic and never having time for us—he now says he wants to change. He wants to enjoy life more."

Maryanne smiled. "So this is good?"

"Really good," Riley agreed. "But so were my dates with Colin and Brendan."

"What are you going to do?"

"I don't know," Riley said. "I know I can't keep dating all three of them…"

"No," Maryanne said. "That would definitely land you on Santa's Naughty List."

"But does that list even really matter?" Riley asked, only half joking.

"Uh, yeah," Maryanne said, "it definitely matters. I saw the guys this morning. They all came down for breakfast asking where you were. They seem like they've already fallen hard for you."

"Oh boy," Riley said. "How is this happening? I don't want to hurt anyone."

"All you can do is listen to your heart," Maryanne said.

"But what if my heart's confused?" Riley asked.

"You'll find a way to figure it out," Maryanne said. "It's Christmas. You just need to believe." She moved a plate of cinnamon rolls in front of Riley. "Here you go. I made something for you."

Riley's eyes lit up. "Cinnamon rolls? One of my favorites!"

"But not your only favorite," Maryanne said. "You also love blueberry muffins, right?"

Riley nodded, impressed. "My mom used to make them for me on special occasions. But how did you know that?"

"Before everyone came to Christmas Camp, we asked them their favorite Christmas dishes for our last dinner tonight. I think so many memories are connected with the food we eat, especially family recipes. I wanted to surprise you with your favorite things, but when I asked your three exes if they knew what you liked at Christmas, they all said you'd never celebrated Christmas with them."

When Riley looked up at Maryanne, she was thankful to see Maryanne wasn't judging her, but she did look curious.

"Anyway," Maryanne continued, "I did some research and found in an interview where you talked about blueberry muffins being a favorite comfort food."

"Wow, you're really good," Riley said. "Are you sure you shouldn't have been an investigative reporter?"

They shared a laugh.

"And then Luke said you liked all things cinnamon, even in your coffee, so I hoped you liked cinnamon rolls. I thought I'd combine the two. I wanted you to have something special. I'm calling these Christmas Lake Blueberry Cinnamon Rolls. Let me know what you think."

"I think you're a genius," Riley said, picking up a fork and diving into the cinnamon roll. It was still warm from the oven, soft and doughy. When she took a big bite, her eyes grew huge. After she had another bite, she put down her fork with a contented sigh. "And now I know you're a genius. These are amazing! I love the cream cheese frosting. That's a favorite of mine, too."

When Luke walked in and saw Riley, he laughed. "Someone looks like a happy Christmas Camper," he said. "Let me guess...you tried the cinnamon rolls."

"Uh, yes," Riley said, "and they're incredible."

"Told ya she liked cinnamon," Luke said to Maryanne.

Riley was licking some frosting off her fork. "Maryanne, you should sell these. You'd make a fortune."

"Well, if you want more, you need to take it to go because we're already late," Luke said. "Caylee took everyone into town—to the community center—to get started on our first Christmas Camp activity for the day. We'll meet up with them there."

Riley jumped up. "Thank you for waiting for me. I'm really sorry I overslept. I'm ready. Let's go."

Maryanne had already put the rest of Riley's cinnamon roll in a bag for her. "In case you need something to nibble on later."

"You're a saint," Riley said as she happily took the bag. "That restaurant in LA would be crazy not to hire you. Have you heard anything yet?"

"Not yet," Maryanne said, "but fingers crossed."

Riley gave Maryanne a quick hug. "Thank you again. This was really thoughtful of you. I've never had a Christmas food tradition so this will be my first."

As soon as she'd said the words and saw Maryanne's and Luke's surprised faces, she instantly regretted it.

She hurried out of the kitchen. "Come on, Luke. Let's go."

As they were driving into town, Riley was relieved Luke wasn't asking her any follow-up questions about not having any Christmas food traditions. The less she said about

Christmas, the better. At least if she didn't want to blow her cover as Miss Christmas.

She was actually really looking forward to doing one of Luke's family's favorite Christmas traditions: volunteering at the Christmas Lake Community Center and helping to put together Christmas meals for families who needed a little extra help this year. The Christmas Camp theme of the day was giving back, and all the Christmas Campers seemed excited it.

When they got to the community center, she joined the Christmas Campers, who were already making great progress. Everyone had paired up to put the boxes together, and she'd paired up with Luke since they both arrived late.

When he pulled two Santa hats out of a bag and insisted they each wear one, she protested until he told her it was also a family tradition to the wear the hats. When she didn't believe him, he called his mom on FaceTime. Apparently, it was, indeed, their tradition. However, since she was also a huge fan of Riley's, she'd told her she could do whatever she wanted. Riley instantly liked Luke's mom.

A few minutes later, the Christmas song "We Wish You a Merry Christmas" had come on, and instead of cringing and rolling her eyes, she'd found herself singing along with Luke and enjoying it.

They were having a great time together. And then Brianna showed up...

Brianna was quick to tell Riley that her family and Luke's had been volunteering together at the community center since they were kids. When Brianna offered to take over for her so she could go do her job spending time with the Christmas Campers, Riley felt like it was more a way to get rid of her than a kind offer. Especially when Brianna happily took Riley's Santa hat and put it on her own head as she smiled at Luke.

Riley was sure that if anyone knew what she was thinking about Brianna at that moment, it would have landed her on the Naughty List.

Two hours later, after successfully packing up more than one hundred boxes, everyone was getting ready to leave when Colin, Brendan, and Tyler showed up.

Riley was surprised to see them since the plan was for her to see them at the dance, but when Colin announced they were just stopping by quickly to drop off personal donations for the center, Riley felt so grateful and moved. Luke was also impressed, letting them know much he appreciated their gesture and how much it would make a difference to the families in the Christmas Lake community.

Before the guys took off, Riley gave each of them a hug and thanked them for being so thoughtful. All three of them had always been generous. Even when Colin and Brendan had been broke, they'd always found a way to give back. It was something Riley had always admired and loved about them.

When it came to Tyler, she'd met him when he was already very successful, but he'd also been one to donate to important causes and support charities he felt were making a difference in the world. He'd also helped her set up her own charity where she could give her books to libraries across the country who didn't have the budgets to buy very many new books. They'd even gotten some other authors on board to donate their books, too.

After all the Christmas Campers had lunch in town, the group headed back the lodge for Riley's Christmas Camp Author Chat. She couldn't wait to hear more of their thoughts and ideas on the kinds of Christmas stories they wanted to read.

This was the activity Riley had been the most nervous about, though, fearing the Christmas Campers would ask her personal questions about her favorite Christmas traditions, which were nonexistent. However, as soon as the chat started, Riley quickly realized she didn't need to worry. The Christmas Campers had all come prepared with a list of their own Christmas traditions to share, things that they thought would be great in her next book.

The conversation had been lively and filled with so many amazing Christmas stories that the chat continued well beyond the hour and a half it had been scheduled for.

Finally, seeing how late it was and knowing that everyone would need some free time to have dinner and get ready for the dance, Riley wrapped up the chat, much to the disappointment for the Christmas Campers. But everyone cheered up when Riley said they could e-mail her their ideas and she promised to look at all of them.

The Christmas Campers all hugged Riley and told her how special this weekend had been but that their favorite part was getting to spend time with her. She genuinely felt like she'd become friends with them and knew that the love they were showering her with was going a long way in helping her get over the ghosts of her Christmases past. There was no denying this Christmas Camp experience was changing her. She was not only starting to open her heart again to Colin, Brendan, and Tyler but she was also starting to open her heart again to Christmas.

The pure joy and love she'd felt at Christmas Camp was giving her some new memories she would always cherish, while also bringing back some of her old Christmas memories, ones she'd thought she'd lost forever.

The memory that was now most vivid was from one Christmas when her dad dressed up like Santa Claus. He'd told her he was one of Santa's helpers, and just because you couldn't see the real Santa Claus, it didn't mean he wasn't always there with you, loving you and watching over you. He'd told her he was just like Santa, that even if he was gone, he would always be with her, always love her, and always watch over her.

That Christmas was the last one they'd spent together before he passed away. He'd given her a silver charm bracelet with a Santa charm on it and told her they'd add a new charm every Christmas. But that had been her last Christmas with her dad, and after that, she had never looked at her charm bracelet again.

But now, by embracing Christmas, instead of feeling the pain of all she'd lost, she actually felt closer to her dad, connected to him, to the memories that were slowing coming back to her.

She smiled as she walked over to the Christmas Wish Santa by the fireplace and peeked inside his bag of wishes.

Caylee joined her. "Looking for something?" she asked in a teasing voice.

"Maybe just an answer to a question," Riley answered. "Hypothetically, if someone had made a Christmas wish and they'd wanted to change that wish, is that allowed?"

Caylee laughed. "Hypothetically?"

Riley nodded. "Hypothetically."

"Okay, I'll play along," Caylee said. "So, *hypothetically,* if someone made a Christmas wish, I think it's okay to change that wish as long as you do it before Christmas."

"So I still have time," Riley said, relieved, then quickly tried to cover her mistake. "I mean, *a person* would have time."

Caylee laughed again. "Yes, you or any person, hypothetically, would still have time."

Their Christmas wish conversation was cut short when an elderly couple, the Silvers, came up and wanted to talk with

Riley. After Caylee excused herself, the couple told Riley they didn't have any children so Christmas was usually pretty quiet for them, but that by coming to Christmas Camp, they felt like they'd met a whole new family, one that now included her.

When they hugged and thanked her again, Riley teared up and said she wanted to thank *them* for bringing so much happiness and joy to Christmas Camp.

After the Silvers walked away, Luke joined her. "I caught the tail end of that," he said. "It sounds like you have a lot of people who want to adopt you into their family."

Riley, smiling, looked over at the group of Christmas Campers who were taking pictures together. "This is really something. I had no idea it would be like this. I've hosted book events before, but I've never had this kind of connection with people."

"That's because it's Christmas," Luke said. "That's what Christmas is all about—sharing memories and connecting with people in your community. Christmas is the time of year that people are at their best and have an open heart, and everyone here has certainly taken you into their hearts."

Riley suddenly fought back tears. "I'm sorry," she said, embarrassed. "I don't know what's gotten into me. I'm never like this…"

"Christmas, that's what's gotten into you, and it's nothing to be sorry about," Luke said as he gently touched a tear that had escaped.

Riley's heart beat faster when she felt Luke's touch.

Caylee reappeared, interrupting the moment. She took Riley's arm. "Sorry, Luke. I'm going to steal Riley away from you. Maryanne and I need to get her upstairs and start getting ready for the dance."

"She's all yours," Luke said.

Riley let herself be led away by Caylee, but when she glanced back over her shoulder at Luke, she smiled when she saw he was still watching her. When he smiled back, her pulse quickened even more.

"Everything okay?" Caylee asked, giving Riley a curious look.

Riley dragged her attention back to Caylee. "Yes. Everything's great."

She didn't miss Caylee's knowing look.

"What?" Riley asked.

"I just thought I saw sparks," Caylee said. "Between you and Luke."

Riley stopped dead in her tracks. "What? That's crazy. You didn't see *anything*."

Caylee put her hands on her hips. "I saw what I saw. You're the one always saying in all your books there has to be a spark, and now you're telling me you don't recognize it in yourself? What about with your exes? Do you have a spark with them?"

"I don't know," Riley answered, feeling flustered.

"Well, if you want to have your own Christmas love story, I'd definitely try to figure it out sooner than later, if I were you," Caylee said.

Before Riley could respond, Colin came up to them holding two glasses of Champagne. He handed them each one. "Riley, can I talk to you for a moment?"

Riley looked back at Caylee.

"Go ahead," Caylee said. "We still have plenty of time, and Riley, weren't you just saying you were looking for something with Colin?"

When Riley shot Caylee a warning look, Caylee just smiled back at her. "You two kids have fun," she said before walking away.

Riley took a sip of her Champagne and smiled at Colin. "What did you want to talk about?"

"Us," Colin said. "I really want to talk about us."

Chapter Thirty-Six

R iley recognized the look on Colin's face. It was the look
he always used to get when he wanted about to talk
about something serious.

"I thought we could do a toast before everything gets going
tonight," Colin said.

Riley held up her glass. "Okay, but then you're going to
need some Champagne. When she saw Maryanne passing out
Champagne, she quickly walked over and took a glass.

"For Colin," Riley explained to Maryanne.

"Good luck," Maryanne said with a wink.

"Thanks," Riley said before taking the glass back to Colin.

When Colin took the glass, he smiled back at her, but then
when they both spotted Paul hovering nearby with his camera, Colin turned to her. "Let's go in the library for a little
privacy."

Riley smiled. "You read my mind."

But as they were turning to go, Paul stopped her. "Riley,
I have that picture you wanted." He walked over and handed
her a printout of her childhood photo with Santa. "Does this
work?"

Riley nodded, looking at the picture. "It works great.
Thank you, Paul."

Colin smiled when he saw that picture. "That's a classic.
You're so cute. Looks like I have some serious competition

with the Big Guy there."

Riley laughed as they headed into the library and was relieved to see they were alone. She slipped the photo into her cocktail purse.

"This is turning out to be quite the night," Colin said. "You should be really proud of all that you've done here at Christmas Camp. People seem to really love it—and you, though that's not surprising. You're very loveable."

Riley laughed. "And you're very sweet and great for a girl's ego.

Colin held up his Champagne. "A toast to Christmas surprises and finding a way back to each other."

Riley hesitated a moment before clinking her glass to his. Looking at Colin, she knew that she'd always love him, but she didn't know if she could see herself *in* love with him.

Caylee's voice was in her head talking about the importance of having that *spark*...

She knew what she needed to do.

She stepped closer to Colin and kissed him.

He was surprised for a moment, but then he kissed her back, putting his arm around her, drawing her in closer. As they kissed, she waited for the spark.

It never happened.

She slowly pulled away and looked into Colin's eyes. She saw so much love and kindness there. It would be so easy to start a relationship with him again. He would always be the safe choice, someone to protect her, who she could count on.

But she had grown over all these years and was a strong person herself. She didn't need the safe choice anymore. She wanted someone who would challenge her, help her grow. So as much as she loved Colin, she didn't see herself loving him the way he should be loved, and she knew they both deserved more than that.

She was about to tell Colin how she felt when Brendan

walked in. He was carrying two glasses of Champagne. "Hey, sorry to interrupt," Brendan said, "but can I steal Riley away?"

For one surreal moment, Riley actually felt like she was on an episode of *The Bachelorette* where the contestants were always cutting in on others' one-on-one time.

"We had just started talking," Riley said to Brendan.

Colin took Riley's hand, looked into her eyes, and smiled a confident smile. "It's okay. We can talk later."

"Are you sure?" Riley asked.

"Absolutely," Colin said and turned to Brendan. "She's all yours."

After Colin disappeared, Brendan handed Riley a fresh glass of Champagne. "I hope I wasn't interrupting something."

Riley gave him shrewd look. "Yes, you do."

Brendan laughed. "That's what I always love about you, Riley. You don't pull any punches. But seriously, I wanted to show you something."

"Okay," Riley said, giving him a curious look.

"It's in my room," Brendan said.

Riley laughed. "You really think that line's going to work on me?"

Brendan laughed loudly. "It's not like that. You know me better than that."

When he held out his hand to her, she took it. "This better be good."

"Don't worry," Brendan said. "It is."

When they got to his room, he set down both of their glasses and walked over to the dresser and picked up an impressive-looking antique globe. It was about a foot tall.

"I wanted you to see *this*," Brendan said, placing the globe on the table in front of her. "I found it in town, and I thought it would make the perfect Christmas present for you."

"It's very nice, but you already got me that beautiful compass," Riley said.

Brendan smiled back at her. "This is different." He picked up a white envelope from the table and handed it to her. "Open it."

When Riley opened the envelope, she was even more confused. She took out a voucher for a plane ticket, but there was no destination or date.

"What is this?" she asked, checking both sides of the voucher.

"Spin the globe," Brendan said, excited. "Pick any spot you want, and wherever it is, we'll go there together. It will be our next trip—the start of a whole new adventure."

When Brendan spun the globe, Riley just stared at it going around and around...

"Go ahead," Brendan said, pointing at the globe. "Pick a spot."

The globe kept spinning, but instead of picking a place, Riley leaned in and kissed him.

It only took him an instant to get over his surprise and kiss her back.

Riley could hear the globe still spinning. She could taste the Champagne on Brendan's lips, but what she couldn't do was feel a spark.

As she gently pulled away, Brendan reached out for her hand. His eyes were full of hope. "That was a great surprise," he said.

Riley struggled to find the words to tell him that while the adventures she'd had with him would always be something she cherished, she was ready to go on new adventures, just not with him. She could be brave now on her own. He had helped her with that. And while she was grateful, grateful wasn't enough to build a relationship on. They'd had a great journey together, and now it was time for both of them to take a different path. Brendan deserved to have someone fall head over heels in love with him, the way she had once. If Brendan had taught her anything it was to always be courageous and to keep moving forward, and that's what she needed to do now, even if it meant she didn't end up with him.

The globe stopped spinning.

"Riley—" Brendan started but was interrupted by Comet barking outside the door.

When Riley went over and opened the door, Comet barked again and then trotted down the hall before stopping to look back at her, almost as if he was urging her to come with him.

Riley turned to Brendan. "Comet wants something. I need to see what's going on."

"I'll come with you," Brendan said.

When they got downstairs, the first person they ran into was Tyler. He was holding two glasses of Champagne and smiled when he saw her.

"Oh no, not again," Riley said under her breath before she could stop herself. Luckily, it didn't look like Tyler had heard her.

"There you are," he said. "I've been looking for you." He acknowledged Brendan with a nod. "Is it okay if I steal Riley for a few minutes?"

"Only if you bring her back," Brendan said, and by the tone of his voice, he was only half kidding.

Tyler handed her the full Champagne glass he was holding, and Riley had to bite her lower lip to keep from laughing. By this point, she didn't even try to argue. She'd seen how it worked on *The Bachelorette*. It was better to just go along with it and follow the Champagne.

"I'll catch you later," Brendan said as he walked off. "The

globe will be waiting."

"The globe?" Tyler asked, confused.

"Long story," Riley said and then took a sip of her Champagne. "Have you seen the library?"

"Yes," Tyler said.

Riley took his hand. "Come on. There's something I want to show you."

By the time they got to the library, Riley's stomach had tied itself into nervous knots. What if Tyler wasn't the one, either? The changes he was talking about making in his life aligned with hers. He had been right when he'd said that of her three exes, he knew her the best *now.* He'd met her after she had grown and changed from dating Colin and Brendan.

Tyler could so easily be the Prince Charming on the white horse, or in this case in the stretch limo, to sweep her off her feet.

Riley couldn't wait any longer. Still holding her Champagne, she kissed Tyler.

He didn't hesitate before kissing her back, and he kissed her with a confidence Riley had always been attracted to. She waited and hoped…but it wasn't there.

Still no spark.

As she pulled back, she honestly wasn't surprised, even if she was a little disappointed. A life with Tyler would have been such an easy life to slide back into. But she wanted more than just easy. She wanted to be challenged, to have success on her own, and to shine on her own, not be someone else's star.

"Well, that was worth waiting for," Tyler said, quickly kissing her again before holding up his Champagne. "A toast," he said with confidence. "To the new Riley Reynolds Library Books Foundation."

When he clinked his glass to hers, Riley just stared back at him. "What are you talking about?"

"This is your real Christmas present," he said. "I've been talking with Margo, and together, we've found a way to start a foundation for you so you'll not only be able to donate books to libraries in need but a percentage of each book you sell will go into a foundation fund that will continue to help libraries. The publisher has agreed to pay that percentage because it's going to get you great publicity. Isn't that wonderful?"

Riley was speechless and still trying to process what he was saying. "When did you talk to Margo?"

"We've been talking all weekend," Tyler said. "She's pretty amazing to work with. She totally gets it."

Riley still had too many questions to be excited. Her first one being, would Tyler still want to do this once she told him she wasn't getting back together with him? She also needed to know a lot more before she put her name on anything.

As if Tyler was reading her thoughts, he jumped in. "Don't worry," he said. "This is just a proposal. It all hinges on your approval and your feedback, but I helped with the legal work to get the ball rolling."

Riley relaxed. "That is amazing. I'm sorry. It's just a lot to take in. I don't even know if my publisher is going to keep me. It all depends on if I can deliver a good outline for this next novel."

"I have faith in you," Tyler said. "You can do this. We make a great team, Riley, and this is just the beginning of what we can do together."

Just as Tyler leaned down to kiss her again, Luke entered the room.

"Oh, I'm sorry," he said, taking a step back. "I didn't mean to interrupt."

When Riley tried to pull back, Tyler took her hand.

"You're not interrupting anything," Riley rushed to say. "Do you need me for something?" She dropped Tyler's hand.

Luke nodded. "There's someone who wants to talk to you."

"Then let's go," Riley said, already heading out the door. She turned back to Tyler. "I'll see you later."

Tyler smiled back at her and lifted his glass. "I'm counting on it. We have a lot to celebrate."

Chapter Thirty-Seven

As Riley hurried out of the library, Luke followed her.

"So I guess congratulations are in order?" Luke asked, his expression impossible to read.

"Congratulations on what?" Riley asked.

But before Luke could answer, Riley heard a familiar voice. "Riley?"

"Mom?" Riley said, stunned. "What are you doing here?" She hurried over and gave her mom a huge hug. Her heart was bursting with love. "This is amazing. I can't believe you're here."

"Surprise!" Riley's mom said as they continued hugging. "You can thank Luke. He made it all happen. He thought you should have family here to celebrate this big event, both Christmas Camp *and* Christmas."

Riley gave Luke an incredulous look. "You did this for me?" Her voice was almost a whisper.

Luke smiled. "You've done so much for my family, coming here and hosting this Christmas Camp, I thought you might want your mom here. I mean, after all, it's Christmas."

Riley went and gave Luke a heartfelt hug. "Thank you." When she stepped back, she looked into his eyes. "This means more than you know."

"My pleasure," Luke said.

"This is the best gift you could have ever given us," Riley's mom added. "And Riley, your stepdad wanted to come, but he thought he'd give us a little girl time. I think he just wanted to stay home and eat all the Christmas cookies."

Riley and Luke both laughed.

"Well, we have those here, too," Riley said. "So he's missing out."

Comet trotted up, sat down next to Riley, and barked.

Riley leaned down and gave him a hug. "Mom, this is Comet."

"Well, aren't you a handsome fellow?" Riley's mom said to Comet. "It's good to see you have a new man in your life—finally."

Riley's eyes flew to Luke's.

He was laughing and looking down at Comet.

But when her mom caught her looking at Luke and gave her a curious look, Riley quickly gave Comet another hug. "Comet is the best."

"But he's far from the only man in Riley's life right now," Luke told her mom.

When Riley gave him a look to zip it, he just smiled back at her.

"What's this?" Riley's mom asked, instantly alert. "You two?" She eagerly pointed at Luke, then Riley. "This is great. I knew I liked you, Luke."

"No," Riley and Luke both said at the same time.

"He has a girlfriend," Riley rushed to finish.

"She has a boyfriend," Luke said at the same time.

Riley and Luke stared at each other.

"I don't have a girlfriend," Luke said.

Riley gave him a look. "Hello, what about Brianna?"

Luke laughed. "Brianna's a friend, not a girlfriend."

"What?" Riley asked, trying to process the news. "But I saw you two together. I see how she is with you…"

"We dated growing up, but that's it," Luke said. "Since I've been back helping my mom, she's wanted more, but I've told her it's not going to happen. We're friends. That's all."

Riley's mom grinned back at Luke. "So then you and my daughter are—"

"Nothing, Mom," Riley interrupted, flustered and embarrassed. "We're nothing."

Luke's eyebrows rose, and for a moment, Riley thought he almost looked…disappointed.

Riley's mom put her hands on her hips. "Then who is Luke talking about, Riley?"

"I hope it's me," Colin said as he came around the corner with Brendan and Tyler.

"Or me," Brendan said.

"It's me," Tyler said with a self-assurance that made both Colin and Brendan frown.

Riley's mom's jaw dropped. "Colin? Brendan? Tyler?!" She looked over at Riley. "This is…unbelievable. All three of your ex-boyfriends are here at this Christmas Camp?"

Riley put her arm around her mom. "It's a long story. I'll explain everything, but right now, I really need to go upstairs and get ready for the dance. My photographer wants me ready for pictures in a half hour, and I'm already running late." She gave her mom another hug. "Are you going to be okay down here, or do you want to come up with me?"

Riley's mom smiled back at her. "I'm just fine. I need to go change, as well. You go get ready and do your job. I'll be here after the dance, and we can catch up." She kissed Riley on the cheek. "I'm so proud of you and so glad I'm here to see this." She looked over at Luke. "Thank you again, Luke, for making this possible."

Colin, Brendan, and Tyler all looked at Luke like they were seeing him in a new light—as their competition.

"Riley," Caylee called from upstairs. "Are you coming up?"

"Coming," Riley yelled back.

She gave her mom another quick hug. "I'll see you later tonight." Then she looked at Colin, Brendan, and Tyler. "And you guys, as well." As she headed up the stairs, she looked back at one person, Luke. He was talking to her mom, and her mom was laughing.

Riley was still smiling when she walked into her room.

With the help of Caylee and Maryanne, Riley was able to get ready quickly. She had to laugh when she got to her room, and they had already picked out her dress. She had to admit they'd done a good job. It was her favorite dress, as well, out of the clothes Mike had sent her. It was another sparkling red gown, but it had a halter neckline covered with red sequins and a soft, shiny, satin skirt in a ballgown style that made her feel like a princess.

Riley had a great time as they helped one another do their hair and makeup, and she wondered if this was what it felt like to have sisters.

Caylee and Maryanne had been more than excited to wear something from Riley's Christmas clothes stash again, with Caylee picking a fun and flirty, short, red sequin skirt paired it with one of the simple black sweaters Riley had brought from home. Maryanne chose another red dress, this one all lace, and it fit her as if it had been made just for her.

As they stood together, arm in arm, and looked into the mirror, they smiled.

"I think we're ready," Riley said.

"We are *so* ready," Caylee agreed, and they all hugged.

"I'll go find Paul," Maryanne said. "He said he wanted to

get some pictures of you before you went down."

"Oh, wait," Riley said, going over to her dresser and opening the top drawer. She took out the picture she'd had Paul print up of her with Santa when she was little. She handed it to Maryanne. "Could you add this to the Christmas Camp memory board for me? If there's a spot for it."

Maryanne held the picture to her heart. "Of course, there's a spot for it. Everyone is going to love that you're sharing this. Thank you. I'll add it right now."

Riley suddenly felt embarrassed. "There's no rush. It's no big deal."

Maryanne smiled at her. "I'll take good care of it."

When Maryanne left, Caylee grabbed Riley's hand. "So what are you going to do about Luke?"

"What do you mean?" Riley asked, confused.

Caylee laughed. "It's *so* obvious that you two have a thing for each other."

"Okay, I'll play. What are you going to do about *Paul?*" Riley countered with a smug smile.

Caylee stepped back. "We're not talking about Paul. We're talking about Luke."

Riley put her hands on her hips. "You go first. I talked to Paul, and it seems like he really cares for you. What happened?"

Caylee paced around the room.

"I mean, tell me he's a bad guy and I'll drop it," Riley said.

"He's not a bad guy," Caylee said, defending him quickly. "He's a good guy. Too good. That's the problem. And he didn't do anything. I did."

Riley waited for Caylee to continue.

When she finally stopped pacing, she sat down on the bed, picked up the Santa pillow, and hugged it. Riley sat down next to her.

"Short version," Caylee said, staring at the Santa. "We dated. It was great. I got deployed to Afghanistan. I didn't want him waiting and worrying about me. I know how hard it can be so I broke if off with him. End of story."

"But is it?" Riley asked. "The end of your story? Because the guy I talked to clearly still cares about you, and I think you care about him."

Caylee jumped up and tossed the Santa pillow on the bed. "Your turn to answer my question. What are you going to do about Luke?"

"There's nothing *to do* when it comes to Luke," Riley said as she walked over to the window and stared out into the night. "There's nothing going on between us. He's only tolerating me this weekend because he has to. Before you got here, he tried to make me leave. Did you know that?"

Caylee locked eyes with her. "Riley, what I know is that I've known Luke almost my whole life. I know what I'm talking about. I see the way he looks at you, *and* the way you look at him. You don't look at your exes like that. Can you honestly tell me that one of them is *the one?* If you can, then I'm wrong and I won't say another word."

Riley laughed. "Promise?"

"Yes," Caylee said, completely seriously. "I promise."

Riley walked over to her desk and picked up one of the Santa figurines. "Colin, Brendan, and Tyler are all great guys..."

Caylee followed her. "Agreed. But...?"

Riley sighed and put down the Santa. "You're right. None of them are the one. There's no spark. Don't get me wrong, I wouldn't base my decision on just a physical spark. I've always believed that kind of spark comes from something deeper than just chemistry. It comes from having the kind of connection, mentally *and* physically, that's undeniable. All three of my exes are great, but I'm different now. I can't go back. To grow, I need to move forward. That's how I'm going to find the kind of love I want and need."

Caylee shot both arms up in victory. "I knew it!"

"*But* that doesn't mean I have a thing for Luke or that he has a thing for me," Riley said. "Don't get me wrong, he's been great putting on this Christmas Camp—you all have been—and I know all the Christmas Campers love Luke and he brought my mom here, but we're two totally different people. He's moving back to Europe, I live in Arizona, and..."

Caylee stopped her by taking her hand and looking into her eyes. "Do you want some advice?"

Riley laughed a little. "I'm guessing you're going to give it whether I want it or not."

"True," Caylee said. She took a deep breath before continuing, looking uncharacteristically serious. "Being in the military, being deployed in a war zone, I've learned you can only live for today. Tomorrow's never guaranteed. I also learned that with my parents. So don't waste the precious time you have making excuses for why you can't be with someone or why you can't be happy. Live in the moment. Grab all the happiness you can, while you can, and figure the rest out if you're lucky enough to get a tomorrow. Does that make sense?"

Riley nodded slowly.

"If you think there might be something there with Luke, you gotta go for it," Caylee said. "You're a romance writer. Isn't it time you wrote your own happily-ever-after?"

A knock on the door interrupted them. "It's Paul," he said through the closed door. "Maryanne said you're ready. The rest of the media is also starting to show up."

"Coming," Riley called back to him.

Then she turned to Caylee. "And what about you taking

your own advice with Paul? You're right here, right now, and so is he. Make this trip count, Caylee. Do it for you. Do it for Paul. Do it for love."

Riley picked up her purse, and when she opened the door, she found Comet waiting for her. This time Comet was wearing a black bow tie and looked very dapper. She smiled as she leaned down and adjust the tie so it was perfect. Tyler had let her borrow his bow tie from their date, although she hadn't told him it was for Comet.

As she started walking down the hall, she saw her mom come out of one of the guest rooms. "Oh, good, I'm glad I caught you," her mom said. "Can you come into my room for just a second? I have something I wanted to give you."

"Sure," Riley said, "but you didn't need to get me anything. You know we don't exchange Christmas presents..."

"I know," Riley's mom said. "It's not from me." She handed Riley a little white jewelry box.

When Riley opened it, she touched her hand to her heart. Inside was the silver charm bracelet her dad had given her their last Christmas together. It still had the one Santa charm on it.

"Do you recognize it?" her mom asked.

Riley nodded as she remembered her dad putting the bracelet on her wrist for the first time and how much she'd loved the Santa charm.

Her mom took the bracelet out of the box and held it up. "I had a few links added so it should fit you now. I thought you might want to wear it tonight."

When Riley silently held up her wrist, her mom happily put the charm bracelet on her. It fit perfectly.

Tears pooled in Riley's eyes, and she blinked them back. "Thank you, Mom," she said, touching the Santa charm.

"Your dad would be so proud of you. I know I am," Riley's

mom said as she gave her a kiss on the cheek. "I was hoping that this year we could spend Christmas together, but *not* in Hawaii. We could stay home and actually celebrate Christmas again, start some new traditions. What do you think?"

Riley hugged her mom tightly. "I think that would be great. I really do."

"Wonderful," Riley's mom said. "But now you better get going. A lot of people are waiting for you."

"You're right," Riley said. "I'll see you soon." As she hurried down the hall, she looked down at her Santa charm and smiled.

When she got to the stairs, her heart skipped a beat. Luke was waiting for her on the bottom step. He looked incredibly handsome in a black suit and white shirt with another red tie that matched her dress.

Caylee's words were echoing in her head: *Live in the moment. Grab all the happiness you can, while you can, and figure the rest out if you're lucky enough to get a tomorrow.*

There was so much she still needed to figure out, but one truth she knew was that she'd been falling for Luke from the start. She'd shut down her feelings because she'd thought he had a girlfriend, and then her three ex-boyfriends had arrived. It was complicated, and adding to that, it was Christmas, which brought so many feelings rushing to the surface.

When she got to the bottom of the stairs and Luke held out his hand, she smiled as she put her hand in his. When their fingers touched, something flashed in his sapphire-blue eyes and she felt it.

The spark.

When she laughed, much of her tension melted away. Here she had been looking for that spark with her exes, but now, when she wasn't looking, that spark had found her.

"You look beautiful," Luke said. "Like you belong in a

Christmas fairy tale."

Riley smiled and blushed. "Thank you. My dad would have loved hearing you say that. He used to make up Christmas fairy tales and tell them to me at bedtime when I was little. It was one of my favorite parts of Christmas."

"Do you remember any of them?" Luke asked.

Riley nodded. "I do. There was *ChristmasElla*, about how Cinderella spent her Christmas, and *Snow White and the Seven Christmas Eves*, and *The Little Mermaid's Christmas Wish*, and lots more."

"That's really creative," Luke said. "Sounds like you come by your storytelling ability naturally."

Riley smiled. "I guess I do."

"Have you ever thought about writing your dad's fairy tales down as a children's book?" Luke asked. "I bet kids would really love it."

Riley felt a bolt of inspiration jolt through her. "Luke, that's a great idea! I have a friend who is an amazing illustrator, and there are so many stories I remember. I wonder if I could really do this..."

"Of course, you can," Luke said. "Remember, it's Christmas. Anything is possible."

Riley was growing more and more excited. "And for my romance novel, I could make my heroine a children's book author who is writing a book of Christmas fairy tales, but she's lost her Christmas spirit and needs to find her own happily-ever-after for inspiration."

"Maybe with the illustrator?" Luke offered.

Riley laughed. "Great idea. I love this. I think it could really work. Everyone has been wanting me to write a Christmas story that I have a connection with, and it has been impossible to come up with anything."

"Why has it been so hard this time?" Luke asked.

"It's Christmas," Riley said. "We have a complicated history." She took a deep breath. "I lost my dad at Christmas."

"I'm so sorry," Luke said.

As Riley looked up into his eyes and saw the empathy there, she realized she'd never told that to anyone before. She never talked about her dad or Christmas, but she was glad she told Luke.

"Thank you," she said. "And thank you for this idea. I think this might be a great way to honor his memory." Before she knew what she was doing, she gave Luke a hug. It just felt right. It all felt right. She could hear his heart beating in his chest, and her own heart matched its rhythm. She was blissfully lost in the moment until she heard someone clearing their throat.

She reluctantly stepped back from her embrace with Luke and turned around to find all three of her exes staring back at her.

Chapter Thirty-Eight

C olin, Brendan, and Tyler all looked handsome dressed up for the dance.

"Riley, there you are," Colin said. "You look beautiful."

Riley smiled back at him. "Thanks."

"Red always was your color," Tyler added.

Tyler stepped forward. He walked over to Riley, leaned down, and kissed her before she even knew what was happening. "You look perfect," he said.

Flustered, she quickly took a step back.

"I'd appreciate it if you didn't kiss *my* girlfriend," Brendan said as he gave Tyler a warning look.

Colin laughed. "Your girlfriend? I think you're both confused. Riley, tell them. You've picked me."

When they all looked at Riley, she glanced at Luke, but he was already walking away.

Upset and knowing what this must have looked like to Luke, Riley turned back to her exes. "Guys, I can't do this right now. My photographer is waiting in the ballroom, and all the media is here. Let me get through this dance. This is our last Christmas Camp activity, and I'll talk you later tonight. I promise."

She hurried off before any of them could protest.

She didn't get very far before she was surrounded by her

Christmas Campers, all wanting pictures with her all dressed up for the dance.

Caylee had finally come to her rescue and escorted her to the ballroom, where Paul and the media were waiting to get interviews and pictures before the dance started.

As soon as she entered the ballroom, she felt like she was being transported into one of her dad's Christmas fairy tales.

Luke and Mike had called in a favor and had a designer friend from Denver decorate, keeping it simple but magical. Bringing the beauty of the outside in, they added dozens of live Christmas trees covered with white twinkle lights. White lights also lined all the wooden beams across the vaulted ceiling like stars in the sky. Mike had even found a band to play classical Christmas songs everyone could dance to so the media outlets would have some great opportunities to get some festive shots.

As Riley made her way to the microphone they'd set up for her interview, she had to admit that Mike had done his job. Not only were there local TV stations from Denver present but he'd also scored some national media.

"Where's Luke?" Riley asked Caylee as they approached the mic.

"I haven't seen him," Caylee said.

Riley quickly scanned the room but didn't see Luke anywhere. She smiled at all the journalists, who were waiting for her to get started.

"We're just waiting for one more person," Riley told them. Then she whispered to Caylee, "Can you go find Luke? He needs to be here."

"I'm on it," Caylee said and hurried off.

But the media wasn't waiting.

"Riley," a reporter in the front row called out, "I'm Ray Davis with the *Denver Tribune*. Can you tell us about your three boyfriends who showed up here? Are they all going to be in this new Christmas novel of yours?"

"No!" Riley answered quickly, then softened her response with a laugh.

The reporter quickly followed up. "'No' to telling us about your boyfriends? Or 'no' to them being in the book?"

"Both," Riley said, getting some laughs from the crowd. She smiled at everyone, trying to hide how uncomfortable this line of questioning was making her feel. "If we can just hold off with questions for a moment, I'd like to start by introducing Luke Larchmont. This amazing place is his family's lodge, and he made this Christmas Camp happen. He should be joining me any moment."

"We don't need to wait," a voice said from the back of the crowd. When the person stepped forward, Riley's eyes widened. It was Mike, with Margo by his side.

Riley did a double take. None of the plans included them coming to Christmas Camp. Their surprise visit instantly made her nervous. *What are they up to now?* she wondered.

It didn't take long for Mike to get through the crowd and claim the microphone. "Hello, everyone. I'm Mike Conneley, Riley's publicist. Luke told us to go ahead and get started with the interviews because we have a dance to put on."

Riley fought to keep smiling as everyone clapped. She didn't understand why Luke wasn't coming. This was his moment to get publicity for the lodge. This was why he did the Christmas Camp.

When she looked over at Margo, who was standing on the sidelines, she found Margo was focused on her phone.

Mike pointed at a female reporter in the first row. "Tammi, from *National Lifestyles*, go ahead with your question."

Tammi smiled at Riley. "Riley, your boyfriends, they looked pretty handsome in the photos we all saw online. Two questions: Who is the one that got away? And are the other two still available? I'm asking for a friend."

As everyone laughed, Riley smiled, but she wasn't thinking about her exes. She was thinking about Luke.

A half hour of questions later, Riley was exhausted, not to mention thankful they were wrapping things up so they could start letting their guests into the ballroom for the dance.

As soon as they were done, she grabbed Mike's arm and took him into the hallway and into a small storage room where they could talk in private. The room was filled with Christmas decorations. She shut the door behind them.

"I think that went well," Mike said, clearly proud of himself.

Riley gave him a stunned look. "I don't even know where to start. All those questions were about my personal life, my ex-boyfriends. We didn't talk about Christmas Camp or the lodge or even my book. What were you doing? Why didn't you change the line of questioning? And what are you even doing here?"

Mike laughed off her concern. "Riley, any media like this is great media for your books. You're a romance writer. People love hearing about your love life and these mysterious three exes. We couldn't have asked for better publicity. They've been eating this stuff up. You saw everyone out there. And Margo and I came because this is a huge deal. I wanted to make sure you handled the media right and didn't take off on us again."

Riley glared at him. She wished she had a dozen snowballs because she would have thrown them at Mike's smug face. When she took a step back from Mike, needing to put distance between them, she accidently ran into a giant plastic Santa. She caught it just before it tipped over.

"Where's Luke?" she asked, putting Santa back in his place. "He didn't get a chance to talk to the press."

Mike shrugged. "He didn't want to do the interview. He said it would be better to stay focused on you. He thought you were going to make your big announcement about Tyler."

Riley gave him a confused look. "About Tyler and the library foundation? I haven't even agreed to that yet."

"No," Mike said. "About you and Tyler getting back together. That he's the *one*."

Riley laughed. "What are you talking about? I'm not back together with Tyler."

"What?" Mike said, confused. "You're sure?"

"Yeah, I think I'd know," Riley flung back at him.

Mike looked perplexed. "Well, that's what Luke said. Did he get the guys mixed up maybe? Are you back together with one of the other guys?"

Riley gave him an incredulous look. "No!" She shook her head, getting more upset by the second. "I'm not back with any of them."

"Well, Luke thinks you're getting back together with Tyler," Mike said. "I was actually giving him a hard time because the way he kept talking about you, I thought he was into you, but he told me he never had a chance."

Riley's heart sank. She'd heard enough. She had to fix this. "Where is he?" she demanded.

"I don't know," Mike said, "but we have to get you back to the ballroom. The dance is starting, and everyone is going to want to see who you have your first dance with. I told the media that whoever you dance with first is the guy you picked for your own happily-ever-after."

"What?!" Riley said, dumbfounded. "I told you, I'm not getting back together with one of my exes. You had no right to assume that, let alone *announce* it! What is *wrong* with you?" Riley pushed past him and out the door.

"Riley!" Mike called after her. "Where are you going?"

She picked up her pace and never looked back. When she went around the corner, she started passing her Christmas Campers as they were heading to the dance.

"I'll be right back," she said as she hurried by them. When she stopped seeing people coming, she took off her shoes so she could run.

She saw her mom approaching with Maryanne, but she didn't slow down. "I'll explain later, Mom!"

Her mom laughed. "Okay!"

She ran into the lobby, hoping Luke would be there, but instead, she found Colin, Brendan, and Tyler all on their phones.

She stopped short. "Have you seen Luke?" she asked, breathless.

Tyler shook his head. "No." He stared down at her feet. "Why aren't you wearing your shoes?"

"Is everything okay?" Colin asked. He looked concerned.

"No, it's not." She started to take off again but then stopped and turned back to the guys.

"Look, this is not the way I planned to talk to you all, but there's a lot of confusion going on right now about who I'm dating, thanks to this media blitz my publicist devised and some misinformation from Luke," Riley said.

"I talked to Luke," Tyler said. "He should be all straightened out."

"What did you say?" Riley asked, afraid to hear the answer.

"He congratulated me on us getting back together, and I thanked him for all his help. That's all," Tyler said.

Brendan and Colin both looked shocked.

"Wait, you two are back together?" Brendan asked. "You picked *him?*"

"Yes," Tyler said, smiling like he'd just won the lottery.

"No," Riley said at the same time.

Tyler's smile turned into a confused frown.

Riley took a deep breath. She had to get control of this out-of-control situation.

All three of the guys sat down in silence.

Riley put her shoes back on. "Please let me say what I need to say without any interruptions and all your questions will be answered."

"Go for it," Brendan said.

"We're all ears," Colin said.

Now that Riley had their undivided attention, she knew she just needed to be honest with them, but suddenly she was nervous, very nervous. But she pressed on. "First, I can't tell you how much it means that you're all here," she told them, her voice full of sincerity. "The fact that you've all taken time from your busy lives to see me means the world to me. I'm flattered. But mostly, I'm thankful to be reminded of how lucky I've been to have you all in my life."

Riley took a moment to smile and make eye contact with each of them. "Having you here this weekend has brought back so many amazing memories," she continued. "You've all taught me so much about love, and even more about myself, and because of you, I know what real love is. And I want that for each of you."

She opened her purse and took out the red heart ornament Colin had given her on their date and walked over and handed it to him. "Colin, you gave me this saying you wanted me to know that I would always have your heart. I'm giving it back to you because someday you're going to find someone who really deserves it."

She looked into Colin's eyes. "I'll always love you, Colin. We had our great love story, and I think we know, if we're honest with each other, that it's time for both of us to start a new chapter."

When Colin took the ornament and looked at her, she could see in his kind eyes that he knew she was right, and she loved him for that.

Next, she took the compass Brendan had given her out of her purse and walked over to give it to him.

"Brendan, you and I have had some amazing adventures together. You gave me this compass so I could always find my way back to you, but you know better than anyone, the best adventures are when you keep moving forward and exploring new things. I will always love you for helping me be brave and fearless. That's why I can give you this compass back because you've already helped me find my way and the strength to go after what I really want. I know there are many more adventures just waiting for you, and I want you to find someone who will love you as fiercely as you love them."

As Brendan studied the inscription on the compass, Riley waited for him to look up at her. When he finally did and they shared a smile, she knew Brendan would be just fine— better than fine—and that he was probably already planning his next adventure.

Lastly, Riley took the diamond star necklace and star ornament out of her purse and gave them back to Tyler.

"Tyler, you showed me a world I never thought I could be a part of. You helped me own my own power and know my worth. You say I'm your star, but honestly, you have been mine. You've guided me and shown me that the sky is the limit. I will always love you for teaching me to never settle for less than I should have. Now I want the same for you. I want you to find someone who can love you the way you deserve to be loved."

During her whole speech, Tyler never broke eye contact with her. When she was done, he nodded. "So you're not picking any of us?" he asked.

"I'm picking me," Riley said. "I am who I am because of all of *you,* and for that, I am so thankful. I want you to find your own happily-ever-afters, and I know you will."

Riley gave each of them a hug. "Now if you'll excuse me. I need to go find—"

"Luke," Colin cut in with an all-knowing smile.

Brendan nodded sagely. "Because he's the one, isn't he?"

"Luke?" Tyler asked, looking confused. "What are you talking about?"

Colin laughed. "We'll explain it to you, buddy."

"Riley, go," Brendan said. "Go get your happily-ever-after."

"I love you guys," Riley called over her shoulder as she ran out of the room.

Chapter Thirty-Nine

Riley rushed into the kitchen calling out for Luke. "Luke? Are you in here?"

Silence.

It had been the same story in the library. Apparently, everybody at the lodge was now in the ballroom because even the lobby was empty now.

She whispered to herself, "Luke, where are you?"

She was about to leave when a log on the fire cracked and popped, lighting up the face of the Christmas Wish Santa next to the fireplace.

When she looked over at the Santa, his bag of toys caught her eye, and she remembered the Christmas wish she had made on the first day of Christmas Camp. She walked over and peered inside the bag and then carefully started looking for the Christmas wish she had made. She knew she'd recognize her scroll because instead of tying the red ribbon into a pretty bow like everyone else, she had triple knotted it and left the ends hanging. It only took a second to find.

She slid the ribbon off and read her wish out loud. *"To write a wonderful Christmas love story."*

She picked up a pen from the table and crossed out the word *write* on her original wish and replaced it with the word *have*.

She read her new wish out loud. *"To have a wonderful Christmas love story."*

As she was putting her wish back into Santa's bag, she caught a flash of light in the big picture window that looked out over Christmas Lake. She went over to the window to see what was happening.

Her heart stopped when she saw the Christmas Lake Christmas tree.

The lights on the tree were flickering. She had never seen them flicker before. They were usually always glowing steady and bright.

"Something's wrong with the lights!" she said in a panic. "They can't go out. They've never gone out..." She knew there wasn't time to get anyone from the ballroom. If the lights went out, years of tradition, of honoring military members, would be over.

She couldn't let that happen.

Without thinking, she ran to the closet and grabbed a random coat and threw it on. She didn't care that it was way too big for her, almost reaching to her ankles. She also grabbed her yeti boots, slipped them on, then raced toward the lake.

It was snowing, and the path was slick. She almost fell several times, but she kept going, never taking her eyes off the Christmas Lake Christmas tree.

"Please don't go out. Please don't go out. Please don't go out," she repeated over and over again. She was moving as fast as she could, but the lights were still flickering.

When she got to the lake, she came to a screeching halt. The ice looked almost blue in the moonlight. But she didn't see the beauty. The only thing she saw was the danger as the memory of her news van almost going through the ice flashed into her mind. She shivered, but not from the cold—from the memory that chilled her to the bone.

She took several steps back. "I can't do this," she said. "I can't."

When she saw the lights on the tree continue to blink on and off, she turned around and yelled, "Luke! Luke!"

But her cries for help were lost in the icy wind that had picked up and was now swirling around her. She looked at the ice like it was her enemy.

She brought her freezing hands up to her mouth to blow warm air into them, and the Santa charm her dad had given her shone in the moonlight. That's when she saw the inscription on the Santa. It said, *Always believe.*

She looked out on the lake, the Christmas tree lights continuing to flicker. She took a deep breath and stood up straighter.

I just have to believe. Luke goes out there every day. He said it was safe.

She held the Santa charm to her heart as she put her first foot on the ice. Then she took another step, and another, and pretty soon she was walking across the lake. She was at the Christmas tree in no time.

As soon as she got to the tree, she realized she didn't even know what to look for, or how to fix it. She started by gently moving the strands of lights on the tree that were blinking.

Nothing happened. They just kept blinking.

The wind was picking up. The lights on the tree were swaying back and forth. That's when she remembered how Luke had shown her how to wrap the lights around the branches so they wouldn't fall off.

She did that quickly the best she could, even though her frozen hands were clumsy. She was down on her hands and knees, trying to look under the tree for the battery pack Luke had talked about when her hand touched something furry and wet.

She screamed and jumped back. Then came a familiar bark. It was Comet, and he was with Luke.

Before she could say anything, Luke scooped her up so she was no longer on her hands and knees. "What are you doing out here!" he shouted at her. He looked angry and worried.

She pointed at the tree. "The lights! There's something wrong with the lights."

"You need to get inside now!" he yelled over the wind as he took off his gloves and put them on her shaking hands. He also quickly put his hat and scarf on her.

"Let's go," he said, putting his arm around her to shield her from the wind."

But she refused to budge. "No!" she insisted. "You need to stay and fix the lights. I'll go. But you stay. Please, they can't go out. They can't go out..."

She took off before he could argue, but he caught up with her. He put Comet's leash in her hand and looked down at Comet. "Go!" he told Comet. "Take her inside."

For the first time, Comet listened to Luke and did just what he was told. He barked and started pulling Riley toward the shore.

When Riley looked over her shoulder and saw Luke was still watching her, she tried to yell out to him but her voice almost disappeared in the wind. "Luke, go back and fix the lights! I'm okay. Go!"

Luke hesitated.

"Go! Hurry!" Riley urged.

"Get inside," he yelled back before turning and rushing over to the Christmas tree.

Comet didn't stop pulling her forward until they got inside the lodge.

She had just taken off her coat and was trying to warm up by the fire when Luke burst through the front door. "Are you okay?" he demanded, checking her hands. "What were you thinking going outside without any gloves or a hat? Are you *trying* to get frostbite?"

Riley pulled her hands away from him. "Why aren't you out there fixing the lights?!"

Luke pointed at the window.

When Riley rushed over and saw the lights were now back to normal, glowing in all their glory, she almost cried she was so relieved.

"There was a loose cable. It's all fixed. It's fine," Luke said as he picked up a blanket off the couch and wrapped it around her.

Now Riley did feel tears in her eyes—grateful tears. She touched the Santa on her charm bracelet and shut her eyes. *Thank you, Dad.*

"Are you okay?" Luke asked, sounding genuinely concerned. "I was in the front yard checking the lights there when the Santa from the sleigh came loose and blew down to the lake. I was running after it when I saw you. You should never have gone out there dressed like that. You could have really been in trouble."

"I know," Riley said. "I'm sorry. I wasn't thinking. I panicked when I saw the lights. I was looking for you. I wanted to explain about—"

But Riley didn't have a chance to finish when Mike stormed into the room. "There you are," he said, pointing at Riley. "Everyone is waiting for you at the dance. This is *your* event, remember? All the media is here. You need to get in there, now. I'll go tell everyone you're coming."

Mike started walking away but then stopped and gave Riley the once-over. "But go fix your hair and your face first. You're a mess." Mike left the room before Riley could say anything.

She picked up a nutcracker, and she swore she would have thrown it him if Comet hadn't barked at her. "Sorry," she said to Comet as she put the nutcracker down. Then she looked at Luke, who had an amused look on his face. "Not sorry," she added.

Luke started to leave the room. "I'll see you at the dance."

"But wait..." Riley started, but he was gone before she could stop him.

A few minutes later, after she'd touched up her hair and makeup as Mike had demanded, Riley entered the ballroom. She was just starting to look around for Luke when Mike hurried over and linked arms with her.

"There you are. My favorite author," Mike said merrily.

Riley gave him a suspicious look. "Did someone spike your eggnog?"

"Just smile and look happy," Mike whispered in her ear. "Everyone's watching."

When he led her onstage, the band had just stopped playing.

He took the mic. "Hello, everyone," Mike said, beaming. "Thank you all for being here—our Christmas Campers, everyone from the Christmas Lake community, and all the media that's helping us share this very...unique Christmas story. And now, without further ado, let's give a big round of applause for Miss Christmas!"

Riley fought to keep smiling when Mike called her Miss Christmas. As she stepped in front of the microphone, she opened her cocktail purse and took out the speech she had prepared.

As everyone clapped, she looked out into the crowd. In the front row stood her mom, looking as proud as could be, and beside her were Caylee and Maryanne, who were clapping the loudest. Also in the front row were her Christmas Camper twins, Carrie and Terrie. They were taking pictures. When they waved at Riley, she smiled and waved back.

As she continued to look around the ballroom, her smile grew. All her Christmas Campers were intermingling with people from the Christmas Lake community. Everyone looked happy and relaxed. Except Margo, who was laser-focused on her phone. When she looked in the back of the room, she saw Colin, Brendan, and Tyler. They all held up their Champagne glasses to her in a joint toast. It was the best gift they could have given her, showing her that they would all be okay. She gave them a grateful smile.

But when she looked around the room, the one person she didn't see was Luke.

She took a deep breath and looked down at her speech again. When she looked back up, that's when she saw Luke standing in the doorway. She stood up straighter and felt more confident as she put her speech back in her purse and smiled at everyone.

"First, I want to thank all of you for being a part of this very special Christmas Camp event," Riley said. "I know a lot of you, especially the press, have seen pictures online and have heard all kinds of different stories about my three ex-boyfriends showing up here to surprise me, so I'm here to tell you what's really going on, the truth."

When Riley looked at her mom, her mom solemnly nodded.

"Starting with the fact that I'm not Miss Christmas—far from it," Riley said. She saw Margo's head jerk up from her phone, and Mike suddenly looked very nervous. She smiled at them both.

They both gave her a warning look.

She ignored it.

"The truth is," she continued, "I haven't celebrated Christmas since I was eight years old."

Whispers began among the crowd.

"That's right. It's true. You can ask my mom, she's right here in the front row. After we lost my dad, we stopped celebrating and spent Christmas at the beach in Hawaii. We didn't do any Christmas activities because I didn't want to. It was so much easier to forget than to remember everything we'd lost when my dad passed away. So imagine my surprise when I found out I had to write a Christmas novel and host this Christmas Camp."

Riley had everyone's attention now. When she saw how confused her Christmas Campers looked, she kept going. She owed them the truth.

"I thought I could just come up here and fake it," Riley admitted. "I was just going to pretend I was like everyone else who celebrated Christmas, especially since my publicist, Mike over here, was marketing me as 'Miss Christmas.'"

When another murmur went through the crowd, Riley saw that people weren't smiling anymore. They looked upset, but she knew she couldn't stop now.

"Then things got really complicated when my ex-boyfriends showed up." Riley laughed, but no one laughed with her. "Everything that happened here during Christmas Camp, I didn't expect. I didn't expect the Christmas Lake Lodge to be so magical. I didn't expect to meet people like Luke, whose family owns this amazing lodge, and Caylee and Maryanne, who have worked around the clock to make sure everyone at Christmas Camp had the best time. I also didn't expect to have so many genuine connections with all of you Christmas Campers, who have come here to support me and have brought so much joy and love. Everyone here has changed me."

Riley smiled at the Christmas Campers.

"So, yes, the truth is, I did fall in love here at Christmas Camp..."

Everyone was staring at her, hanging on her every word.

"This weekend I've been reminded of how special Christmas really is and that what matters most are family, friends, faith, your community, spending time with the people you love, honoring old traditions, and creating new ones. I've fallen in love with Christmas again. It has opened by my heart, and now, as they say at Christmas, anything is possible."

Riley looked back at Luke, but she couldn't read his expression.

"I want to thank you again for being here and taking this journey with me. I hope you can forgive me for how this story started. Please know how thankful I am, and that with your help, I've finally remembered the true meaning and magic of Christmas."

She looked out at the audience and smiled a heartfelt smile. "Merry Christmas, everyone." They were two words she hadn't said in a very long time, and it felt wonderful. "Merry Christmas!"

As Riley started walking away from the mic, everyone started clapping and cheering. The applause got even louder when she went over and hugged her mom.

"I'm proud of you, honey," her mom said. "And Dad would be proud of you, too."

"I love you, Mom. Merry Christmas."

"Merry Christmas," her mom said and then looked into her eyes. "Now, go get your happy ending." She looked over at Luke.

Riley, nervous, wrung her hands together. "I don't know, Mom…"

"Yes, you do," Riley's mom said, giving her a nudge. "Just trust your heart and trust Christmas."

As Riley walked to the back of the ballroom, she could feel

everyone's eyes watching her.

She walked up to Colin, and an excited murmur swept through the crowd. "Merry Christmas, Colin," Riley said as she hugged him. "Thank you for loving me."

"Merry Christmas, Riley," Colin said, smiling back at her.

She did the same thing with Brendan and Tyler, completely confusing the crowd.

It wasn't until she walked toward Luke that the crowd grew completely quiet. You could have heard a piece of tinsel drop.

Like the rest of the crowd, Luke looked confused when Riley stopped in front of him.

"What are you doing?" he asked her quietly so no one else couldn't hear.

When Riley smiled at him and met his eyes, she didn't feel afraid anymore. She knew that no matter what happened she was following her heart. She'd had three great loves in her life because she'd trusted her heart. It hadn't let her down yet.

When the piano player in the band began to play the classic Christmas song "The Christmas Waltz," Riley took Luke's hand. "Will you dance with me?"

Luke looked around. "What about Tyler?"

"What about him?" Riley asked. "I'm not with Tyler, and I'm not with Colin or Brendan. They're my past. I'm looking for my future, a future that could start with this dance…So what do you say?"

"To a dance or to a future?" Luke asked, completely serious.

Riley leaned in and whispered in his ear, "To both."

She pulled back and smiled at him. For a moment, he was silent.

Riley held her breath.

When Luke slowly smiled back at her and she could see the passion in his eyes, she didn't want to waste any more time.

She kissed him, and when he wrapped his arms around her and kissed her back, she didn't just feel a spark—she felt *fireworks*.

Everyone cheered, with Colin, Brendan, and Tyler cheering the loudest.

After the kiss, Riley looked into his eyes and smiled a smile that was filled with love. "Merry Christmas, Luke," she said softly.

"Merry Christmas, Riley," Luke said before kissing her again.

Chapter Forty

One Week Later, Christmas Morning

"Ho! Ho! Ho! Time to get up and go! Ho! Ho! Ho! Let's go! Go! Go!"

Riley awoke to the Santa alarm clock in her room at the lodge. But this time, instead of yanking the batteries out of Santa, she sang along as she jumped out of the sleigh bed. With the enthusiasm of a cheerleader, she danced around in her new red silk pajamas.

"Let's go! Go! Go!"

She couldn't wait to celebrate her first Christmas with her mom, stepdad, and Luke at the Christmas Lake Lodge.

It was hard to believe a week had already gone by since the Christmas Camp dance. Riley smiled remembering her first kiss with Luke and how the dance had also sparked some other possible romances—Tyler dancing with Margo, Mary-anne dancing with Colin, and Brendan dancing with Rachel, one of the pretty Christmas Campers from Tennessee.

After the dance, Luke had invited her and her family to spend the next week leading up to Christmas at the lodge with Caylee, Comet, and his mom, who would be able to make it home for Christmas after all.

As hard as it had been to say goodbye to her Christmas Campers, Riley felt confident that the friendships they'd formed would last far beyond the holidays. For a Christmas present, Paul had made her a special Christmas Camp album that included all her favorite pictures. She would cherish it and the memories always.

As for the Christmas Camp itself, her publishing team had called it a huge success. They had gotten a ton of positive publicity and had signed off on Riley's idea for her first Christmas novel to be about a children's author who was writing Christmas fairy tales and fell in love with her illustrator. Riley also got the greenlight to do a children's book featuring her dad's Christmas fairy tales.

The Christmas Camp had also inspired Luke to move forward with his career. When his mom had arrived at the lodge, he'd announced the exciting news that they had a new buyer for the property, and he wanted his mom to take the deal.

When the offer turned out to be from him, his mom had been thrilled to keep the lodge in the family. Luke had decided he owed it to his family's legacy, the community of Christmas Lake, and to himself to use his expertise to turn the lodge into a Green-friendly property. He wanted to try to set an example of what other small lodges and inns in the area could do to help compete with the new big luxury resorts.

For Riley, what she'd loved this last week was spending time with Luke enjoying the simple things in life. They'd spent every day together doing different Christmas activities. Luke had shared some of his family favorites, and Riley had shared some from the Google list she'd made. She'd even gotten everyone to go caroling and had loved every second of it.

She'd also sent her favorite New York bartender a picture of her making a snowman with Luke and captioned it, *He's the one.* Alex had congratulated her by sending her his Grandma Lola's secret mulled wine recipe, the recipe she'd tried to get from him for years. It had truly touched her heart because Alex had always told her he could only share the secret recipe with family.

After Luke shared his family's secret hot chocolate recipe with her, she'd asked Alex if she could share Grandma Lola's recipe with Luke. He'd agreed, and when she'd sent him the secret hot chocolate recipe, he'd gotten a kick out of Luke's personal secret ingredient, little chopped-up pieces of York Peppermint Patties. She couldn't wait for two of her favorite guys to meet.

The more time Riley spent with Luke, the more she realized how truly compatible they were. She felt as if she'd known Luke forever, and he was already her best friend. Her heart hadn't been wrong, and the spark between them only grew brighter with each new day.

Riley had a lot to celebrate and be thankful for. Her only disappointment had been when she'd stopped by Merry and Bright wanting to get Luke one of the Christmas Lake Christmas Angels and Lisa had told her they'd sold out already. Riley had been excited to carry on the tradition and give the angel to Luke, someone she was starting to care very much for.

Now, as she got dressed to go downstairs for Christmas morning, the smell of peppermint hot chocolate and her new favorite blueberry cinnamon rolls filled the air, making her mouth water.

When she heard a bark at the door, she hurried to open it, eager to see her four-legged best friend, Comet. He didn't disappoint. She laughed when she saw he was carrying a big wrapped Christmas present in his mouth and he wearing a new ugly Christmas sweater. This one had a bunch of Santa cats all over it.

"Well, don't you look puuuurfect," she said to Comet, laughing at her own joke. He proudly dropped the Christmas present at her feet.

"Well, Merry Christmas to you, too, Comet. What do we have here?" she asked.

She unwrapped her gift at a speed that would have made Caylee proud and then laughed loudly. It was a new ugly Christmas sweater. This time it was an emerald-green hooded sweater with a giant elf face on it. When she checked out the hood, it had fuzzy pink elf ears and a pointy top. On the front of the sweater was a pinned note that said, *Wear me!*

She laughed again and looked at Comet. "Let me guess. Another family tradition?"

When Comet barked and ran down the hall, Riley only hoped he wasn't going to get another sweater.

After a hilarious, lively Christmas breakfast where everyone wore their new ugly Christmas sweaters, Luke led them all out to the lake to make Christmas snow angels. It was a new tradition he'd just come up with, and everyone agreed it was a good one.

While people took pictures with their snow angels, Riley stood back and noticed that, once again, her angel wings and Luke's angel wings were touching.

"So what do you think it means that our snow angels' wings are touching?" Luke asked as if reading her mind.

Riley smiled as she thought about it for a moment, then looked into Luke's eyes. "I think it means we're supposed to be together, here and always."

Luke smiled back at her. "I like that. I like that a lot."

They stood side by side, hand in hand, with their own shoulders touching as they turned back to look at their angels.

"Okay, everyone, it's time for my favorite Christmas tradition," Caylee called out.

As everyone followed Caylee down to the lake and stepped on to the ice, heading for the Christmas Lake Christmas tree, Riley hesitated for a moment.

"Are you okay?" Luke asked.

Riley looked at the ice and took his hand. "I am now."

Once they were gathered the beautifully lit Christmas tree, they all joined hands. Then one by one, each of them shared a memory, honoring members of the military they knew and all the brave men and women who served their country.

When everyone was ready to head back to the lodge, Luke playfully pulled Riley behind one of the Douglas firs and kissed her.

"I have a present for you," he said with a boyish smile.

"I thought we agreed we weren't doing presents," Riley said. "That we were going to make memories instead."

Luke nodded. "We are...*after* you open your present."

Riley laughed. "You're impossible." She looked around. "So where's my present?"

Luke pointed at the tree.

Riley raised an eyebrow. "You're giving me a tree?"

Luke laughed. "No, the tree is where you'll find your present."

But Riley didn't see anything.

"Look closer," Luke urged.

Loving a challenge, Riley started moving around some of the branches. "There's no way you can hide anything in here," she said. "These branches are too thick."

"Did I say it was in the tree?" Luke asked with a mischievous grin, then kissed her again.

Riley pulled away, laughing. "Stop distracting me."

She circled the tree, and that's when she spotted it. It was just peeking out from a patch of snow—a little tin box about the size of a shoebox.

Excited, she scrambled to pick it up and lifted it in victory. "Got it!"

Luke laughed as they walked over to what had become their favorite bench and sat down together. "Open it," he said.

She gave him a look. "You sound just like Caylee."

"No, Caylee would've already opened it for you."

They both laughed.

As Riley started to lift the lid off the tin box, Comet came running over and sat down at her feet and tried to poke his nose inside the box.

"Comet, hold on," Riley said, laughing as she moved the box out of his reach. When she finally removed the lid, she found something wrapped in burlap inside.

Her eyes flew to Luke. "Is it...?"

He just smiled back at her.

She carefully took out the burlap bundle and slowly unwrapped it until she found the Christmas gift she'd dreamed about.

A Christmas Lake Angel.

She carefully picked it up and held it to her heart. "How did you get this? I went to Merry and Bright, and Lisa said they were sold out."

"They were," Luke agreed. "But Paul helped me out."

"Paul?" Riley asked. "How could he help?"

"Paul *Harrison*, of the Christmas Lake Harrisons, is the great-great-grandson of Thomas Harrison..."

"The original artist?! Thomas who made it for Cynthia?!" Riley said, both shocked and excited. "Paul is part of that family? The family that makes these angels?"

Luke chuckled and nodded. "He is. When I told him why I wanted to give you this angel, he had his dad make one more Christmas Angel this year, just for you."

Still holding the angel to her heart, she looked into Luke's eyes. "What did you tell him?"

When Riley looked into Luke's eyes, she could see the love.

He smiled back at her. "I told him that you're my Christmas ever after and that I want to spend every Christmas and every day with you."

When Riley kissed him, she felt so much hope in her heart and knew her Christmas wish had come true.

She'd gotten her very own Christmas love story, and this was only the beginning...

Acknowledgments

Christmas is the time of year I always look back on the great loves of my life. I am forever grateful for the lessons they've taught me about how to love and be loved. I've learned to never settle, go all in, be fearless, and follow your heart in love and life. This has guided me on my journey to write *Christmas Ever After* and to take a leap of faith in starting my own publishing company, HawkTale Publishing, to champion uplifting, heartwarming, and empowering storytelling.

I'm truly thankful to my new creative team, editor Danielle Poiesz of Double Vision Editorial, Libby Murphy of Radiant Content & Design, Ingram Spark's Justine Bylo and Leigh Cheak, and the entire Ingram family. To my other beloved edit elves, my mom, Lao, and my second mom, Kathy, I couldn't do this without you. To my dad, who always inspires me, and Margaret for always being there. And to the rest of my family, I'm thankful for you every single day. Finally, to my trusted tribe, Jeryl, Lee, Heather, Lorianne, Clint, Brenda, Denise, Marybeth, Amy, Tim, Hope, Greta, Samuel, Rob, Jim, Wendy, Bob, and Delia and Tom, your continued belief in me and unwavering support is everything.

Meet Karen Schaler

KAREN SCHALER is a three-time Emmy Award–winning story-teller, screenwriter, author, journalist, and national TV host. Karen has written original Christmas movies for Netflix, Hallmark, and Lifetime, including the Netflix sensation *A Christmas Prince,* Hallmark's *Christmas Camp,* and four books, *Christmas Ever After, Finding Christmas, Christmas Camp, and Christmas Camp Wedding,* earning her the nickname "Christmas Karen" in the press. Karen has also created a real-life Christmas Camp experience for grown-ups, held around the world, where she carefully curates and hosts magical holiday activities from her movies and books. For Karen's novel *Finding Christmas* she also wrote the movie. Traveling to more than sixty-five countries, Karen is the creator and host of Travel Therapy TV. All of Karen's stories are uplifting and filled with heart and hope.

Visit karenschaler.com to sign up for Karen's newsletter for special book deals, giveaways, sneak peeks, and more.

Books by Karen Schaler

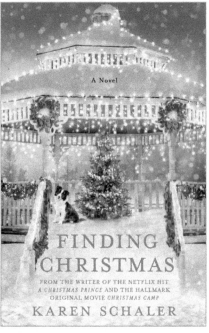

ADDITIONAL FICTION TITLES
Christmas Camp Wedding (novella)

NONFICTION
Travel Therapy: *Where Do You Need to Go?*

Christmas Ever After
Recipes

One of the things I love to do when writing all my Christmas novels is share some of my own Christmas traditions, and that includes some of my favorite family recipes, some recipes I've created, and some fun holiday activities that I hope everyone will enjoy.

Merry Christmas!
Christmas Karen

Christmas Lake Blueberry Cinnamon Rolls

Makes 9 Rolls
Prep Time: 2 ½ hours to let the dough rise twice.

Ingredients:

DOUGH

- ¾ cup almond milk (can also use regular milk), heated to 110°F
- 2 ¼ teaspoons quick-rise or active yeast (¼-ounce package)
- ¼ cup granulated sugar
- 1 egg, room temperature
- ¼ cup unsalted butter, softened to room temperature
- 3 cups bread flour, plus more for dusting
- ¾ teaspoon sea salt

FILLING

- 2 cups frozen blueberries (wild blueberries are best)
- ⅔ cup brown sugar (light or dark)
- 2 tablespoons ground cinnamon
- 1 teaspoon nutmeg
- 6 tablespoons unsalted butter, softened to room temperature

FROSTING

- 1 16-oz can of cream cheese frosting

Instructions:

DOUGH

1. Warm milk in microwave for 40–45 seconds, until around 110°F. It should feel warm but not hot to the touch.
   NOTE: Do not overheat milk, or it will kill the yeast. If milk is too hot, just let it cool down to 110 degrees before adding yeast.

2. Add heated milk to a large mixing bowl and sprinkle yeast on top.

3. Add in melted butter, sugar, salt, and egg. Mix well.

4. Slowly stir in flour with a wooden spoon, a little at a time to get right consistency, until dough begins to form. Don't add too much flour. Dough should be slightly sticky but not stick to fingers. Form dough into a ball.

5. Use your hands to knead the dough for 8–10 minutes on a well-floured surface. Dough is fully kneaded when you press on it and it springs back and you cannot easily pull it apart.

6. Put dough ball to a well-oiled bowl to prevent sticking, and cover with plastic wrap and a warm towel. Place in warm area. Let dough rise until doubled in size (approx. 1 hour to 1 ½ hours).

FILLING

1. Combine sugar, cinnamon, nutmeg, and butter.

2. Keep blueberries frozen until right before use.

ADDING FILLING TO THE DOUGH

1. After dough has doubled in size, transfer to a well-floured surface and roll out into a 12x16-inch rectangle.

2. Spread cinnamon filling evenly over dough, making sure to hit the corners.

3. Add frozen blueberries, spreading blueberries out evenly.

4. Tightly roll up dough, starting from the smaller 12-inch side. End with seam down, and pinch dough together to seal.

5. Cut into 1-inch sections with a very sharp knife or unflavored dental floss. You should get nine large pieces.

6. Place six cinnamon rolls in a 9x13-inch baking pan lined with parchment paper, and four rolls in a 9x9-inch pan lined with parchment paper. (You can butter pans if you prefer.)

7. Cover both pans with plastic wrap and warm towels. Let rise until doubled in size (approx. 1 hour).

BAKING

1. Preheat oven to 350°F. Remove plastic wrap and towels. Bake cinnamon rolls for 18–20 minutes until just slightly golden brown on the edges. You want to underbake them a little so they stay deliciously soft and gooey in the middle!

2. Take out of oven and immediately remove from pans.

3. Use half the frosting to frost immediately so it melts into the rolls. Then wait ten minutes to add the rest of the frosting.

4. Serve immediately.

Enjoy!

Christmas Lake Gingerbread XOXO Cookies

Makes 36 Cookies

Ingredients:

- 2 ¼ cups all-purpose flour
- 1 tablespoon ground ginger
- 1 tablespoon ground cinnamon
- ½ teaspoon ground cloves
- ½ teaspoon allspice
- ¼ teaspoon salt
- 1 teaspoon baking soda
- 1 tablespoon finely cut candied ginger (optional to add spicy flavor)
- ¾ cup (1 ½ sticks) unsalted butter, softened
- ½ cup brown sugar
- ½ cup granulated white sugar
- 1 egg
- 1 tablespoon fresh-squeezed orange juice
- ¼ cup molasses
- 36 Hershey's Kisses of your choice

Instructions:

Note: Mix all ingredients by hand for best results.

1. Preheat oven to 350°F.
2. Sift together the flour, ginger, cinnamon, cloves, allspice, salt, and baking soda. Stir in candied ginger, if desired.

3. In a large mixing bowl, cream butter and brown and white sugar until fluffy.

4. Beat in egg, and then stir in fresh orange juice and molasses.

5. Gradually stir in the flour and spice mixture to the butter and sugar mixture.

6. Mold dough into small walnut-sized balls.

7. Place 2 ½ inches apart on an ungreased cookie sheet.

8. Gently flatten with hand, until dough is about 1-inch thick.

9. Bake for 8–10 minutes.

10. Let cookies cool on cookie sheet while adding one Hershey's Kiss on top of each cookie.

11. Transfer to wire rack or parchment paper to cool completely.

12. Store in airtight container to keep cookies soft and chewy.

Enjoy!
XOXO

Christmas Ever After
Activities

My mom lives in Washington state and loves watching all the birds in her backyard. This gave me the idea to create some special edible outdoor ornaments for them so they could also have a wonderful Christmas. I hope you enjoy making these and sharing them with the feathered friends in your life as much as we do.

Christmas Lake Edible Birdseed Ornaments

Materials needed:

- Cookie cutters (we use stars, trees, hearts, and angels), greased
- ¾ to 1 cup birdseed (smaller seeds without large sunflower seeds work best)
- 1 packet (¼ oz) unflavored gelatin
- ½ cup boiling water
- Your favorite Christmas ribbons
- Recyclable straw
- Parchment paper

Instructions:

1. Prepare cookie sheets by putting down parchment paper. Set aside and cookie cutters.
2. In a large bowl, add ½ cup boiling water to your unflavored gelatin. Stir until completely dissolved.
3. Add 1½ to 2 cups of birdseed to the gelatin, and mix well.
4. Pack birdseed firmly into your cookie cutters.
5. Using a straw, create hole for your ribbon to hang the ornament.
6. Place in cool place or refrigerate for several hours, or overnight, until completely dry.
7. Gently pop your birdseed ornament free from cookie cutter.
8. Thread your favorite Christmas ribbon through the hole and hang outside on a tree, pole, or hook.
9. Watch your feathered friends enjoy their Christmas gift!

Christmas Lake Pine Cone Bird Ornaments

Materials needed:

- Pine cones (opened)
- Peanut butter
- Birdseed (small seed is best without the large sunflower seeds)
- 12-inch strips of Christmas ribbon or twine
- Small brush

Instructions:

1. First, the fun part: go on your own scavenger hunt for the best pine cones.
2. Gently clean off any debris from your pine cones using a small brush.
3. Cut twelve-inch strips of ribbon or twine, and loop around the top of the pine cone, underneath the first layers of petals, and tie a double knot. Then tie the two pieces of ribbon or twine together with another double knot, creating the hanger. *NOTE: Be sure to do this before adding the peanut butter.*
4. Using a brush (or butter knife) spread a generous amount of peanut butter over the pine cone, making sure to cover all the tips.
5. Roll your pine cone in a bowl of birdseed until completely covered.
6. Hang outside for your feathered friends to have their own Christmas feast.

Christmas Ever After
Green-Friendly Christmas Tips

I've found there are so many easy and affordable ways we can all have a more ecofriendly Christmas and do our part to protect and cherish our natural resources. Here are some of my favorite tips, just small things that can help make a big difference.

- **Use LED lights.**
  We all love the sparkle, but when picking lights, look for LED lights that use about 80% less energy than regular lights and can last almost ten times longer.

- **Put lights on a timer.**
  Set all your indoor and outdoor lights, including your Christmas tree lights, on a timer. This way, you can enjoy them when you want but turn them off when you're not using them, like at night when you're sleeping.

- **Green Christmas tree**
  For the ultimate ecofriendly Christmas tree, use a live tree that's potted so you can re-plant your tree after Christmas, creating a wonderful memory that will last, as well.

- **Be mindful about your food.**
  During the holidays, it's so easy to buy and make more food than you need. Purchase only the quantity you need so there's less waste. Also, if you can purchase produce that's grown locally, it's great to support local farmers and businesses.

- **Shop online.**
  Let your fingers do the shopping! Shopping online saves you from driving around and using up gas.

- **Green-wrapping paper**
  Use paper made from recyclable products. Also, save any wrapping paper, bows, and ribbons that you get so you can re-use it next season.

- **White Elephant re-gifting**
  Having a white elephant gift exchange is my grandma's favorite thing to do every Christmas. In my family, everyone brings something they've received in the past to "re-gift" during the white elephant exchange. This can also be something you have at home that you no longer have use for, but the idea is to "recycle" a gift.

MERRY CHRISTMAS!